MOMENT OF TRUTH

Ginny barked "*Freeze!*" in a voice that threatened to crack the floorboards. Her .357 lined up straight on his face.

He didn't freeze. Maybe he was too scared. He wheeled away as if she'd already fired.

Inadvertently he blundered against the door and knocked himself down. Snow blew across him from the porch. Eighteen inches of it had accumulated outside, and it was still falling.

Ginny rushed forward, crouched nearly on top of him. Then she corked the muzzle of her gun on his nose.

Eyes white with alarm, he gasped out, "Don't shoot! I killed her! I confess! Don't shoot me!"

I stopped. Ginny didn't need me. Not now. Maybe she never did.

THE MAN WHO TRIED TO GET AWAY

Stephen R. Donaldson

TOR®

A TOM DOHERTY ASSOCIATES BOOK
NEW YORK

THE MAN WHO TRIED TO GET AWAY

Copyright © 1990, 2004 by Stephen R. Donaldson

A Tor Book
Published by Tom Doherty Associates, LLC
175 Fifth Avenue
New York, NY 10010

www.tor.com

Tor® is a registered trademark of Tom Doherty Associates, LLC.

ISBN 0-765-34127-1
EAN 978-0-765-34127-3

First edition: November 2004
First mass market edition: November 2005

Printed in the United States of America

0 9 8 7 6 5 4 3 2 1

To
Real and Muff Musgrave
friends to treasure

Note:

This novel has been slightly revised since its original publication.

Of course, I lost weight. People do that after they've been shot in the gut. But I could afford a little weight. Cooking for Ginny had given me more pounds than it did her. My real problem was movement.

Muy Estobal's bullet had torn me up pretty good inside, even if it did leave my vital organs alone. And I hadn't done myself any favors with all that hiking around the night after I got shot. The doctor told me that if I walked to the bathroom with my IVs nailed to my arms every hour or so until he started hearing "bowel sounds," he would maybe consider removing my catheter. As a special reward for being such a good patient.

That was easy for him to say. El Señor didn't want him dead. It wasn't his problem I might die because of the simple fact that I couldn't get out of bed.

I needed to move. To escape from the hospital. Before el Señor sent Estobal's replacement after me.

So far I'd only been stuck here for forty-eight hours, and it was already driving me crackers. If they hadn't given me so many pills, I wouldn't have been able to sleep at night. I would've stayed awake the whole time, watching the door. Expecting to see some goon with at least an Uzi come in to blow me away.

Ginny hadn't been much help. She kept telling me that there wasn't any danger, there was too much heat on el Señor, he couldn't afford to risk having me hit so soon. Which should've been true, I suppose. And I should've believed her. I'd believed her when she first said it.

Hadn't I?

But after that, unfortunately, I got a phone call.

It came during the day, when the hospital switchboard was on automatic, and the winter sunlight and the blue sky outside my window made everything I could see look safe. But I must not have been feeling particularly safe, because I believed my caller right away.

When the phone rang, I picked it up and said, "Huh," because that's easier than hello when your whole torso is strapped with bandages and you don't feel much like breathing deeply anyway.

A voice I almost knew said, "Get out of there. He wants you. You're a sitting duck."

Then the line went dead.

Cheered me right up, that did.

When I told Ginny about it, she looked just for a second like she believed it, too. Her gray eyes sharpened, and the lines around her broken nose went tight. But after that she grinned. "Probably somebody's idea of a joke."

Oh, sure. I'd killed Muy Estobal, el Señor's favorite muscle. Together, Ginny and I'd disrupted el Señor's revenge on a man who'd ripped him off and murdered one of his people. Everyone around him probably laughed out loud whenever my name came up.

But my caller wasn't finished.

The next day, the doctor heard gurgling in my guts— bowel function struggling back to life—and took out the catheter. I got the thrill of starting to feed myself hospital gruel, which tasted like pureed dog food. And I was encouraged to get out of bed and actually stand until pain made my head ring like a gong, and my famous bowels hurt like they'd been shredded.

I was horizontal again, holding on to the bed and doing my best not to gasp, when the phone rang.

This time my caller said, "I mean it. You haven't got much time. He wants you dead."

I felt like I was inches away from recognizing that voice, but I couldn't pull it in. Gremlins in spiked boots raced up and down my intestines, distracting me.

"Who?" I asked. At the moment I didn't care how much it hurt to breathe so hard. "Who wants me dead? Who are you? Why are you warning me?"

The line switched to a dial tone.

So when Ginny stopped by for her daily visit, I made her get the .45 out of my locker and leave it where I could reach it.

"You're taking this too seriously." She sounded bored. "El Señor is practically paralyzed right now. The cops are watching everything he does. Even crooked cops are going to be honest for a while, with this much heat on. The commissioner is talking about 'wiping out organized crime in Puerta del Sol.' The newspapers are jumping up and down. I get interviewed at least once a day. Fistoulari Investigations never had so much publicity. I'm actually having to turn clients away.

"Brew, you're safe. Just relax. Get well."

Just relax. Why didn't I think of that? "If this is supposed to be a joke," I muttered past my bandages, "I'd hate to meet whoever's doing it when he's in a bad mood."

"You sure you can't identify the voice?"

I shrugged. It wasn't very comfortable, but it was better than arguing.

"I'll check with the switchboard on my way out." Now she was humoring me. "Maybe they can take your line out of the automatic circuit. If we screen your calls, maybe we'll find out who's calling."

I wanted to say, Don't screen my calls. Get me out of here. But I didn't. I let her go. She and I had too many problems, and the worst of them was that we were afraid of each other. We hadn't had a straight conversation in months because we were both too busy trying to control each other's reactions. She was afraid that if she said or did the wrong thing, I'd go get drunk and never be sober again. And I feared that I might push her back into being the lost woman she'd become after she lost her hand.

She wore her "prosthetic device" now, the mechanical claw that took the place of her left hand. Which was an improvement. But she still wore it like a handicap instead of something familiar, something she trusted. I figured that the only reason she wore it was to appease me. She was afraid of what I might do if she didn't. She had it on to protect me. Or to protect herself against me.

I loved her. I used to think she loved me. But it didn't show. Everything was twisted. We might as well have been chained together by our various fears. So I didn't tell that her I was too scared to stay in the hospital by myself. I didn't want to add to her worries.

Unfortunately the switchboard couldn't take just one line off automatic. The next day, I got another call.

By then I'd spent twenty-four hours expecting it. I was just a touch jumpy when I reached for the phone. Ol' nerves-of-steel Axbrewder. Weak as spaghetti in that damn bed, I fumbled the receiver onto the floor and had to pull it up by the cord to answer it.

"Sorry," I said.

"Don't hang up," I said.

"Tell me what's going on," I said.

Impressive, no?

The silence on the line sounded like snickering.

"How did you get my number?"

"Hospital information," the voice I almost knew replied. "Anybody in Puerta del Sol can find out what room you're in just by asking. You're a dead man."

Leaving me with that cheery thought, my caller put down the phone.

A couple of hours later, Ginny showed up. I told her about the call, but she didn't seem particularly interested. Instead, she studied me as if I were exhibiting strange side effects to a new medication. "This has really got you going," she commented. Observant as all hell.

"Think about it," I snarled as well as I could. "How many people hate me enough to consider this kind of joke funny?"

But my vehemence didn't ruffle her. "Think about it yourself, Brew," she replied calmly. "How many people love you enough to give you this kind of warning?"

That stopped me. Who would know that el Señor actively wanted me dead? Only someone close to him. And who in that group would give a good goddamn what happened to me? Which one of his people would risk warning me?

No one fit that description.

I made an effort to look more relaxed. "I guess you're right. It must be a practical joke. Some minor sociopath dialed the number and liked my reaction. Maybe he even dialed it at random." I was trying to play along with her. Defuse anxiety. But the idea that I wasn't worried was pure bullshit and moonshine, and I couldn't keep it going. "It's just a coincidence that I've actually got enemies."

"No, you don't," she retorted, grinning. Maybe she found it funny when I sounded so pitiful. Or maybe she was just keeping her guard up. "That's what I keep trying to tell you. El Señor is paralyzed. There isn't anybody else."

I liked her grin, no matter what it meant. But it didn't cheer me up. Things like immobility and helplessness put too much pressure on my morale.

I was recovering too slowly. Where the hell were my recuperative powers when I needed them? Movement is life. I was running out of time.

I waited until Ginny left. Then I climbed vertical and practiced lugging the tight lump of fire I called my stomach around the room. Unfortunately that just aggravated my discouragement. About the time that pain and exhaustion got bad enough to make me sob, I decided to lie down and just let el Señor kill me.

Teach her a lesson, that would.

Self-pity may not be my most attractive quality, but I'm damn good at it.

So she took me completely by surprise when she came in early the next morning, before any phone calls, and asked, "Can you walk out of here?"

I stared at her.

"Well, can you?"

I stared at her some more.

She sighed. "If you can get out of bed," she explained with elaborate patience, "put your clothes on, and walk out of here, we're leaving. I've got a job for us."

That early in the morning, I was still muzzy with sleeping pills. Nevertheless a few dopey synapses in my head went click. Before I could question them, I said, "You believe those phone calls."

She nodded sharply.

"I can't talk the cops into protective custody, but hospital security is watching your room most of the time. And the nurses here remember you." She gestured with her left arm, and her claw gave me a flash of stainless steel. She'd lost her hand to a bomb in this hospital. "They're doing what they can to keep an eye on you."

She didn't let me interrupt. "It isn't enough. If you don't get out of here today, I'm going to move in with you."

I shook my head without realizing it. "Why didn't you tell me? Why did you try to make me think you were laughing at me?"

"I didn't want you to worry," she snapped. "You're supposed to be recuperating, not lying there in a muck sweat."

"Aye, aye, Captain Fistoulari, ma'am, sir," I muttered.

In a fine display of moral fortitude and physical courage, I closed my eyes.

"Brew." Her patience slipped a notch. "I'm serious."

"So am I," I said through a haze of drugs and fear. "Go away. This stinks."

"What's the matter? Those calls obviously bother you. Don't you want to get away from them?"

"Yes," I admitted. "But not like this." In fact, the whole idea made me cringe. I was tired of being protected. Not to mention being protected against. "If it's a real job, the last thing you need is a half-ambulatory cripple on your hands. And if it's a nursemaid exercise for my benefit, just to keep me out of trouble, I don't want it." For a few months now I'd believed in myself enough to stop drinking—but that, as they say, was tenuous at best. The last thing I needed was one less reason for self-respect. "You said you're turning clients away. Pick a job you can do by yourself. Leave me alone."

Unfortunately that shut her up. She didn't say anything for so long that I finally had to open my eyes to see if she was still in the room.

She was.

She stood at the window with her back to me, hiding her face against the morning. Something about the line of her back, the way she held her shoulders, told me that I'd hurt her.

"Ginny—" I wanted to explain somehow, if I could just think of the words. But nothing came out of my mouth.

After a while she asked the glass, "Why is this so hard?"

"I don't know." My usual frightened contribution to our relationship. "Everything we do to each other matters too much."

She turned.

With the sunlight behind her, I almost missed the fighting light in her eyes. Wearing the conservative suits she preferred, her respected-private-investigator clothes, her blond hair tidy around her fine face and her mouth under control, she looked like nothing so much as an up-and-coming businesswoman, lean and ready. Except for her broken nose, and that light in her eyes, and her claw. The punk who broke her nose was long dead. She'd shot him more than once, just in case he missed the point the first time.

"It's a nursemaid job," she said straight at me, "a piece of cake. You may remember the commission suspended my license." Her tone dripped pure acid. "It's temporary, but for the time being there are only certain kinds of jobs I'm allowed to take. And the fee is real. You know I can't afford to ignore that. And it's out of town. Up in the mountains, where el Señor isn't likely to find you. It'll give you a week where you don't have to do anything worse than walk around."

I did my best to shake my head in a way that would make her believe me. "I don't care about that. I—"

She cut me off.

"*Listen*. Just once, listen to me. I suppose I could take what money I've got and borrow the rest and just buy you a plane ticket. You could disappear. Make it hard for el Señor to find you.

"But that won't work. We've tried it before, and it never works. You end up drunk somewhere, and eventually I have to come get you.

"Or I could go with you. I could sit around watching you until we both went walleyed or my money ran out. That won't work either. You know it won't.

"The only thing that ever does you any good is a *job*. As far as I can tell, you only stay away from alcohol when you've got people depending on you.

"Well, this job isn't exactly hard. We can't take on anything difficult with you in this condition. But it's still a *job*. It'll give you something to do, people to take care of. I don't have anything else to offer.

"I don't care whether you want it or not. We're going to accept that job if you can just *stand*."

For a second there I felt so sick that I wanted to throw up. Absolutely puke my life away. I had an existential knife in my guts. She was protecting me again. Protecting against me again.

But then, all of a sudden, it occurred to me that knives

cut both ways. Whether she intended it or not, she was offering me a chance to take care of myself. A chance to get up on my feet and make some of my own decisions.

So I relented. I wasn't exactly gracious about it. In fact, I was angry as hornets. But I said, "I don't know why I bother arguing with you. I don't like nursemaid operations. I don't like being nursemaided. But I haven't got any better ideas. In any case, you're going to take care of me no matter what I do. I don't have the strength or the willpower to stop you. This way I can at least try to return the favor."

Ginny glared at me. The flash of her claw in the light reminded me that she had her own reasons to hate being taken care of. She'd been dependent on me for six months after she lost her hand—and she was only just now starting to get over it. Sounding bitter, she rasped, "Is it the sleeping pills, or are you always this perceptive?"

I ignored her irritation. The pain in my stomach lost its metaphysical significance. A job. Something to *do*. I wanted that, no question about it. As soon as I agreed to go back to work, I forgot that knives do only one thing, and it isn't called healing.

Helping myself up with both hands, I got out of bed.

2

I remembered getting dressed. I'd done it once before, when the hole in my gut was more recent. But that time I'd been too full of drugs and panic to have much rational grasp on what I did to myself. This time I knew where every single suture inside me was, and I could feel it pulling.

One thing you've got to say for us private investigators. We know how to have a good time.

Technically, of course, Ginny is the private investigator. She's Fistoulari Investigations. I'm just the hired help. I haven't had a license for this kind of work for years—not since I tried to help a cop who happened to be my brother apprehend a purse snatcher and accidentally shot him. Under the influence of alcohol. Amazing how the things we love best are the things that hurt us most. I couldn't remember the last time I had one entire day where the idea of a drink didn't sound like heaven.

But I didn't drink when I was working. In fact, I hadn't had a drink since the day I figured out that Ginny needed me as badly as I needed her—since the day she lost her hand. But that was starting to change. She wore her claw now, did things for herself. Every time I saw her, she was more the woman I used to know, the Ginny Fistoulari who could go after Satan himself and not take any prisoners.

Which was a good thing, as far as it went. The only problem was, it left me with fewer ways to protect her. Or to protect myself against her.

On the other hand, getting dressed was *work*, no question about it. And we had a job to do. That was at least useful as a distraction.

She watched me have fun with my shirt for a minute or two. Then she said, "Why don't I go get your paperwork done? That way we won't have to wait around for discharge." She knew how I felt about having an audience while I suffered.

I shook my head. I wanted her to go away, that was a fact. But I also wanted her to watch me struggle into my clothes. I wanted her to have no illusions about my physical condition. And if she stayed, she could talk to me. Help me through the peculiar ordeal of putting on my underpants.

For no particularly good reason, I said, "That doctor's going to have a spasm when he hears about this."

"No, he won't." She was sure. "I talked to him earlier. If you're well enough to get dressed, you're well enough to go home. All we have to do is keep an eye on you—take your temperature, watch for infection, that sort of thing. I already have your pills." Gazing innocently at the ceiling, she finished, "I didn't tell him about the job."

Well enough to get dressed. At the moment, that was debatable. Also trivial. She'd obviously spent some time getting ready for this case. That held my interest.

"Tell me about the job," I asked to keep her talking. "Who are we nursemaiding besides me?"

"You'll love it." She made a studious effort not to wince every time my face twisted. "For once I've got us something easy. Might as well be a vacation.

"Does the name Murder on Cue, Inc., mean anything to you?"

I shook my head again. If Murder on Cue, Inc., was a company that arranged assassinations, I planned to send them after the bastard who invented underpants.

"It's a small outfit, only two people as far as I can tell. Unless they have a secretary hidden away somewhere. Roderick Altar and his wife. They run what they call 'mystery camps.' They get people who like to try to solve crimes, play at being Sherlock Holmes for a few days. Then they hire actors and plan a scenario and take the whole crowd to some secluded place where the real world won't get in their way, and they stage a murder or two for these people to puzzle over. Nobody except Altar and his wife knows the difference between the actors and the guests. Whoever solves the murder wins."

"Be the first kid on your block to catch a killer," I muttered. With my underpants on, I had to rest for a while. I couldn't look at Ginny. I didn't want to see whatever was in her eyes. "Don't these people have anything better to do?"

"Apparently not." As a matter of policy, Fistoulari Investigations doesn't sneer at people with money. They tend to pay better than people who don't. But I could tell that Ginny shared my visceral reaction to Murder on Cue, Inc.

"So what do they need us for?" I asked to deflect myself from my socks. "Don't they want to catch their own killers?"

"Security," she answered.

She didn't elaborate.

At last I had to look up at her. "What the hell do people who think killing is some kind of game need security for?"

She shrugged. She was studying me intently, trying to see into my wounds—trying to understand them. "According to Altar, he's just the organizer, the guy who pulls the practical details together, like where these people stay, how they get there, what they eat, who feeds them. His wife's the murder enthusiast. She hires the actors, plans the scenario. She even screens the guests. I guess Murder on Cue is her hobby.

"He says he wants security for the insurance. Supplying protection for his guests and their belongings, he gets better rates. But his wife has different ideas—he says. She wants security because—how did he put it?—'the presence of private investigators makes the ambience more credible.' And it gives the guests some extra competition. Solve the crime before the professionals do."

My brain must've been in worse shape than I realized. I actually got both socks on before I thought to ask, "You mean she isn't going to tell us who the actors are? What the scenario is? We're supposed to play the same game they're playing?"

Ginny gave me a tight little smile. "Playing *along* is part of the job. Mrs. Altar won't tell the guests who we are, and we aren't supposed to either. The only thing they'll know is that two of them are investigators. But we don't really have to try to solve the crime. In fact, we don't really have to do much of anything.

"Our main job is just to keep an eye on the general safety of the situation. Apply a little common sense. Keep the guests from getting carried away. According to Altar, they've never had any trouble. He doesn't want to start now."

Maybe I'd finally grown accustomed to the pain. I closed my eyes, lifted one foot into my pants—and was amazed to discover that I'd survived the experience. I still felt like I was performing an appendectomy on myself with an apple corer, but aside from the usual lightheadedness and agony I was doing fine.

Trying not to pant—trying to prove that I really did have a wit or two inside my skull—I produced another question. "What do you know about this Altar? And his wife."

"Do you want help?" She meant with my pants.

I ignored her offer. After a moment she pretended that she hadn't said anything.

"Roderick and Sue-Rose Altar. I haven't met her. He's in his early fifties. Not exactly fat, but he likes food more than exercise. Used to be a venture capitalist, until he made too much money to justify working. Now he manages his investments. And takes care of Sue-Rose and her enthusiasms.

"I don't have your talent for snap judgments"—a reference to my ingrained preference for intuition over reason—"but if you pushed me I'd say he's just a bit bored with Sue-Rose and her enthusiasms and his whole life."

That settled it. A nursemaid job if ever there was one. If Murder on Cue had ever put on a mystery camp where anything actually happened, Roderick Altar probably wouldn't have been bored. I should've gone back to rejecting the whole idea. Unfortunately I'd thought of another reason why I couldn't do that. Ginny wouldn't abandon me—and the harder I made it for her to protect me, the more likely she was to get hurt herself. So I kept my opinion of useless work to myself.

Almost like I'd done this sort of thing before, I put my other foot into my pants and pulled them up.

Someone should've applauded, but my audience didn't bother.

Get off the bed. Tuck in my shirt. Thread a belt through the loops. Buckle it. Keep your breathing shallow and act like you aren't about to fall on your face. A dazzling performance, Axbrewder. So maybe it was just a nursemaid job. If it required me to stand and walk and possibly even shake hands, it was going to be as much as I could manage.

"What about your coat?" Ginny asked. "You want help with that?"

I wavered and wobbled in front of her. For some reason, she looked taller than I was—which should've been impossible, considering that I'm six-five and she isn't. Maybe it was déjà vu, a reminder of all the times she'd come looking for me, looking for a way to rescue me from myself, and I'd stood there unsteady with drink and let her pretend that she needed me. Whatever the explanation, I didn't like it. So I asked the kind of question that usually got me in trouble.

"Why us?"

I'd caught her with her mind somewhere else. Probably

still trying to guess how far I'd be able to walk. "Why us what?"

"Why does Roderick Altar want Fistoulari Investigations?" Speaking distinctly was as close as I could get to sarcasm. "You don't usually do this kind of work."

"I asked him that." She still wasn't thinking about my question. A frown knotted the bridge of her nose, and her eyes kept flicking away from me as if she didn't enjoy what she saw. "He said he must've heard my name somewhere. Or read it in the paper. I told you I've been doing interviews."

Which finally struck me as odd. She ordinarily didn't have much patience for the media. So I put in, "Why?"

"Trying to keep a high profile," she explained absently. "As long as we're news, we'll be harder to hit.

"But I don't think he actually cares who we are, or whether we're any good. He isn't that interested."

What she said made perfect sense, of course. But I still hated it. I suppose the truth was that I'd been angry at her for a long time. She should've let me drink myself into my grave, instead of rescuing me over and over again. And she should've been stronger when she lost her hand, instead of putting the burden on me—refusing to wear her claw, requiring me to take care of her for six months because she felt so crippled, so much less than a human being, not to mention less than a woman, that she didn't have the courage to do anything except hurt.

Now that she'd returned to being herself—put on her claw and taken control of the situation—I was even madder. Her vulnerability had been my only defense against my own weaknesses. It had compelled me when nothing else worked. The less she needed me, the more helpless I felt.

Our feelings for each other had gotten pretty twisted over the years.

If there was one true, clear thing hidden away inside me anywhere, it was that I wanted to get those feelings untwisted. And as far as I could see, work was my only way to untwist them. A nursemaid operation was a lousy opportunity, but I didn't have any others at the moment.

I stuck to the point of my questions.

"You still haven't answered me. Didn't you tell me Murder on Cue has been doing mystery camps for a while now?"

Ginny made an effort to come back from wherever her head was. "So?"

"So Roderick Altar has hired security before, too, and it wasn't us. So what went wrong? Why wasn't he satisfied with whoever it was? Or has he really had some trouble he isn't telling us about?

"Why have we got a nice safe job like this right now, just when we happen to need it, and it's the only thing the commission will let us handle?"

I had her attention now. "Are you serious?" she asked, staring at me. "Is this really the way your mind works? Axbrewder, you're sick. Or they're giving you too much medication. Coincidences do happen, you know. Every event in life isn't aimed at you."

But that wasn't my point. "In other words," I countered, "you didn't ask him. You let him offer you this job, and you didn't even ask him why."

The tip of her nose had gone white, which usually happens when she's furious. Ominously quiet, she said, "All right, Brew. Spit it out. What's your problem now?"

Luckily I knew her well enough not to take this anger personally. She wasn't mad at me. She was mad because I'd touched a nerve.

I looked at her straight. "You don't usually miss that kind of question. You aren't thinking hard enough about this job. You're thinking too much about me."

"It's a nursemaid operation," she snapped back. "How much thought do you think it requires?"

I didn't try to answer. I didn't have to. As soon as she heard what came out of her mouth, she caught herself, and her eyes dropped. "All right," she said again. "I get the message. I do worry about you too much. There's no job so simple it can't get messy if you don't pay attention to it.

"Put on your coat. Call a nurse when you're ready to go." Without waiting for my opinion, she headed toward the door. "I'll meet you at the discharge exit."

In some way I'd shaken her self-confidence. Maybe I'd just reminded her that she had as many reasons to be angry as I did. Or maybe she was still more vulnerable than she liked. Disgusted at herself, afraid for me, and more desirable than any other woman I knew, she left me to figure out the pain in my gut for myself.

3

The coat was too much for me. Ginny had unearthed a thick and somewhat ratty three-quarter-length sheep-skin from my closet—a relic of more prosperous times—and I couldn't face hauling it up my arms and over my shoulders. Instead I pushed the buzzer to call a nurse. Then, while I waited, I retrieved the .45 and hid it in one of the pockets of the coat. The coat was pretty heavy anyway. Maybe no one would notice the extra weight.

The hospital staff must've had orders to get rid of me as soon as possible. A nurse arrived with a wheelchair almost right away. Without any discernible sense of loss over my departure, she put my coat on for me, helped me sit down, and gave me a ride to the discharge exit. By then Ginny had finished swearing on her soul to pay every conceivable penny of my bill. She and the nurse maneuvered me into the passenger seat of her creaky Olds. The nurse slammed the door.

Ginny started the Olds. To distract myself from the many pleasures of sitting in this position with miles of tape strapped around my ribs and every suture straining, I asked, "Now what?"

Spinning the wheel one-handed, Ginny took us out of the parking lot. Instead of looking at me, she watched the traffic for ambushes or tails. Her purse lay open beside her so that she could reach her .357. Just in case.

"The camp doesn't start until tomorrow," she said, "but today we have an appointment with Mrs. Altar. Look the place over, find out what she wants us to do. I told you it's

up in the mountains. I gather Murder on Cue is renting an
entire hunting lodge for the week, complete with staff. A
place called Deerskin Lodge." She tried not to sneer when
she said the name, but she couldn't help herself. Then she
added in a different tone, "It's a good three-hour drive. Can
you stand it?"

I didn't answer that. I was too busy showing off my he-
man private investigator stoicism. "The Altars like isolation."

Ginny nodded. "Adds to the appeal of the situation.
Makes the guests feel like they really do have to solve the
crime, or else they might get killed themselves. Also prevents intrusion from the real world."

Leaning on the accelerator, she took the Olds up the access ramp onto the freeway and began the long climb out
of the valley where Puerta del Sol sprawls along the Flat
River. The sky was gray with winter, and a temperature in-
version trapped a pall of woodsmoke and exhaust fumes
over us. Nevertheless the San Reno Mountains reared up
ahead like they didn't give a damn about such things, filling the whole eastern horizon.

"According to Roderick Altar," Ginny concluded, "they've
used this lodge several times now, very successfully. The
setting is perfect, and the staff knows what to do."

"Duck," I snorted cryptically.

"Huh?"

"The staff knows what to do. Which is duck. They don't
want to get hit by flying bullets when all those amateur
sleuths start apprehending each other."

"My, my." Ginny Fistoulari making polite social conversation. "You're in a good mood this morning."

With an effort, I swallowed more sarcasm. Her comment had the effect of making me realize that I had one
more reason to dread this job, one I hadn't admitted yet. I
hated nursemaiding and being nursemaided. I hated the
things she and I did to each other. And I also—this came as

a surprise—didn't want to make a fool of myself in front of eight or ten crime buffs. After all, "detection" and "investigation" aren't the same thing. The guests probably knew a hell of a lot more about "detection" than I did. "Mystery" camp was their game, and I wasn't likely to be good at it.

What fun.

Hunkered down into my pain, I concentrated on surviving the drive up to Deerskin Lodge.

The freeway ran through Pico Canyon and across the high plains to the east of the San Renos, but we turned off while we were still in the mountains. For half an hour or forty-five minutes, we had good clear road. It went in the direction of Puerta del Sol's ski resorts, and no one is more willing to invest in good clear roads than ski resorts. After the resort turnoff, however, the driving conditions deteriorated. We'd had an unusual amount of snow Tuesday night, and today was the next Monday. At this elevation, at this time of year, the temperature extremes chew hell out of the pavement.

We slogged up into thick pine forests and unexpected meadows, but I was in no condition to appreciate your basic winter wonderland scenery, sunshine glistening everywhere, white draped over the trees, nothing on the ground except snow and game tracks. I was too busy hurting every time the Olds lurched into a pothole or skidded over a patch of glaze.

But eventually I got tired of stoicism. "Why do they start on Tuesday?" I asked Ginny, just to break the silence.

By now she must've been sure we weren't being followed. Instead of watching the rearview mirror, she concentrated with a kind of aimless ferocity on her driving. "A group of hunters left the lodge yesterday. The staff won't be ready for more guests until tomorrow."

"And how long does our job run?"

"Seven days, counting today. Everybody's supposed to go home Sunday night."

How nice. A week of keeping amateur Sherlocks from shooting each other. There was just one problem. "What do we do after that?"

Obviously, she wasn't on my wavelength. "After what?"

"After this week. El Señor won't give up on me that fast. We'll still have the problem this job is supposed to solve."

Ginny flicked a glance at me, then turned her eyes back to the road. Carefully she ruddered the Olds around a shiny curve. "By then you should be stronger. According to your doctor. The more you move around, the faster you'll recover—as long as you don't do anything crazy. And the commission probably won't keep me suspended much longer. We can find a job that'll get us out of town. We won't be restricted to hand-holding operations."

I didn't like the sound of that. I didn't want to spend the rest of my life hiding. But there was no point in complaining about it. The rational vestiges of my mind understood that Ginny was just trying to keep me safe. One job at a time, one decision at a time. That was all anyone could do.

At the moment, however, I didn't feel equal to it. I wanted to get away and never come back. Some problems you can't do anything with except run.

I made Ginny stop the car and help me into the backseat. Getting in was tough, but once I'd stretched out on my back my insides hurt less. As long as I didn't get carsick, I'd probably survive the rest of the trip.

"Take a nap," Ginny said over her shoulder. "I'll wake you up before we get there."

"Fine," I murmured as if I had that much common sense. But I didn't sleep. I spent the time trying to figure out what was wrong between us.

I didn't regret the bodyguard job that ended up with Muy Estobal's bullet in my gut and Estobal himself dead and el Señor angry at me. We'd needed that job. Without it, Ginny might not have recovered her essential self-esteem, her ability to function. Now she'd resumed being the woman I liked and desired and trusted.

So what was wrong? Why did I get the impression that we didn't love each other anymore? Why were we still afraid of each other, angry at each other?

Actually, her feelings weren't hard to understand. She was angry at me because I'd pushed her into opposing el Señor. I'd forced her into the position of having to wear her claw or quit altogether. And because after all this time I still wanted a drink. I'd been a drunk for too long, and I wanted a drink for the same reason every drunk wants one. To prove I deserved it. Confirm my worldview, as they say. Reassure myself with the certainty of my own unworth. Which didn't exactly make me an easy man to trust.

But why was I angry at her? Was it simply because she kept me away from alcohol? Was it because nothing she did ever solved any of my problems?

On some level, I knew that being angry at her and being angry at myself were the same thing. But at the moment I couldn't pin down why.

She didn't break the silence until she stopped. Then she said, "Time to shift. I told Altar you're injured, but I don't want anybody to think you're incapacitated."

Oh, well. I was about as ready as I was likely to get. While she opened the door, I rolled off the seat to get my arms and legs under me. Then I crawled backward out into the snow and stood up.

Sort of. My posture wasn't notably upright. But at least I could breathe the sharp winter and look around.

The air tasted cold and clean, like someone had just invented it for the first time. On the other hand, the wood smoke over the lodge reminded me that there was usually nothing new or even particularly clean about the things people did indoors.

Nevertheless I had to admit that Deerskin Lodge was a good place for a mystery camp—isolated, self-contained, and beautiful. We stood on a rise at the front gate, with the lodge and its outbuildings below us at the end of a driveway at least a hundred yards long, in the bottom of a hollow with mountains on three sides, a barbed wire fence around the whole spread, and the next phone a good hour or so away by car. The real world sure as hell wasn't going to intrude here—which, when I thought about it, struck me as a mixed blessing.

Most of the hollow had been cleared, but the people who built the camp had obviously tried to preserve as many of the original trees as possible. In fact, the middle of the lodge roof had a particularly patriarchal longneedle pine growing out of it. And a dozen or so evergreens still occupied the hollow, most of them down near the buildings.

Aside from the lodge itself, I counted six outbuildings. Most of them looked like cottages, and I jumped to the brilliant conclusion that they housed the staff. I couldn't tell how many of them were occupied, but two had smoke whispering from their chimneys and vehicles parked outside, a battered old sedan, a stretch pickup truck, and a Land Rover.

At a guess, the lodge looked big enough to feed, shelter, and recreate twenty people or so, with room left over for plenty of closets, complete with skeletons. It had been built in a haphazard—i.e., rustic—way around its central tree, but one wing plainly included a kitchen, and the others probably held bedrooms. Unlike the trees, the pitched roofs had shed the snow, baring their shingles. Small vent windows under the eaves let air in and out of the attics.

Out front stood a van that could've carried ten people and their living room furniture. If that was Sue-Rose Altar's idea of transportation, you had to admit she at least knew how to take her hobbies seriously.

Ginny studied the terrain with a wistful look on her face. After a minute she murmured, "Kind of makes you wish we really were on vacation, doesn't it. This would be a good place to relax."

For absolutely no good reason at all, I suddenly wanted to burst into tears. The joys of convalescence. I would've been willing to sacrifice actual body parts to make our relationship into one where we could take vacations together.

The expression on my face must've revealed more than I wanted. Holding me with her gray stare, she asked carefully, "You all right?"

I wasn't equal to answering that question. Instead I told her one of my usual lies. "I don't like feeling this weak, that's all. Don't worry about it."

Like the rest of my lies, this one wasn't a lie because it was untrue. It was a lie because it wasn't enough.

She went on studying me. "We'll have to spend some time with Mrs. Altar. Hang on as long as you can. But if you need a break, let me know. I'll arrange something."

Still taking care of me.

When I nodded, we got back into the Olds. With pain throbbing in my chest, and my skull full of something that felt like grief, I concentrated on the road while she drove us down to the lodge.

Sue-Rose Altar must've seen us coming. She emerged onto the porch, a wide wooden structure that covered the front of the building, and waved at us while Ginny parked beside the van.

She was a tidy little woman, older than she appeared at first glance, with perfectly waved gray hair and a sparkle of childlike enthusiasm in her eyes. She wore a sable fur coat so lustrous that it may still have been alive, and her boots were clearly designed for feeling pretty indoors instead of for sloshing around in the slush.

For Ginny's sake, I took a deep breath and tried to get out of the Olds as if I did that kind of thing every day.

Mrs. Altar greeted us delightedly. "Ms. Fistoulari. Mr. Axbrewder. How wonderful." I noticed right away, however, that she didn't risk her boots in the snow. Nothing gets past the hardened private investigator.

Leaning over the rail of the porch, she continued, "Did you have any trouble finding this place? I hope so. I love being so isolated. It's just perfect. I get so excited before one of my mysteries, Rock can hardly stand me. Come up, come inside. Let's get to know each other."

Ginny gave me a look, just checking that I was still ambulatory. Then she put on her professional smile and led the way up half a dozen steps to the porch.

"Mrs. Altar." She didn't make any effort to hide her claw as she shook Sue-Rose's hand. "Pleased to meet you. I'm Ginny Fistoulari. This is Mick Axbrewder."

I lagged behind, doing my utter damnedest to pretend that I knew how to get up steps.

"Your husband," Ginny added, "said you would help us get oriented, let us know what to expect, that sort of thing."

"Buffy," Mrs. Altar burbled. "Call me Buffy. Rock is so formal, but I don't let him get away with it." She didn't seem to be aware that I hadn't caught up with Ginny yet. "I'll call you Ginny and Mick. We'll all be on a first-name basis by suppertime tomorrow. It's going to be great fun."

That did it. Nobody calls me Mick. My friends have better sense, and my enemies don't like the results. Before Sue-Rose "Buffy" Altar could go on, I surged up the stairs and said almost politely, "Call me Brew. I prefer Brew."

Just for a second everything seemed to stop. Mrs. Altar blinked at me uncertainly. Ginny ignored me in a way that suggested she'd done this on purpose. I stood motionless with pain thudding in my guts and sweat creeping past my hairline despite the cold.

Then Mrs. Altar recovered her composure. "Well, of course. Brew. How nice. Rock told me you've been hurt. I think it's very brave of you to come out and work for us so soon after your injury. But this will be just like a vacation.

We'll all have loads of fun. Come inside, and I'll show you around."

Her fur positively gleamed as she turned and moved briskly toward the door.

I gave Ginny my usual look of bloodcurdling happiness. She continued retailing her professional smile, no discounts for personal friends. Softly, as if she weren't sure I could follow the conversation, she murmured, " 'Rock' must be her husband."

"Oh," I said intelligently.

She went after Mrs. Altar. I shambled along behind her as well as I could.

Inside the air was warmer—but not as much warmer as I'd expected. Apparently Deerskin Lodge relied on fireplaces for a lot of its heat. The large room we entered had three of them, but they weren't lit.

Built around the tree trunk, the room itself was a high-ceilinged lounge with waxed wooden floors, knotty pine paneling, rough-cut beams, any number of stuffed animal heads for decor, and sturdy furniture sprawling everywhere. The atmosphere had a faint tang of ashes, the kind of smell you get when a chimney isn't working right and the fireplace has a minor back draft.

"This is the den," Mrs. Altar announced. I wasn't sure she'd ever stopped talking. "This is where we gather to reveal how we solved the crime. If we solved it. That's my favorite part of the whole week. Don't you just love those scenes in books where the famous detective explains his reasoning and takes everyone by surprise? I like to see how people react to the mysteries I've cooked up for them.

"This time we have eight guests. That makes fourteen people altogether, eight of them, me and Rock, you two, and our two actors. But remember, I want you to act like guests as much as you can. That's part of the fun, not knowing who the real detectives are. You can make up any cover you want, I don't mind, I like surprises."

"What can you tell us about the guests?" Ginny put in when Mrs. Altar paused for breath. "The more we know, the better we'll do our job. And the better cover we can figure out."

Buffy gave her an arch glance. "I'm sure that Rock told you we don't want to reveal who the actors are—or what the mystery is. That's part of the fun, too. We'll all be on the same footing." All of us, of course, except Rock and Buffy. "But I'll be glad to give you the names."

"Please," Ginny replied with just a hint of asperity.

"Well, let's see." Mrs. Altar made a show of consulting her memory. "There's Mac Westward and Constance Bebb. They're famous—they're 'Thornton Foal,' the novelist. They like to come to camps like this for ideas and atmosphere. Then there's Houston Mile and Maryanne Green. Houston has been to two of my camps before, but I've never met Maryanne. He always brings a different woman with him.

"There's Joseph Hardhouse and his wife, Lara—and Sam Drayton and *his* wife, Queenie. One of them is a doctor. Sam, I think. Yes, that's right. Joseph owns a chain of restaurants. Oh, and Catherine Reverie and Simon Abel. They're from back east. They want to try running a mystery camp of their own, and they're coming to see what it's like—see how Rock and I do it."

Yep, that was it. Counting on my fingers, I got up to ten. Eight guests and two actors. Just enough suspects to be a challenge. Not enough to be realistic. I thought it would be a good idea to sit down, but I couldn't find an excuse, so I stayed on my feet and tried not to sway too much.

"Why do the rest of them come?" Ginny asked. She meant, Why do grown people waste time on something like this? "You explained Mac Westward and Constance Bebb. Simon Abel and Catherine Reverie. What about the others?"

"Why, for the same reason I'm here," Mrs. Altar replied

with polite astonishment. "They love mysteries. They like to be involved."

Oh, naturally. Why didn't I think of that?

I could tell from the shape of Ginny's smile and the tightness around her eyes that she shared my reaction. She wanted a better explanation.

The truth probably had something to do with liking excitement and safety at the same time. Thrills without risk. Like riding the roller coaster in an amusement park instead of, say, tackling white-water rapids in an open canoe.

No doubt about it. I was going to have a wonderful time.

"Come on," Mrs. Altar continued. "Let's look around."

As we crossed the den, I was vaguely surprised that the floorboards didn't creak. Wooden floors usually don't like me much. But Deerskin Lodge had been built to last.

The next big room was the dining room. It had a fireplace at either end, massive wrought-iron lighting fixtures, and one long table of polished pine, with enough heavy chairs to seat at least fourteen people. But I ignored details like that. Instead I focused on the fact that the walls were decorated mainly in gun cabinets.

Rifles on one wall. Shotguns on the other. Handguns interspersed here and there. I recognized a Winchester .30–30 carbine, a Purdy that looked powerful enough to buckle plate steel, even a General Patton Commemorative six-shooter. They were all mounted for show instead of use, all closed behind glass doors. But when I touched the latch on the nearest door, I found that it wasn't locked.

Under each of the cabinets were rows of drawers. Mrs. Altar had already moved out of the room, still talking, but Ginny paused to watch while I pulled a drawer open.

It was full of ammunition. In this case, rounds for the .30–06 Remington mounted level with my nose.

I checked three or four drawers. Each held ammunition for the guns in the cabinet above it.

Murder on Cue might as well hold its mystery camps in

an arsenal. Rock and Buffy had enough firepower at their disposal to slaughter an entire regiment of paying guests.

Ginny wheeled away from me and cut into our guide's monologue. "Mrs. Altar."

Sue-Rose stopped. "Please, call me Buffy. I mean it. I really can't abide formality."

"Mrs. Altar." Ginny put a snap in the name. "I want all these guns taken down and locked away. Somewhere where your guests can't get at them."

Mrs. Altar positively gaped in surprise. "Whatever for?"

"You've hired Fistoulari Investigations for security. Those guns are a security risk. Your guests could shoot up half the county before we realized they have that little common sense."

"Oh, really." Mrs. Altar frowned in vexation. "You can't be serious. What kind of people do you think come to my mystery camps? Rapists? Child molesters? This is recreation, fun. Our guests have always been responsible members of society. We've never had the least trouble.

"We only need security for the insurance. Rock must have explained that to you. You don't have to worry about it. The job you're really being paid for is to play along with our mystery, help us enjoy it."

"I don't know anything about that," Ginny retorted, "and I don't care." She wasn't actually angry. She just sounded angry to make her point. "You hired me for security, and I mean to take it seriously. That includes routine safety precautions. Locking those guns away is definitely a routine safety precaution."

Of course, she could've suggested locking up the ammunition instead. But that idea had a couple of problems. For one thing, it made her look like the kind of woman who backed down—which could make her job a lot harder later on. And for another, she knew as well as I did that a gun without ammunition is more dangerous than ammunition without a gun. If nothing else, people can hit each other with guns. They don't usually throw ammunition at each other.

But Mrs. Altar didn't care about things like that. Unlike Ginny, she *was* angry. "I've never heard anything so ridiculous. What good is a hunting lodge full of empty gun cabinets? What kind of atmosphere is that?" If she kept this up, she'd scorch the hair on her coat. "If we expected trouble, any trouble at all, do you think we would have hired *you?*"

When she heard what she said, however, she had the good grace to look a bit embarrassed. "I mean, Brew just got out of the hospital. Knowing you aren't at your best, we would never have hired you if we weren't sure there would be no trouble."

"I appreciate that, Buffy," I put in. "But guns are dangerous anyway. People want to touch them. You say your guests aren't the kind of people who shoot each other. That makes the situation even more dangerous. People who don't know much about guns are the ones who have accidents.

"We aren't criticizing anyone. We aren't even complaining." Axbrewder's best imitation of sweet reason. Sometimes when Ginny acts fierce I back her up by acting soft. "The whole point of a precaution is to prevent trouble, not cause it."

"Humor me on this one," Ginny put in, sarcastic now instead of angry. "I'm the only security you've got. If I walk out, you won't have time to hire anybody else. Locking up the guns won't ruin your mystery. But without two professionals to play against, your guests might not have anywhere near as much fun."

Obviously Mrs. Altar was accustomed to getting her own way. On the other hand, she must've been able to see that Ginny wasn't bluffing. Frowning her irritation, she said, "Oh, very well. You can talk to Art about it. He should be around here somewhere. But Rock will be very displeased by your uncooperative attitude."

Still fuming to herself, she led us out of the dining room toward the kitchen wing.

Ginny cocked an eyebrow at me.

"Makes you wonder," I whispered, getting even with her for encouraging Buffy to call me *Mick*, "who used to do security for them."

She snorted. "All right," she whispered back. "I admit it. I should've found out more about how we got this job. I should've asked who used to do it, and why they aren't doing it now. You satisfied?"

I wanted to say something about just how satisfied I was, but we were already entering the kitchen, and Mrs. Altar had stopped to introduce us to the two people there.

Speaking as someone who probably should've spent his life being a short-order cook instead of prying into other people's misery, I was impressed by the kitchen. Deerskin Lodge had the equipment to take first-class care of its guests. The room was nearly as spacious as the den, with gleaming stainless steel food lockers built into the walls, massive conventional, convection, and microwave ovens, plus two huge gas cooktops and more appliances than I could count on short notice—can openers, coffee mills, Cuisinarts, blenders, knife sharpeners, the lot. Not to mention utensils and pots and pans, most of them hanging from racks bolted to the beams. Also a Hobart dishwasher big enough to double as a car wash.

With a kitchen like that, Christ wouldn't have needed a miracle to feed the five thousand. I could've done it myself, if I were healthy.

Both people in the kitchen were working. The woman sorted what looked like a few hundred bags of groceries— supplies for Murder on Cue, Inc. She was exceptionally pretty in an exceptionally pale sort of way. Her long wavy hair was so blond it was almost white, and her skin seemed outright translucent, letting all the light around her shine in to her bones. Somehow her eyes managed to appear deep without having any color. She didn't wear rings or bracelets, but from her neck a small silver crucifix hung on a fine chain.

She met Mrs. Altar's greeting soberly, without a smile. The depth of her eyes and the lines of her face gave the impression that she was a woman who never smiled at anyone.

"Brew, Ginny," Mrs. Altar said, still sounding miffed, "this is Faith Jerrick. She's the cook for the lodge."

Instinctively I distrusted Faith Jerrick's cooking. She was too thin to have much appreciation for food.

"That's Art over there," Mrs. Altar continued, pointing at the man. "Arthur Reeson. He's the manager."

At first all we could see of Reeson were his legs. The rest of him was buried under one of the cooktops. The noises he made suggested that he was repairing the stove's innards. But when he heard his name mentioned, he disimmured himself and stood up.

His dark good looks contrasted strangely with Faith Jerrick's paleness—black eyes, black hair, swarthy skin made even darker by a premature five-o'clock shadow, grease stains, and pipe dope. He was nearly as tall as I am, and his tight work shirt betrayed an indecent amount of muscle. Like the cook, he didn't smile, but his expression only resembled a glower because his skin and brows were so dark. It was nothing personal.

"Art," said Mrs. Altar, "this is Ginny Fistoulari and Mick Axbrewder. They'll be with us for the rest of the week." Deliberately disavowing us, she added, "Ginny wants to ask you something."

When he heard our names, Reeson's eyebrows went up. But they didn't stay up. Instead he showed us his stains to apologize for not shaking hands. Then he nodded unnecessarily at the cooktop.

"Pilotless ignitions are a great idea." His voice sounded permanently hoarse, as if he'd done too much shouting in his life. "If you get a gas leak, they don't blow up the kitchen. But they're a sonofabitch to fix.

"What did you want?"

As a general rule, Ginny wasn't what you could call reluctant to assert herself with strangers. But she knew how to be civil about it. "Mr. Reeson," she replied evenly, "Mr. Axbrewder and I are private investigators. Mr. Altar hired us to keep an eye on the safety and security of his guests for the next week. I'm concerned about the guns in the dining room. They're a hazard, especially around inexperienced people. I'd like them locked up somewhere. I don't care where, as long as you can keep the key to yourself."

Art Reeson's eyebrows went up again. Maybe they were on automatic, went up and down by themselves. "That's unusual," he said, almost croaking. "I've never been asked to do that before. What's changed?"

"I can't answer that," Ginny said without a flicker. "I don't know who did security for Murder on Cue in the past. I have no idea why they didn't object to the accessibility of those guns. But *I* object, Mr. Reeson. I'd object in the same way if Deerskin Lodge kept cases of gelignite lying around."

Reeson didn't exactly avoid her eyes, but he didn't precisely meet them, either. "I'll have to ask the owners. They make the rules around here. I can't touch the guns myself without permission."

In a tone that didn't invite discussion, Ginny said, "Please. As soon as possible."

Brightly Mrs. Altar remarked, "Well, that's taken care of, then," as if a particularly thorny dispute had been successfully negotiated. At once she started talking to Faith Jerrick.

"Now, Faith, I hope you have some truly special meals planned for my guests. You've done wonderful things for us in the past. I expect you to surpass yourself."

"Yes, ma'am," the cook replied distantly.

Mrs. Altar looked Faith up and down, and sighed. "And please call me Buffy. You know I prefer that."

"Yes, ma'am," Faith repeated. Unlike Reeson, she had the gift of avoiding people's eyes without making a point of it. Apparently she was a woman who didn't argue much—and didn't pay much attention to arguments.

With a sable shrug, Mrs. Altar turned back to Ginny and me. "I don't know why I bother," she admitted. "I've never been able to get her to use my name. Shall we go?" She gestured us out of the kitchen. As soon as we reached the relative privacy of the hall, she added, "In fact, I don't think I've heard her say more than four words. Yes, no, ma'am, and sir. I think she isn't, you know"—Buffy tapped her forehead—"all there."

Inspired by my usual instinct to come over all manly and protective in the presence of frail women, I muttered, "Maybe she just doesn't have anything she wants to say." But Mrs. Altar ignored me, and Ginny had the decency not to laugh out loud.

All this moving around had just about finished me. At the moment I wasn't especially conscious of pain. My guts had taken on a generalized throbbing that felt bearable simply because it was diffuse. But the strain of convalescence and movement and concentration had used up my strength. And I couldn't imagine what contribution I was making. Nobody would miss me if I took a little rest somewhere.

I managed to catch Mrs. Altar before she launched another monologue. "Buffy, is there a phone I can use? I should check in with our office." Which was patent bullshit, but maybe Mrs. Altar wouldn't know that. "You can show Ginny the rest of the lodge while I'm on the phone."

Fortunately Ginny could take a hint when she's in the mood. "That's right," she said promptly. "Your husband gave me the impression that Deerskin Lodge has more staff than just Faith and Art. You can introduce me to them and finish showing me around while Brew makes his calls."

"All right." Unlike the matter of the guns, this request didn't trouble Mrs. Altar. "There's only one phone. Our guests aren't supposed to spend their time talking to the rest of the world. But naturally a phone is a necessity. It's in the manager's office. This way."

She steered us down a hall away from the den. In a moment she stopped in front of a door with a mail slot. "Of course," she was saying, "the lodge doesn't need a formal manager. The owners have an office back in Puerta del Sol. And the staff has been here for a long time. They know what to do. But Art uses this room to do his paperwork— bills and files, registrations, reservations, I don't know what all."

The door wasn't locked, so she had no trouble letting us in.

It was an office, all right. I recognized it right away by the filing cabinets and desk, the adding machine and phone. Everything possible was made of wood—rustic as all hell—but the oak of the desk and chairs didn't quite match the blond pine paneling and floorboards. Which probably didn't matter because the lodge's paying guests weren't expected to come in here.

Ginny stayed outside. After a quick glance around the room, she told me, "We'll come back for you when we're done," and set Mrs. Altar into motion again with a touch on her arm. Together they receded down the hall.

I heard Mrs. Altar say, "There are only two other people here. Petruchio and Amalia Carbone. Truchi and Ama. He works with Art and takes care of the grounds. She's the housekeeper. They'll be around somewhere, but they'll be busy. I don't think I've ever seen either of them when they weren't busy."

Left to myself, I went into the office and closed the door. I wanted to lie down, but the room lacked a couch, and I didn't think I could come up with a decent excuse for sprawling on the floor, so I sat in the chair behind the desk. It was the biggest one in the room, and it had solid armrests. Also it tilted, so that I could adjust my guts into a somewhat more comfortable position. All I wanted was to hurt less and go to sleep for a while.

But there's something about sitting at someone else's desk that makes you feel like looking in the drawers. I resisted the impulse briefly. Then I decided what the hell. I was a private investigator. Poking my nose in where it didn't belong came with the territory.

Of course, I didn't find anything interesting. The drawers held perfectly ordinary files and supplies—grocery receipts, boxes of paper clips, stuff like that. But my knees didn't quite fit the desk, and my position while I looked through the drawers shoved them high up under the writing surface.

One knee bumped something.

Probably one of the supports. So what? And this was my first day out of bed. I had no business hunching forward and twisting the sin out of my stomach to look under the desk.

I did it anyway.

I found a pistol in a holster glued to the wood where the person at the desk could reach it easily. I unsnapped the holster, pulled out the gun.

It was a Smith & Wesson .44 with a long, underlugged barrel, the kind of gun you use when you want to hit something small and far away and make sure it stays dead.

For no special reason except I'm an intuitive fool and can't resist the impulse to jump to conclusions in all directions, I suddenly felt sure that Art Reeson liked guns. The owners didn't use this desk, he did. He liked being surrounded by weaponry.

He probably didn't want to do what Ginny had asked him.

I hesitated. Apparently he'd worked for Deerskin Lodge for a long time—and the owners certainly wouldn't keep a manager who made a regular practice of waving guns around. Murder on Cue had never had any trouble. Maybe he was just indulging an innocent fetish.

Nevertheless where I come from people who like guns that much are always trouble. No exceptions.

Sometimes being intuitive helps. And sometimes it makes you look like an idiot. But I was too tired and sore and possibly even feverish to be reasonable, so I made a snap decision. Swinging open the cylinder, I poured out the shells and dropped them into the bottom of one of the drawers. Then I put the .44 back where I found it.

After that, like a man with a job well done, I leaned back in the chair, closed my eyes, and napped the nap of the just.

4

Ginny came back for me without Mrs. Altar in attendance.

I didn't know how she managed that, and I didn't ask. I was just glad Buffy wasn't there to see how thorough my incapacitation had become.

From somewhere, Ginny produced a glass of water and any number of pills. My antibiotics, she said, and one or two things to help manage the pain, but I knew her well enough to be suspicious. I was morally certain some of those pills were vitamins. She believes in vitamins, the more the merrier.

After the pills, she led me to the dining room, where Faith Jerrick put some soup on the table for us. Chicken noodle, of course. It tasted like she'd made it all by herself, fresh from a can. Compared to hospital suet, however, it didn't taste too bad.

Eventually I felt good or at least stable enough to ask about Mrs. Altar.

"Gone back to the city." Ginny watched me for indications I might someday recover my health. "I gather she wants a final rehearsal with her actors. She'll pick us up with the rest of her guests early tomorrow afternoon."

"What're we supposed to do in the meantime?"

Ginny shrugged. "Finish here. Get you as much rest as possible." She considered for a moment, then added, "I don't want to go back to the apartment. El Señor's goons might find us. We'll check into a motel." Nothing about the process seemed to interest her much. She lacked the mothering instincts to be a good nursemaid. On the other hand, she stuck by her own decisions. "I packed our suitcases this morning," she concluded. "They're in the Olds."

Without warning, I felt sorry for myself again. For the next week, at least, I wouldn't even be able to choose my own clothes.

Obviously a nap hadn't improved my mood. But I still had a job to do, so I did it. I told her about the gun I'd found.

I didn't mention emptying it. Probably too embarrassed.

She did her best to look involved. "So what does the famous Axbrewder intuition tell you about Art Reeson?"

It was my turn to shrug.

She drank down the rest of her soup. Then she said, "My sentiments exactly."

When we were done, we drove back to Puerta del Sol. We checked into a motel. She helped me wash up because I couldn't handle that job by myself yet. I ate more soup. Then I got as much sleep as I could.

Several times during the night, I looked over at her. She was sitting up in bed, staring at the ceiling like a woman who wanted badly to be somewhere else. Her claw lay dead on the nightstand beside her.

When I saw her like that, she scared me. I would've said something, but I didn't trust myself. If I pushed her in the wrong direction—toward giving up on me—I'd be lost. Under other circumstances, I would've at least stayed awake with her. As it was, I couldn't even do that.

But the next morning I felt better.

A misleading statement. The truth was, I felt like I'd spent the night wrestling with the Angel of the Lord, and all I'd gained from the experience was a whole new collection of aches and pains. And yet I did feel better. The nature of my hurts had changed. They felt less like I'd committed seppuku recently, more like the consequences of wild overexertion. Easier to live with.

So I ate my antibiotics and vitamins. I let Ginny take my temperature. I practiced dressing myself. I experimented with motel restaurant Cream of Wheat—which wasn't a success, unless you happen to like lumpy Elmer's glue. Then Ginny and I spent a bit of time deciding on our "cover" so that we'd know what to tell Murder on Cue's guests.

The whole time she looked miserable. I suppose she might've told me what was going on if I'd asked her a direct question. But I didn't have the nerve.

At last it was time to go. We were supposed to meet Roderick and Sue-Rose Altar in the parking lot of the Camelot Hotel a little before one. According to Ginny, Rock and Buffy chose the Camelot because that's where their out-of-town guests stayed.

We arrived a few minutes early, but the van beat us anyway. Somehow it managed to look even bigger than it did up in the mountains. I've lived in apartments that were smaller.

The sliding door stood open, and a man in a suit waited beside it, looking bored. For winter in Puerta del Sol, the day was warm—he didn't need an overcoat. For that matter, I didn't need my sheepskin. But I didn't have anywhere else to keep the .45.

"That," said Ginny as she wheeled the Olds to a stop near the van, "is Roderick Altar. Sue-Rose must be getting the rest of her group together."

When we climbed out of the Olds, the man glanced at us and nodded. If he was surprised to see Ginny carrying our suitcases, he didn't show it. Instead he murmured, "Ms. Fistoulari." Then he asked, "Mr. Axbrewder?"

He didn't offer to shake hands, so I didn't either.

He was about his wife's height, pudgy and going bald. The remains of his hair were plastered across his scalp to disguise a patchwork of liver spots. The tight merino wool of his suit expressed money, but his face only conveyed a lack of interest. He looked like a man who used to get excited years ago—before the extra flesh on his cheeks and jowls sagged, dragging him down. Only a woman who called herself Buffy would've called him Rock.

"My wife's inside." He indicated the hotel unnecessarily. "She should be out in a few minutes." Then he said, "Before she gets here, I want to talk to you."

That was fine with me. I wanted to talk to him, too.

Ginny and I paused in front of him, waiting for the dullness to fade from his eyes.

It didn't. In a flat tone, he said, "My wife tells me you objected to all those guns."

"That's right." Ginny didn't offer to justify herself.

Altar nodded. "It's about time someone did. I don't like guns. In fact, I don't like hunters. They're a hazard."

Well, well. That was a surprise. Buffy Altar had apparently overestimated her husband's passion for the ambience of Deerskin Lodge.

He'd given me an opening for the questions I wanted to ask. Unfortunately Ginny had questions of her own, and they weren't the same. Before I could go ahead, she said, "I gather you don't share your wife's enthusiasm for these mystery camps. Why is that, Mr. Altar?"

He looked toward the hotel. Obviously he didn't want Buffy to hear his response. When he'd satisfied himself that she wasn't about to materialize from the asphalt, he replied, "I just told you. I don't like hunters. 'Solving the crime' is hunting in another guise, that's all. It's an unequal contest. Even if our murderers were real—and armed— they wouldn't stand a chance. We have them outnumbered. Secrecy is their only hope. As soon as they make a mistake, we can overpower them. The exercise is trivial by nature."

Ginny smiled sharply. Altar may not have been interested in what he was doing, but all of a sudden she was. "I'm not sure I understand," she commented. "Most people wouldn't draw that parallel between game animals and murderers."

Rock didn't take offense—but he also didn't take fire. "I'm not saying I approve of murder. I'm just explaining why hunting doesn't appeal to me."

"But aren't you what they call a venture capitalist?" Ginny was a hunter herself, born and bred. "Isn't that 'hunting in another guise'? Hunting for the right people and the right opportunities to make money?"

For the first time Altar's fleshy features lifted, and his eyes showed a hint of energy. "'Hunting' is the wrong word. Or it's hunting for the opposite reason. The whole point of venture capitalism is to find valuable underdogs, the victims of unequal contests, and help them overcome bad odds, beat systems that are organized to defeat them. It's like hunting in order to help the game escape."

"Or," I put in, "like hunting for murderers to help them get away."

Just for a second, I thought Altar might laugh. He actually did smile. "Well, I wouldn't want to go that far." This time he made an overt show of verifying Buffy's absence. Then he told us in a conspiratorial whisper, "But I've been known to disturb a few clues, just for the fun of it. Make the crime a little harder to solve."

Ginny's smile had a different quality altogether. "You devil," she said distinctly. "I can see we're going to have to keep an eye on you."

At once he hooded his expression. "You'll never catch me," he murmured. "I'm too good at it."

Well, at least now we knew why he was willing to work with Sue-Rose on Murder on Cue, Inc. He wanted to sabotage her hobby. I didn't know whether to laugh or snarl.

But I didn't waste time deciding which. While he was still in the mood for revelations, I said, "Tell me, Mr. Altar. How did you happen to choose Fistoulari Investigations for this job?"

That subject clearly didn't interest him at all. "Oh, I heard about you somewhere," he said with a shrug. "Someone told me you do good work. I had my doubts when Ms. Fistoulari said you were in the hospital recently. You've been injured? But I took your reputation into account. And the job isn't challenging."

And, I added for him, if one of the hunters you don't like isn't at his best, so much the better. But I kept that to myself.

"I gather you've been doing this for a while," I continued. "We aren't the first security you've hired. Who had the job before we did?"

Unfortunately Rock Altar wasn't listening. Even Ginny had stopped paying attention. Instead they both watched a souped-up blue Camaro roar into the parking lot as if the driver had blood on his mind.

Automatically Ginny braced herself. Her hand found its way into her purse. But I didn't react. The sun was shining, and the sky was as clear as a dream. And the parking lot was too public. No one in his right mind would try to shoot me here. Besides, the Camaro had its windows up. When goons with guns drive by to blow you away, they always have their windows rolled down.

So much for my chance to ask Altar how we got this job.

The car skidded into a nearby parking space. The doors burst open. A woman jumped out of the passenger seat. A man stood up from the driver's side.

"You're a menace!" the woman shouted. "You nearly got us killed! I've never been so scared."

She laughed happily as she protested.

"Hey, I got us here," the man retorted. "And we aren't late. You said you didn't want to be late."

He was laughing, too.

They ran into each other behind the Camaro. She made a pretense of trying to slap him. He hugged her so hard that her feet left the ground. They laughed some more.

"Dr. Drayton," Altar murmured without too much disapproval. "Mrs. Drayton. Glad you could make it."

I remembered their names. Sam and Queenie Drayton.

Apparently they were local—a conclusion I jumped to because they hadn't spent the night at the Camelot. But I didn't care where they were from. I didn't even care why he considered it a good idea to drive like a drunk kid. What I wanted to know was, Where did she get a name like Queenie?

She subsided while her husband turned to size us up. He wore a tweed jacket and good slacks that didn't match the scarf flung carelessly around his neck. With his strong jaw and wavy hair and perfect teeth, he looked more like a movie star than a doctor. In fact, his face betrayed altogether too much pleasure for a doctor. Maybe he had some kind of low-stress specialty, like Facial Blemishes of the Rich. Or maybe he was one of Buffy's stooges.

On the other hand, it was easy to understand why any man would be happy in Mrs. Drayton's company. She wasn't beautiful—maybe she wasn't even pretty. But her hazel eyes looked straight at the world, afraid of nothing, and her wide mouth seemed to fill up with joy when she smiled. She had a slim, athletic, endearing body. Her coat hung open, and the way her breasts moved under her cashmere sweater gave the impression that she didn't wear much support. Or need it.

Down, Fang, I said to myself.

Fang didn't pay any attention.

"Mr. Altar?" Drayton asked, looking at me.

"I'm Roderick Altar," Rock answered. He didn't offer to shake hands with Sam Drayton either. "This is Mr. Axbrewder and Ms. Fistoulari. My wife is inside." He nodded toward the hotel. "We should be ready to go in a minute or two."

Drayton didn't seem to mind not shaking hands. He gave his wife a squeeze, then let go of her. "I'll get our bags."

Fishing out his keys, he unlocked the Camaro's trunk and produced two large suitcases and a black medical bag.

For an actor's prop, his bag looked unusually authentic. Used and familiar.

Altar opened the back of the van. Drayton heaved his suitcases and the bag inside. Then, since our suitcases were handy, he put Ginny's and mine beside his. Ginny thanked him with a nod. I thanked him by making a studious effort not to grin at Queenie.

Sue-Rose chose that moment to emerge from the Camelot with the rest of her guests in tow, followed by a bellhop pushing a luggage cart the size of New Hampshire.

Eight of them, by actual count. I reviewed their names to myself, but across the parking lot I couldn't guess which name went with which person.

Buffy beamed at all of us. As soon as she was close enough to be heard, she said, "I'm so glad you could all make it. This is going to be wonderful. Let's load up and go. I can't wait to get started. We'll introduce ourselves when we're on our way."

Sam and Queenie shared a look and a shrug to contain their laughter. Ginny and I didn't have any last-minute messages for each other, so we just nodded. Altar stood at the van's sliding door like a butler who didn't care whether he got fired, and all the rest of us piled in while the bellhop filled up the back.

Unfortunately piling in didn't come easily. It necessitated too much stooping, which put too much pressure on my guts. By the time I reached a seat, I thought I was going to pass out.

I found myself in what would've been called steerage on an ocean liner, the bench seat across the rear of the van. Other passengers had better accommodations, individual "captain's chairs" with armrests and ruffled upholstery. The Altars sat up front. She took the driver's seat, obviously in charge. He slumped beside her, slowly sinking from view. Behind them, Ginny had the seat closest to the door. She'd already begun talking to the man across from her, but I couldn't tell anything about him except that he had broad shoulders and the slickest hair I'd seen since Brylcreem went out of fashion.

Next came a man about the size and general shape of a mushy dirigible, possessively holding hands with his companion, a small flushed creature who, like Rock, looked like she was being consumed by her chair. Then two men, one of them handsome, the other not. Then two women matching the opposite descriptions. I occupied one of the corners, with Sam Drayton beside me, Queenie beside him, and the last woman beside her.

I didn't know what to make of the fact this woman had already taken notice of me. Ordinarily I'm used to being noticed—too big to ignore. But she didn't seem struck by my size. Which should've pleased me, I suppose. She had dark brown wavy hair swept back from her face with elegant casualness, and her makeup emphasized her beauty artlessly. Gloss or moisture glistened on her parted lips. Her wide brown eyes were soft and intent.

Us virile-type males are supposed to jump right up and salute when attractive women look at us like that. But for some reason I wasn't pleased. In fact, I didn't like it at all. Intuition again. I suspected her of looking at me like that because she knew I was in pain.

Buffy fired up the van. She was talking to Rock—in a moment she would address the rest of us. Before that happened, however, the woman beside Queenie Drayton reached her hand toward me and said softly, "We should introduce ourselves. I'm Lara Hardhouse."

Somehow I twisted my torso enough to get my arm free. As I shook her hand, I noticed that her fingers were cool, caressing. I tried to keep my pain from showing, but it made me sweat helplessly as I muttered, "Axbrewder. Call me Brew."

To distract everyone from the spectacle of my obvious

discomfort, I introduced Sam and Queenie. The three of them shook hands. But they didn't pay much attention to each other. As soon as he finished with Lara Hardhouse's fingers, Drayton leaned over and put his mouth close to my ear.

"I don't like the way you move," he whispered. "What's the problem?"

So much for my theory that he wasn't really a doctor.

"Abdominal injury." I didn't bother to whisper. Ginny and I'd decided to use my limitations as part of our cover. "I've only been out of bed for a couple of days. A vacation is supposed to help me heal."

Drayton glanced at my belly. Then he nodded toward the front of the van. "You should sit in one of those chairs. More comfortable."

"I *should* do a lot of things." All this courtesy wore on me. "Taking my pills. Getting more exercise. Improving my personality. Unfortunately I just get cranky when people tell me what I *should* do."

The doctor smiled as if he understood perfectly. "Convalescent blues," he pronounced. "That's a good sign. It means you're finally well enough to realize just how lousy you feel. Don't worry, it doesn't last."

He turned away, wrapped his hands around Queenie's, and proceeded to ignore me.

Too bad Lara Hardhouse didn't do the same. Instead she kept her gaze on me, her eyes moist with sympathy.

Mrs. Altar didn't make any announcements until she had the van rolling in the direction of the freeway. But after that she couldn't contain herself.

"Well, this is wonderful." We could all hear her. The van was as quiet as a mausoleum. "I get so excited before one of my mysteries. Rock keeps telling me that Murder on Cue is a business, but I can't think of it that way. I just love it. We've done everything we can imagine to give you a crime you'll enjoy. Haven't we, Rock?"

Rock's reaction—whatever it was—remained hidden by his chair back.

"Now," Buffy went on as if we were all about to start singing campfire songs, "it's time for introductions. I'm Buffy, most of you know that, and this is my husband, Rock. You'll all probably start from the assumption that he and I didn't 'do it,' but that's precisely why you shouldn't be too sure we're innocent.

"Let's work toward the back. Tell us who you are and what you do and why you're here."

She paused expectantly.

The man beside Ginny looked over to her, giving me a glimpse of his profile. His face had aggressive lines—sharp brows, a nose you could've used to open cans, a chin like clenched knuckles—softened by a wide flexible mouth. His jet-black hair lay slicked back from his forehead like a streak of grease. Ginny murmured something I couldn't hear—she may've told him to go first—and he nodded.

Turning farther to scan the rest of us, he said, "I'm Joseph Hardhouse." Like his mouth, his voice was flexible, capable of all kinds of inflections. "I own Granny Good's." Granny Good's was a chain of family-style restaurants based in Denver. "We make a lot of money, but the work is almost as boring as the food." He smiled humorously. "I take vacations like this to get away from worrying about the price of hash browns, or cooks who don't wash their hands enough."

Sam and Queenie Drayton chuckled. I didn't hear any other reactions.

"Murder fascinates me," Hardhouse continued, "the whole question of why people kill each other. To be fair, I should warn you that I think I know the answer. If I'm right, that gives me an advantage this week." His tone concealed whether or not he was joking. "But I don't like to lose, so if I'm wrong I'll never admit that I said anything like this. You'll only find out what my answer is if I win."

"That isn't fair!" Buffy protested in good-natured reproach.

"Neither is murder," Hardhouse countered. "That's part of what makes it interesting."

Still smiling, he passed the introductions to Ginny.

She studied him briefly with an expression I hadn't seen on her face for a long time. Then she announced calmly, "Ginny Fistoulari. Mick Axbrewder and I run a construction company in town." She did it again, set me up for people to call me *Mick*. There was nothing I could do to stop her. "Last week he didn't watch where he was going and nearly impaled himself on a bundle of rebar. But I can't make him rest unless I stand over him, and then I don't get any work done myself, so I signed us up for this. At least he'll be away from heavy equipment. And if the mystery gives him enough to think about, he might not drive both of us crazy."

I should've been angry. She knows I don't let anybody call me Mick. But as I listened I realized what she was doing. That Mick and her joshing tone dissociated us from each other. It disguised our relationship. Which might conceivably make our job easier.

I didn't like it. But I decided to let her get away with it, at least temporarily.

Obliquely I noticed that we were on the freeway now, picking up speed. The van ran almost silently, and I couldn't feel any vibrations from the road. For some reason, that made me nervous, as if we'd lost contact with reality.

The dirigible heaved himself around to look up and down the aisle. His smile was like too much butter icing on a cake, so rich that I could feel my cholesterol level rise. Maybe it explained his bad teeth. Still holding hands with his companion, he said, "Ah'm Houston Mile, and this here pretty little filly is Maryanne Green." His accent was so thick you could've used it to stucco houses. "We're from the great state of Texas, where Ah've got a few little ol' oil wells and just a bitty stud farm."

"Now don't you be too modest, Houston," his "filly" put in, her voice as sweet as his smile. "You raise the finest Arabians in the state, and you know it. Why, just last year," she informed us, making sure we understood Houston Mile's finer qualities, "place and show at the Kentucky Derby were sired on Houston's farm."

From where I sat, I could see dimples and devotion, but not much else.

"Well, Ah am a mite proud of them long-legged heartbreakers," Houston responded, "if Ah do say so mahself. But not too proud to exercise mah brains ever' once in a while. Ol' Buffy and Rock do put on a fine mystery. Stumped me ever' time so far, and that's a fact."

At that Buffy laughed happily, and Houston Mile licked his fat lips as if he wished he were licking Maryanne Green.

I could tell right away that I had a lot in common with both of them.

The handsome man behind Maryanne was next. He actually got out of his seat, offering all of us a good look at him, but he didn't smile. He had one of those faces that was too young for itself, as if it hadn't made up its mind what it would be when it grew up. He must've been at least thirty-five, but he looked about nineteen. Now that I could see him clearly, I wondered why I'd thought him handsome. His features were too soft for that, almost malleable.

"I'm Simon Abel," he said seriously. I seemed to hear a hint of Boston in his voice. "I'm here with Cat Reverie." He indicated the woman sitting in front of me, and she stood up, too. "This is a working vacation for us. I used to be a housepainter. She ran a hairdressing salon. But we saved up, and now we want to go into business for ourselves. We want to run our own mystery camps. We came to see how Rock and Buffy do it."

A housepainter? Simon Abel looked about as much like a housepainter as Sam Drayton did like a doctor. I decided to reserve judgment until I got a better look at his hands.

Cat—Catherine—Reverie, on the other hand, looked exactly like a woman who ran a hairdressing salon. Her lush auburn hair swept down onto her shoulders as if you were supposed to write a poem about it. Her bulky sweater and long skirt concealed her figure in a way that made you think you'd find it stunning if you got a glimpse of it. She was pretty in a professional fashion, as if she were just an advertisement for herself, not a real woman.

Her smile was the exact opposite of Simon Abel's. "Of course," she beamed, "the reason we want to run a mystery camp is because we love mysteries. Miss Marple, Nero Wolfe, Marlowe, they've always been my favorite books."

With an air of studied naturalness, she smoothed her skirt under her and sat back down.

Until Abel folded himself into his chair again, I didn't realize that he hadn't actually looked at anyone except Cat Reverie while he stood.

That left two people who needed no introduction, mostly because they were the only ones left who stood a reasonable chance of being Constance Bebb and Mac Westward, the famous novelist. For their sakes, I hoped they really were famous. To me, they looked like the sort of writer you've never heard of. The woman wasn't more than middle-aged, but she had the prim graceless air of a worn-out schoolteacher. Despite his corduroy jacket and turtleneck shirt, the man made me think of mashed potatoes that someone forgot to put in the refrigerator a few days ago.

He remained in his seat and didn't say anything. She rose to do the talking for both of them. "I'm Constance

Bebb," she said as if she weren't sure we'd done our home-work, "Connie, and this is Mac Westward. We're collaborators. Together we write the Thornton Foal novels."

There she paused like she expected a round of applause.

Somewhat to my surprise, she got it. *I'd* never heard of Thornton Foal—and I was still looking for Buffy's shills. But Maryanne Green and Cat Reverie clapped enthusiastically, Simon Abel breathed, "Wow!" and Joseph Hardhouse arched his black eyebrows. Queenie Drayton shifted forward as if she recognized the name happily.

Now that she had her applause, however, Constance Bebb didn't seem particularly interested in it. "Thank you," she said dryly. "It's nice to know that some people still read.

"We like attending mystery camps," she continued in the same tone. "They give us ideas. The experience of thinking about someone else's puzzles is invaluable. And guessing who did it in books is too easy. A reader doesn't have all the distractions that make real crimes so difficult to solve. Camps like this help us make our own books convincing."

Mac Westward nodded like a man drifting into senility.

Constance Bebb sat down. Lara Hardhouse, Sam and Queenie Drayton, and I introduced ourselves. Hoping it would do some good, I stressed *Brew*. Then Buffy Altar took over again.

"You're a wonderful group. I think this camp will be the best we've ever had."

The way she drove showed that she knew what she was doing, but I had to keep reminding myself. The tone of her enthusiasm didn't inspire confidence. I didn't trust people who had such a pleasant relationship with their own lives.

"You all know what we'll be doing, so I don't need to explain too many things. We'll be at Deerskin Lodge for a vacation. It's as simple as that. All we have to do is relax and enjoy ourselves—until the mystery starts.

"But there are a few points I want to emphasize." A few

of which she was especially proud. "Four of the people in this van are professionals. Two of you are actors, and two of you are private investigators. For you, there's one absolute rule. You can't reveal who you really are. All the rest of us are counting on you to keep your real reasons for being here secret.

"With everyone's cooperation, we can make our mystery really unique. For instance, one of our actors is probably here to be the murderer—unless it's me or Rock—but that doesn't mean the other will be the victim. The victim could be any of you. But that doesn't mean you're out of the game. You'll be informed that you've been killed, and we do ask that you play along, but you'll be informed in a way that doesn't reveal who killed you. After that, you can continue to try to solve the crime yourself. The only restriction—since you're dead—is that you won't be allowed to ask any questions. You'll only be able to listen and observe.

"Doing it this way has tremendous advantages. Because the victim doesn't have to be one of the actors, we can have more than one victim. We can have a whole series of murders. In fact, that's one of the ways the murderer can win. He can win, of course—or she—by not getting caught. Or he can win by killing us all.

"And since the victim doesn't have to be one of the actors, we can't guess the murderer simply by knowing who the victim came with. That's partly why it's so important for the actors and the private investigators to keep their identities secret.

"Now." Buffy's speech was like her driving—her enthusiasm concealed her expertise. "How will you be informed that you've been murdered? We used to use notes, little pieces of paper that said something like, 'There's an adder in your bed. As soon as you pull back the covers, you're dead.' But that made life too easy for the murderer. He could leave his notes anywhere. There was too little connection to the crime. And the notes always gave you the chance to argue that you didn't pull back the covers of your bed, so you weren't dead.

"Instead we now use blue marbles. The murderer has a supply. If you find one in your purse or your pocket, you're dead. If you pull back the covers and see a blue marble in your bed, you aren't dead, but if you find the marble after you're in bed, you are. Of course, if you don't find the marble at all, the attempt on your life failed. To kill you the murderer has to put it where you'll be sure to find it."

At this point Joseph Hardhouse made a show of turning out his pockets.

"No," Mrs. Altar laughed. She'd seen him in the rearview mirror. "Nobody's been killed yet. Our murderer doesn't want to take the chance that we might stop and call the police. In fact, nobody will be killed for at least a day. That will give us all the time to become familiar with Deerskin Lodge, to get to know each other a bit—and give the murderer time to figure out the best way to start killing us."

My pain had one advantage. It gave me an excuse for the way I looked. My companions weren't likely to realize that most of what showed on my face was disgust. The idea that fourteen grown men and women would spend the next six days hunting for blue marbles should've been funny, but I was in no mood for it.

Luckily for me, the speech was almost over. "Oh, just one more thing," Buffy said after pausing long enough to make me think she'd finished. "The weather forecast. You'll all be delighted to hear that we have a big winter storm coming in. We should get it sometime tomorrow or the next day. The mountains are supposed to get at least a foot of snow. We'll be practically snowbound—I hope."

Oh, good. More ambience.

For the first time in twenty-four hours, it occurred to me to wonder whether those guns had actually been locked away.

The rest of the guests seemed appropriately excited by

Mrs. Altar's announcement, but Mac Westward chose this occasion to emerge from his silence. In a cold lumpy voice, he asked, "Will we be safe?"

Apparently the surprise of hearing Westward speak acted as a catalyst on Rock. As soon as Buffy answered, "Oh, of course," her husband pulled up his head and faced the back of the van.

"Deerskin Lodge," he said firmly, "is fully supplied and equipped for the worst winter weather. If necessary we can live there comfortably for weeks. There is a phone. We can call for help if we need it. And if the line goes down, the manager, Arthur Reeson, has a snowmobile he can use to reach the nearest town. I think we can all count on our safety, Mr. Westward."

In response the male half of Thornton Foal folded his arms over his chest and subsided.

Now that Buffy was done, the guests started talking to each other. Most of them seemed genuinely excited about this vacation. Almost simultaneously, Simon Abel and Catherine Reverie leaned across their respective aisles to tell Mac Westward and Constance Bebb how thrilled they were to meet one of their favorite writers. Joseph Hardhouse acted like he was eager to resume a conversation with Ginny, but Houston Mile interrupted him. Despite his accent, Mile knew how to enunciate clearly when it came to money, and his voice carried—I heard him ask Hardhouse how much profit could be made in the restaurant business. Maryanne Green listened as if she were entranced.

To distract myself from the particular smile Ginny focused on Hardhouse, I turned to Sam Drayton and asked the first brilliant, insightful question I could think of.

"What's your specialty, Dr. Drayton?"

He looked at me, grinning like a movie star. Just for a second, he hesitated. Then he said privately, so that the women in the next row wouldn't hear him, "Rebar accidents. You know what I mean—puncture wounds with blunt rods, slow poisoning, that sort of thing. Amazing how busy it keeps me."

He took me by surprise. "In other words," I muttered, keeping my voice as quiet as his, "you don't believe me."

He nodded. "Just getting poked in the stomach wouldn't do enough damage. Having one of those rods rammed right through you would do too much. You wouldn't even think about a vacation like this."

Too bad the other people on the bench seat were listening. Queenie Drayton I could tolerate—I already had an almost adolescent crush on her. But Lara Hardhouse was another matter. She took everything we said too seriously.

However, I couldn't do anything about Lara or Queenie, so I concentrated on Drayton. "You think I'm faking it. You think I'm one of the actors."

Still grinning, he mouthed the word *no*. "You're no actor. The pain is real. I just don't buy your explanation."

As if she'd been holding her breath, Lara said in a little bursting whisper, "Mr. Axbrewder is a private investigator."

"Good God." She startled me, which helped me sound convincing. "What makes you think *that?*"

Both Sam and Queenie stared at her, but she didn't hesitate. "You aren't just *in* pain," she explained. "You *know* about pain. All about it. I can see it in your face. You work with it all the time, you live with it. You aren't the kind of man who takes this kind of vacation."

Well, shit. So much for my cover. But I couldn't just give up on it. Constance Bebb and Cat Reverie might've overheard what we were saying. And I wanted to do whatever I could to make Lara less interested in me.

"You're wrong," I said straight at her. "I just look like this because I'm an alcoholic."

That was a mistake. Sam Drayton nodded to himself, and Queenie looked away as if she were embarrassed. Their reactions were about what I expected. But Mrs.

Hardhouse suddenly became so interested in me that her whole face burned with it.

At least I didn't have to put up with any more conversation for a while.

5

I nstead of probing me, Murder on Cue's guests talked to each other. I suppose I should've been listening—you never know when a "clue" will crop up. But between them Sam Drayton and Lara Hardhouse had given me a scare. And that made me want to go to sleep. It was like having a hole in my moral guts as well as in my stomach. Leaning my head against the wall of the van, I closed my eyes and tuned out my fellow travelers.

Ginny wouldn't be amused if the people around me already believed I was a private investigator.

Buffy would be livid.

I was in pretty sad shape if I couldn't even get through the first hour of a nursemaid job without screwing up.

I wanted a nap, but I didn't really expect to get one, not under these conditions. So I was surprised when I jerked open my eyes, blinked my vision into focus, and found that we were already high in the mountains. It must've been the deterioration of the road that woke me up. Sunlight glittered on the leftover snow, still clean and mostly unmarked, and the trees arranged themselves against the hillsides and the sky like they were posing for a travel poster. For a minute there I felt completely disoriented, as if someone had changed the world around me and all the rules were different.

I hoped I hadn't been snoring.

During my nap, some of the guests had traded seats. Cat Reverie now sat opposite Simon Abel, talking with Ginny and Joseph Hardhouse. Lara Hardhouse had moved across from Mac Westward, where apparently she'd actually succeeded at engaging him in conversation. Sam and Queenie Drayton listened quietly. I had Houston Mile beside me, with Maryanne Green beside him and Constance Bebb in the other corner. Maryanne was quizzing Connie about Thornton Foal while Mile supervised. He smelled like petroleum oozing through an inadequate buffer of breath mints.

When he noticed that I was awake, he showed me how bad his teeth were. "Feelin' better, son?"

Well, no. I felt disoriented and bitter—not to mention bloated, as if my guts were filling up with blood. So I nodded and gave him a smile as convincing as his.

"Like Ah say," he continued, "Ah've done this before. Crime is intriguin', and ol' Rock and Buffy put on a fine show. It do challenge a man to keep up." Then he paused and peered at me expectantly.

A moment or two passed before I realized that this remark was intended as a question.

I didn't want to encourage him. "Not me," I muttered. "This is Ginny's idea. She's the boss. I'm just here because bed rest makes me crazy."

In response he chuckled and leered. "Ah know what you mean, son. Bed ain't good for but one thing, and rest don't come into it."

With one hand, he stroked Maryanne's upper thigh.

Luckily for me, touching Maryanne distracted him. He turned to lean over her and left me alone.

Eventually we reached the gate and the long driveway that led down to Deerskin Lodge. Buffy stopped to announce our destination and let everyone take a look. Then she drove down into the hollow and parked in front of the lodge.

One by one, we off-loaded ourselves into the mud and slush. I was the last one out.

By the time I'd dragged my sore carcass between the

seats and through the door, a man had emerged from the lodge to deal with the luggage. He had a peculiarly old-world face, with creased sallow skin, a drooping off-white walrus mustache, and bland innocent eyes—the kind of face you'd expect to see on some Mafia don's simple-minded cousin. He wore a battered old peacoat which concealed his frame, but the way he handled the suitcases convinced me that he was strong.

He must've been Petruchio Carbone, Truchi. He and his wife, Amalia, were the only members of the staff I hadn't met.

I half-expected Art Reeson to put in an appearance. Welcome the guests as Deerskin Lodge's official representative. But he didn't show.

Mrs. Altar had already reached the steps to the porch, keeping her contact with mire and muck to a minimum, but the rest of us stood around near the van and studied the mountains and trees and buildings, the absolute sky. Getting used to being here. Ginny had joined a little cluster that included Joseph Hardhouse and Cat Reverie. I edged closer to her, looking for some hint to help me interpret the way she dissociated herself from me. But her glance in my direction was studiously impersonal.

Under the circumstances, however, I couldn't help noticing that her entire face had changed since the parking lot of the Camelot. Now she looked fascinated rather than disinterested. The lines of her jaw and nose were keen, and her eyes shone like glass after you clean away a film of dust and oil.

I also couldn't help noticing that she seemed to have lost the self-consciousness—or the shame—that used to make her hide her claw. Now she treated her stainless steel hand as if it were as much a part of her as anything else.

And, on top of all that, I positively and entirely couldn't help noticing that her attention and keenness were focused on Hardhouse. She actually reached out to him a couple of times, touched his arm gently, like a girl hoping to be asked out on a date. His pleasure, which shone like his hair, was divided sort of equally between her and Catherine Reverie, but she ignored Cat to concentrate on him.

That hit me hard. Harder than it should've, probably, but I wasn't exactly at my best. I'd known Ginny for years, loved her for years, but I hadn't seen her look at me like that since I could remember.

All of a sudden, I knew what introducing me as Mick meant. She was leaving me on my own—abandoning me, as they say, to my own devices. She'd done what she could for me by bringing me here, putting me in a safe place. That was enough. Now she intended to pursue her own interests.

At the moment those interests had nothing to do with me. Instead they revolved around Joseph Hardhouse.

The insight left me numb with shock. Instinctively I tried to retreat.

When I turned away, I found myself blinking dumbly into the face of Lara Hardhouse.

She stood close to Mac Westward. Something about the way she accompanied him conveyed the impression that she'd appropriated him, probably without his being aware of it. But the ache in her eyes was aimed at me, and it was so intense that it practically stopped my heart.

She regarded me like she understood what had just happened.

Because I was numb with shock and couldn't afford to think, I pushed that possibility away. Instead I decided— on no basis whatsoever—that I knew what troubled her. Her husband was a philanderer, and it was killing her. She worked to make herself beautiful and share his recreations, trying to win him back, but nothing could make him love her the way she wanted. She needed help. She didn't look at me like that because she pitied me. She just thought we had something in common.

We did. But I didn't want to think about it. All I wanted was distance from my own dismay.

By then Buffy had started talking again, making a speech of welcome. I came in on the part where she said, "Truchi will take care of your bags. Unless they don't have tags on them." Pleased with her own humor. "In that case, you'll have to sort them out for yourselves.

"Come inside, and I'll show you where your rooms are. Once you've had a chance to settle in and freshen up, you can get oriented and do a bit of exploring before dinner."

I didn't know what else to do with myself, so I lurched along behind the group toward the stairs and the porch.

"This is the den," Buffy announced as she led us into the big lounge with the tree trunk and the stuffed heads. The room was considerably warmer than yesterday, heated by fires crackling in all three fireplaces—which solved the back-draft problem. "The dining room and kitchen are that way." She pointed in their direction. "The bedrooms are along these other two halls. There are more rooms than we need, but we'll be scattered to give you all"—she smiled a mystery lover's smile—"as much privacy as possible."

As if she were heading up a regatta, she steered us toward our quarters.

Sam and Queenie Drayton shared a room, of course. So did Houston Mile and Maryanne. And Rock and Buffy. I wasn't surprised that Connie, Mac, Simon Abel, and Cat all had separate rooms. But I was a little taken aback by the fact that Joseph and Lara Hardhouse weren't together.

Neither were Ginny and I. Her room was down the other hall from mine.

On top of that, I didn't much care for my room. Sure, it had a bathroom and a bed, which were about the only things I absolutely required. But the bed looked to be about a foot too short, and the chairs were delicate. Chintz and doilies mostly decorated the room, and on the walls hung sepia prints of hunters standing over dead beasts. It was the sort of room where you'd expect vacant women to sit and knit while they waited for their menfolk to come home from putting holes in animals. Or people.

I sneered at it in an attempt to distance myself.

I needed as many ways as I could find, so I was glad when I heard a knock on my door, and Petruchio Carbone came in with my suitcase.

He tilted his head to ask me where I wanted him to put my stuff.

"On the bed." I didn't have any better ideas. "I'll take care of it later."

With a shrug, Carbone flipped my suitcase onto the coverlet like it weighed practically nothing—which it probably did. Then he moved toward the door.

I wasn't eager to be left alone. To stop him, I asked, "Have you worked here long, Mr. Carbone?"

He paused, looked at me with an air of impersonal sorrow, scratched his head as if the question were more complex than I realized. After a moment he said uncertainly, "Ten years?"

"So you know Mr. and Mrs. Altar? You've seen their mystery camps before?"

His shrug was eloquent without actually shedding any light on the subject.

"What are they like?" I didn't care. I was just trying to survive. "How do the camps go? What do you think of all this?"

He fixed me with his simpleminded-cousin gaze. Under his mustache, his mouth looked like he'd never smiled in his life. "Since I'm working here," he said distinctly, "everybody who comes is crazy. I pay no attention."

He left to finish distributing luggage among the guests.

Crazy. Sure. Including me. I slipped off my sheepskin and draped it over my suitcase. Then I lowered my pains into a particularly flimsy rocker and tried to imagine how I could endure being here for an entire week. Cut off from

Ginny. Left alone to watch her while she looked for love or at least excitement elsewhere.

Fortunately I was still numb enough to function when she knocked on my door and walked into the room. Her eyes held a fighting gleam, and she didn't bother to ask how I was doing. Before I could muster what courage or anger I had left, she said sharply, "Come on, Brew. I want to show you something."

When she issues orders like that, I obey. No matter what. Trying to conserve my physical resources, I got up slowly—but I got up.

She strode out of the room. I followed.

Ahead of me and pulling away, she went down the hall to the den, then veered off toward the dining room.

When I caught up with her, she was standing in front of the gun cases.

All the guns were still there.

For some reason, my eye caught on a .22 rimfire Winchester with a pump action that looked like a brand-new design pretending to be old. And over on the other wall hung a by-God varmint pistol, one of the best—a Kimber Predator with bolt action and a scope sight.

More for completeness than to satisfy my curiosity, I touched the latches on the cases again. Still open. The drawers under the cases still held ammunition, neatly arranged so that the loads for each weapon were directly below it.

After a moment I realized that I was whistling softly through my teeth. I didn't really care about the danger. I was just grateful for the distraction.

Ginny didn't look at me. "What do you think?" she asked quietly.

"I think," I replied profoundly, "one of us is going to have to have a talk with Rock. Or Buffy." I kept my voice down as well. "Or both."

"I know that, you idiot," she rasped. "I meant, what do

you think we should do about the guns? Take them ourselves? Make Reeson lock the cases and give us the keys?
How far should we push this?"

"That's what I meant, too." I didn't like being called an
idiot, but I was in no mood to object. "Whatever happens,
it has to come from the Altars. And Reeson has to do it. If
we intervene ourselves, we'll blow our cover. Which will
make dear sweet Buffy furious. She'll fire us. Then we
won't have anywhere to go except back into town."

Into el Señor's range of fire.

Now Ginny looked at me. She was furious herself, but
when I didn't drop my eyes, she twisted her mouth into
something that might've been intended as a smile. Leaning
close to me, she whispered, "God, I hate it when you're
right."

With a flash of her skirt, she stalked away in search of
Mr. or Mrs. Altar.

Again I followed her.

She damn near collided with Buffy as Mrs. Altar came
through one of the doorways with Sam and Queenie Drayton, Joseph Hardhouse, and Catherine Reverie.

"Ah, Ginny, Brew." Buffy wore a smile so bright you
could've used it to read by. "We were just going to take a
walk around the grounds—the 'policies' of the Lodge, as
they say in those wonderful old British novels.

"Will you join us?"

"Can you wait a minute?" Ginny countered. The
change in her voice astonished me. I'd expected assertiveness—take-charge Fistoulari in full cry. Her professional integrity was at issue. But instead she sounded
positively amiable. "Brew and I have a problem. We need
to talk to you."

"Oh, not right now," Buffy protested with a girlish pout.
"We had our hearts set on a walk. Freshen our appetites for
dinner. Isn't that right?" she asked her companions.

None of them contradicted her, although Sam muttered

something that could've meant anything, and Queenie seemed to be stifling a secret laugh.

"Tell you what," Buffy rushed on. "Rock and I'll make time for a quiet chat after dinner. I'm sure we'll be able to straighten everything out."

Which indicated that she knew what Ginny wanted to talk to her about.

Ginny acquiesced gracefully. Another surprise. "That'll be fine," she said with no hint of irritation. "Maybe I'll come on that walk with you after all."

Queenie looked up at me. Under other circumstances, I could've drowned in her dark eyes. Her voice was like music as she asked, "What about you, Brew?"

But I was already floundering. I shook my head stupidly.

She smiled and shrugged, and Buffy led her party toward the front door. Cat Reverie clung to Hardhouse's arm. The way she tucked her hip against his thigh gave me the impression that walking wasn't her preferred form of exercise.

Ginny accompanied them outside contentedly, as if she'd never been angry in her life.

Calling "Wait for me," Simon Abel hurried past to catch up with them. Then they were gone.

I stared after Ginny's back for a long time after the door closed. What was going on here? Who was that woman? The Ginny Fistoulari I knew wouldn't have taken no for an answer from a Sherman tank. Not where her job was concerned. She would've insisted on a private conversation. What made her so easy to get along with all of a sudden?

Hardhouse, that was the answer. She'd swallowed her irritation and assertiveness for his sake. No, worse than that. Her determination had evaporated as soon as she saw him.

She was gone. Just like that.

I needed a drink.

It would probably make me sick, but at the moment I didn't care. Now I had a hole in my heart as well as my stomach, and this numbness wasn't going to last much longer. When it wore off, I would be in serious trouble.

Unfortunately—or fortunately, depending on your point of view—I didn't get a drink. On my way toward the dining room to locate a liquor cabinet, I met up with Roderick Altar.

He appeared especially vague, blurred by his lack of interest in his own thoughts. But he didn't hesitate when he saw me. "Mr. Axbrewder," he said as if I were what he'd just been thinking about, "I need to talk to you. Is Ms. Fistoulari around? Can you come to the office for a moment?"

A session with Rock wasn't what I'd had in mind, but I didn't dismiss the opportunity. When you're floundering, you'll grab hold of anything—which in my case happened to be my job. The client wants talk? The private investigator gives talk. Especially when he also has things to discuss.

"She's out," I explained, "but I'm here. In fact, I was looking for you." Some lies are easy. "We have a problem."

I thought I caught a glimpse of relief on his features. Maybe he didn't want to face Ginny with what he had to say. "This way," he muttered with his usual lack of ceremony and walked off in the direction of the office.

Since yesterday a new stack of papers had appeared on the desk. Guest registration forms, all filled out—probably by Rock. He made himself at home in the big chair behind the desk. I envied him his assurance, but I didn't argue. Hardship puts grit in your soul. Bracing my stomach in one of the less comfortable chairs, I waited for him to begin. The dullness of his gaze made it hard to think of him as a venture capitalist—or as any other life-form that liked risk.

But at least he didn't beat around the bush. Without any of his wife's social shuck-and-jive, he said, "You noticed the guns." His eyes didn't quite meet mine.

I nodded. "We weren't amused."

Rock sighed. "I wasn't either. I've just had a talk with Art Reeson. Did you meet him yesterday?"

I nodded again.

"He spoke to the owners of the lodge yesterday afternoon. I gather this was after you and Ms. Fistoulari told him you wanted the guns locked away. Apparently they refused permission. They say they accumulated their collection at considerable expense, and they're proud of it. It's part of the *appeal* of Deerskin Lodge.

"They take the position that we knew the guns were here. We could have objected to them before we hired the lodge. In addition, we've hired the lodge in the past without objection. Therefore they're unwilling to ask Reeson to take on the extra effort and inconvenience of easing Ms. Fistoulari's mind.

"And yours, of course," he added as an afterthought.

"I see," I said. I wasn't sure I liked being an afterthought. "And how do you feel about that, Mr. Altar?"

He shrugged without shifting his eyes, which were focused on the middle of my shirt. "As I told you, I don't like guns. They're an unnecessary opportunity for accidents, even a temptation. On the other hand, we've never had any trouble. Our guests come here to *play* at crime, Mr. Axbrewder. Most of them would be horrified to encounter the real thing." After a moment's hesitation, he said, "I'll go further than that. I think most of our guests play at crime in order to defuse their horror of the real thing. They're afraid of being victimized. Safe danger, safe hunting, create the illusion of invulnerability."

Then he spread his hands. "I would prefer to let the matter drop."

I was tempted to let myself get involved in a discussion about motivation. But my personal danger seemed too real. I needed to stick to business. So I asked, "What if we don't?"

Rock frowned as if he didn't understand the question.

"What if Ginny and I don't agree to let the matter drop? What happens then?"

That at least brought his gaze up to mine. When he met my eyes, I saw the toughness that had been missing until now—the toughness that had been atrophying from disuse ever since he'd become Buffy's partner in Murder on Cue, Inc.

"Then," he said slowly, "you'll look like a fool. Whatever you do, the guns will remain where they are. And your identities will be exposed to no purpose. That will significantly reduce your value to us. I doubt that your fees will be worth paying solely for the sake of lowering our insurance rates."

"I see," I said again. "Leave the guns alone or get fired."

Rock faced me without blinking. He didn't like guns. He didn't even like Murder on Cue. But on this subject he was prepared to back his wife as far as necessary. He couldn't possibly know that Ginny and I couldn't afford to be fired right now. As far as he knew, we might take a stand and refuse to budge. He accepted that risk.

Like it or not, I had to respect him.

So I tried a different tack. "Mr. Altar, do you have any idea how much trouble Ginny and I'll be in if those guns are involved in an accident, or even a crime, and the commission holds an inquiry? We'll be held responsible. We could lose our license." That is to say, Ginny could lose her license. "We *know* better than to leave guns like that just sitting around."

He shook his head. "I think not. You were hired at the last minute. The circumstances here weren't under your control." The way he lowered his eyes suggested that he was trying to negotiate. "If necessary, I'll testify that you did your best to have the guns locked away."

That was slim. The commission already disapproved of Ginny for keeping me on the payroll. We were both under investigation for our run-in with el Señor. Altar's testimony wasn't likely to improve our credibility much.

Nevertheless his offer at least made it possible for us to avoid getting fired. And it gave me something else I wanted.

An opening.

While he thought we were still dickering, I asked for the second time, "Tell me, Mr. Altar. How did you happen to choose us for this job?"

That took him by surprise. He glared up at me. "I've already explained that. I—"

I interrupted him. "You didn't finish. You didn't tell me who had the job before we did."

He obviously wanted to ask what this had to do with the question of the guns. But he swallowed his curiosity, at least for the moment.

With a perfectly straight face, he said, "Lawrence Smithsonian and Associates."

When he mentioned that name, the bottom fell out.

"In fact, I've known Lawrence for years, at least by reputation. You must know him, too—he's highly regarded in banking circles around Puerta del Sol. And Murder on Cue has always had a good relationship with his company. We would have used his people as a matter of course, but just two days ago he was forced to pull out. Some sort of professional emergency. He couldn't tell me the details, but he needed all his people.

"He gave me your names."

Altar said all this blandly, easily. He had no idea what he was doing to me. "Now that I think about it, that's where I first heard of Fistoulari Investigations. Lawrence assured me that you would be perfect for the job. I trusted his judgment, of course."

Lawrence Smithsonian. Ginny called him "fat-ass Smithsonian." He was the one who got us into trouble with el Señor in the first place. Another recommendation. He'd sent us a client who'd killed one of el Señor's numbers runners. Which was about as charitable as helping us step in front of a locomotive.

And now we were here because of him? What the hell was going on?

Suddenly the whole game had changed. If Smithsonian got us this job, we could be sure of one thing. He did it out of malice.

And he knew something about it that we didn't.

My throat had gone dry. I had to fight to make my voice work. "Did Smithsonian—" I choked, stopped, tried again. "Did your friend Lawrence happen to say *why* he thought we'd be perfect for this job?"

"Well, I wouldn't call him a friend." My reaction clearly baffled Rock. "He's only an acquaintance. But no." He consulted his memory. "He didn't explain. However, he did imply we would be doing him a favor if we took you on. I had the impression he owed you a debt and wanted us to help him repay it."

A debt. Oh, right. Absolutely. Smithsonian didn't owe us a debt. He owed us blood.

I got to my feet. That nice protective numbness was gone. My head reeled, and a hum filled my ears. For some reason, however, problems like that didn't seem to affect my balance. I went toward the door almost steadily.

"Mr. Axbrewder." Altar must've called on resources he hadn't used for a long time. His voice snapped after me, but softly, softly, just a threat of the whip, not an actual blow. For the first time, he sounded like his nickname was more than a whim of Buffy's. "What about the guns?"

I wanted to laugh, but if I'd tried it would've come out falsetto with panic. "Don't worry about the guns. It's too late now."

He wasn't satisfied. "Will Ms. Fistoulari agree?"

"It's too late for both of us." That was all I cared about. But it wasn't the answer he wanted. I stopped with my hand on the doorknob and grinned back at him like a banshee. "She'll leave the guns alone. That's the least of your problems."

Back in my room, I spent the rest of the time before dinner cleaning my .45.

This was going to be a hell of a vacation.

6

My gun was a .45 Glock with enough stopping power to maim an automobile, but it didn't do me any good. The only actual use I'd ever gotten out of a firearm was shooting my brother. On the other hand, I didn't spend all that time cleaning it in order to use it. I did it to calm myself down. Basically I'm a tidy soul. I like to clean things. Back in Puerta del Sol, I would've scoured Ginny's apartment. Here I cleaned my .45.

By the time I was done, I'd reached a decision. I wasn't going to tell Ginny about Smithsonian.

It scared me spitless, but I was too stubborn to back down.

After all, why was I here? Not to get away from el Señor—that was Ginny's reason for bringing me, not my reason for coming. I was here to protect *her* from el Señor. And to start taking care of myself. So that I wouldn't be so vulnerable to her.

Joseph Hardhouse gave me an immediate, tangible reason to desire less vulnerability. As far as I could figure out, the only glue holding me and Ginny together these days was the chemical reaction between her protective instincts and my weakness. Now that she'd put me somewhere safe, at least for a week, the glue had already begun to break down. What did I have to lose by facing Rock's information on my own?

As of now, Lawrence Smithsonian was *my* problem. If Ginny wanted problems, let her think about what she was getting into with Lara's husband.

Unfortunately reasoning my way through the puzzle

Smithsonian represented wasn't easy. I had nothing to go
on except intuition.

Well, start from the facts. Lawrence Smithsonian, bless
his piggy little heart, had sent us the job that led to Ginny
killing our client and me killing Muy Estobal. So what? He
wasn't exactly one of the world's sweethearts, but he could
not have premeditated the whole thing. Even if he'd actively wanted to get us into trouble with el Señor—which
by itself was plausible, considering his dislike for Ginny—
how could he have known we would take the case? How
could he have known how it would turn out? Fat-ass Smithsonian was just nasty, not prescient.

So why was I scared now? What was the danger? He
knew something about this job we didn't. What, for instance? I had no way to figure that out. Assuming that
Ginny and I'd just gotten ourselves into another disaster
of his devising—well, what exactly *was* the disaster?
How did I arrive at the conclusion that this camp was anything more than a nursemaid operation? What did I use
for evidence?

Intuition. That's all.

And something else. Something that nagged at me and
refused to come clear.

But I was in no mood—and no condition—to suffer over
it. The back of my brain would talk to me when it damn
well felt like it, not one heartbeat before. And I had other
agendas.

I still meant to have a drink. If Ginny wanted to get
burned playing with Joseph Hardhouse, that was *her* business. I had an entirely different fire in mind.

By the time I finished cleaning my weapon, I heard
chimes out in the hall. When I opened the door, I saw a
woman walking away from me, beating rather aimlessly on
a small xylophone. From the back, she looked like a cross
between everyone's favorite grandmother and the Pillsbury

Doughboy. Amalia Carbone, the housekeeper, announcing dinner.

Until Cat Reverie emerged from the room across from mine and smiled at me, I didn't realize that I hadn't heard Buffy's companions return from their walk. No banging doors, no creaking floorboards, no talk, nothing. The rooms had better insulation than I'd expected.

A couple of things surprised me about Cat's appearance. She'd changed her clothes. Now she wore a drop-dead gown, black and slinky, which showed enough cleavage to reanimate a corpse. And she seemed glad to see me.

"Brew." She beamed up at me. "Good timing." Slipping her arm through mine, she hugged my biceps. "You can escort me to dinner."

I'd seen her walk with Hardhouse, so I was braced for the way she tucked her hip against my leg. Immediately I noticed that her posture had one particular advantage. It made her look like her breasts might come out of her dress at any moment.

But I wasn't interested in her. She wasn't Ginny. She wasn't even Queenie Drayton. I didn't pull my arm away—but I also didn't smile. With my usual charm, I asked, "What's all this about? I thought you were after Hardhouse."

Just for a second, her smile flicked away. Nevertheless she recovered quickly. "I am," she admitted in a tone that contained a world of possibilities. "But you could persuade me to change my mind. I like men.

"No," she amended at once, "that's not quite right. I like strength. I like muscle and toughness. Unless I'm losing my touch"—she chuckled as she squeezed my arm—"you have both.

"Take me to dinner," she commanded before I could respond. "Maybe later I'll find out whether I'm right."

While I groped for a snappy retort, I was interrupted.

A door slammed behind me. A hand came down on my shoulder.

Simon Abel.

He glared at me, lines pinched around his mouth. Unfortunately anger didn't suit his too-young face. Instead of lending him force, it only made him look like a petulant kid.

"If you don't mind," he snapped, "she's with me."

He gave me a problem. Nobody touches me—not like that. No matter how weak or wounded I am. But Cat's face wore a laughing expression for my benefit, and I didn't like that either. I didn't want to take sides between them.

So I pulled my arm out of her grasp and caught him by the wrist. Holding him hard enough to make him wince, I put his hand on her shoulder for him.

"Take her," I said with a malicious grin. "She's yours."

Then I strode ahead of them toward the dining room. For a few paces, anyway, adrenaline helped me walk like a normal person.

God, I wanted a drink. More and more, I couldn't think of any other way to stand being myself.

Most of the crew had already assembled in the dining room when I arrived. And most of them had changed for dinner. Ginny and Mac Westward were the only exceptions. Hardhouse had produced an actual dinner jacket, and Lara's gown rivaled Cat's. Houston Mile and Rock had on suits, Buffy and Maryanne Green wore dresses which would've done justice to an Easter service, and even Constance Bebb gave the impression that she'd donned her best tweed. As for the Draytons, Sam looked merely elegant and movie-actorish in a sports coat and cream scarf, but something about Queenie's silk blouse and flowing skirt almost broke my heart.

Feeling more than ever like the ugly duckling, I hunched into the room and glowered democratically at everybody.

Cat and Simon followed a moment later. They were both flushed, but for different reasons, and they didn't touch each other. Cat headed toward Hardhouse. Abel stood in the doorway, looking baffled by his own anger.

"Ah, here we are at last," Buffy announced happily. She may've been immune to awkward situations. "Please don't think dinner is a formal occasion. Some of us just like to dress up. It makes us feel that we're taking part in an Agatha Christie novel.

"Why don't we sit down?"

Smoothly she assigned seats. No haphazard arrangements for Sue-Rose Altar. After a bit of shuffling, we were all in our places, Rock and Buffy at the ends of the long table, Maryanne, Westward, Lara Hardhouse, Drayton, Ginny, and Simon along one side, Joseph, Cat, and me, then Connie, Mile, and Queenie down the other. Everywhere we looked, gun cases loomed behind us. Either the guns didn't belong there, or we didn't, I couldn't decide which.

When we were seated, Buffy rang a little bell, and Amalia Carbone appeared. I hadn't seen her face before. More than anything, she looked like someone you could trust to make spaghetti sauce.

Faith Jerrick trailed behind her. A demure net contained Faith's fine, almost white hair. She wore her crucifix outside her blouse. She didn't look at any of us.

Both she and Ama carried bottles of wine. From opposite ends of the table, they started offering wine to the guests.

I was never much of a wine drinker, but I knew the difference between white and red. Suddenly my pulse began to clamor in my head, and my throat felt too tight to breathe. I'd arrived without expecting it at a crisis. The mere idea of alcohol made my whole body constrict with eagerness. I stood on the brink of something irrevocable— a choice more important than I could measure. I deserved a drink, didn't I? Wasn't that the one true thing I could say about myself? I was an alcoholic, and alcoholics drink because they deserve to drink. Being sober was just a smoke screen, a way of hiding the truth—of pretending to be something I wasn't.

And Ginny didn't give a shit. Obviously. She didn't look at me. She'd already cut me off. She sat too far away from Hardhouse to focus her attention on him, so she talked to Sam Drayton. Even he held more interest for her than I did.

Self-pity is a wonderful thing. It justifies whatever you want. I couldn't think of one reason why I shouldn't get stone drunk as fast as possible. When Faith brought the red wine to my place, I nodded, and she filled my glass.

Looking at it, I realized for maybe the first time in my life that wine can be as lovely and seductive as rubies. It lacked whiskey's tranquil amber promise, but its attractions were still powerful. The lights in the dining room made my glass seem deep enough to drown in.

"Let me propose a toast." Buffy raised her glass. She was in her element. Her smile sparkled like her earrings, and her skin appeared to glow. When she looked that happy, I could understand why Rock went along with her hobby.

We raised our glasses. She paused dramatically, as if she knew what this moment meant to me, then said in a clear voice, "To a beautiful murder and an elegant solution."

Ginny gave me a glance like a sneer, but she didn't watch while I brought my glass to my mouth.

Lara watched. Her own wine forgotten, she stared at me intently, almost avidly, as if she were hungry for the implications of my drinking. Her lips were parted and moist, unmistakably ready to be kissed, and a dusky smolder filled her eyes. All of a sudden, she was the loveliest woman in the room, and every ounce of her was aimed at me.

Her intensity went through me like a kind of panic. Abruptly—too abruptly for grace, never mind discretion—I put the wine down untasted and picked up my glass of water. Conspicuously late, I joined the toast.

Everyone at the table seemed to stare at me. Ginny's

face had an odd congested look, like conflicted fright. I couldn't read Lara's reaction, but Sam gave me an unabashed grin, and Queenie murmured almost too softly to be heard, "Good for you."

As if in acknowledgment, Hardhouse proposed another toast. "May we all get what we want most this week." His voice grated on my nerves, but I drank with the group anyway.

His toast made his wife blush. Maybe it had something to do with infidelity.

Then Houston Mile started to chuckle. "Son," he said down the table at Hardhouse, "if Ah required an opportunity such as this to get what Ah want most, Ah wouldn't bother. Ah'd purely lie down and die."

"You must have simple wants, Houston," Hardhouse replied. "Perhaps you aren't very ambitious."

"Oh, Houston is ambitious," Maryanne Green put in, sounding rather breathless. "He's amazing, really. He can do anything. No one ever beats him—no one ever says no to him."

That I doubted. There were people right here who were perfectly capable of saying no to Houston Mile. But accuracy wasn't the point—not to Maryanne, anyway. Her words seemed to inflate Mile, take up some of the slack in his appearance. Somehow she made him look less bloated, more like he fit inside his skin.

He gave an aw-shucks grin. "How that woman do talk," he said expansively. "Ah'm just a good ol' boy from down home, if Ah do say it mahself. But I got no qualms about mah taste in horseflesh. Or womanflesh."

Now it was Maryanne's turn to blush.

"Don't let Mr. Mile mislead you," Rock put in unexpectedly. His air of vague disinterest may have been a disguise, concealing the man who liked to tamper with clues. Without looking at any of us, he explained, "He's been to two of our mystery camps. At the first, he was the first to solve the crime. At the second, he was the only one to solve it."

Buffy clucked disapprovingly. "Now, Rock, you shouldn't tell them things like that. You'll embarrass Houston. And you'll intimidate everyone else."

Embarrass Houston Mile? No chance. In fact, he said as much himself. "Ah'm not embarrassed, Buffy. Ah got mah reputation to maintain. Tell you what," he said to the rest of the table. "Ah'll lay you a small wager, whatever you like, Ah already know Buffy's actors. Ah got 'em figured. *And* Ah know which of us is supposed to be detectives."

Faith and Ama had brought out food. Cream of broccoli soup, I think it was. But eating didn't prevent us from listening hard.

"Fascinating," Queenie Drayton breathed. "Are you really sure?" When Mile nodded, she went on, "I'll bet with you. I think I have it figured out as well. What shall we bet?"

At once Mile flapped his fat hands in protest. "Miz Drayton, a gentleman don't wager with a lady."

"Oh, come on," Cat Reverie chimed in eagerly. "In this day and age? Don't you have women's liberation down there in Texas? Go on, bet with her. I want to know what you both guess. Maybe you aren't as good at this as you think."

Her challenge didn't ruffle Mile. He acceded easily. "Miz Drayton, if you insist Ah'll wager the princely sum of ten dollars that mah figurin' is righter than yours."

"Done," Queenie said without hesitation.

"So tell us," Cat demanded. "Start with the actors. Who do you think they are?"

Simon had his face buried in his food. Ginny was smiling unaccountably at Hardhouse. From where I sat, it looked like she was wasting her time. While she spoke, Cat Reverie kept one hand clamped to Hardhouse's thigh. However, everyone else paid close attention to Queenie and Mile.

Everyone except Mac Westward. He paid no attention to anything except his wine.

"No!" Buffy insisted before either Mile or Queenie could answer. "If you're right, you'll ruin the fun for the rest of us. And if you're wrong, you'll help us eliminate possibilities.

"I'll tell you what. Write your guesses on a piece of paper. Give them to me. When the camp is over, I'll read what you wrote. Then the rest of us can judge who wins the bet."

I had to give her credit. Sue-Rose Altar knew how to run a mystery camp.

Cat pouted, but both Queenie and Mile accepted Buffy's terms. For the moment, anyway, they kept their faces studiously blank, bluffing each other like mad.

As if he'd been ready for this since the beginning of time, Rock produced a sheaf of paper. He passed a sheet to Queenie, a sheet to Mile. Then he supplied pencils.

Queenie and Mile wrote briefly. She chewed the end of her pencil between names and glanced up and down the table, apparently suppressing a giggle. Mile approached the exercise more laboriously.

When they were done, they both folded their lists and handed them to Buffy. She unfolded the papers and read them solemnly, as if this were a momentous occasion. I waited for the background music to swell, playing the "suspense" theme from *The Deerskin Lodge Murders*.

She couldn't keep it up, however. When she read Mile's list, she burst out laughing. "Houston Mile, you should be ashamed of yourself." But then she put both papers away in her purse.

Mile favored us with an oleaginous grin, exposing his bad teeth.

I turned toward Cat to catch her reaction.

Apparently she'd already lost interest in guessing games. Instead she leaned toward Hardhouse. Now she had both hands on his leg under the table.

Mac Westward cleared his throat. He was gazing up at the ceiling as if it had a message written on it. After squinting upward for a minute, he read it to us.

" 'Mystery Camp of Fools.' Good title."

For the first time, Connie Bebb spoke. "Do you think we could get away with it? It may not be original enough."

Westward didn't answer. His attention returned to his wine.

Faith and Ama brought the next course—prime rib with sweet potatoes and homemade dressing. Unfortunately the soup was already as much food as I could handle. I tasted enough of the meal to raise my opinion of Faith Jerrick. After that I concentrated on water to keep myself from thinking about wine.

Gradually the conversation became general. Ginny and Sam Drayton began discussing ozone depletion in the troposphere, of all things. Cat was consumed—the perfect word for it—with Joseph Hardhouse. Beside me, Connie dipped at her food like a recent graduate of Miss Manners' school for "excruciatingly correct behavior."

Buffy kindly kept Simon Abel off the conversational streets. At the other end of the table, Maryanne Green worked so hard to strike some kind of spark from Rock that I feared she might do herself an injury. But I could hardly make out what either pair said. That left me with the disturbing prospect of Lara Hardhouse.

Nominally, at any rate, she was talking to Westward. In fact, she'd actually succeeded at getting him to listen to her. He tilted toward her with his elbow propped on the arm of his chair and his chin braced on his palm. While she spoke, he stared abysmally at her food, as if he found it depressing.

She kept her eyes on me, however. Her gaze held an appeal, a need almost strong enough to be called supplication. She might've been asking—begging?—me to rescue her from something.

Whatever it was, it couldn't have been Westward. If she'd left him alone, he might've fallen asleep. But instead she was telling him what she thought was wrong with most mystery novels.

"It's the puzzle," she explained. "How did the murderer get into the locked room. Why isn't there any blood. Who could have switched glasses with the victim. It all gets in the way. It's only an intellectual game, like a crossword puzzle—it prevents you from caring about what happens. It's just curiosity, not suspense. Real suspense is emotional, not intellectual. It has to do with liking one of the characters and not knowing whether he'll be the next victim. It has to do with hating the murderer and wanting him to get caught—or liking him and not wanting him to get caught.

"I don't care whether Mr. X must've killed her because he's the only one who knows how to remove wine corks with an ice pick. I care that he did it because he was in love with her and couldn't stand seeing her sleep with anyone else."

There Lara paused as if she were waiting, not for Westward's reaction, but for mine.

I was mildly surprised to see that he did react. Without shifting his stare—or his posture—he mumbled, "You're right. But you're also wrong."

Lara and I both gave him time to go on. He didn't. Instead he drank more wine.

"Mac's being cryptic," Connie announced primly. "He's had too much to drink." If Westward felt the effect of her jibe, he didn't show it. "The subject happens to be one we feel strongly about."

She didn't raise her naturally soft voice. Nevertheless, its firmness took over the table. Everyone stopped talking to hear her. Buffy in particular watched and listened as if she were studying at the feet of a priestess. But even Cat Reverie and Houston Mile stopped whatever they were doing to pay attention.

"Mac means," Connie said, "that you're right about intellectual puzzles, but you're wrong about suspense.

"The problem with building a mystery novel on an intellectual puzzle is the implicit assumption that anyone is capable of anything. This is debatable in itself, but the puzzle goes one step further. It implies that everyone is *equally* capable of anything. Therefore the only way to distinguish between equal possibilities is to focus on *how* the crime was committed rather than on *why*.

"But surely this is nonsense. Everyone is *not* equally capable of anything.

"If we reject that assumption, the mystery becomes, Who *is* capable of this particular crime? Which one of the characters has the capacity for it? But even if we accept that anyone is capable of anything, we still have to recognize that different people—being different, *unequal*—require different kinds of stress to bring out their latent capabilities. The mystery becomes, What kind of stress would make a given individual capable of this particular crime? Is that kind of stress present?"

Buffy was too excited to sit still. "But surely," she said, unconsciously echoing Connie, "one of the capabilities you're talking about is the ability to commit the crime in a way that will conceal or confuse who did it. That's an intellectual ability. Whether a murderer gets caught doesn't depend on what kind of person he is. It depends on how smart he is."

Constance Bebb, however, was at least one half of Thornton Foal, the famous novelist. She didn't suffer interruption gladly. In an austere tone, she replied, "We wouldn't be interested in these crimes if they weren't committed by people who were smart or desperate or unscrupulous enough to try to avoid the consequences of their own actions.

"Nevertheless the true function of the mystery novel is not to construct the physical or intellectual puzzles you complain about, Mrs. Hardhouse"—Connie didn't pretend that she wasn't snubbing Buffy—"but rather to search and analyze character, to probe emotional puzzles, to define the resources and restrictions which make one individual incontestably him- or herself and no one else. The true detective identifies who did it by understanding that only one unique person could have committed this particular crime under these particular conditions of stress."

By then Cat had apparently had all the edification she could tolerate. As Faith and Ama began to clear the plates, she announced brusquely, "I want some port. Do you have any port?"

But Connie was determined to finish her speech. While Faith returned to the kitchen, Connie went on talking.

"So you see, the suspense of the novel does rest on a puzzle. But it is an emotional puzzle, a psychological puzzle. And the better the construction of the puzzle, the more suspense it generates. Why do you like a certain character? Why do you care what happens to him or her? Is it because you understand them, or because you don't? Is it because you believe they are capable of the crime, or because you believe they are not? And how accurate are your beliefs? The best mystery novels—like the best crimes— search and analyze the reader, the observer, by the very process of searching and analyzing the participants. Ultimately the suspense of the story arises from the fact that we ourselves are being tested by it."

When she finished, Mac Westward raised his glass like a salute and drank a silent toast to his collaborator.

I couldn't help myself. She made me look at her in a new way. Softly I murmured, "You're starting to make me wish I'd read more mystery novels."

"You should," she replied like a stern aunt. "There is no more profound question than the question of murder."

I doubted that. From my perspective, the question of suicide went deeper. I didn't have too much trouble thinking about what made people decide to kill each other—or not. But self-murder was more like alcoholism. It was fascinating, almost compulsory, but I couldn't get my mind around it.

On the other hand, I had no intention whatsoever of mentioning a subject like that in front of a group like this.

In any case, I didn't get the chance. "You're very persuasive, Ms. Bebb," Hardhouse put in with an amiable chuckle, "but I think that last assertion was a little too sweeping.

"Murder is only murder—you want somebody dead, so you do something about it. We all feel that way sometimes. And, as you say, under the right provocation we'd all act on it. A man comes home from work and finds his wife in bed with another man, so he shoots them both. We can all sympathize. But there's no mystery in it. It doesn't really 'search' us.

"I think Buffy is right. What makes a murder interesting—what makes it 'profound'—is the desire to conceal it. To *benefit* from it. Crimes of passion are just that, passionate, emotional. They don't mean anything except that one person got upset, so another person ended up dead. Deliberate, premeditated, *concealed* crimes, on the other hand"—he smiled like the blade of a table saw—"have interesting implications."

They sure did—at least from my point of view. Especially if you were the intended victim. But I kept my mouth shut. Now was no time to mention el Señor. And I was busy watching Ginny.

Her eyes practically glowed at Hardhouse. She seemed to find him more desirable by the minute. When she spoke, she sounded like she was challenging him—but she didn't look that way.

"Does this have something to do with your theory about why people kill each other?"

He flashed an avid smile at her. "I can see," he admitted, "it was a mistake to bring that up. I've made myself more obvious than I realized. If you want to play fair," he added humorously, "you should try to forget I said any of this."

Right.

Several of the guests may've wanted to pursue the subject, but at that moment the port arrived. Faith set an elaborate crystal decanter down in front of Cat, and Hardhouse immediately busied himself filling her glass. Then he offered port to the rest of the table. By the time everyone had turned him down, new conversations were underway.

I had to do something about the way I felt before it got out of hand. Also I couldn't stomach the sweet sick smell of port. More by luck than skill, I managed to catch Ginny's eye. After that I stood up and excused myself.

Queenie looked at me mischievously. "Do you play bridge, Brew? If this were a Christie novel, we'd all spend the rest of the evening playing bridge. We need some way to pretend we don't know one of us is going to be killed."

If she'd asked me that earlier, I might've said yes. Any excuse to spend some time in her company. But now I was too strung out.

"Sorry," I said—and tried not to wince at the sound of loss in my voice. "I only play bridge when I drink."

Walking roughly to hurt my guts—I needed the distraction—I went to my room.

Ginny took forever to arrive. At least twenty minutes. She'd left my pills and vitamins on an especially delicate end table. I considered flushing them down the toilet. I considered smashing the end table. Finally I took some of whatever was in the bottles. Maybe if I tried to stay healthy, she'd give me another chance.

When she knocked, I told her to come in. She stuck her head past the door, but didn't accept my invitation. "I'm going to go corner Rock and Buffy," she said in a vaguely impersonal tone. "You want to come? Don't if you're too tired. I can handle it."

I beckoned her in. "That's what I want to talk to you

about," I lied. I needed some way to insist, and this was as good as any. "I've already cornered Rock."

"Oh?" At least I had her attention now. She moved into the room and closed the door behind her. Her claw resembled a surgical implement in the lamplight. "How did that come about?"

I was sitting on the bed. In a better world, I would've faced her standing, but I didn't trust my legs to hold me. In a far better world, I would've met her gaze.

"After you went on that walk"—I did my best to sound noncommittal—"he came looking for us."

I paused. After a moment Ginny asked, "What did he want?"

"Apparently the owners of the lodge told Reeson not to lock up the guns." I had a talent for reporting conversations, so I repeated what Altar had said almost word for word.

She didn't like it, but she didn't get mad. Frowning hard, she muttered, "Well, I can't say I'm surprised. Just disgusted. Common sense must be an antisurvival trait. If too many people had it, we'd collapse from overpopulation." Then she asked, "What did you tell him?"

I was tempted—just tempted—to get mad myself. If she cared about stuff like that, she shouldn't have left me to talk to him alone. But that would just give her an excuse to turn her back and walk out. Which was about the last thing I wanted.

So I said, "I told him we'd let the matter drop."

She nodded slowly. "That's probably what I would've done. Approximately. I don't want to get fired. I can't risk going back to town with you in this condition."

My condition. No question about it, I was really starting to hate my condition.

I could tell she wanted to leave, but the expression on my face must've stopped her. Looking at me a little harder, she asked, "Was there something else we need to talk about?"

Something else? Surely you jest. What else could there be? El Señor wants me dead, and Lawrence Smithsonian went out of his way to get us this job, and I'm losing you. I've got a hole inside me you could drive a truck through. No, there's nothing else we need to talk about.

"Brew?" Her tone betrayed her concern. I still had the capacity to worry her. "What's going on?"

I had to do better than this. Too much was at stake.

Touching the bed with my palms, I said almost like I wasn't begging, "Stay with me tonight."

Her eyebrows went up. Her eyes flicked to the bed, then back to my face. "You just got out of the hospital," she observed with studious neutrality. "Are you that well?"

I shook my head. The truth, Axbrewder. Tell her the truth. Just this once.

"I'm that lonely."

She moved closer, leaning over me so that I had to look straight into her eyes. For a long moment, her gray gaze seemed to search me all the way to the back of my brain. Instinctively I held my breath. She didn't smile or glare or do anything else to reveal what she felt.

Abruptly she pulled away and went back to the door. As if it were the last thing she would ever say to me, she replied, "God loves you. Sit on your hands."

Then she left.

It's an old joke. This guy takes a girl he doesn't like to the prom. She's miserable, she wants romance. Trying to get him to be nice to her, she complains, Nobody loves me, and my hands are cold. He says, God loves you, sit on your hands.

In other words, Take care of yourself. For a change.

I couldn't stay awake. One advantage of convalescence. Since I had nothing better to do, I went to bed.

7

When I got up the next morning—later than usual for me—there didn't seem to be any victims. Not yet, anyway. No strangled hilarious screams during the night. No blue marbles reported anywhere. As Buffy had promised. I didn't exactly distrust her—but I didn't exactly trust her, either. Or Deerskin Lodge. Or Murder on Cue, Inc. Just to be sure, I checked the roll.

Listening shamelessly outside one of the bedrooms, I heard Houston Mile and Maryanne Green giggling. At least he was giggling. She may've been whimpering.

Sam and Queenie Drayton were on their way to their room as if they wanted to do some giggling of their own.

Off to one corner of the den, Rock and Westward sat smoking cigars at each other, engaged in a silent fumigation contest.

Near one of the fireplaces, Buffy, Connie, Simon, and Ginny—of all people—sat at a card table, apparently playing canasta. I hadn't realized that Ginny knew how to play canasta. In fact, I hadn't realized that she knew how to hold cards with her claw. But she did both without any obvious strain.

That left Joseph and Lara Hardhouse unaccounted for. And Cat Reverie. Maybe they were still asleep.

My stomach hurt almost as bad as my soul, and anyway I hate the whole world until I've had some coffee. Ignoring various greetings, I shambled toward the kitchen in search of caffeine.

In the dining room I found a breakfast buffet, complete

with sweet rolls, scrambled eggs congealing over a can of sterno, orange juice, and—yes—coffee.

I also found Lara. She sat at the table, pushing her food back and forth on her plate.

Just my luck. The perfect breakfast companion. I had to admit that she looked as beautiful as ever, but the darkness in her eyes announced a restless night as plainly as a billboard. Whatever ate at her had become hungrier.

I wasn't what you could call grateful that she'd kept me away from the wine at dinner. Frightened was more like it. Something about the nature of her attention scared me.

Hoping she'd leave me alone, I poured myself some coffee. But as soon as she realized that I didn't mean to say anything, she started to talk.

"That was a brave thing you did last night." Her voice was like a caress. "Ginny doesn't treat you very well. It would have been easy to have a few drinks, to drown your sorrows." She made the cliché sound more poignant than I would've believed possible. "I admire courage like yours."

Involuntarily I stared at her. Courage? Are you kidding?

Slowly she turned her coffee cup around and around in its saucer, but her eyes ignored her hands. "I wonder," she murmured, "if you realize how attractive your courage makes you. Some women believe a perfect body and a healthy libido are what they want in a man, but I like courage"—she moistened her lips—"and pain. They give me hope."

I faced her with my mouth practically hanging open. No question about it, she was too many for me. There was more going on here than I could guess. And my famous intuition didn't come to my rescue. It needed caffeine, just like I did.

Fortunately, we were interrupted. Hardhouse and Cat Reverie came into the dining room, so absorbed in each other that they actually held hands.

When they saw Lara, neither of them blushed. Neither of them even had the grace to look flustered. They let go of each other, however—that was something. With an empty laugh, Cat headed for the coffeepot. Hardhouse faced his wife as if the lines of his pugnacious features and the slickness of his hair held a message only she could read.

The way I felt about Joseph Hardhouse had one advantage. Seeing him had the effect of kick-starting my brain. All of a sudden, the sheer shamelessness of his attitude, and Cat's, seemed too blatant to be real. I recovered my ability to jump to conclusions.

"Don't tell me. Let me guess," I said almost pleasantly. "You actors have all the fun. Tonight you'll switch partners and go through the same charade again. Is this Buffy's idea of a murder scenario?"

In unison, like they'd been practicing it for weeks, Hardhouse, Lara, and Cat turned to gape at me.

Then Lara protested, "Oh, Brew! How could you think—?" Her voice was practically a moan. Turning her face away, she blundered up from the table and fled the room.

Cat broke into a smile that made my skin crawl.

Hardhouse took a step toward me. His eyes looked as hard as his jaw, his forehead. With the index finger of his right hand, he tapped me gently over the heart. "Nobody here is an actor," he articulated. "I play for blood, not sport."

Cat aimed her smile at him as if she understood.

"But even if we're all actors," he continued, "it's no business of yours. You have your own wounds, and they're about as much as you can handle. You don't need any more trouble."

I had to say something, so I rasped, "Actually, trouble is what I'm best at. Wounds just sharpen my concentration."

Listen to me, Hardhouse. Don't mess with Ginny.

I waited until he dropped his hand. Then I took my coffee out to the kitchen.

I didn't have any particular reason to be there. I just needed to leave the dining room—and I didn't want to face

Ginny in the den. For the first time, it occurred to me that I wasn't the only one who stood to get hurt in this situation. Axbrewder at his unselfish finest. If Ginny was attracted to Hardhouse, so attracted that she couldn't stay away, he might do her real damage. She might end up looking at me the way his wife did.

On the other hand, she wasn't what you could call helpless. If he wanted to mess with her, he might wake up one morning with a stainless steel prosthetic device installed in his chest.

He was right about one thing, anyway. It was none of my business. Even though the thought of them together made me want to scream my heart out.

Thinking about Ginny reminded me of my pills. They hadn't done me any good last night, so I decided to ignore them. I started on the coffee.

The kitchen was deserted. Faith Jerrick must've been busy elsewhere. For a second I thought I caught a faint whiff of gas. Maybe Reeson wasn't done working on the stove. Maybe he just hadn't done a very good job. Or maybe I was wrong. The smell faded when I tried to verify it.

After a while I noticed a hard rhythmic thunking sound in the distance. It seemed to come from outside the lodge.

Sipping my coffee, I wandered over to one of the windows.

The day was overcast, and it looked cold. Wind fussed through the branches of the evergreens like it was in a bad mood. Apparently, the snowstorm Buffy had promised us was on its way.

Not far from the cottages and the rear of the kitchen, Art Reeson stood chopping firewood.

He was good at it. The ax rose and fell like an extension of his arms. He didn't put any apparent effort into it, but chips flew from every cut. The logs almost seemed to fall into sections by themselves. He'd taken his jacket and shirt off, despite the cold, and his back steamed delicately.

Well, if he could stand the weather, so could I. My coat was back in my room, but I had on a heavy sweater to conceal the bulk of my bandages. After I finished my coffee, I limped out through the kitchen and down the steps.

I didn't have anything particular in mind. He and I could discuss the guns again, but that was just an excuse. All I really wanted was to get away from Murder on Cue for a while.

He saw me coming and stopped. The overcast made his black hair and dark skin look less stark, more natural—more like a way of blending into the generalized gray. If the clouds got any thicker, he might be completely invisible. Maybe night was his natural element. He scowled at me, but he didn't seem angry. For all I knew, that scowl was his version of a smile.

"What's the matter, Mr. Axbrewder?" he asked. His voice still sounded like it'd been hoarse for years. "You walk funny."

I scowled back. Two could play that game. "Old war wound."

He looked me up and down. Then he shrugged. "You're a bad liar." It was definitely possible that his scowl was a way of smiling. Or of concealing a smile.

"Really?" I drawled. "Most people think I'm pretty good."

"Most people," he pronounced with the same assurance he had when he swung his ax, "don't know anything about liars."

"And you do?"

"We're all liars, Mr. Axbrewder. Most people don't know anything about themselves."

"And you do, Mr. Reeson?" I repeated.

Now he smiled. If his scowl was a smile, his smile must've been a glare of anger. "Call me Art. We don't really need all this firewood. But I didn't have anything better to do this morning. Faith and the Carbones do all the real work around here. Come have a cup of coffee with me."

I gave him a grimace, just to remind him that he hadn't answered my question, but I didn't hesitate. "Sure." The cold was worse than I'd expected. I'd already started to shiver.

"Good." He sank his ax into the stump he used for a splitting block. From a tree branch nearby, he retrieved his shirt and wool jacket. While he pushed his arms into the sleeves of his shirt, he led me toward one of the cottages.

Smoke gusted from its chimney, and a Land Rover sat out front. Ama and Truchi Carbone probably lived next door—that house was obviously occupied as well. So where did Faith Jerrick live?

I learned the answer as soon as Reeson took me inside. She lived with him. We found her in the immaculate little living room, sorting laundry. Her method for folding towels and sheets made them look starched and ironed, permanently creased, and her stacks were as precise as the arrangement of the furniture, as clean as the floorboards and walls and curtains. If she'd met my gaze—just once— I might've considered her the ideal woman. My whole life, I've wanted to meet a woman as tidy as I am. And she had profound eyes.

But she didn't meet my gaze. She didn't look at Reeson either. She glanced up when we came in, but she didn't actually appear to focus on us.

"I offered Mr. Axbrewder a cup of coffee." Reeson's tone eased in her presence. "He's going to tell me about an old war wound." If he was laughing at me, it didn't show.

"Call me Brew," I put in. Then, rather awkwardly, I added, "Don't go to any trouble."

I said that because her reserve made me uncomfortable. As if I were intruding somehow.

But apparently she didn't mind the intrusion. Setting her

laundry aside, she said, "Please sit down, Mr. Axbrewder. You're welcome here, in God's name."

Still without actually facing either of us, she left the room. Through the doorway, I heard her making kitchen noises.

I raised my eyebrows at Reeson. " 'In God's name,'?"

His shrug didn't commit him to anything. "She's religious," he murmured. "More than religious. Ecstatic. God talks to her. She prophesies. Some time ago, I guess she decided I agree with her. I used to try to argue with her, but now I leave her alone. Let her think what she wants about me.

"She's a good woman." Which sounded like an odd thing to say in that noncommittal fashion. "We all have our ghouls and beasties, Axbrewder. And we all have ways to keep them at bay. Religion is hers, that's all."

And mine was alcohol, I suppose. Which explained why I was in such bad shape without it.

"What's yours?" I asked.

He smiled again. "I try not to let people lie to me. I get scared when I think I'm not hearing the truth."

That wasn't quite what I expected to hear. I thought he would make some reference to guns.

"Your 'old war wound,' for instance," he continued. "I get nervous when I hear things like that."

I was developing a distinct preference for his scowl.

On the other hand, he didn't have any obvious weaponry nearby. Maybe he could've hidden a derringer in one of the seat cushions, but I doubted it.

We were still on our feet. For some reason I wanted to stay that way, so I forced myself to sit down. "What difference does it make?"

He sat down too. Like his ax work, all his movements were natural, relaxed. "I'm the manager here." His voice stayed husky. "I'm responsible for what happens. You and Fistoulari are security for Murder on Cue. I can understand why you wanted the collection locked away. What I can't understand is why somebody who can hardly walk takes on a job like this.

"The Altars would hire a blind man if he helped jazz up their mysteries." Reeson clearly had no great opinion of Buffy and Rock. "But why do you want the job? If anything goes wrong, you'll be useless. That makes me think you're playing some other kind of game. It makes me nervous.

"Tell me about your 'old war wound,' Axbrewder."

Faith came back into the room, carrying a tray with two melmac mugs, a creamer and sugar bowl, and a steaming pot. "Mr. Axbrewder." She offered me a mug. I declined cream and sugar. "Art." He took a mug and a bit of sugar. She put the tray down, then poured coffee for both of us. After that she went to stand behind his chair. Still not quite looking at me, she rested her fingertips on his shoulders.

He reached up gently to stroke her fingers, but he kept his attention on me.

"I got shot," I said bluntly. "About a week ago."

"Guns," Faith breathed. Just for a second, I received the full depth of her gaze. Then she slipped out of focus again. "They are evil, and all things done with them. God is love. He has no use for guns."

Which probably explained why Reeson didn't have any in sight.

But he wasn't deflected. His scowl intensified. "Who shot you?"

Again I asked, "What difference does it make?"

"You were shot"—in spite of its hoarseness, his voice had force—"but you're still alive. Maybe you're on the run. Maybe you're hiding out here. Maybe whoever shot you is coming after you."

That was a little too shrewd for my taste. I didn't mind sitting in his living room sparring with him about how grown men keep the ghouls and beasties at bay, but I didn't like where this conversation was going.

"He isn't," I said with a grin of my own, as humorless and bloody as I could make it. "I broke his neck."

Take that and be warned.

Distinctly Faith said, "I will pray for your immortal soul, Mr. Axbrewder."

I wanted to laugh out loud. Humorless and bloody with a vengeance. "Pray for *his*, Ms. Jerrick. Three other people might've died if I hadn't gotten him first." Ginny among them. "He was a professional killer, and I couldn't stop him any other way."

Gravely she replied, "I pray for all who are lost to the Lord."

By this time Reeson's scowl looked positively joyous. "You must be made of iron, Axbrewder. But you still haven't told me why you took on a job like this when you can hardly walk."

I took a slug of coffee to hide my bitterness. It was still hot enough to scald my tongue. "I'm not 'on a job like this.' Ginny is. Murder on Cue only needs one of us. I'm just here so that she can make sure I take my pills while I recuperate."

I'm a better liar than he thought. This time he believed me. Or he acted like he did, anyway. Abruptly he slapped his thighs and rose to his feet, as smooth as a piston. But when I started to get up, he stopped me. "Axbrewder, I sympathize. Let me know if there's anything I can do to make it easier. Those people over there"—he meant the guests—"would drive me crazy. They're all spinning lies as fast as they can. That's the whole point of these mystery camps. Give them a chance to practice their illusions. Come over here anytime you feel the need to get away. We'll do our best to tell each other the truth.

"You two stay and talk to each other. I need a shower."

Scowling heavily, he kissed Faith.

Maybe she was as religious as she sounded. Maybe she spent so much time communing with God she didn't need to look anyone else in the eye. But there was nothing spiritual about the way she kissed Reeson back. Her whole body concentrated on it.

Fascinating. She may've been the perfect woman after all. But I didn't let that distract me. "Before you go, Reeson," I put in, "answer a question for me. Do you know who did security for Murder on Cue the last time they were here?"

His eyebrows did a little jump on his forehead, but he hardly hesitated. "Sure. I don't remember the guy's name, but I remember who he worked for. Until now, they did all the security for the Altars. Lawrence Smithsonian and Associates.

"Do you need to know who specifically? I could look it up."

"No. I'm just curious. Do you happen to know why he didn't object to those guns?"

"I told you. The Altars would hire a blind man if they thought he'd add to the fun. That guy was just f"—he glanced at Faith sharply, caught himself—"just kidding around. The life of the party. For him it was a vacation. You and Fistoulari are the first security they've had who take the job seriously."

"Thanks." I was done, so I let him go.

When he left the room, Faith moved to sit in the chair he'd vacated. Apparently she'd taken his suggestion as a commandment. But she didn't offer me any small talk.

Studying her made me rethink my position. Maybe I didn't really like perfection. Ten minutes with a woman who never looked me in the eye, and I'd spend the rest of my life drunk.

Since Faith refused to look at me straight, I didn't have anything to restrain me, so I asked one of my less tactful questions. "You're a devout woman, Ms. Jerrick," and you sure as hell know how to kiss, "but you aren't married. Why do you live with Art?"

Maybe she didn't look at people, but she definitely heard what they said. From her scalp to the skin of her arms, she blushed. She was so pale normally that I hadn't realized she had so much blood in her.

Nevertheless she didn't evade the issue. "Art and I are married in the sight of God," she answered firmly.

Her assertion was open, as they say, to more than one interpretation. A cynic could've had a field day with it. Unfortunately—or fortunately, depending on your point of view—it doesn't take much to make me ashamed of myself. Her blush was enough. Backpedaling furiously, I said, "I'm the kind of man who jumps to conclusions. Right now, I'm jumping to the conclusion that he's the reason you work here. Wouldn't you rather live closer to your church—closer to people you can worship with?"

That put her on more secure ground. "Mr. Axbrewder, I don't choose my life." As fast as it came, the red faded from her skin. "Choosing belongs to the Lord. It is in His hands. My task is not to choose, but to serve. It is a wife's responsibility and joy to serve her husband, just as it is the soul's responsibility and joy to serve God. Art lives here. He works here. What else would you have me do?"

"Don't you get lonely?"

"Lonely?" She seemed genuinely surprised. "How could I be lonely? Art is with me. The Lord is with me in all things, rising and sleeping." Her tone began to hint at the ecstasy Reeson had mentioned. "My soul is a guest at God's great feast. Only the lost are lonely, Mr. Axbrewder."

Damn her, anyway. She was right. Only the lost are lonely. But I didn't enjoy hearing it from her. I was more than a bit lonely myself.

My backpedaling had become a rout. The Lord had made her mighty against His enemies. Mostly trying to cover up my disarray while I looked for an escape, I asked, "What about Art? Why does he work here? He seems like a man"—as soon as I said this, I realized that it was true—"who could do anything he wanted."

The lines of her face gave me the impression that she was mildly disappointed. She didn't want to answer practical questions, she wanted opportunities to witness for the Lord. But apparently her concept of service included answering practical questions.

"He likes the isolation. He likes the balance between office work and physical exertion. And his job is very flexible, Mr. Axbrewder. He sets his own hours, he works when he chooses, he takes vacations whenever the mood strikes him. The owners trust him completely." She was proud of this. "They leave the lodge entirely in his hands."

What, entirely? Something about that sounded wrong to me. "But surely he checks in with them on a regular basis? He calls them when decisions need to be made?"

He called them about the guns?

"How should I know?" She was serene in her ignorance. "It's not my place to watch how he serves his employers. But why should he call? He has worked here for years. He has proven his faithfulness. Good service is rewarded with trust."

You mean he *didn't* call about the guns?

No, I was wrong, I had no business jumping to a conclusion like that. Under Faith Jerrick's influence, my intuitive instincts were starting to blow fuses. Or maybe in some obscure way I was being seduced.

"Speaking of good service, I'd better go see how my partner is doing." I reached my feet with an ungainly heave. "Like Art, she doesn't really need anyone to check on her. But when I don't do it, I feel like I'm goofing off."

Faith stood up gracefully, gave me a polite nod. I left in a hurry.

Outside, the wind slapped my face, and the cold jolted into my lungs. Which had the effect of restoring my rationality. Very therapeutic. The weather was deteriorating. Clouds heavy with snow boiled across the treetops. Dimness filled the air like dusk. If I stayed out here long enough, I might recover active sanity. Or freeze to death.

Or maybe they came to the same thing.

In the meantime, however, I didn't know what to do with what I was thinking. Reeson never called the owners about the guns? That made no sense. He'd been the manager here—the *trusted* manager—for years. No matter how much he liked guns, he knew how to be responsible. And Faith loved him—Faith, who hated guns. I was losing touch with reality, no question about it.

And yet I couldn't stop wondering if he really was a man who used telling the truth to keep the ghouls and beasties away.

8

My sweater didn't protect me from the cold. You'd think all those bandages would be good for insulation, but they weren't. My guts felt like they were being gnawed on by wind and chill.

Unsteady as a drunk, I lurched back to the lodge.

Through the kitchen to the dining room. Not a Hardhouse in sight, blessed be the Name of the Lord. On general principles, I stayed there long enough to eat a piece of dry toast. I needed time to get warm. Also time to brace myself to face the crew in the den.

Ama Carbone went through the room carrying an armload of sheets and towels to the laundry. Like Faith, she kept busy trying to make the world clean.

I should've helped her. Laundry is something I understand.

Instead I braved the den.

Murder on Cue's guests had rearranged themselves in my absence. The canasta game was finished. Apparently the Hardhouses had gone to ground somewhere. So had Ginny. Which I took as a bad sign. But what the hell, in my condition I took everything as a bad sign. Houston Mile, Maryanne Green, and Cat had joined the rest of the group. Rock and Westward had given up their smoking contest.

Mile was telling a story. Everybody else listened.

He stood beside one of the fireplaces, leaning a pudgy arm on the mantel in the relaxed shitkicker pose of a good ol' boy raconteur—what my brother used to call a "raccoon-tuner." His timing was good, I had to admit that. I hadn't heard the first half of his story, but everything he said sounded by-God funny, and most of his audience laughed harder and harder as he went along. It had something to do with a half-naked girl and a hoe—a hoe-er. A whore, get it?

Hearing his story promised to be more fun than I could stomach, so I headed for my room.

As I left, I saw him glare in my direction. He didn't like it when people walked out while he was the center of attention.

Well, good. Now I knew how to insult him. If I ever needed the information.

After that, however, my luck improved. In the hall outside my room I met Queenie Drayton. Without Sam.

"Hello, Brew." Her voice might as well have been music.

Involuntarily I stopped in front of her. Or maybe we stopped in front of each other.

"Sam," she explained in a tone of affectionate disgust, "has a talent for falling asleep at the most awkward times. It comes with being a doctor, I suppose."

I couldn't tell whether it was all that life in her eyes or the way her breasts stroked the inside of her flannel shirt that made me want to propose marriage.

"What's everyone else doing?" she finished. "Is anything going on?"

I hadn't had a crush this bad since high school. Maybe I should've been embarrassed. But she didn't seem to need it. I muttered something incoherent about Houston Mile and stories. Then I pulled myself together.

"Come to my room," I suggested. "I'd like to talk to you." Lamely I added, "And you'll miss the punch line."

Laughter carried down the hall. She cocked her head to it for a moment—which reminded me that she liked to laugh herself. Then she gave me a smile like a gift.

"I think I should warn you, Brew. When a man invites me to his room, he almost always ends up telling me the story of his life."

I snorted to disguise my pleasure. "I'll try not to be that boring."

Before she could change her mind, I steered her to my door.

Amalia had already cleaned my room. The bed was made, and I had fresh towels. Like Faith, she got her job done.

I ushered Queenie inside, closed the door, seated her in one of the chairs, settled my bulk on the bed. Quickly, so that I wouldn't lose the opportunity, I said, "Tell me something. How did a real honest-to-God human person like yourself come by a name like 'Queenie'?"

She responded with a chuckle deep in her throat. "You're trying to turn the tables on me."

"Sure," I admitted. "Why not? I already know the story of *my* life. Believe me, you can live without it."

"But you can't live without mine." She was teasing me.

I made an effort to match her. "It's all I have left."

Unfortunately that almost came out like I meant it. My interest was genuine, but I didn't want to sound pitiful about it.

Her eyes never shifted from my face—a stunning contrast to Faith Jerrick. In her gaze I seemed to see shadows pass across the background of her mind, hints of understanding, glimpses of empathy. At the same time she went on trying to heal me with the warmth of her smile.

"Well, for one thing," she said, "it's not a nickname. It's my real name. I wish I could say it's a family tradition. I used to tell people that in college, when I was feeling especially self-conscious. 'My mother's name was Princess, so I'm Queenie.' But you know, in a funny way that's almost the truth.

"It was my father's idea. 'Princess' was his pet name for my mother. They had a houseful of sons, and when I finally came along he was so delighted he lost his common sense. I guess he always wanted a daughter. And he doted on my mother. He thought she hung the moon.

"My mother tried to warn him. Queenie isn't the kind of name you give a child if you want her to have a comfortable social life. But I guess he couldn't imagine the whole world wouldn't feel the same way he did about me."

I concentrated on her like a puppy. When she stopped, I murmured, "They loved you. They loved you down to the ground."

She chuckled again. "It wasn't fair, really. They gave me a terrible handicap with my peers. At least when I was a teenager. I don't mean the name. They deprived me of the definitive adolescent experience—thinking my parents didn't love me. Believing they didn't understand me.

"I could hardly talk to my friends for years. We didn't have anything in common. Their parents were all mean and hateful and petty—just like the parents of teenagers are supposed to be. Sometimes," she concluded happily, "I felt so left out I could hardly stand it."

"Poor you," I agreed. "You've suffered awfully."

"Does it show?"

"I'm afraid so." If she kept this up, I might start feeling better—and then I'd be in real trouble.

She pursed her lips. Which made me think about kissing her. With just a hint of seriousness, she said, "Maybe that's why men tell me the stories of their lives. They're all so unhappy, and they know I'm a kindred spirit."

"No." The temptation to be serious was more than I could bear. "It's because you're real and happy, and you've got room in your heart for the things you hear."

Also because she was profoundly beautiful. Not pretty or glamorous—something more. But I didn't let myself say that.

She went on gazing into my eyes, the lines of her expression as clear as words. They said, I've got room for you, too. If you want to talk.

Which was exactly *not* what I wanted.

"So tell me," I said, changing subjects with all the delicacy of a bulldozer, "what names did you write down for Buffy?"

Just for a second, Queenie looked startled. She probably thought she knew what this conversation was about, and I took her by surprise. In a musing tone she said, "Brew, there's more to you than meets the eye."

I shrugged. "That's the bandages. If I took them off, you could see everything."

With an odd air of chagrin, she caught her lower lip between her teeth, held it. But she never looked away, never flinched. "In other words," she murmured slowly, "the truth about you is in the wound. Not in the man who was wounded.

"I don't think Buffy wants us to talk about our guesses." She didn't miss a beat. If I needed the subject changed, it was changed. "She'd love it if we were wrong. But she doesn't want to take the chance we might be right. She wants us to work it all out for ourselves. Alone."

Too true. On the other hand, I didn't give a flying fuck at the moon what Sue-Rose "Buffy" Altar wanted. Except she was my client, so I had to make at least a token effort to keep my job. "I'll make it easier," I responded. "Just tell me who the actors are."

"Why does it matter?" she countered. Doing a little probing of her own. After all, she loved mysteries.

"Come off it, Queenie," I retorted. "You know why it matters."

By which I intended her to think I meant, You know I'm a private investigator. What I really meant, however, was, It matters because of Ginny. I need the truth about Joseph Hardhouse.

"All right." Her smile took on a suggestion of glee. "I think the actors are Houston and Maryanne."

I couldn't keep my face from twitching. "Why them?"

She didn't hesitate. "I don't think he deserves his reputation as the resident hotshot. He isn't that bright. And he's too slimy to live. Do you know, he actually tried to put his hand up my dress at dinner last night? He's got to be faking it. Or else he doesn't like his 'little filly' as much as he claims.

"As for her—if she isn't an actress, she'll set women's liberation back fifty years. No self-respecting woman would treat that man that way unless she was acting."

Well, I had to agree. No self-respecting woman would. The key word, however, was "self-respecting." Maryanne was acting, all right. But it wasn't because Buffy paid her.

"Thanks," I said, lying through my teeth, "that helps."

"In other words," she observed acutely, "you don't believe me. You think Houston Mile really is as slimy as he seems."

Considering the noises I'd heard from Mile's bedroom this morning, I replied, "No. I think he's even slimier."

Queenie studied this idea. "And Maryanne puts up with it. She *feeds* it." She shivered. "That's disgusting."

Almost at once, however, she recovered her good humor. "OK. I can live with that." She didn't mind being contradicted. She was playing a game she enjoyed. "I've been wrong before.

"Now it's your turn. Who do *you* think the actors are?"

I shrugged again. "Joseph and Lara Hardhouse?"

Her eyes widened. She closed her mouth. Then she actually looked away from me, *looked away*— She was like me, too good at jumping to conclusions. And this time she'd jumped to a conclusion full of pain.

"Brew," she said softly, as if she wanted to warn me or comfort me somehow, "I can only tell you one thing about Joseph. He isn't acting. That isn't an act."

Oh, good. Just what I wanted to hear.

"So what you're saying is"—when her gaze came back to me, I looked away, I couldn't face her honesty anymore—"I might as well kiss Ginny good-bye."

Since I wasn't looking, I didn't see Queenie get to her

feet. The next thing I knew, she stood at the door. But she paused with her hand on the doorknob.

Carefully she said, "Talk to Sam."

I glared at her. "Why?"

Her smile was another gift, better than the last one. "Because he's worth talking to."

A beat or two later, she added, "Don't forget, you still owe me the story of your life."

She didn't wait around for my reaction. Shutting the door gently behind her, she walked off.

I needed a drink, I told myself. I needed to get drunk. But I didn't believe it. Somehow alcohol had lost its allure. What I really needed was to punch someone's lights out. Break a few bones. Rearrange the world I lived in.

After a while, I began to think that even Mile's stories would be an improvement over my own company, so I followed Queenie out of the room.

The hallway was turning into a great place to meet people, make new friends, have interesting conversations. Before I'd taken two steps, Simon Abel appeared.

"Brew," he asked immediately, "have you got a minute? I'd like to talk to you."

Unless I was going deaf in my old age, he sounded anxious about something.

Well, talking to people was my job, whether I understood what they had in mind or not. On top of that— As soon as I heard his tone, I realized that I wanted something from him.

"Sure," I said, "I've got minutes coming out my ears," and led the way back into my room. He knew Cat Reverie better than anyone else here. That made him a potential source of information about Joseph Hardhouse.

I offered him a chair, but he shook his head—he was too tense to sit. I, on the other hand, needed more rest. Even though I was in the mood for violence, all this exertion wore me out. I lowered my pain onto the bed again.

He shoved his hands into his pockets, took them out again. Looked around the room. His soft features worked to assume a shape that didn't fit them. On a hunch, I decided not to give him too much help. He conveyed the impression he was just a kid, despite his chronological age—and kids usually aren't good liars. Unless you help them.

"Brew," he announced after a certain amount of obvious dithering, "I owe you an apology."

"Huh," I replied intelligently.

"I was wrong last night. Before dinner. I shouldn't have jumped on you like that."

"Huh," I said again.

"Cat isn't your problem," he explained. "It isn't your fault she likes to flirt."

Fixing him with my best blank stare, I asked, "You call that flirting?"

"Oh, yes." Once he got started, he was in a hurry to have his say. "I know she talks like she wants to screw every man she's ever met who isn't dead between the legs. And when you look like she does, you don't have any trouble getting a response. But she doesn't mean it."

I had trouble keeping my stare blank. Who did he think he was kidding?

"It's like a knee-jerk reaction with her," he continued. "She does it to everybody. She doesn't believe how beautiful she is. She doesn't believe men would be attracted to her no matter what she did. She doesn't really believe she can be loved. She has to go looking for it. She has to prove to herself over and over again that she can get a reaction.

"It isn't really sex she wants. She wants to believe in herself. But you can't prove love. Nobody can make you believe they love you. *Sex* you can prove. Flirting is a close as she can get to proving she can be loved."

He astonished me. Not because I thought he was right—or wrong—about Cat Reverie, but because I hadn't expected him to reveal so much of himself so quickly.

"So why are you doing it?" I asked bluntly.

Apparently he had the innocent man's ability to miss the point of what he'd just said. "Doing what?"

"Still trying to prove you love her. You just told me you know it can't work."

He had an answer ready. "Because I *do* love her.

"Brew, I think of her as a woman who's lame. Emotionally lame. And it breaks my heart to see her so—so unsteady on her feet. Unable to believe in herself. So I keep trying. When she flirts with someone like you, and I act jealous, it does her good. It *sustains* her. It doesn't cure her self-doubt, it can't, but at least it contradicts her preconceptions. It contradicts the idea that she can't be loved."

This speech had a practiced sound. He knew it too well. But I still suspected that he was telling me the truth about himself.

"Bullshit," I remarked politely.

Which was obviously not the reaction he'd expected. He stared back at me. A flush of anger or embarrassment crept into his face.

"Do you think—?" he began.

"Listen." I had no business acting so superior, but sometimes it's a useful technique. "It can't work. I'll tell you why.

"You want her to believe she's lovable. You're trying to prove it the only way you can—by showing it. But your way of showing it just demonstrates that she has the power to hurt you. She flirts. You get jealous. Fear and pain. So what are you really showing her? That she's a woman who hurts people. She even hurts people who love her.

"How much self-esteem do you expect her to learn from lessons like that?"

He didn't take his own life lying down, I had to give him that. I could see confusion, rage, hurt, shame, all written in red across his features. Unfortunately for him, he had to choose one before he could answer. That took him a moment, and the delay made him look foolish. The real secret of life, as all us wise men understand, is to keep moving like you know what you're doing, instead of standing still while you sort it out.

Finally he was ready. Trying to pretend that he hadn't already missed his chance, he protested, "What the hell gives *you* the right to criticize *me*? Who the hell are *you*?

"Aren't you the one who wanders around with a constant wince, soaked in self-pity, putting yourself down, showing everybody how much you hurt?" His voice rose. He knew how to shout—something else he'd practiced. "Aren't you trying to demonstrate to all of us how rotten Ginny is, just because she has the hots for Joseph and doesn't care about you anymore? Aren't you trying to persuade *her* she's rotten?

"You think I want to teach Cat she's unlovable? What about *you*, Axbrewder? *What about you?*"

I smiled at him. I'm belligerent when I'm cornered, and I don't take the truth gracefully. On the other hand, I didn't have the actual strength to bounce up off the bed and remove his head for him. So I said, "Nice speech, Abel. There's the door. If you don't make your exit now, you'll ruin the effect."

For his own obscure reasons, he didn't continue raging. He also didn't leave—at least not immediately. Instead he stood where he was and gaped at me, blushing like I'd caught him with his pants down.

Poor guy. He probably didn't deserve to look so silly. I made an effort to contain my anger. "I didn't mean to be critical." Wincing again, but what the hell. "You're right, I was out of line. What you and Cat do with each other is none of my business."

All his reactions seemed odd. Now I'd reassured him somehow. Practically smiling, he muttered, "Damn straight," like he hadn't really learned to swear yet. Then he walked out of the room while I groped to understand him.

As soon as the door closed, however, my anger came back in a rush. *Aren't you trying to persuade* her *she's rotten?* He'd turned the tables on me. Instead of telling me about himself, he'd exposed me. *Persuade her she's rotten.* Was it that bad? Was that the real point of all my wounds and helplessnesses, my drinking and guilt? To convince her that she didn't deserve anything better? So that she wouldn't walk away from me?

Christ, Axbrewder. You're a prince.

No question about it. I definitely needed to do something violent.

I also needed an answer about Joseph Hardhouse. Unless that and violence came to the same thing. Almost desperately, I left my room to look for Lara.

That may not have been one of my more sensible decisions, but it was the best I could come up with on short notice.

Unfortunately looking for her meant that I had to deal with the people in the den.

Fortunately Houston Mile no longer held the stage. He must've done enough raccoon-tuning to content him for a while. Now he sat with Mac Westward and Maryanne Green under a moose head with a rather moldy set of antlers. In fact, he seemed to have Westward trapped. He spoke quietly, but his voice carried. Everyone in the room heard him describe some of the more pleasurable aspects of greenmail. Maryanne sat beside him, palpating his knee from time to time—hanging on every word.

Westward, however, didn't look trapped. Behind his usual cold, lumpy expression, he looked like a novelist considering new motives for murder.

On the other side of the big tree, Ginny and Constance Bebb shared a private discussion. I knew Ginny well enough to see that Connie had her full attention, and she didn't want to be interrupted. Which was fine with me. I didn't know what to say to her anyway.

Buffy and Rock sat with Simon Abel and Cat as far as they could get from everyone else. Just because I'm the kind of guy who thinks things like that, I thought they all looked furtive.

The Draytons and the Hardhouses weren't present.

I wandered over to the front door and went out onto the porch. Pretending that I wanted to check on the weather.

Outside, conditions had deteriorated. The wind had died down, apparently because the air had grown so gray and thick that it was hard to shift. As a result, the cold seemed less bitter than before. A few flakes rode the breeze like advance men, testing opportunities for the snow behind them. The idea that Deerskin Lodge's position in the bottom of this hollow would provide shelter was an illusion. The hillsides and the surrounding mountains made the wind swirl. More snow would probably fall here than anywhere else.

I scanned what I could see from the porch. If I were more diligent, I would've taken my coat and gone for a walk, just to get a better picture of my situation. How many doors did the lodge actually have? Where were they? What were the best ways to get from one place to another?

I didn't do it. At the moment I didn't give a shit about being diligent. What I really wanted was to learn something horrible and dangerous about Joseph Hardhouse. Then I wouldn't have to feel so wrong toward Ginny. I could justify my reactions.

I succeeded. In a manner of speaking.

Avoiding observation from the den, I moved down the porch, away from the windows. And when I reached the corner, I spotted Hardhouse and his wife.

To all appearances, they were taking a stroll together

among the trees. I only saw them in glimpses between the dark trunks. But they were unmistakably holding hands.

While I watched, they stopped. Hardhouse put his back against a tree. They wrapped their arms around each other and kissed like they meant business.

9

When Ama called us to lunch, Buffy and all her guests responded with excitement. Lunch marked the passage of time, the heightening of suspense. The moment approached when someone would be killed.

The only one not excited was me. My convalescence didn't seem to be going especially well. I felt vaguely feverish, slightly giddy, and the pain in my guts had taken on a new, rather watery dimension. On top of that, I was so sleepy you could've sold me over the counter as a soporific.

In spite of my condition, however, I noticed that Cat Reverie and Hardhouse had lost interest in each other. Instead Ginny had turned up the rheostat of her focus on him. Meanwhile Lara was being even more attentive to Mac Westward. And Sam and Queenie Drayton seemed almost insufferably fond of each other.

But I didn't care. After lunch I went back to my room and climbed into bed.

I wanted to sleep for the rest of the week. Unfortunately I started dreaming about snow. And Muy Estobal. And Lawrence Smithsonian. Snow was pain, and I crawled through it forever until I found myself with my arms locked around Estobal's neck and no way to let go. He was too strong for me, he broke me apart piece by piece, and I couldn't defend myself because I was full of tequila, *tequila*, of all things, but I hadn't drunk it, no, that was el Señor's doing, he'd forced it into me, and Smithsonian watched me cling to Estobal and die, grinning like a self-righteous moray eel.

Which wasn't the way it actually happened, of course. Smithsonian hadn't been there when I killed Estobal. And I hadn't been full of tequila. Nevertheless my dream seemed inevitable, truer than reality. I felt almost grateful when a knock on my door woke me up.

"Come in," I croaked like I was dying.

Whoever was outside tried to come in. Apparently, I'd locked the door.

When did I start locking my door? I could sort of remember having done it, but I couldn't remember why. To keep Ginny out? Or Lara Hardhouse?

Trying to scrub the incoherence off my face, I stumbled out of bed.

When I got the door open, I found Mac Westward there.

Blinking at me as if he couldn't believe his senses without corroborative testimony, he asked, "Were you asleep?"

I shook my head. "I had to get up to answer the door anyway."

The situation didn't seem to require courtesy—or even intelligence—so I left the door open and got back into bed.

Westward stood in the doorway for a while. Eventually, however, he reasoned his way to the conclusion that I'd invited him in. He entered the room and closed the door.

Sounding more than ever like an inedible vegetable, he observed, "You're hurt worse than I thought."

I couldn't get Smithsonian out of my head. "Everything is worse than I thought," I remarked profoundly. "Did you come to watch?"

"It's tempting. The Altars outdid themselves with you. You would be the perfect victim."

Until he said that, I hadn't realized that he was capable of sarcasm.

"Westward"—I lacked the energy to look at him, so I kept my eyes closed—"you came to see me. I didn't invite you. It's *your* job to make sense, not mine. What do you mean, 'The Altars outdid themselves'?"

He paused. Maybe he was searching for a comfortable chair. But I didn't have to wait long before he began to explain.

"Two of us are actors. Two are private detectives. There are twelve candidates. But I can eliminate Connie and me. You may not know who we are, but too many other people do. And I can eliminate the Draytons. No actor—or detective—would choose medicine as cover. His ignorance would be too easily exposed.

"We're left with eight possibilities.

"Mr. Axbrewder"—his voice took on a pedantic tone—"I'm morally certain that if Joseph and Lara Hardhouse were hired to be here, they were hired as actors rather than as detectives. That leaves only six people who could conceivably be detectives.

"Whom would you suspect? Houston Mile and Maryanne Green? Impossible. No one could trust a man like that—except possibly another Texan. What about Simon Abel and Catherine Reverie? Improbable. In my view, they both lack substance.

"Only you and Ms. Fistoulari remain.

"I grant that you, too, are an improbable candidate. You were born to be murdered, not to prevent murders. But Ms. Fistoulari is entirely credible. And if she is a detective, you must be also."

All right, already. So Mac Westward was more awake than I'd realized. So what? As far as I was concerned, he could announce the murderer right now and take a bow. Buffy would be furious, of course—but the rest of us could go home.

"Mr. Westward," I said in the general direction of the ceiling, "you didn't come here just to persuade me that I'm a detective. Why don't you cut out the rest of the lecture and tell me why you *did* come?"

He thought about that briefly. Then he asked, "Do you mind if I smoke?"

"Yes," I said. "Cigars make me puke."

Hell, it was my room, wasn't it?

His silence conveyed a shrug. "I notice," he commented after a moment, "that you didn't ask me why I'm sure the Hardhouses aren't detectives."

I kept my mouth shut. I didn't want to think about anything that involved Joseph and Lara.

He ignored my silence. "It's because they take the initiative. An actor might do that in a situation of this kind. A detective, never. If a detective has his own agenda when he's on a case, he's useless. His job is to react to circumstances, not create them."

Oh, good. Just what I needed, another sermon. Why did everyone in this fucking place think I required their wisdom?

"Get to the point, Westward."

"The point? You really are a belligerent and unhelpful man. Perhaps I should reconsider my assumptions. It may be that your relationship to Ms. Fistoulari isn't professional. You may not be a detective—you may simply have the misfortune to be her lover. That would explain your attitude."

I do believe I'd hurt his feelings. Whatever brought him to me was something he cared about more than he liked to admit.

"However," he went on, "you're still the only one who can advise me. For my needs, your attitude may actually be a benefit rather than a handicap."

That was too many for me. I opened my eyes. In fact, I sat up and dropped my legs over the edge of the bed.

"*Advise* you?" I demanded. "Me?"

"Why not?" He didn't meet my gaze. Instead he stared at one of his cigars, watching the way he rolled it back and forth between his fingers, crinkling the wrapper. "You're the only one here who may be able to understand my predicament."

"Which is?"

He took a deep breath, let it out with a sigh. As if he were reading the words off the cigar band, he said, "I think Lara Hardhouse wants to have an affair with me."

Oh, my. In fact, My goodness. What have we here?

Mac Westward, you're scared. You're scared of that woman.

"And what makes you think I'll understand?"

He still didn't look at me. "I also think she wants to have an affair with you." For a moment, he fell silent. Then he added, "If you want to know the truth, I think she wants you more than me. But she can't have you. You're invulnerable. You're too full of self-pity to care what anybody else wants." The male half of Thornton Foal was actually sneering at me. "She's picked me to be your replacement."

"Westward"—for his sake as well as my own, I made an effort to pull myself together—"maybe I'm as full as self-pity as you think. Maybe that even makes me invulnerable. But I'm not stupid. It doesn't matter what Lara Hardhouse wants. No one in his right mind would want her. That woman is trouble."

When I said that, he stiffened. "She's *in* trouble. It's not the same thing."

Oh, well. With a sigh of my own, I asked. "What kind of trouble?"

"Her husband," Westward said promptly. "He has affairs himself—he has so many that his women have to stand in line. First Catherine Reverie. Then your Ginny. Queenie Drayton will be next. And he treats Lara like dirt. She needs someone to value her, someone to cherish her. She needs to believe that she doesn't deserve what he does to her."

Bullshit, I thought. Crap and bovine droppings. But I didn't say that out loud. After talking to Simon Abel, I didn't feel righteous enough. Instead I tried a different approach.

"Let me see if I understand," I said in my best Sardonic Uncle Axbrewder tone. "You didn't really come here for advice. You came because you want a clear field. You want me to promise that I won't try to get into Lara's bed ahead of you."

Westward was an interesting fellow. I was morally certain, to use his term, that he was spitting mad. But he didn't glare at me, or raise his voice. He didn't even turn red. On the other hand, he did peel the wrapper off his cigar. Then he stuck the cigar in his teeth and lit it. Even though his hands shook.

"Mr Axbrewder," he articulated, "what do you think the life of a 'famous author' is like? Autographings? Fans? Glamour and groupies? Nothing could be farther from the truth.

"The average mystery novel sells less than five thousand copies in hardcover. And less than forty thousand in paperback. *If* it's published in paperback. *Nobody* reads mystery novels. Even the people here who recognize the name 'Thornton Foal' don't actually *read* his books. I know that from listening to their conversations. Connie and I don't attend mystery camps because we like them. We attend because without the tax write-off we can't afford vacations. Neither of us owns a home. No bank will loan us money."

For a moment, he hung fire. Then he mustered his courage and got to the point.

"I don't get very many chances with women."

Which explained why he thought that I would understand. And why he feared that I would get in his way.

His honesty deserved an honest response. Cutting right to the heart of the matter, I replied, "You say you want advice. Here it is. Watch your back."

"Thanks," he snorted bitterly. Puffing a cloud of smoke in my direction, he stood up and stomped out.

Damn cigar. The room smelled full of smoke and loneliness. But that didn't stop me from lying back down in bed and pulling the covers up to my ears.

I slept longer than I expected—which should've done me good, I suppose. When I woke up, however, the sensation of fever in my head had intensified, and my intestines felt like they were sloshing around inside my belly. Oh, well.

Unfortunately my health didn't seem like a good enough excuse to stay in bed for the rest of my life, so I got up. I did my best to hide my wounds under a clean shirt and sweater. Then I went out to face the world.

I found Connie alone in the den. She sat at the card table, playing a kind of solitaire I'd never seen before. Apparently everyone else had found something else to do.

When I entered, she looked up and said, "Good afternoon, Mr. Axbrewder," without quite smiling. Maybe she would've welcomed a chat, but her manner didn't actually encourage it, and anyway my head was too fogbound for small talk. Instead of joining her, I went to a window to look out at the weather.

A premature gloom had taken over the world, but I couldn't see anything else. The heat of the fireplaces and the cold outside blanked the glass with mist. But I heard voices, so I moved to the door and stepped out onto the porch.

Buffy must've been ecstatic. She was getting all the ambience she could decently want. The snow came down as thick as rain, so thick that the gusts and swirls of wind hardly registered. At a guess, we already had six inches on the ground, and the depth of the early dusk promised more. For most practical purposes, Deerskin Lodge would be as isolated as she could wish.

I had a different reaction. Snow reminded me of Smithsonian. And Smithsonian made me think of people getting shot.

The people outside didn't share my memories—or my mood. All this ambience filled them with glee. Laughing like schoolkids, Sam and Queenie had tackled Cat and Simon in a snowball fight, and Maryanne pranced through the middle of the battle like a cheerleader. As soon as they saw me, however, all five of them scooped up snow and flung it in my direction.

Waving my hands to ward off attacks, I retreated into the lodge.

But then I didn't know what to do with myself. Indecisively I stopped to watch Connie's game. Like almost everything else I'd seen since we arrived, her version of solitaire made no sense to me. After a minute I gave up trying to follow it.

"Tell me," I asked, "are mystery camps usually this boring?"

She raised her head, studied me gravely. "Usually," she replied, "they're worse."

For some reason, this failed to improve my humor.

Before long the combatants came inside, laughing with each other, scattering snow. When they'd warmed themselves at the fires, they dispersed to dress for dinner. That and Ama Carbone's performance on the xylophone brought me to the belated realization I'd slept most of the afternoon away.

What this unaccustomed capacity for sleep meant I had no idea. Was I recovering? Slipping into peritonitis? Did I care? Not especially. When Murder on Cue's guests had gathered, I accompanied them into the dining room.

We sat in the same arrangement as last night, with artillery and wrought-iron fixtures impending over us. Faith and Amalia served a dinner generically indistinguishable from the previous one—perfectly acceptable and maybe even tasty food, if your stomach could handle it. Cat Reverie demanded port again, and when the decanter arrived she commandeered it possessively, as if she wanted to prevent anyone—but especially Hardhouse—from sharing it. Other than that, none of us admitted that we might be less than happy with each other. The general mood was one of barely contained eagerness.

Mile bared his rotten teeth like a pouncing predator. Westward had an unexpected spot of color on each cheek, and he drank less than last night. Excitement seemed to ease Lara's troubles somehow. She fixed her deep dark eyes on me repeatedly, but behind her somber expression she seemed less aggrieved, more at rest. Maryanne burbled like a kid. Drayton smiled at everything—except during those brief moments when he noticed that I wasn't eating. And Buffy positively bristled with anticipation. Even Ginny had a glow that I hadn't seen for a long time, at once satisfied and hungry, as if she'd found something to nurture her and intended to have more of it.

The sight felt like a knife in my wounded guts. I tried to distract myself by thinking about Lara. Unfortunately she resembled Connie's card game. I needed someone to tell me the rules. Did she feel better because she'd had a reconciliation with her husband, or because she knew that she could use Westward to get even with him?

I had no trouble staying away from the wine. Fever was good for me, apparently.

As a group, we tried to act normal for a while. But at last Queenie couldn't stand it. With a deliberate shiver, she burst out, "Someone say it. Tonight one of us will probably be murdered."

"Isn't it wonderful?" Buffy chimed in. "Don't you just feel like you've never been more alive in your whole life?"

Both Hardhouse and his wife nodded sagaciously. Westward nodded, too, but I was sure that he had no interest in murder.

"Well, Buffy," Mile drawled, "Ah wouldn't purely agree with them sentiments. Life is where you find it. If you've never stood there and seen a bitty ol' oil well turn gusher— why, Ah'd say there's all kinds of ways of feelin' alive. Give a man a pretty little filly and let him teach her to run"—on cue, Maryanne produced a schoolgirl blush— "and you'll learn somethin' about feelin' alive.

"But a situation like this one here, now, it do have its advantages. Knowin' Ah might be killed, knowin' Ah got to outsmart me a killer or die—why, it purely makes me feel like a gusher mahself."

The leer he aimed at Maryanne wasn't easy to misinterpret.

"Why?" I hadn't intended to say anything, but Mile brought out the contentious side of my personality. "No one will actually die. Why do you care who it is? Why do you care if it's you? We're all safe. There aren't any"—just for a second, I fumbled through my fever for the word I wanted—"any consequences."

Ginny gave me an unreadable look. Rock nodded vaguely.

Buffy wanted to protest, that was obvious, but Sam forestalled her. As if he were practicing his bedside manner, he said, "You're right, of course. This isn't the real world. In the real world, crimes have consequences. There you have to care about them. Here you don't.

"But none of us are confused about that, Brew. We know it isn't the real world. It's a vacation. And," he added seriously, "it only works because we've all agreed to make it fun for each other."

All except me, I thought. But maybe I was wrong. Some of the other guests may've made entirely different agreements.

Nevertheless I felt actively betrayed when Ginny put in, a bit too intensely, "Sam's right, Brew. You should make an effort to get into the spirit of the occasion. It might speed up your recovery."

I heard what she said. I even heard what she meant. Getting into the spirit of the occasion worked for *her*. She was recovering just fine. Without me.

There was nothing I could say to that, so I shut my mouth.

General conversation. Food. Anticipation. Some of the

other guests viewed the world through a haze of wine. Personally, I viewed it through a haze of fever. Dessert. Coffee. I didn't have any coffee. It might reduce the haze—and I needed the haze. It was my only protection.

When dinner ended, we went into the den and sat around the fireplaces and tried to pretend that we had something in common. Somehow I found myself cornered by Drayton. He must've made it happen on his own because I sure as hell didn't have a hand in it.

"Are you all right, Brew?" he asked seriously. "You don't look good." I smiled like one of Reeson's ghouls and beasties. Oh, sure. Absolutely. Of course. I feel great. "The truth is," I admitted for the second time, "I got shot. I think my entire life has a hole in it."

He ignored the metaphysical implications. "Shall I take a look?"

I shook my head. "You're on vacation, doctor."

For a moment, he studied me soberly. "You know, Brew," he said after a while, "I can think of worse things than practicing a little medicine on my vacation."

I considered my options. Queenie had told me to talk to him, but I doubted that she'd had a medical consultation in mind. For no clear reason, I trusted both of them. Maybe I trusted him because he'd married to her. That in itself was a significant recommendation. Or maybe I was just sentimentally vulnerable to people who knew how to love each other. But whatever the explanation, I didn't want to talk to him in my present condition.

"I'll let you know," I answered as well as I could. "I've got enough pills to stock a drugstore. They're bound to do me some good eventually." Then I added. "Thanks for the offer."

He frowned like he thought I was making a mistake, but he shrugged and left me alone.

Some time later, I noticed Cat Reverie trying to catch my eye. When I finally met her gaze, she gave me what they call a "meaningful look." Then she moved away in the direction of the dining room.

I had no intention of following her. None whatsoever. Completely out of the question. On the other hand, however, Ginny had told me to *get into the spirit of the occasion*. And avoiding how I felt about that was probably the most important thing in my life at the moment. The spirit of the occasion, sure.

Making no effort to be inconspicuous, I lumbered after Simon Abel's girlfriend.

I caught up with her in the dining room. She'd acquired the decanter of port and two glasses. Faith and Ama had cleared away the dinner dishes. I could hear the Hobart running in the kitchen. It sounded the way my stomach felt.

Cat treated me to her best imitation of arch allure. "Come to the parlor," she said. Like the spider to the fly.

"The parlor?" I hadn't known that the lodge had a parlor.

"It's this way."

The spirit of the occasion. I followed her some more.

Clearly I should've done some exploring. Then I would've known about the parlor, a medium-sized room complete with a thick Persian rug, a fireplace, a couple of windows, a wet bar, two deep armchairs, a love seat, and altogether too many doilies. The fire burned like the mouth of hell. Truchi or Reeson sure kept busy stoking all these blazes.

Cat closed the door behind me. "Have some port?" She waggled the decanter.

Well, I could make an effort to get into the spirit of the occasion, but I didn't want to be ridiculous about it. Sighing, I shook my head.

She shrugged, poured herself a glass. Then she put the decanter and the extra glass down on the wet bar. Outside the windows, the world had gone black. If I stood close to the panes, the light behind me showed snow still coming down as if the heavens themselves had broken. A foot of it so far? More than that? But past the short reach of the light everything disappeared, swallowed by dark and cold.

Slowly Cat ambled to the other side of the fireplace. We faced each other across the front of the hearth. She stood with her hips cocked so that the tight sheath of her dress stretched over her breasts. Her nipples hardened against the fabric, as alluring as the look in her eyes—and just as premeditated.

"I get the impression," she said, "that you don't like me."

Opening gambit. Now it was my move. "I get the impression," I countered, "that we've already had this conversation. What happened to Hardhouse? Did he decide to go back to his wife?"

Apparently my brand of seduction didn't trouble her. She chuckled deep in her throat. "Back to his wife? Not Joseph. A man like that never goes back."

"Then what went wrong? You can't expect me to believe that he got tired of you in just one night."

Now she laughed out loud. "Well, thanks for that, anyway. I'll take it as a compliment." Hints of firelight caught in her eyes, cast a shade of unnatural red on her cheek. "I didn't get tired of him, either. He has"—she grinned salaciously—"a lot on the ball. But I like variety.

"I like strong men." She hadn't tasted her port yet. Still carrying her glass as if it made her more desirable, she started toward me. Her hips pulled against the sides of her dress. "As many as I can get."

Well, this was fun. If she had her way, I was about to become another notch on her garter belt.

Smiling nauseously, I said, "That's interesting. Simon says you do it because you have a self-esteem problem. You're trying to prove that you can be loved because deep down inside you don't really believe it."

Just for an instant, she faltered. Maybe Abel meant something to her after all. But her Avid Temptress pose met the challenge. She reached me. Her empty hand stroked the front of my sweater. Softly she pronounced, "Simon is a wimp."

I wanted to croak out a laugh—or a cry for help. "And you think I'm not?"

Languorously—I think that's the right word—she raised the hand with the glass and rested her wrist on my shoulder. Her free hand slipped to the back of my neck, drawing us closer. Her belly rubbed against my lower abdomen. Her breasts brushed my bandages.

"You're hurt, sure," she breathed up at me. Firelight filled her eyes. "But under all that pain you're made of iron. I can see it.

"Kiss me. Hurt me if you want to. I love strength. I love strong men. I want to be kissed hard."

For some reason I thought I heard a shot.

At exactly the same instant, a tidy circle appeared in one of the windowpanes.

Poor Catherine Reverie, determined and doomed.

I wasn't holding her. My arms still hung at my sides. She had no one to catch her. She thrashed like a convulsive and went down, splashing blood and bone and gray meat from an appalling hole in the side of her head. In the process, she spilled her port all over me. It soaked into my sweater, rich and cloying, and it made me stink. The glass rolled off into a corner somewhere and broke.

The spirit of the occasion. Sweet Christ.

This was going to be one *hell* of a vacation.

10

Ignoring the pressure on my guts, I dropped to my knees and lifted her in my arms as if I thought I could make a difference. But Catherine Reverie was the deadest looking body I'd seen in a long time, all the grace and desire and confusion blown out of her. Her blood added its stain to the port on my sweater. The rug was definitely ruined.

After a while, I realized that I wasn't accomplishing anything. There were things I ought to do. If I could just figure out what they were.

Ginny would know.

I lowered Cat to the rug—lowered her gently, not because she cared, but because I did. Heaved myself upright. Lurched to the door and opened it.

"Ginny," I panted. "Come here."

She would never hear me if I didn't do better than that.

"Ginny!"

She emerged from a room just a few doors away, flashing her gray eyes and her claw. The room must've been Joseph Hardhouse's. Why else would he appear right behind her as she strode into the hall? On the other hand, they both had all their clothes on. They didn't even look rumpled. Her right hand clutched her purse.

Relief twisted along the pain and the sloshing wetness in my guts.

"Brew?" Ginny snapped. Her attention focused on me, sharp, capable, and complete. It steadied me almost immediately. "What is it? What's happened?"

Other people heard me shout as well. They came into the

hall from the den, Drayton first with Mile and Maryanne behind him and others trailing. But Ginny arrived first. I pointed her into the parlor. Then I shifted my bulk to block the doorway.

Hardhouse glared at me, his face dark with irritation. His hair formed a carnivorous streak across his skull. But I didn't let him pass.

Chewing unladylike obscenities, Ginny scanned the parlor, Cat's body, the windows. Quickly, carefully, she jumped over Cat to the fireplace, then reached around to the windows one at a time and pulled down the blinds. Which should've occurred to me. If a sniper wanted to kill one of us, why not all of us? Maybe he'd only left me alive because I'd knelt down beside the body, out of the line of fire. I wasn't doing my *job*.

As soon as she'd covered the windows, Ginny wheeled toward me.

"What happened?" she demanded. "Did you see anything?

"Were you," she continued as if the smell of port filled her attention and no other question mattered, "drinking with her?"

She jerked me off balance as effectively as a magician doing misdirection. I gaped at her and did nothing to prevent the guests from pushing past me into the parlor.

Drayton and Hardhouse stooped beside the corpse. Hardhouse's anger had shifted. Now he looked both furious and ecstatic. In contrast, Sam concentrated too hard to show any reaction.

"Shee-it. Shee-it." That was Houston Mile. His face had gone pasty, like rancid cooking oil.

When Maryanne saw Cat, she gave a little squeal and tried to throw herself into Mile's arms. He shoved her away so hard that she sprawled on the love seat. Warding off panic with both hands, he backed toward the corner and wedged himself in as if he were trying to hide.

Just for a second, Maryanne stared pure hate at him. Then she began to bring great wrenching sobs all the way up from the pit of her stomach. They shook her whole body, but they didn't make a sound. She was as quiet as Cat.

Buffy, Rock, and Connie all seemed to appear at the same time. Buffy arrived bright with anticipation. Presumably she believed that one of her murders had been committed. She went right up to the body like she meant to congratulate Cat for an outstanding performance.

Then she broke into screams.

She had a throaty yowl, full of harmonics and horror—it went right into my bones. And she didn't stop. She screamed and screamed—

"Rock!" Ginny yelled. "Make her shut up!"

He didn't do it. Cat's body fixed his attention as if it were the only thing left in the world.

A lot of people react that way to violent death. They can't integrate something so far outside their range of experience. It changes the meaning of everything they know.

From the floor, Sam muttered through his teeth, "What did she do to deserve this?"

Buffy went on screaming.

Like a schoolmarm with a young bully to discipline, Connie stepped forward and smacked Buffy twice across the face, hard.

Shocked, Buffy covered her stinging cheeks with her hands and sobbed into her palms.

By then Lara and Mac Westward had arrived, holding hands demurely, like kids on their first date. But the sight of Cat changed his entire face. His usual congealed expression vanished, and his eyes burned sharply. He shoved past me and actively shouldered Hardhouse out of his way so that he could kneel beside Cat as if he wanted to study her—as if after years of writing about murder he wanted to see what it really looked like.

Hardhouse surged to his feet, glaring dark emotions in all directions.

"Brew!" Ginny barked through the confusion. "Who's missing?"

"*Joseph.*" The sheer intensity of Lara's whisper made her voice carry. *"What have you done?"*

So softly that I almost didn't hear him, he hissed back, "Nothing. I didn't do it."

"Queenie Drayton," I answered Ginny. I still had a job to do. "Simon Abel."

But Queenie wasn't missing. She appeared as I said her name. She paused in the doorway to assess the situation. If she were shocked or frightened, she didn't let that deter her. As soon as she saw where she was most needed, she went to the love seat and put her arms around Maryanne.

Maryanne buried her face in Queenie's neck and continued sobbing.

Ginny cut through the crowd toward me. Her purse lay on the floor under one of the windows. Her fist gripped her .357, and her claw moved like a threat.

"Joseph!" she cracked out, as convincing as a whip, "Sam! All of you! No one leaves this room until we find Simon!

"Rock, you're supposed to be in charge here. Go to the office, use the phone. Call the nearest cops. Do it *now*."

Her voice lashed him into motion. He left the parlor like a frightened sleepwalker.

"Come on, Brew," Ginny commanded.

I followed her out into the hall and swept the door shut.

She knew where Simon's room was. She'd been paying attention when Buffy handed out living assignments. Faster than I could move, she headed into the den and down the other hall. I was a good ten steps behind her when she reached Abel's door.

She didn't wait for me. Before I got there, she turned the knob and threw the door open.

Ginny! She should've waited, she needed me to back her up. Pulling out the .45, I lurched into a run.

The room was empty.

"Damn it," I panted thinly, hardly able to breathe, "don't *do* that. You know better."

She ignored me.

As soon as I stopped swearing at her, I noticed the cold. Abel had left his window open.

Snow had fallen on the sill, on the floor inside the window. Not a lot, maybe no more than an inch. Just enough to make it obvious that the snow hadn't simply settled there. It had been disturbed on the floor and the sill. As if Abel had gone out that way.

Ginny pulled the blind down. Then she checked the bathroom. I checked the closet. Nobody there either.

Haste and panic made pain throb in my abdomen. My guts seemed to flop around loose inside me. A minute passed before I realized what *was* in the closet.

"He's still outside," she said.

And, "He won't get far."

And, "We need to get all the blinds down. Maybe Cat isn't his only target."

"Ginny," I said like a choked fish.

On the floor of the closet, I could see a bit of snow. It looked like the remains of a footprint.

A rifle stood poorly concealed in the corner.

Ginny looked at it. She studied the snow. Using one of Abel's shirts so that she wouldn't ruin too many fingerprints, she picked up the rifle and sniffed the muzzle. Then she showed it to me.

I recognized it from the collection in the dining room— a Winchester .30–30 carbine. Its muzzle gave off the unmistakable smell of cordite and burned oil.

I put the .45 away.

"Why," I asked the cold and the fever, "didn't he close the window? Did he think we wouldn't check his room?"

"Maybe he isn't very smart." Ginny gave me the Winchester to carry. "Let's check the cases, see if anything else is missing."

I nodded. Maybe I was being stupid. I simply couldn't imagine Simon Abel blowing that hole in Cat's head.

We moved more slowly now. We had more reason to be cautious. From the hall we reached the den. We couldn't hear Buffy sobbing. We couldn't hear voices at all. Like the rest of the rooms, the parlor was too well insulated.

Don't be stupid, I told myself. Not now. Maybe he didn't mean to kill her. You can't judge the intent by the wound it makes.

We encountered no one in the den. Or in the hall between the den and the dining room. Or in the dining room. The Hobart in the kitchen had finished running. For a second I assumed that the kitchen was empty, too. Then I heard noises that sounded like flatware and plates being stacked.

"Sonofabitch," Ginny gritted under her breath.

At least half a dozen guns were missing.

I remembered some of them. The Purdy shotgun. A Ruger .357 Magnum. And, of all things, the General Patton Commemorative.

The rest could've been anything.

Reeson was bound to have an inventory. He could tell us what kind of firepower we were up against.

But it didn't make sense. Anyone who needed that Purdy or the Ruger would have no use for a Commemorative six-shooter.

Unless he—or she—knew nothing about guns.

"Looks like we're in for a siege," I commented, feverishly casual.

"Sonofabitch," Ginny repeated.

She led the way into the kitchen.

We found Faith Jerrick there alone, taking dishes from

the Hobart and piling them neatly on one of the counter-tops. She raised her head when we came in. I'd never seen her look anyone in the eye, but she sure as hell looked at Ginny's revolver. As she stared at it, she turned so pale that I seemed to see the pure color of her bones through her skin. One hand crept up to the fine chain around her neck and clutched at her crucifix.

At first Ginny and I didn't say anything. We concentrated on making sure that Faith didn't have company.

I carried the Winchester like a club—which I guess made it obvious that I wasn't about to do any shooting. Faith kept her attention on Ginny. Voice shaking, she prayed, "May God forgive you for what you do."

Just for an instant, Ginny flinched in surprise. Then she glanced at her .357 and made a disgusted gesture. "There's been a murder," she rasped. "The killer is outside. He may want to shoot someone else." Then she jumped to a decision. "But you should be safe. If anybody wanted to kill you, they could've done it long ago. And they wouldn't have shot one of the guests.

"We need Reeson. Can you go get him? I could send Brew, but I want him with me."

She wouldn't be in danger. Unless she accidentally encountered Cat's killer.

I should've gone. That was my job. But I didn't have the strength for it. And Ginny was in charge.

Faith jerked a nod. Like a woman who would've panicked and run if such things hadn't been forbidden by her religion, she turned for the back door. In this case, however, her religion probably had more to do with Reeson than God.

We had to keep moving, search the rest of the lodge. We couldn't just stand around waiting for Reeson. But before we could start, we heard something that sounded exactly like the front door of the den opening. We heard boots stamping the floor.

Ginny headed in that direction fast. Changing my grip on the .30–30 as I stumbled along, I did my best to keep up. I wasn't more than five steps behind her when she charged into the den.

Simon Abel blinked at us. He wore a heavy winter coat and cap, but I couldn't make out the details. They were caked in snow. Snow clung in clots to his legs and feet. He looked like he'd been out making snow angels.

Ginny barked, "*Freeze!*" in a voice that threatened to crack the floorboards. Her .357 lined up straight on his face.

He didn't freeze. Maybe he was too scared. He wheeled away as if she'd already fired.

Inadvertently he blundered against the door and knocked himself down. Snow blew across him from the porch. Eighteen inches of it had accumulated outside, and it was still falling.

Ginny rushed forward, crouched nearly on top of him. Then she corked the muzzle of her gun on his nose.

Eyes white with alarm, he gasped out, "Don't shoot! I killed her! I confess! Don't shoot me!"

I stopped. Ginny didn't need me. Not now. Maybe she never did. I could afford to take a few moments, try to get my breath back. Find some answer to the pain.

Altar came into the den. Presumably he'd just left the office. He moved slowly, almost aimlessly, like a man who couldn't remember why he was here.

He didn't seem to notice Ginny or Simon. When his eyes managed to focus on me, he said in a blank voice, "The phone is dead. The snow must have pulled down the line."

I've always tried to be a responsible member of society. Still holding the Winchester, I went around Ginny and Abel to close the door.

11

It was just as well I shut the door. Snow had already started to drift in from the porch. Outside it blanketed everything, as thick and terminal as volcanic ash. I suppose the phone lines could've come down under that kind of weight.

Now that Ginny had Simon on the floor, she didn't quite know what to do with him. He'd confessed too fast for his own good. Which probably didn't make her feel like trusting him. Reaching down, she clamped her claw in his coat to haul him upright.

"Mr. Altar!" Abel gabbled, "Rock, I only did what you told me, I was only doing my job, tell her, don't let her shoot me!"

Something about the particular tone of Simon's hysteria penetrated Altar's fog. For the first time, he shifted his attention toward Simon and Ginny. Slowly a flush spread across his face. In a moment he looked almost crimson, on the verge of a heart attack. Bunching his fists, he hissed, "*You fool!* You weren't supposed to *do* it!"

In our respective fashions, Ginny, Simon, and I all gaped at him.

When he realized that we were staring at him, Altar's rage paled out. He blinked at us. "He's an actor," he muttered as if he were apologizing. "He was supposed to be acting. He wasn't supposed to *do* it."

"It's a little late for that," Ginny panted as she pulled on Abel's coat.

He tried to untangle his feet so that he could cooperate.

"No, wait." He was as confused as the rest of us. Or he was good at acting confused? "What are you talking about? What's going on?"

Before anyone could answer, an idea as terrible as Ginny's .357 struck him, and he jumped away from her so fast that her claw lost its grip. The fingers came together with a metallic snap.

"Cat?" he asked. "*Cat?*"

I suppose I should've grappled for him, helped Ginny keep him under control. But I felt feverish and unloved, and too much snow had fallen, and Simon Abel was an actor who'd been hired to do a job. On top of that, Ginny didn't want my support. Instead of exerting myself, I said, "The parlor," and pointed him in the right direction.

He turned and ran.

Ginny gave me a glare that would've curdled blood and went after him.

He headed straight for the parlor, threw open the door, rushed into the room.

The atmosphere was tense, as if half the people there had just stopped shouting at each other. You could almost hear Mile sweat.

From behind I couldn't watch Abel's face. But I saw everyone else flinch away from him. Even Sam Drayton. Even Hardhouse.

He ignored them. Maybe at the moment he didn't know that he had an audience. He went rigid with shock. Then he let out a howl, broken off when he flung himself down beside Cat's corpse, scrambling to take her up in his arms.

Ginny kept her gun on Abel, mostly to show the rest of the group that she was still in charge. I set myself in the doorway and took a quick inventory of the guests. I had an active desire to avoid any more surprises—to be sure that no one could come at my back, except maybe Rock.

Queenie must've been good at comforting people. Maryanne was stable now, if not exactly calm. She acted frightened at the sight of Simon—or at the sight of Ginny's gun—but she didn't start crying again. Queenie faced us all with her arm around Maryanne and waited to find out what was going on.

Connie approached comforting Buffy in a completely different way. Her manner was stern, authoritative, and her mouth kept a tight inflexible line, like it was held in place by C-clamps. Her eyes watched everyone with impartial suspicion.

I couldn't tell whether Buffy felt comforted. Mostly she just looked catatonic.

Joseph and Lara stood close to each other, as close as they could get without actually touching. His jaw jutted aggressively. A strange intensity that might've been eagerness or dread glittered in her eyes.

The sight of them together made me shiver.

Mile had recovered from his initial panic. Now he tried to bluster—or he did until Simon came into the room. Then he shut up. I could almost see anxiety ooze from his pores.

Sam Drayton and Westward didn't seem to be doing anything in particular, except ignoring Mile. Sam was accustomed to crises and death. We could count on him. In contrast, Mac's detachment and curiosity struck me as loony, essentially unreliable.

No question about it, I was getting feverish. Another shiver went through me. Sounding positively amiable, I commented to the group, "Doesn't look much like a murderer, does he."

Sam, Mac, and Joseph turned to stare at me.

I waggled the rifle. "This is probably what he used. He won't be shooting anyone else for a while."

While Simon rocked Cat and hugged her like he was trying to squeeze the death out of her, Ginny attempted to get Buffy's attention.

"Buffy. *Mrs. Altar.*"

But Buffy, as they say in hospitals, was unreactive.

"Brew, where's Rock?"

I glanced down the empty hallway, then looked back at Ginny and shook my head.

"I want to know what the Altars hired Simon to do," she demanded as if she expected the rest of us to come up with the answer. "I want to know what went wrong."

Simon surprised me by hearing her. He lifted his face out of Cat's hair. In the kind of voice you sometimes get from junkies and drunks, people who have had too many neurons blasted, he said, "They hired me to kill her."

Buffy didn't react to this, either. But Drayton had other ideas. He turned on Simon.

"Why would they do that? They've been running mystery camps for a long time. Why would they suddenly decide they want someone dead?" He pointed at Cat. "And why *her?*"

"She was unfaithful," Simon answered in the same voice. Maybe he hadn't noticed the blood on his clothes. "I loved her. I did everything I could to take care of her, make her happy. That's what men are supposed to do, isn't it? Take care of women who need them? But she didn't care. She wanted other men. She wanted sex—sex with everybody. Except me. They hired me to kill her. The jealous lover."

Sam wanted to protest. Probably we all wanted to protest. But Ginny objected first.

"No, Simon. That isn't quite right." She spoke softly now, almost gently, like she didn't want him to feel threatened. "You're an actor. The Altars hired you to *pretend* to kill her. She's an actor, too. They hired her to *pretend* to be the victim. That was the scenario. A jealous lover and his wanton girl friend. They didn't want you to really kill her."

"No, of course not," Simon agreed. He was nearly as unreactive as Buffy. "I wouldn't do that. I love her."

"You just did," Hardhouse pronounced, each word as

harsh as a blow. "You shot her through the window." He flicked a glance at me that could've meant anything. "Unless it was Brew you wanted to kill, presumably because he was fooling around with her, and you hit her by mistake."

In unison, Sam, Queenie, and Mac opened their mouths. Like me, they hadn't considered this possibility before.

It had never occurred to me that Ginny might've had a better reason than lack of trust for not sending me out after Reeson.

"No, of course not," Simon repeated. Obviously he hadn't understood Hardhouse. But a few seconds later it hit him. "Wait a minute." His face changed radically. He was too young for himself—or his personality had too many unintegrated pieces. Nothing looked natural on him. His dismay as he put Ginny's .357 and Cat's corpse and the rifle together seemed artificial, manufactured in some way. "You think I *killed* her? You think *I* killed her?"

No one responded.

Abruptly he dropped Cat, let her head thud back to the rug. Then he jumped to his feet and started shouting.

"Weren't you listening? I love her! I've loved her for years! I wouldn't kill her!"

"You confessed, boy," Mile put in, apparently trying to create the illusion that he'd regained his self-possession. "We heard you. We got us enough witnesses to hang you."

"No, you don't understand!" Simon shot back. "I was confused. I thought you were talking about the *camp*— about the *mystery*. The reason we're all here.

"I'm an actor. Cat and I were hired to put on a mystery for you. She was supposed to act as promiscuous as she could, and I was supposed to 'kill' her for it. With one of those blue marbles. Then you could try to figure out who did it.

"When"—he faced Ginny with a gulp—"when you waved that gun at me and yelled, I panicked. I thought you were taking the camp too seriously. Right from the start, I thought you were a little crazy. I didn't know you were talking about a *real* murder."

The blank stare he got back for this speech wasn't lost on him. Whatever else you said about him, you probably had to admit that he was an experienced actor. He knew he was "dying."

"*Look*." He pulled his coat open and shoved one hand into his pocket so suddenly that Ginny automatically tightened her grip on the .357. Maryanne winced. Connie's mouth clenched disapprovingly. But what he brought out wasn't a weapon. It was small collection of blue marbles. "*I was hired to pretend to kill her*. They wanted me to kill as many of you as I could before you caught me.

"*You* heard Rock in the den." Simon turned his appeal on me. "He hired me. He admitted it."

I ignored him. His reactions, and Ginny's, and the fever made me feel that I'd lost contact with reality.

"That's true," Ginny answered Simon in a leaden voice. "I'm sure almost everything you say is true. You're an actor. You were hired. But that doesn't prove anything. It doesn't mean you didn't kill her."

He was working himself up into a frenzy of protest. "Why would I do that? I loved her!"

"For the same reason you were supposed to kill her," Hardhouse retorted. He seemed to be enjoying himself. "She screwed around. You loved her, and she didn't love you back. You couldn't stand watching her get into every bed except yours.

"You must have planned this from the beginning, as soon as Rock and Buffy offered you the job. You figured that pretending to kill her would be the perfect cover for really killing her."

"That's insane!"

Simon wanted to sound hot and indignant and righteous, command the stage in a way that would make all of us believe him. I could see that. Unfortunately a sob burst out of

him, ruining the effect. "I didn't do it," he insisted as hard
as he could. "I didn't kill her." But he only managed to look
pathetic.

"Miz Fistoulari," Mile drawled, getting to be more like
himself by the minute, "you have purely done us a service.
Ah confess, Ah was a mite worried we was all likely to get
shot. But you got him, and we're safe.

"Ah always knew there was somethin' fishy about him."

He spread his arms to Maryanne. "Commere, you pore
li'l filly," he said like he actually thought he could soothe
her. "We're safe now. No sense cryin' about it."

The Lord works in mysterious ways, His wonders to per-
form. Maryanne got up from the love seat and went into
Mile's hug like a kid who needed her daddy.

Just for a second, Queenie's face twisted as if she
wanted to puke. But she didn't say anything.

"We *are* safe, now, aren't we, Ginny?" Connie asked
sternly. "He must have shot her. Who else could have done
it? And you have his rifle. Surely we can tie him or lock
him up somewhere until the police are able to get through
this storm."

Ginny hesitated. She looked at me, frowning. She hadn't
had much time to think—but she was already a good distance ahead of me. "If I were you," she said slowly, "I
wouldn't jump to that conclusion."

The room started to tilt. I had to put my hand on the door
frame to hold it steady. Her warning was aimed at me more
than Connie and the rest of the guests. Fortunately no one
else saw me lose my balance. They all concentrated like
mad on Ginny.

"What do you mean?" Connie demanded in her best
irate schoolmarm manner. "Why do you think we aren't
safe?"

"Miz Bebb's right," put in Mile. He'd wrapped himself
around Maryanne like melting margarine. "We can't be in
danger. Who else could have shot her?"

Abel insisted again, "I didn't do it," but no one listened.

"I don't know." Ginny kept looking at me as if she could see fever radiate from my skin. "But a couple of details worry me. Rock says the phone is out. We can't call the police. We'll have to wait until morning and then see whether Reeson or Carbone has a vehicle that can drive in this kind of snow."

"Buffy mentioned a snowmobile," Maryanne put in. "Or Rock did. I'm sure of it."

Ginny nodded. "The second point is that more guns are missing." Steadily, as if she didn't notice the sting of apprehension around her, she added, "If Simon took them, he didn't put them the same place he put the rifle."

Alarm, protest, panic—voices all going at once.

"Guns."

"Where did you put them?"

"How many of us were you planning to kill?"

"What's happening to us?"

For a minute, I lost contact with the room. As it tilted, my brain slipped a few cogs. As if I wanted to change the line of reasoning that made me so sick, I ran backward to the question of the snow on Abel's windowsill.

"Calm down!" Ginny demanded over the noise.

At once the whole group collapsed into silence.

"You're intelligent people," she went on. "Brew and I are professionals. Reeson has at least a four-wheel drive, as well as the snowmobile. We'll figure out what to do. There's no immediate danger. Just don't stop using your heads."

Use my head. Sure. I lifted my weight off the door frame and moved precariously toward Simon.

He looked at me like I might club him with the Winchester. Probably he was under too much stress to realize that I didn't mean him any harm. I took him by the arm and pulled him toward a corner of the parlor, out of the way.

Ginny gave me another glance, then decided to leave me

alone. "Sam," I heard her say, "go find Rock. He's wandering around the lodge somewhere. But if you can't track him down in a couple of minutes, come back here. I sent Faith after Art Reeson. At the time, I thought she'd be safe. Now I'm not so sure. If they don't show up soon, we'll have to organize a search."

"Right." Sam paused to give Queenie a quick kiss. Just in case. Then he left.

"Simon," I said, shivering as if I could feel the draft in his room, "tell me something. Are you a fresh-air nut?"

He didn't need to be a good actor to peer at me like I'd lost my mind.

"Do you always leave your windows open?"

His soft features twisted into a laborious squint, as if he thought his life depended on his ability to distract me. "Brew, help me," he whispered. "I didn't kill her. You know that. They're going to turn me over to the cops. I'll be convicted if somebody here doesn't believe me."

"Relax." I smiled like I'd just escaped from an institution. "The cops aren't that good at convicting people these days. Tell me why you left your window open."

If he kept scrunching up his face so hard, he'd break something. "Is this a gag?" His voice jerked above a whisper. He forced it down again. "I didn't kill her. Why are you talking about windows?"

I really didn't have the strength to argue. And I wasn't going to explain—I didn't want to plant ideas in his head. Which left me without a lot of alternatives. But I still had some muscle, and I still had a grip on his arm. I started to squeeze, grinding my fingers into his biceps.

"Simon," I said softly, "just answer the question."

The pain made him gasp almost immediately. "I didn't."

"Didn't what?"

"Leave my window open. I never leave my window open." Speaking faster and faster to stay ahead of the pain. "I keep it locked. I live in L.A. Cat did, too. We just said we were from back east for cover. If you don't lock your windows, everything you own is gone when you come home."

I eased my grip. "For some reason," I remarked distantly, "I'm not surprised."

I'm sure he would've liked to rub his arm, but I hadn't actually let go of him yet. "What has my window got to do with this?" he asked. "What difference does it make?"

"If you're telling the truth, it probably makes a lot of difference." Although at the moment I couldn't have explained how or what to save my soul. I was just trying to do my job—just trying to account for the facts. "If you're lying, it doesn't make any difference at all."

Feeling light-headed, I shifted my attention back to Ginny.

She was saying, "On the drive up here, Rock told us we had nothing to worry about if we got isolated. That's still true—as far as it goes. We can keep Simon under control. We only have a problem if he isn't the one who killed Cat."

"Why do you keep saying 'if'?" Hardhouse asked. Maybe it was my imagination, but he sounded almost seductive. "What makes you think Simon didn't do it?"

Ginny smiled humorlessly. "Professional skepticism. When you look at a picture, and one detail doesn't fit, sometimes the whole picture is wrong. Why did he take all those guns? Where did he put them? What did he plan to do with them? Until he answers questions like that, I'm going to keep saying 'if.' "

"She's dead," Buffy murmured for no apparent reason. "It's my fault." She wasn't talking to any of us. "We're stuck here. We're going to die. It's all my fault."

"Nonsense," Connie put in, quietly but firmly. "You couldn't have known this would happen. And you had the good sense to hire Ginny and Brew. We'll all be fine."

"I didn't take 'all those guns,' " Abel insisted. He sounded tired, as if I'd worn him out. "I don't know what you're talking about. I don't know anything about guns. I didn't shoot Cat."

With his usual charm, Mile told Simon to shut up.

When I noticed Art Reeson in the doorway, I couldn't decide whether to feel relieved or worried. Rock and Sam stood right behind him. He and Rock wore a certain amount of snow, but most of it was on him. His coat shed cakes of the stuff, he had snow in his hair, even snow in his eyebrows, snow packed on his legs. For a moment, he didn't say anything. He just looked at Cat and me and Ginny like he wondered how much trouble we might give him.

In a lame voice, Rock explained, "I couldn't think of anything else, so I went to find Art. But he was already on his way. Then Sam found us."

"Mr. Altar says the phone's dead." Reeson sounded more than ever like he'd done too much shouting, and his hoarse rasp made what was left of my stomach twist. For some reason I felt sure that I wouldn't like what came next. "That shouldn't have happened," he continued. "We have snow up here all the time. It never pulls down the phone lines."

The liver spots on Rock's scalp gave him a diseased appearance. He said, "Art checked the cars."

"We've never had trouble with the phones," Reeson insisted. "That made me nervous. I wanted to be sure we've still got a way out of here."

He stopped.

"Don't drag it out," Ginny drawled. "Tell us the good news."

Reeson shrugged. He didn't have any trouble looking at her straight. "Nothing works. The van, Truchi's truck, my four-wheel drive—even the snowmobile. They've been immobilized. Somebody took the rotors out of all the distributors.

"We can't leave. We can't get help. We're stuck."

Probably Maryanne whimpered or groaned. Probably Mile swore. Probably Queenie said something like, "Oh, no!" But I couldn't be sure. Mac Westward was laughing too loud.

12

Apparently Reeson didn't know whether to take offense or not. He ignored everyone who tried to question him—Hardhouse, Drayton, even Ginny. "What's so funny, Mr. Westward?"

Mac stopped laughing like someone had flipped a switch and turned the sound off. "Nothing. Nothing at all. This is just perfect. It's just like in all the novels."

"Don't say that, Mac," Queenie murmured as if she knew she couldn't stop him. "Don't say it."

He said it without pausing. "A group of people get together for something they think is innocent. But it isn't innocent at all. They're cut off, isolated. Then the murders start. They try to figure out who's doing it before they all die, but they can't. Finally there are only two people left. One is the murderer. The other isn't. But the reader doesn't know which is which. The classic murder mystery. Thornton Foal wrote a book just like it several years ago."

Then he started to laugh again, cackling like a gooney bird.

"*Mac!*" Connie's command was like the way she'd slapped Buffy, sharp and to the point. "*Pull yourself together.*"

Westward stopped again. Without transition he went all red and puffy around the eyes, like he was allergic to laughter.

"This is crazy!" Houston Mile protested at Reeson. He could've used authority lessons from Connie, but he did his best. "Ah won't *have* it. You are *incompetent*, boy, and

Deerskin Lodge'll be liable!" I hadn't realized that he knew such big words. "How'd you allow this to happen?"

Reeson fixed Mile with the sort of glare I've always wished I could produce—the sort that makes people turn pale. He hardly raised his voice, but we all heard him.

"Did you call me 'boy'?"

Mile probably wanted to yell some more, but the words didn't come out. Instead he gaped like he had something nasty stuck in his throat.

"I must have misheard you," Reeson commented without a trace of humor.

"All right," Ginny put in quickly, "that's enough. Both of you *boys* can show off your macho to each other later. We have a problem. We need to make some decisions.

"If we stay cooped up in this room, we'll start hitting each other. Let's go to the den. Brew, Art—make sure the windows are covered." She didn't want anyone to take potshots at us.

Sam nodded sharply. "Good idea."

"Who?" Maryanne quavered. "Who's left? Why would anybody want to shoot at us?"

No one took any notice of her.

"I'll go with you," Hardhouse said to Reeson and me. Offering to share the heroics.

Reeson didn't thank him. Neither did I.

Lara made no effort to hold him back.

"If you don't mind," Connie said firmly to Ginny, "I'll take Buffy to her room and stay with her. She doesn't have anything to contribute at the moment. And she's in no condition to be left alone. If you can't make decisions without me, let me know."

As an idea, that one stank. We should all have stayed together. Nevertheless Ginny gave her permission with a nod.

I didn't argue the point. Reeson, Hardhouse, and I returned to the den.

We weren't particularly nervous about shutting the

blinds and closing the curtains. Reeson and Hardhouse probably believed that Simon qualified for the role of Cat's murderer. And I was half giddy with the smell of port and blood, not to mention the hot liquid sensation burbling in my guts. When we were done, Reeson stoked up the fires while Hardhouse went back to the parlor to let Ginny know. Soon everyone except Connie and Buffy was in the den.

Ginny kept Abel covered, although he didn't make any threatening moves. Probably thinking too hard to actually do anything. Holding hands, the Draytons sat down on one of the couches. Mile sat down, too, collapsed fatly into a heavy armchair, but Maryanne stayed on her feet, behind his chair with her hands on his shoulders. The balance between them had shifted subtly. They were both scared, but now she was the one doing the comforting.

In contrast, the Hardhouses had resumed acting like an estranged couple. More changes. Still participating in the heroics, he placed himself on guard duty at the entrance to the hallway that led to Buffy's room. She came over to me.

"Brew." She reached out, but my expression must've warned her against touching me. Her hands faltered in front of my chest, fluttered back to her sides. "Are you all right? You look awful." Fortunately she kept her voice low. "What did she do to you? What was that woman doing to you?"

It took me a moment to realize that her question had something to do with sex or alcohol.

I shook my head. Assuming that I wanted to talk to her at all, now wasn't the time.

If Westward noticed Lara's attitude, he didn't show it. He had other things on his mind. Whatever had started him laughing earlier was gone. Now he looked almost as lost as Rock. The bafflement in his eyes made me wonder whether he even knew who he was without the other half of Thornton Foal.

I stayed on my feet, ostensibly guarding the front door.

Ginny had Simon sit down. She pointed out seats to Lara

and Mac. Then she took a chair herself, sitting where she could see everyone. Reeson she left squatting by the nearest hearth, tinkering with the coals. Deliberately she put her .357 down on an end table by her right hand.

"Art," she began before anyone could get the impression that she wasn't in charge, "what about Faith and the Carbones? They're stuck in this with us. Shouldn't they be here?"

"Faith didn't shoot anybody," he said flatly, like he'd missed the point of the question. "I told her to stay home with the doors locked. If you want to get at her, you'll have to go through me."

But he hadn't missed the point. "The Carbones need to know," he went on. "They have a right. But they didn't shoot anybody either. They've been here longer than I have. They like the job and the hours and the place. As far as I'm concerned, you're all better suspects."

I accepted that. So did Ginny. "All right," she said, sounding as steady and uncompromising as he did. "That's good enough for now. You talk to them when you get the chance."

Reeson nodded at the flames.

"We have several things to consider," she continued to the back of his head. "We need you for all of them. You're the manager here—you know what our resources are, what we can do. Like it or not, we're dependent on you."

He nodded again. The firelight in his eyes gave him a look of sharp concentration.

Ginny raised three fingers and touched them one at a time with the tips of her claw. "First, we need some way to get a message out of here, call for help. We can't wait around for a thaw—or for one of us to find those rotors. Second, we need to keep Simon out of trouble"—she smiled bleakly—"until the cops get here." Simon winced at this, but she ignored him. "Third, we need the rest of those guns locked up. We can't let anyone else appropriate any artillery."

Before Reeson could respond, Maryanne protested in a wobbly voice, "You still sound like you think Simon didn't do it. Like you think we're still in danger. I don't understand."

"That can wait." Ginny was in no mood for interruptions. "Right now, we need to figure out what we're going to do."

Sam released Queenie's hand, shifted forward in his seat. "I don't think so, Ginny. I'm sure you're right about the practical situation. But we also have an emotional problem. We're all scared. A woman has been murdered. We need to know who did it. I don't mean that the things you listed aren't important, but we need this first. If Simon *didn't* do it, this is a life-or-death issue for all of us. The cops can't help us. Locking Simon up won't help us. And we may need those guns.

"What do you know that we don't, Ginny?"

Mile and Mac muttered their agreement. Maryanne nodded eagerly. Queenie put her hand on Sam's shoulder, a touch of approval. Hardhouse stuck out his jaw and watched Ginny with his eyes smoldering. Off in his own world, Rock mumbled something that sounded like, "How did he get them?"

Ginny pulled in a deep breath and scanned the room. Then she gave in.

Facing Simon, she said, "I'll go first. After that it's your turn."

While his eyes widened, she turned to the rest of us. "I won't bore you with the standard lecture about circumstantial evidence. I won't talk about how 'things are never what they seem'—except you'd be amazed how often that turns out to be true. I'll keep it simple.

"I know Joseph didn't do it. I was with him in his room. I know Brew didn't do it. Cat wasn't shot at close range. What about the rest of you? What alibis have you got?"

"We were in the den," Sam returned promptly.

"All of you?"

He thought for a second. "No. Houston and I. Maryanne." He looked around. "That's all."

"Queenie?" Ginny asked.

Queenie didn't hesitate. "I was in our room. Alone."

"Lara?"

Lara raised her hands to her face as if she were hiding a blush. "Mac and I were out on the porch," she said awkwardly. "Talking. Isn't that right, Mac? We came inside when we looked in the window and saw the den was empty."

"Yes!" Mac confirmed almost assertively. "We were together. Neither of us did it. This is crazy."

"Unless you did it together," Ginny retorted, smiling like a Venus flytrap. "Team murder is dangerous. You never know how far you can trust your partner. But it's an efficient way to kill somebody and not get caught.

"What about you, Rock?"

"How did he get all of them?" Rock muttered. He hadn't heard a word Ginny said. "That's what I don't understand."

Ginny shrugged. "What about Connie? What about Buffy? Anybody know where they were?"

No one answered.

"You see the problem. Only nine of us have alibis. Only seven of them look good on paper. How many of you are willing to swear Connie or Buffy or Rock or Mac or Lara or Queenie isn't capable of murder?"

"Well, speaking for myself—" Queenie put in.

Ginny overrode her. She had no intention of wasting time on a general discussion. "Your turn, Simon," she announced. "Give it your best shot."

He was readier now than he'd been earlier—he knew his role. Just for a second, he faced her sincerely and said, "Thanks." Then he got started.

"I know I'm the obvious suspect." He tried to control his tension by clenching his fists. "I'm the one who came inside all covered with snow right after—" He swallowed hard. "I can't prove I was just taking a walk because I didn't like what she was doing with Brew. Joseph was bad enough. Two men in two days was more than I could stomach. I can't prove I'm innocent.

"But look at what you're accusing me of. *Think* about it. I stole some guns—how many?" He glanced at me. "I don't even know how many are missing. But I stole them. I hid the rest, took that rifle, and went outside. I disabled all the vehicles, just to make sure I couldn't escape. Did I mention I've got a death wish? I've been planning to get caught all along.

"Anyway, then I shot Cat.

"How did you find the rifle?" he asked Ginny.

"You left your window open," she answered. "You climbed in through the window, hid the rifle in your closet, then went out again to come in innocently through the front door."

"*Right*, of course, how could I forget. I went back to my room through the window and ditched the rifle in the most obvious place I could think of, just to prove I knew what I was doing when I hid the rest of those guns." He rolled his eyes, spread his hands at the ceiling. "Then I went outside again and came in at exactly the right moment to make you all believe I shot the woman I love. And of course the first thing I did when Ginny caught me was *confess*."

His hands slapped down onto his thighs.

"How *stupid* do you think I *am?*"

He silenced the group. He had no talent for righteous indignation—we weren't bowled over by the power of his performance. Nevertheless his simple logic silenced us. When you added it up the way he did, it really did sound stupid.

After a minute, Ginny repeated, "You see the problem."

"Since you put it that way"—Hardhouse grinned

wolfishly—"I have to admit you've got a point. I don't think I've ever hired a *busboy* that dumb."

Mac steepled his fingers judiciously. "Unless he's being clever instead." The professional novelist speaking. "He may be trying to conceal his guilt by making it appear stupidly obvious."

"Oh, come on!" Simon protested. "Damn it, what do you people use for brains? If I wanted to kill her, this is the *worst* place to do it—and the worst conditions. Here we know one of us did it. I was sure to get caught. Why didn't I do it back in L.A., where I could dump the body and nobody would ever know she was even missing? Do you think this is the first time she's ever cheated on me? Do you think—"

Ginny cut him off. "That's enough. The point's been made. You're the only suspect we've got, but that doesn't mean you're the only suspect there is." To the rest of us, she added, "Use your heads. If we want to stay alive, we need to make sure Simon can't shoot anybody else. And we have to assume he didn't shoot anybody at all. We have to plan for the possibility there's still a killer loose around here."

Reeson had turned away from the fire to watch Ginny closely. When she stopped, he said softly, "You know, you're good at this. That makes it interesting."

In a plaintive tone, like he was tired of waiting, Rock asked, "How did he get all those rotors? Weren't any of the cars locked? Didn't you have the snowmobile in a shed somewhere? Wasn't the shed locked?"

Ginny's grasp on the situation had apparently improved Reeson's humor. Cheerfully he scowled. "Did you lock your van, Mr. Altar?"

Rock blinked blankly. "No."

Reeson shrugged. "Why should you? Why should Faith or Truchi or I lock any of our vehicles? Nobody steals cars up here. Or snowmobiles either. And nobody immobilizes them. We depend on them too much.

"Most of the time," he concluded, "we don't even take the key out of the ignition."

"Good," Hardhouse commented. "I like it. You're right—this makes it interesting." He sounded sarcastic, but I detected relish. "It's looking like more fun all the time."

"At any rate," Sam rasped, "it looks like more fun than convincing the cooks to keep their hair out of the soup. Right?"

I got the distinct impression that he'd decided he didn't like Joseph Hardhouse.

Hardhouse grinned. "You should try it. After six months in the restaurant business, you'll think having your teeth extracted is more fun."

"Too bad it makes so much money," Sam retorted. "Otherwise you could quit with a clear conscience."

Hardhouse didn't have to grope for a comeback. "Maybe if I quit and became a doctor," he said, "I wouldn't have such trouble keeping my conscience clear."

"Listen." Ginny snapped her claw to get their attention. "Bicker on your own time. We've got more important things to worry about right now."

Sam held up his hands to show that he was finished.

From my point of view, the smile Hardhouse aimed at Ginny looked positively voracious.

"If I've made myself clear," she went on, "we're back where I started. We have decisions to make."

"Not really." As smooth as a hydraulic lift, Reeson rose to his feet. "As you pointed out, I'm the manager here. And as *he* pointed out"—with a jerk of his head, he indicated Mile—"the lodge doesn't want any liability suits. That makes the situation my responsibility. I'll take care of it. I don't mean I'm going to catch your killer for you. But I can solve some of the other problems.

"Over the years, I've done a fair amount of winter camping. I have the gear and the experience to cope with this weather. In the morning, I'll hike out of here. If conditions aren't so bad outside the valley, I can probably reach a phone by the end of the day. Otherwise it may take me two days. But the Carbones and Faith can handle everything here while I'm away."

"You should take one of us with you," Ginny remarked. "Winter camping isn't exactly safe alone."

"I should," he agreed, "but I won't. I don't have two sets of gear. And my tent only sleeps one. I'll be all right.

"Before I go," he continued, "I'll tell Truchi to hide the guns somewhere. He won't let any of you know where they are. That way"—his glare conveyed a secret humor— "none of you will be tempted to declare yourselves vigilantes and shoot up the lodge."

"Wait a minute," Mile protested. "Wait a goddamn minute." Reeson had touched a sore point in him—a point sore enough to push him past his fear. "We need them guns. If Ginny's right—and Ah don't say she is—we got to defend ourself. We got the *right* to defend ourself. How're we goin' to do that with no guns?"

"Well, I don't rightly know, Mr. Mile," Reeson drawled back, aping Mile's accent. "Maybe you folks is just goin' to have to place your trust in God—and Miz Fistoulari."

Mile flushed. Obviously he wasn't accustomed to mere employees who talked that way. But he also wasn't accustomed to facing down men with Reeson's talent for toughness. Probably hoping that only Maryanne could hear him, he muttered, "Sonofabitch," and collapsed back in his chair.

"Guns aren't for amateurs, Houston," Ginny said harshly. "I'd rather have one killer on my hands than a roomful of armed amateurs trying to defend themselves."

Tired of feeling useless, parked by the front door and forgotten, I tried to make a contribution. "Even experts miss sometimes," I said through my fever. "The goon who shot me did. But the really amazing thing is, amateurs never do. They always hit *some*thing."

Ginny nodded and turned back to Reeson. "What about Simon?"

"That's harder," he admitted. "The lodge doesn't have any rooms you can't get out of if you're locked in. And I suppose you don't want to do anything as 'inhumane' as tying him to a chair for the next three or four days. I don't know what else to suggest." Then he thought of something. "Except the wine cellar."

"Wine cellar?"

"It isn't really a cellar," he explained, "just a room off the kitchen. Only one door, no windows. There's a padlock on the outside. I think Ama has the key.

"It's insulated so it stays cool, but it doesn't get cold. We can put an electric heater in there. And it has room for a cot and a chair, maybe even a table. We have plenty of card tables.

"You could use it."

"No!" Simon said.

"Good," Ginny said.

"You don't understand," Simon protested. "I get claustrophobia. I'll go crazy in there."

Right away I didn't believe him. He sounded like he was acting again.

Ginny didn't believe him, either. "On the other hand," she answered with an edge in her tone, "once you're locked in the wine cellar, we'll all know you're innocent if somebody else gets killed. And you can be reasonably sure you won't be the next victim."

In other words, she wasn't willing to take the risk that he really was Cat's killer. Personally, I was glad I didn't have to make the decision. Since I didn't think he had anything to do with the murder, I probably wouldn't have had the heart to lock him up. And when I turned out to be wrong, I'd have real trouble living with myself.

Ginny got to her feet, holding the .357 again. Her movements lacked Reeson's oiled precision, but she looked ready and dangerous in her own way. "Anybody got any problems?" she asked the room. "Anything else you want to discuss?"

Maryanne bent down and murmured something in Mile's ear. He nodded without speaking. Somewhere under his fat, he'd probably clenched his jaws, but it didn't show.

Sam and Queenie looked at each other. Then she said for both of them, "Tell us what you want us to do."

I liked her so much it made my back teeth hurt.

Mac studied Lara. He was slowly returning to normal— only the specificity of his concentration on her betrayed the state of his emotions. Apparently the shock of Cat's murder had already become secondary to him. His loneliness ran so deep that what Lara represented was more important.

As for her, she returned his attention like he had the power to make her insides melt.

In contrast, Rock now seemed like he was actually present in the room. He'd finally caught up with the rest of us. He met Ginny's question by raising his head and doing his best to look decisive. "This is what we hired you for. Although God knows we didn't want this to happen. You're in charge."

Joseph Hardhouse echoed Rock. "We'll do whatever you say." But he added a vibration to the words, a second or third harmonic, that echoed painfully in the core of my heart.

Ginny approved with a sharp nod. "I have handcuffs in my purse," she told Simon. "I'm going to put them on you while Art rousts out the Carbones. Once Ama makes the wine cellar comfortable, I won't keep you cuffed.

"Joseph," she asked, "will you get my purse? I left it in the parlor."

He nodded and went.

I still had nothing useful to do. Ginny was too good at this sort of thing.

"Before Art leaves," she continued, scanning the room, "maybe he and Truchi can do something with Cat's body so it doesn't"—she was deliberately harsh—"start stinking up the lodge.

"In the meantime, the rest of us should search for those missing guns."

So that's what we did. Or rather, that's what they did. Leaving Simon cuffed to one of the armchairs, Ginny split the guests into teams and put them to work. Judging by her choices, she trusted no one except the Draytons. She let them work together—alone. But she paired Mac with Rock and sent Lara to keep an eye on Mile and Maryanne. Hardhouse she kept to herself. Each team she assigned a wing of the lodge.

She didn't need a degree in medicine, however, to see that I was in no condition to do any searching. Instead she told me to take Connie's place with Buffy so that Connie could join the hunt.

That made sense, of course. I couldn't stay on my feet much longer. Nevertheless it felt *wrong*. I was her partner. I should've done this job with her. To hell with the fact that my head no longer felt successfully attached to my neck. She still needed a partner.

But I didn't argue the point. Instead I told myself that she knew what she was doing. If I didn't lie down soon, I was going to fall down. And I wanted to get away from Hardhouse.

Tossing the Winchester to Reeson, I went to relieve Connie.

In the Altars' room I found Buffy asleep on one of the twin beds. Shock and unconsciousness had wiped the camp-activities-director look off her face, the deliberate cheeriness and competence. Now she seemed both older and younger, the way some people do when they're scared—worn-out and vulnerable.

Connie sat in a rocking chair beside Buffy's bed, watching over her, as prim and austere as one of the Fates.

"Well, Mr. Axbrewder," she asked me, "what's been decided? What's being done?"

She required an answer, but I'd lost the ability to concentrate. Ginny needed a partner. People were searching the lodge. I should've been one of them. As if this were the crux of the whole situation, I said, "You're supposed to call me Brew."

"That," she retorted with some asperity, "was when we were all guests together at a mystery camp. Now there's been a murder. You and Ms. Fistoulari are the professionals in charge until the police arrive." Apparently she could tell that I had no idea what her point might be. "To be effective," she explained, "you must have authority. I intend to grant you that authority."

"Oh, good," I said. I didn't want authority. I wanted to lie down.

Restraining impatience, Connie repeated, "Mr. Axbrewder, what's been decided? What's being done?"

She had a right to know. Somehow I told her.

She spent a moment absorbing the information. Then she pronounced, "You shouldn't have any trouble with Mrs. Altar. I expect she'll sleep for quite a while. Use the other bed and get some sleep yourself. I'm sure Mr. Altar won't object."

Mutely I obeyed. As if she were the one with all the authority, I went to the bed and eased my guts into prone.

I must've been in worse shape than I realized. An entire swimming pool sloshed around inside me, but that didn't prevent me from becoming one with the mattress almost immediately.

Maybe because she understood how Buffy and I felt, Connie didn't switch the light off. That turned out to be a good thing. It helped me identify where I was when Buffy's crying woke me up.

Softly she sobbed into her pillow, clamping it over her face like she wanted to suffocate herself.

The swimming pool sensation in my gut was worse than ever. I had difficulty heaving all that water upright. But I got myself over to her bed somehow. Sitting beside her, I pried one of her hands loose so that I could hold it.

"Buffy." I sounded like a rusty band saw, but that was the best I could do. "Buffy, it's all right. Don't worry. It's going to be all right." Pure bullshit, but I didn't even notice. "We'll take care of everything."

Clinging hard to my hand, she pulled her face out of the pillow. Her hair was a fright, and the skin around her eyes looked like one of those plastic surgeries where the patient goes into collagen rejection.

"She wasn't supposed to die," she gulped between sobs. "I never wanted her to die. I didn't want anybody hurt. It was just supposed to be fun.

"Now she's dead and it's my fault. It's all my fault."

"No, it's not." I comforted her like she was a sick kid. "Don't be silly. It's not your fault. No one blames you."

That must've been what she wanted to hear. It seemed to help her stop sobbing. Nevertheless she had to protest against it, probably because she wanted it so badly.

"We're here because of me. Because I wanted to do this. Murder on Cue is mine. Rock doesn't care about it. He only helps out because he's my husband. I put us in this situation. I made it happen. Cat wouldn't be dead if I hadn't."

I repeated myself like a half-wit. "Don't be silly." Fortunately as my voice limbered up I sounded a bit more soothing. "That's like blaming the guy who built the lodge for making a place where someone might be shot. It's not your fault."

Gradually she relaxed. Her breathing still shuddered and caught going in and out, but the pressure to sob grew less inside her. Her damaged eyes searched my face as if I were someone she could believe, someone who told the truth.

"I've never seen a dead body," she said in a small voice. "Nobody I care about has ever died. Even my parents are still alive. My favorite teacher from high school is still alive. I never knew my grandparents. When I saw her there in all that blood—" Her mouth quivered pitifully. "I keep thinking this is going to ruin my life."

Most days, I think that people who let the presence of blood and pain in the world ruin their lives deserve to have their lives ruined. But this time, for some reason, her concern just reminded me that I didn't smell so good. I needed clean clothes and a shower and a fresh outlook on life.

So I didn't dismiss her self-pity. Instead I said, "Maybe it won't. It's too soon to know." Then I tried a distraction. "Tell me more about Rock. What does he get out of doing this?"

"I used to worry about that," Buffy admitted. She was too stunned or vulnerable to question what I asked her. Hell, she hadn't even questioned my presence in her room. "He doesn't like mysteries. I thought he would. He's usually good at puzzles. But there's something about this kind of puzzle he doesn't like. I don't know what it is. I used to worry that if he helped me with something he wasn't interested in, he'd lose interest in me."

She paused. I didn't hurry her.

"But then I found out," she went on, "Why he does it. How he stays interested. What he does to stay interested." She was thinking in pieces—but at least she was thinking. "Houston told me. The first time he came to one of our camps.

"You mustn't underestimate Houston, Brew," she insisted. She wanted me to believe whatever it was that Mile had told her. "A lot of people don't like him." With unexpected acid in her voice, she commented, "I think most of the women he brings with him don't like him."

Then she resumed, "But he's devious. That makes him good at mysteries."

She took a deep breath, and a quiver ran through her. Faltering as if she feared my reaction, she revealed, "He told me Rock tampers with the clues. He makes it harder for us to figure out who did it. That's how he stays interested."

So she knew. I couldn't decide whether to be relieved or amazed. From the beginning, it had nagged at me that Rock was willing to sabotage his wife's beloved hobby. But if she knew—

"You don't sound upset," I said. "Doesn't it bother you?"

"Oh, no," she replied quickly. Too quickly? "Do you know what it's like when you're getting older and bit by bit your husband starts to look like he's dying of boredom? It takes the heart out of you. There's nothing you can do about it. You try to look good. You work at it. But you can't make yourself younger. So you try to catch his mind instead—since you can't catch his eye anymore. But Rock doesn't like mysteries."

She let an old sigh out of the bottom of her lungs. "I want him to stay interested. I'm glad he's found a way to do it. And now that I know about it, I can enjoy it. I don't know what he'll do, of course. But just knowing he'll do something makes the mystery better. It puts more pressure on everyone, even the actors.

"It's become a game he and I play with each other." She smiled in a wan attempt to convince me that she was content. "Almost a way of courting each other. If you know what I mean."

Actually, I thought I did. In a perverse sort of way, it even seemed reasonable.

But I didn't buy it. It was too damn convenient.

After all, Roderick Altar didn't like hunters. He wasn't just uninterested in Buffy's game, he disapproved of it. And he'd talked me out of taking a stand about those guns. If they'd been locked up, Cat might still be alive.

Where did he draw the line? How serious did the game have to get before he played it honestly? The last thing Ginny and I needed to worry about right now was a man who couldn't or wouldn't make the distinction between killing people with blue marbles and killing them with actual bullets.

When the door opened, however, and Rock and Ginny came into the room, my immediate concern evaporated. He didn't look like a man who meddled with murders. He looked like a man who needed sleep. He'd gone gray with fatigue, the color of lead and strain. Most of his body seemed to slump on his bones. The sight of him reminded me that he'd freely admitted tampering with Buffy's clues. That odd piece of honesty made him appear less dangerous now.

Instead of mentioning my worries, I asked, "Did you find anything?"

Rock didn't respond. Dumbly he shuffled across the room, sat down on the edge of his bed, and stared morosely into his empty hands. It was Ginny who said, "Not a thing. If you don't count Mile's collection of pornographic paraphernalia."

She sounded distant rather than tired or disappointed, as if the waste of the search had no real importance. Or less importance than other things.

"Come on, Brew." She surprised me by resting her claw gently on my shoulder. "We've done all we can for tonight. The sun'll be up in a few hours. I want to see you in bed before I collapse myself."

She'd stopped trusting me. She'd stopped using me. But she hadn't stopped taking care of me.

I could see that she was in no danger of collapsing.

I sighed and struggled to my feet.

We left Rock and Buffy sitting on the edges of their beds. The only obvious difference between them was that she looked at him but he still didn't look at her.

Probably I should've confronted Ginny then. The halls were empty, no one else was around. I wasn't likely to get a better chance. I should've said, I'm your partner. Stop treating me like an invalid. Stop charging into rooms without me to back you up. Stop telling other people to do my job.

But I funked it. I told myself that I didn't have the strength. The truth was that I didn't have the courage. The simple effort of walking to my room exhausted the last of my resolve. If she hadn't stood over me and made me do it, I wouldn't have taken off my clothes before I crawled into bed.

After all, I *was* an invalid. I couldn't change that just by hating it.

Instead of saying what I needed to say, I murmured, "Simon's window bothers me. It doesn't fit."

Ginny looked at me as if her brain were somewhere else entirely. "What do you mean?"

"He didn't have to make himself look so guilty. He could've shot Cat and stashed the rifle, then closed the window and joined us through the lodge. Even if he had a reason to come in through the front door, he could've closed his window first. By the time we searched his room, the snow would've melted. You wouldn't know the window was ever open."

"You don't think he did it." She still wasn't paying attention.

"No, I don't." I couldn't be honest for myself, but I could do it for Simon.

She shook her head. "Joseph says the same thing. According to him, Simon doesn't have the right kind of motive. That's part of his theory about murder, I guess. Jealousy is too primal. If Simon killed Cat, he'd want her to know it was him. He'd do it face-to-face. He wouldn't attempt a charade as elaborate as this one looks.

"It doesn't matter whether I agree or not. Locking Simon up is still a good idea. It protects the rest of us. Since he can't kill anybody else, whoever wants us to think he's guilty won't risk destroying the illusion."

She was way ahead of me. As usual. For once, I found that reassuring. She didn't love me anymore, and she couldn't treat me like a real partner, but she was still Ginny Fistoulari. She knew what she was doing.

Before she left my room, I rolled over and sank back down into the depths of the pool.

13

When I woke up, I found sunshine splashed brilliantly across the rugs in my room, and the doilies looked positively luminous, and I was in a completely different world of fever. I felt as clear as crystal—and as empty as glass. Like a computer with no software to run it. Precise and useless.

Obviously I'd slept too long.

I blinked at the ceiling for a couple of minutes without once wondering why my curtains were open. The snowstorm had blown past, that was the important thing. Reeson could get out of here. Maybe we could even count on him.

Apparently the sun had been up and doing its job for a while now. Piously setting a good example for the rest of us. No doubt I'd missed Reeson's departure. But I felt too clear and empty to be disturbed by the mere fact that I lay abed like a debutante after a ball when theoretically I was fifty percent in charge of keeping everyone else alive. Fever seemed to be the solution to all my usual emotional difficulties.

On that philosophical note, I got out of bed.

I needed a shower badly. I could still smell blood and port on my skin. On top of that, a distinct whiff of something rank rose from the general vicinity of my bandages. But of course the bandages prevented me from taking a shower. And I was probably too weak for so much exertion. I didn't bother with it. I didn't bother with shaving. I knew I was supposed to take my pills, but I didn't bother with them, either. What good did being clear and empty do me, if I couldn't make my own decisions like a grown-up?

On the other hand, I drew the line at wearing my dirty clothes again. Axbrewder the cleanliness freak. I dragged a heavy cotton sweater over my head, hauled up a pair of pants. The only thing I put in my pockets was my .45.

My feet seemed incredibly far away, almost impossible to reach. Finally I dismissed the problem of socks. Instead I pushed my toes into a pair of loafers Ginny had packed for me. Then, feeling better than I had for days, I went out to face the world.

It was a good thing that my head was so clear. Otherwise I might not have been able to keep my balance. My legs had different amounts of strength, and I listed to one side as if the freight inside me had shifted.

I didn't find anyone in the den. They were all outside, standing on the porch or up to their knees in the snow. When I joined them, none of them paid me much attention. Reeson must've gotten a late start. They were all watching him go—watching their hope trudge out of sight over the white horizon. I could see his tracks in the snow, running up the driveway to the gate at the rim of the valley.

I spotted him in time to see that he didn't turn or wave. He just plodded away, a small black figure disappearing into the background of white snow and dark trees.

Despite the end of the storm, the air hadn't become significantly warmer. And a steady wind blew. Reeson's trail had already started to fill in and fade, erased by powder. In an hour or two all sign of his passing would be gone. The snow wouldn't hold a trail until the sun or the air made it wet enough to stick.

"Mr. Axbrewder." Connie Bebb had noticed me at last. "I'm glad you got some sleep. You needed it."

Then Lara Hardhouse turned. Even though she stood at Mac Westward's shoulder, she flashed me a smile that would've looked friendly if it hadn't held such unmitigated desire.

She and Mac had kept to the porch, along with the Altars and Connie, Houston Mile and Maryanne Green. Of that group, only Lara and Mac didn't seem the worse for wear. Connie looked wan and thin, stretched too tight. A quick frightened little twitch worked the corner of Maryanne's mouth, as if she feared being hit. She tried to control it by compressing her lips. For his part, Mile had the sluggish self-absorbed air of a reptile about to molt.

Rock and Buffy now resembled each other the way old married couples sometimes do. From him she'd picked up a gray tone, the leaden weight of defeat. From her he'd acquired puffy eyes and a frenetic glance. If he'd had any hair, it would've stuck up in all directions.

Apparently Simon Abel still occupied the wine cellar. But Faith Jerrick stood on the porch, too, along with Amalia Carbone. Amalia's husband, Petruchio, had joined Sam and Queenie Drayton, Joseph Hardhouse, and Ginny out in the snow. They'd clustered together like the official farewell committee, supervising Reeson's departure.

When Connie said my name, Ginny and Hardhouse looked at me in unison, as if they'd achieved a new partnership during the night.

The sunlight reflecting off all that clean snow made them squint, but it didn't trouble me. I was clear and empty, and the brightness passed through me without leaving a mark.

Sam and Queenie faced in my direction as well. I had no idea how well they could see me.

In my vacant fashion, I was surprised to see that Faith didn't wear a coat—or even a sweater. Nothing more than a long apron warmed her blouse and skirt. As pale as she was, I would've expected her to be susceptible to chill, one of those delicate creatures whose feet are always ice. But she didn't look cold. Folding her arms under her breasts, she stared up at the spot where Reeson had disappeared as if she could still see him—as if she'd burned his image into her retinas. Maybe that was why she never looked at other people directly. She couldn't actually see anyone except him.

"Does he really know what he's doing?" I asked her. Since my life probably depended on him, I had a personal interest.

I couldn't be sure that she'd heard me until she said, "Oh, yes." Naturally she didn't so much as glance in my direction. "Art always knows what he's doing."

Does he? I thought. He must be impossible to live with. But I didn't say that out loud.

As if my arrival were a signal, the people out in the snow started moving. Truchi strode off toward one of the cottages, unhampered by anything as minor as eighteen inches of snow. Ginny and Hardhouse approached the porch, with Sam and Queenie behind them.

As she came up the steps, Ginny blinked the glare out of her eyes to look at me closely. Now I didn't need intuition to tell me that something was happening to her, something important. I could see it in the muscles around her eyes and mouth. They must've been clenched for so long I'd gotten used to seeing them that way. Otherwise the change when they relaxed wouldn't have seemed so dramatic.

"I came to your room," she said almost casually. "Before Art left. I was going to wake you up. But when I saw how hard you slept, I decided to leave you alone." She almost smiled. "But I opened your curtains, just in case you wanted to wake up."

She was gone. Lost to me. Like people, relationships die. They can even be killed. The only problem when that happens is that you have to go on living.

Fortunately the fever protected me. Instead of pissing and moaning and generally feeling sorry for myself, I shrugged a bit and said, "Thanks."

She didn't trust my reaction. Frowning now, she asked, "Are you all right? You don't look good." A moment later she demanded, "Have you been taking your pills?"

Hardhouse slipped his hand under her arm like he wanted to get her away from me. "Brew's a big boy," he said. "He's old enough to take his own pills."

Briefly she did me the courtesy of ignoring him. "Isn't that right?" Ginny murmured to me. "I'm supposed to stop taking care of you? That's what you want?"

But Hardhouse didn't mean to be ignored. "You're too good at it," he commented helpfully. "He needs to learn the truth about himself. He can't do that when you cover for him."

She glanced at him quickly, as if this perception had the power to change her life.

Obviously the two of them had spent some time talking about me. Somehow I got the impression that his idea of "the truth" wasn't very flattering.

I opened my mouth and pretended to laugh, but nothing came out.

With him somehow indefinably in charge, he and Ginny led the way back into the den. The Altars, Mile and Maryanne, even Connie followed like sheep. Ama Carbone did the same, but not from any herd instinct. She just had work to do.

Faith Jerrick remained on the porch, watching the point of Reeson's departure as if the simple intensity of her yearning could ensure that he came back.

Sam and Queenie stopped in front of me. Concern filled their faces.

"Don't say it," I said, groping for the right note of amiable lunacy. " 'You don't look good.' If I hear that one more time, I might believe it."

The Draytons were holding hands, gripping each other hard. With my new clarity, I didn't have any trouble noticing the whiteness of their knuckles. Softly, speaking per-

sonally to Sam despite the fact that I could hear her, Queenie observed, "You could help him whether he wants it or
not. I don't think he has the strength left to stop you."

He scowled, not at her, but at what she said. "I don't like
doing that. I'm not sure it's ethical. And it doesn't usually
work. As soon as he recovers a bit, he'll just go back to trying to kill himself."

"That's not your problem," she countered. "You've helped
people before when they were too sick or hurt to ask for it."

"Sure. But this is a different situation. In the hospital, or
my office, I can always assume that people want my help,
even if they're too far gone to ask. I'm entitled to assume
that under the circumstances. I don't think I can assume it
here."

She conceded with a sigh. "I just don't like feeling so
helpless."

"May I say something," I put in, "or is this a private
discussion?"

Both Sam and Queenie faced me.

"Sam is right," I told her. "It's none of your business."

Without quite meaning to, I hit a nerve. Her eyes filled
with tears. His face went hard, as if I'd just lost his
friendship.

"Faith," he said steadily, "Brew hasn't had any breakfast. Take him inside. See if you can get him to eat something. If he won't go with you, I'll drag him."

"Yes, Dr. Drayton." Being given something to do
seemed to release Faith from her trance. Not glancing at
any of us, she moved to the door and held it open.

Queenie's tears had more effect on me than Sam's anger.
The fever only defended me from my own pain, not hers.
But I couldn't think of anything useful to say, so I turned
away and let Faith escort me back into the lodge.

Following her, I shuffled into the kitchen. Along the way
I noticed that the guns were gone from the cases in the dining room. Truchi, at least, was doing his job.

In the kitchen, Faith pointed me at a stool at one of the counters, then moved to a refrigerator and began pulling out food.

I sat down and watched her.

I probably should've told her not to bother, but my mind was elsewhere. The empty cases had reminded me of Art Reeson and Cat Reverie and how helpless we all were. Or maybe I just wanted a distraction from Ginny and Hardhouse—and Sam and Queenie. So I asked Faith, "Is this what he does on his vacations? Go camping in the dead of winter?"

Apparently she didn't consider my question unexpected. In her condition, no reference to Reeson was unexpected.

"Sometimes."

There's nothing like a one-word answer to inspire the imagination. "Do you mean he sometimes goes camping on his vacations? Or he sometimes goes camping in the dead of winter?"

She thought about this while she put a plate of cold toast and bacon in front of me, along with a pot of strawberry jam. "Would you like something hot? I can warm up the bacon. Or scramble some eggs."

Instead of gagging, I waited for her to get around to my question. I felt sure that she wasn't being evasive. She simply lived in a mental world very different from mine.

After a moment, she said, "Both."

"Do you go with him?" I was trying to evaluate Reeson's ability to get through the snow and save us.

"No," she answered without hesitation or rancor. "Why should I?"

I shrugged. "Keep him company?"

She stood across the counter from me, her arms folded over her midriff again. If she cared that I hadn't touched the food, she didn't show it.

"I would if he asked me, of course," she explained as if the subject were somehow profound. Her manner was more subdued than the last time I talked to her. If anything, that made her more convincing. "But I have no reason to go, expect to please him. I don't need to go anywhere. God is with me wherever I am. That's all I need."

"I see." I didn't see at all. "Sometimes he goes camping in the winter. Sometimes in the summer. And sometimes he doesn't go camping. If he wants a vacation, he does something else. And you don't go with him."

She nodded gravely.

"Where does he go when he doesn't go camping?"

"You'll have to ask him, Mr. Axbrewder." I hadn't offended her. I'd just touched something outside her chosen world. "He doesn't take me with him, so I don't know where he goes."

"You mean, even when he does something besides camping for his vacation, he doesn't take you with him?"

"Why should he?" Her calm was perfect. "While he's away, I have God for company. And after he goes away, he comes back."

She said this as if it accounted for everything.

Not to me, it didn't. "But why doesn't he tell you where he goes?" I pursued. "Doesn't he even leave phone numbers, in case you need to get in touch with him? What about emergencies?"

Clearly I lacked the capacity to ruffle her. "What emergencies do you imagine I'm afraid of, Mr. Axbrewder? Truchi and Ama are here." Almost as if she were looking at me, she went on, "*God* is here. If you could believe in Him, you would know there is truly nothing to be afraid of."

"I'm trying," I muttered. Bafflement seemed to breathe a fog across the blank glass of my emotions. "It just doesn't make sense." For a second there, confronted by her immaculate and irreducible self-absorption, I felt something surge behind the clarity and the emptiness and the fever— something that tasted and smelled and even hurt like utter rage. *Nothing to be afraid of*. No question about it, I would've been better off with her religion, all my questions answered and no more need to think.

Where else did she get so much *trust*?

I had to get away from her before I lost my balance entirely. At the moment I didn't give a shit whether she thought I was rude or not. I got up and lurched out of the kitchen.

When I reached the den—which seemed unusually far away, like I'd taken a wrong turn somewhere—I found it practically empty. Maryanne Green sat alone in front of the embers of one of the fires, as if she'd been left behind. A deer's head with glassy death in its eyes leaned over her. She looked up when she heard me shuffling over the floorboards. Something in her expression warned me not to join her.

Too bad. I needed help—I needed to escape Faith emotionally as well as physically—and Maryanne was the only resource available. I sat down beside her and asked the first question that came into my head. "Where's everyone else?"

"Most of us were up all night." She didn't turn her head—and she didn't try to sound anything except bitter. "We couldn't find the guns. But Simon is in the wine cellar. We're supposed to be safe now. Ginny said she wanted to get some sleep. Everybody else thought that was a good idea."

Her tone did what I wanted—it hooked my attention. "But not you."

For maybe the first time, I looked at her closely and noticed that she wasn't young. Until then I'd assumed that she was practically a kid. She had a fresh face, and I felt sure that Mile preferred girls to women. But the skin around her eyes had too many fine lines, and her cheeks weren't resilient enough.

"Houston didn't want sleep," she answered. "He's scared, I guess. When he's scared, he does things to me. It reassures him. Maybe he isn't on top of the world. Maybe he can't do everything he wants. But at least he can do what he wants to me.

"But I'm scared, too. He doesn't understand that. Ginny scared me. If she had just let me think Simon did it, I might have been able to stand it. I might have been brave enough. But now I'm scared. I've never been so scared. And what he does hurts. It hurts a lot. Sometimes I think it's going to be more than I can bear."

Her voice trailed away, dying like the coals in the fire.

I could guess what happened. "So you told him no."

She nodded dumbly.

"And he threw you out."

She nodded again. "He says he won't even pay my way home." Then, before I could come up with a reply, she added, "I could kill Ginny for this."

She sounded perfectly sincere.

Suddenly my balance failed. Like Faith, Maryanne touched something in me that I didn't understand and couldn't use, a mad blank anger. "Oh, come on," I rasped. "What do you want her to do? Ignore the chance that Simon is innocent? If he didn't kill Cat, someone else did. And if it's someone else, we don't know what his motive is." Or hers. "Which means we can't predict what'll happen next. Maybe we'll all get shot at. Ginny is just doing her job."

Maryanne didn't try to answer me directly. I'd missed the point. She had a completely different grievance. Glaring at me like I'd just crawled out from under a rock, she countered, "But she isn't much of a woman, is she."

Oh, boy.

"I don't know what you see in her. Or Joseph sees. It isn't fair. She wants to be a man. She throws her weight around and tells everyone what to do and swears like a man. She humiliates you. And you lap it up. You ought to hate her, but instead you follow her around like a puppy. She's castrated you, and you think you like it. And Joseph can't wait to get his hands on her. He ought to know better—a man like that. *He* ought to know better.

"Do you know where they are right now?"

No, don't tell me that. Do *not* tell me that. More than anything else, I didn't want to know where Ginny and Hardhouse were right now. Otherwise I would burst with fever and fury.

"It's none of my business," I said as quickly as I could, trying to stop her.

I didn't stop her. But at least I deflected her.

"Cat was someone I could understand," she went on. "I can't figure out why you didn't like her. She wanted you to be *male*. She wanted to revel in your maleness. That made her a woman, a real woman. And Lara's a real woman, in her own way. I don't know how she manages to see anything *male* about Mac, but at least she wants Joseph to be himself. She likes him the way he is."

As an interpretation of Lara, this stunned me. But I didn't interrupt.

"Even Queenie is a woman." Maryanne concentrated on the coals as if she thought that she could make them blaze by scowling at them. "She has too many opinions, and she wants everyone to take them seriously. But she doesn't get in Sam's way. She knows he's a man. She wants him to be a man.

"Not Ginny." Maryanne actually shuddered, a hard quiver of revulsion. "She doesn't want you to be a man. If you tried, she'd try to prevent you. She wants to make us all *afraid*.

"Why does she do it? What does she get out of it?"

"I have a better question." I was full of panic, terrified of my own emotions, and I couldn't afford to think about Ginny. "Why do *you* do it?"

Poor woman, she knew exactly what I meant. I'd asked her real question for her, the question that made everything else hurt. She turned a gaze like hate at me, and her bitterness came up from the bottom of her heart.

"What makes you think I have a choice?"

I spread my hands helplessly.

"Look at me," she demanded. "Do you see anything that makes you think I have a choice? I'm not young. I've never been able to get a husband. There aren't any jobs I know how to do. I guess it isn't considered a good thing anymore to be a woman, but that's what I am. That's all I am. And I'm not beautiful like Cat. I don't have Lara's talent for looking mysterious and passionate. I don't even have breasts like Queenie. Mine sag, and they have stretch marks, and my hips are puffy." She may have wanted to weep, but her bitterness didn't allow her anything that direct and simple. "I don't have a choice."

"Then," I said softly, like it was my job to break her heart, "you better go back to Houston."

She gave me a look of pure black murder—but she didn't hesitate. Jerking to her feet, she knotted her hands in the front of her blouse and wrenched at it so one of the seams tore and a few of the buttons popped. They clicked to the floor and rolled away, whispering across the wood.

"I'll tell him you attacked me," she said in a dead voice that didn't match her eyes at all. "That'll get him excited." But an instant later she thought better of it. "No, he'll never believe it. He has your number—he knows what you're capable of. I'll tell him it was Joseph. He'll believe that."

Looking more attacked than any woman I could remember, she turned and strode out of the den. Only the defiant flounce of her skirt showed that she knew she was really her own victim.

So much for clarity and emptiness. Maryanne seemed to sweep all that away in her wake, leaving me frantic. Now my head felt like it was being pumped up with confusion, inflated like a balloon, and emotions I didn't want to recognize expanded in me.

Am I really like that? Have I got it as bad as she does?

Have I made myself such a cripple with Ginny that I no longer have any choice?

I must've been sicker than I realized. I'd lost the center of myself, and I couldn't contain the fever. Without being entirely aware of it, I slumped forward like I was fainting and thudded to my hands and knees on the floor.

Luckily that jolted me out of my tailspin. The pain was therapeutic. I was too old to abase myself like this, begging the fireplace and the empty den to take pity on me. And I didn't want to look ridiculous, even to myself. So I took a few deep breaths, then got my legs under me and stood up.

Just to prove that I could do it, I hunched over to the hearth and tossed two or three fresh logs onto the fire. After that, I retreated to the chair and collapsed.

All that exertion made my head explode. Fortunately, it didn't hurt. I simply lost consciousness with a burst like a popping bubble.

I had no sense of time, so I didn't know how long I was out. And as far as I could tell I didn't dream. I didn't have that excuse for being so disoriented. Nevertheless my confusion went right to the bone.

I felt hands on my shoulder, but I didn't know what they were. They shook me, shook me so hard that my head lolled around like my neck was broken, but they had no meaning. Then I heard someone coughing—coughing violently enough to bring up their shoes. A voice knotted with strain choked out, "Mr. Axbrewder! Mr. Axbrewder! Wake up!" Male or female, I couldn't tell.

And I didn't care about any of it. I didn't consider it worth waking up for until a spasm took hold of my lungs and ripped me open from the top of my head to the pit of my stomach.

I tried to lurch upright, but I'd begun coughing too hard

to get my legs under me. When I opened my eyes I could see smoke. Smoke as thick as acid filled my eyes and chest. Spasms pulled claws through my ruined abdomen.

"Wake up!" the voice wailed thinly, like the small cry of a newborn. Then it frayed into retching.

The lodge was on fire? I couldn't tell.

Scrubbing at my tears, I cleared my vision enough to see oily gray-white smoke as it erupted from the fireplace in great billows, swelled outward like the end of the world.

The lodge wasn't on fire. But this was no ordinary smoke. No wood in all the world burned like this, even with fresh logs on the fire and the chimney plugged.

I made another effort to get up.

Amalia Carbone had me by the shoulder. I couldn't make out details, but I recognized her general shape. She strove to haul me to my feet, save me somehow, but she didn't have the muscle.

It helped that I wasn't alone. Old reflexes kicked in. She wanted to rescue me. If I didn't move, we might both die.

The smoke made me gag as if my lungs were full of blood, but I reached one hand to Ama's head and pulled her ear down to my mouth so that she could hear me.

"The doors," I gasped. Despite my desperation, I could scarcely force out a whisper. "Inside. Close them." So that everyone else doesn't asphyxiate. "Then get help."

Then I braced myself on the arms of the chair and climbed upright.

When she saw that I could stand, Ama let go of me and disappeared into the smoke.

My vision swam with tears, and I couldn't straighten my spine. Coughing clenched my guts. But I didn't make a sound, that was the odd thing. I couldn't even hear myself gag. Ama moved in shrouded silence. But then I heard doors slam. One. Two three. The two bedroom wings and the hall to the dining room.

Hunched over nearly to my knees, I blundered toward the front door.

For a while I couldn't find the knob. And for a while after that I couldn't get the door open because I was leaning against it, holding it shut. I'd stopped coughing, overtaken by a spasm that locked up all my muscles until my head whirled for air and I felt like I would never breathe again.

Then I wrenched the door past my bulk and stumbled outside.

I couldn't stop. Trailing an outrush of smoke, still in spasm, I pitched down the steps and fell on my face.

After a minute or two I started spitting blood into the white pure drifted snow.

14

I lay there and retched, bringing up bile and blood. The absence of pain astonished me. Apparently the circuit in my brain which acknowledged pain had gone into overload and shut down. I hadn't had much air recently, and fire filled my lungs, but I hardly noticed. For the moment, anyway, that stuff had no personal impact.

I didn't start to think again until sweet clean cold oxygen finally cleared my wits. Then I raised my head and saw the impression my face had made in the snow.

It was red and dark, as dark as blood from the heart. Not a lot of blood, but enough to get my attention.

I'd torn open some of my sutures.

Someone had just tried to kill me.

From my perspective, lying there in the snow while my body cooled and spasms trembled through me, the evidence seemed irrefutable. I'd been alone in the den. Asleep. God knows how long. And wood didn't burn like that, not like *that*. So someone must've put something in the hearth, something to produce all that acid smoke. And blocked the chimney so that the smoke wouldn't escape. The easy way to do it would've been from the roof. Drop the stuff down the chimney and then pack it with snow.

Whoever did that must've done it because I was alone in the den asleep.

Simple.

Unfortunately, what came next wasn't simple at all.

It wasn't Simon Abel who had just tried to kill me. He'd been locked in the wine cellar all night—

And Cat—

For some reason, I remembered a voice.

It said, *Get out of there. He wants you. You're a sitting duck.*

Sweet Christ.

At least my mental circuits were still out. Even the implications of that memory didn't hurt.

But I had to move. Snow was soaking into my clothes. And lives depended on me. This mess revolved around me somehow. I had to prevent as much of it as I could from spilling over onto innocent bystanders.

Which meant that I needed Ginny.

Which meant that I had to move.

Oh, shit. This was going to be such fun.

The temporary stay of pain I'd been granted helped. All I had to deal with was my weakness. God. I felt *weak!* My entire body hardly contained one useful muscle. Just holding my head up tested me to my limits.

Too bad, Axbrewder. Weakness was just an excuse, another way of trying to evade my responsibilities. Like booze. And self-pity.

So move, already.

Somehow I climbed to my feet.

Around me the lodge and the snow and the dark trees veered unconscionably from side to side, and I couldn't get anything into focus. But I fought to keep my balance. Eventually I found myself blinking in bright sunlight at the driveway out of the valley.

The wind had erased all sign of Reeson's departure. As far as I could tell, he'd never left.

When I turned and let my head tilt back, I was able to see the roof of the den. Sure enough, the snow all around the chimney had been trampled down, shoved aside.

And the roof was probably easy to reach from the attic.

That made sense, anyway.

A step at a time, I forced myself up onto the porch.

That close to the front door, however, I realized that I couldn't go back in through the den. Harsh smoke still poured outward, looking for me. If Ama had gone for help—if she'd made it out of the room all right—the help hadn't come yet. In fact, there was a good chance that no one knew what had happened. Too many closed doors stood between the bedrooms and the den.

I didn't mind. I didn't want to talk to anyone except Ginny.

Shuffling like a cripple, I tottered back down the steps and around the lodge to the nearest door, the outside entrance to one of the bedroom wings.

The wrong one, of course—the wing with my room, not Ginny's. But I couldn't afford to let minor frustrations upset me. If I did, I might lie down and never move again.

Creeping down the hall as if I actually wanted to catch people by surprise, I went to Joseph Hardhouse's door.

That was reasonable, wasn't it? Ginny had been spending a lot of time in his company. It was more efficient to check every possibility along my way, instead of going to her room and being forced to double back. Wasn't it?

Apparently I was in no mood to be honest with myself.

But Hardhouse might be taking a nap. If so, I didn't mean to wake him up. At least that's what I told myself. For all practical purposes, I looked like a wounded abominable snowman. If I woke him up, he'd ask questions. I didn't want to deal with that.

So I turned the knob quietly and eased the door open. In near-perfect silence I peeked inside.

Oh, well. People who sneak around deserve what they get. Life has a way of insisting on honesty, whether you have the courage for it or not. Hardhouse lay on the bed. So did Ginny. They were both naked. He thrust his hips between her legs, hard as a ram. She clung to him and made small groaning sounds I hadn't heard for a long time—sounds I used to love.

She wore her claw.

For some reason that was what hurt—that small detail closed the circuit, restored me to pain. She wore her claw. After everything she'd lost, he made her feel like a woman again. No, more than that. He made her feel so much like a woman that the claw didn't matter, it couldn't stifle her desirability.

It was too much. Entirely too much. I closed the door—gently, gently, so that she wouldn't see me—and did my best to walk away.

I didn't get far. Doors stretched along the walls, but I couldn't tell which one was mine. Tears filled my eyes, and I couldn't see through the blur. Clutching at the nearest doorknob, I turned it and fell like an axed tree into the room.

The rug caught me. I made almost no noise.

Providentially, as you might say, it was the Draytons' room.

They, too, were in bed together, with their arms around each other, naked. But they heard me come in. When I toppled, they jerked up like I had them on strings.

"Brew!" Queenie gasped.

I hardly saw either of them. Sam seemed to arrive beside me without going through the middle stages of getting out of bed and standing up. With no apparent effort, he rolled me onto my back. Checked my pulse, my skin, my respiration. At the same time, he snapped, "Get my bag."

Queenie obeyed. She didn't step back to pull a robe around herself until he had what he needed.

With a pair of scissors he cut my sweater open. Then I heard him say, "Christ, Brew. What have you done to yourself?" But I couldn't get his face into focus, so I had no idea whether he expected an answer. Maybe he was just making conversation.

More work with the scissors. Somewhere past the pain I felt the pressure on my stomach ease. He must've cut off my bandages. After a moment he said, "Well, that's not too bad." Then he demanded, "Haven't you been taking your antibiotics? This is a serious infection."

Like the last one, that question may've been rhetorical. He didn't wait for an answer. Instead he checked my face, wiped my mouth, stuck a finger in around my teeth. "You're bringing up blood," he announced. "That's bad, but I can't tell how bad yet. The infection may make your sutures leak. Or you may have torn them open. If you're just leaking, I can probably help you. If the sutures are torn"—for some reason he sounded angry—"you need emergency surgery."

"Can you do it here?" Queenie asked.

"I don't know. I'll have to think about it. We'll see how he responds." Sam wrapped something around my arm and pumped it tight. Slowly he let it loosen. "He's lost blood, but his pressure is strong. That's good. He hasn't been bleeding long. Or he hasn't bled much."

On the principle that I should be grateful for small blessings, I tried to smile. But my heart wasn't in it.

"Get a glass of water," he instructed crisply. "Maybe we can locate some more good news."

Apparently I'd stopped crying. Why, I didn't know. But my vision finally improved. When Queenie came back from the bathroom with a glass, I was able to focus on her.

"Brew," Sam said firmly, "Queenie will hold your head up for you. Don't try to help her—keep your abdomen relaxed. But drink as much water as you can."

I nodded incrementally. He adjusted his stethoscope. Kneeling beside me, Queenie wedged an arm under my neck and tilted my head off the rug. Then she put the glass to my mouth.

When she did that, incandescent memories burned through me.

I was out of bed, where I had no business being, no business at all, because I'd only been shot a few hours ago, but I needed to catch a killer and maybe rescue Ginny from el

Señor, that was my only justification. And the killer handed me a glass of water. Smiling. *Axbrewder, you look terrible. What are you doing to yourself? How about a glass of water? Drink this. You can't last much longer.* So I drank it. But it wasn't water, oh, no, he was a killer, all right, and he knew what he was doing.

He gave me vodka.

I gagged and thrashed against Queenie's arm, twisted my head away, fought a recollection of pain as hot as a magnesium flare. Alcohol, my favorite stuff on God's earth, had nearly eviscerated me.

"Brew, relax!" Sam commanded. "Let Queenie hold your head! We're trying to help you!"

Wildly I looked at him, at her, as if I needed some other kind of help, anything to get me away from that glass of water. But this was a bedroom in Deerskin Lodge, and the other room where I'd swallowed vodka and nearly died was days and miles away, although the snow remained the same. I had no idea who'd killed Cat—and tried to kill me. If I couldn't trust the Draytons right now, I was a goner anyway.

I didn't relax very well. But I raised one hand and helped Queenie steer the glass to my mouth.

Sam put his stethoscope on my stomach and listened while I drank. The water tasted like the air outside, sweet, clean, and cold, and once I got started I gulped at it until it was gone.

Sam listened hard for a minute, then looked at me. "Well, I think we can say your bowels haven't gone into shock. You're luckier than you deserve. Since I'm the only doctor here and it's up to me, I'm going to guess you haven't torn any sutures." He nodded to Queenie, and she lowered my head to the floor. "I'll clean you up and apply a clean dressing. But first I'll give you an injection."

He returned to his bag. I let him take his time. I had places to go, things to do. But for the life of me I couldn't imagine how I would bear them.

"This," he announced when he was ready, "is the thermonuclear device of antibiotics." He swabbed my arm vigorously with something that smelled like Betadine. "I'll give you regular injections while my supply lasts." Then he poked a needle into my skin. "If you go back on your pills right away and take them *religiously,* you may be able to fight off this infection."

After he pulled the needle out, he withdrew. Maybe he'd gotten tired of working on me naked. When he returned, he was wearing a sweater and slacks.

"I'll start on your bandages in a couple of minutes," he said. "Maybe by then you'll be strong enough to stand.

"In the meantime, why don't you tell us what in hell you think you're doing?"

Tough ol' Axbrewder, as hard as plate steel and twice as remorseless. As soon as I heard the question, I started crying again.

"Brew," Queenie breathed, "oh, Brew, what's happened? What's going on?"

I would've cried a lot harder, but I couldn't make my stomach muscles cooperate.

"All right." Sam studied me without flinching. "Don't try to talk right now. Take it easy. That's what you should be doing anyway. You're safe here. You can rest as long as you want. Believe it or not, even this will pass." Apparently he knew how much comfort that thought would be. Frowning, he added, "Eventually."

No. Positively not. I refused. Despite the fact that I whimpered like a baby, I absolutely declined to lie here and rest while Cat's murderer wandered around loose. Not when she'd been killed for me.

"I can't."

"The hell you can't," Sam retorted harshly. "I'm your doctor. If I tell you to lie there and rest, by God, you're going to lie there and *rest.*"

"No." I shook my head, rolled it weakly from side to

side. "No." I needed to articulate one of the first principles of my life, but all I managed was a small sound like a beaten child. "I can't."

"Why not?" Queenie put in. "Why not? Talk to us, Brew. Tell us what's going on."

I couldn't argue with her. I needed help. Without the Draytons, I might not even be able to stand.

"Ginny and Hardhouse are having an affair." I went on crying. "I caught them."

Sam and Queenie looked at each other. Maybe they were dismayed. Or maybe they just felt sorry for me. Probably everyone here already knew about Ginny and Hardhouse.

"You can't do anything about that." Sam's roughness had shifted to another pitch. "You've spent too much time lying to each other. You can't undo the past."

"You don't understand." I had to do better, had to get through to him somehow. "I need her. Simon didn't shoot Cat. The killer was aiming at me."

Queenie pulled a sharp hiss of surprise through her teeth.

"Oh, shit," Sam said fervently.

They both stared at me, frozen with shock.

"He just tried again," I said because I had nothing left.

They believed me. I could see it on their faces. Maybe my damaged condition convinced them.

"How—?" she began in a small voice. "Why—?"

"Later." Sam swallowed hard to make his throat work. "I don't think Brew has time to explain right now."

No question about it, he was good at emergencies. With a shudder, he threw off his shock. Before I could do anything more than nod, he dug back into his bag and came out with another needle and syringe.

"All right," he said for the second time. "This will help you manage the pain, and it won't put you to sleep. Once we get you on your feet, you'll be able to stay there for a while. That's as much as I can do." He swabbed at my arm again. "But you'll have to pay for it."

Before I could ask him what he meant, he stuck the needle in and said, "You can start by taking some advice."

I blinked at him. Advice?

"I'm not your doctor now," he continued. "This is too important. I'm your friend. You can believe that. Queenie and I are your friends. Too many people here have something to gain from your weakness. The killer certainly does. Joseph and Lara do. Perhaps even Ginny does. And everyone else has something to lose. So listen to me. *Listen*."

Lara had something to gain? Ginny did?

I didn't ask. I listened.

"You need Ginny. The two of you need to trust each other. Our lives may depend on that. The time has come for you to start telling the truth. I'm sure you think you're honest. You're certainly honest about your opinion of yourself. If I put you on the evening news, you would tell the whole country what a shit you are. But that isn't good enough. You have to tell the truth about what you feel. What you want. Nobody will ever trust you until you trust yourself. And truth is the only trust that counts.

"Do you hear me?"

Unlike the first injection, this one got my attention. It hurt with a glow that spread out from my arm into the rest of my body, lighting my sore nerves with warmth, comforting my torn and abused tissues. It resembled the amber peace drunks live for, the state of grace which sometimes comes in the still space between not enough alcohol and too much. There was a difference, however. This glow didn't protect me. I felt several distinct pains at once, and none of them faded. The shot simply warmed away their ability to paralyze me.

"I said, do you hear me?"

Oh, I heard him. I may've been damn near crazy, but I

knew when I was being cared for. I looked at him straight and took hold of his arm.

"Help me up."

He and Queenie shared a searching glance. Then she braced me on one side, and he supported me on the other, and they eased me to my feet.

The effort made my head swirl. My guts throbbed in the distance, like drums announcing disaster. When Sam pulled away, I could hardly stand without him. But Queenie kept me upright until he came back with rolls of bandages and more Betadine swabs.

"This will hurt," he said calmly, "but you may not notice any difference."

Tearing open the swabs, he began to scrub at my belly.

It hurt, all right. So what? When he strapped me into a new dressing, it put so much pressure on my guts that I had trouble breathing. I didn't care. He was making it possible for me to do what I had to do.

After he finished, he studied me for a while—felt my pulse again, stroked the muck sweat off my forehead, peered into my pupils. Then he told Queenie to let go of me.

She obeyed.

I stayed on my feet.

"Good." He nodded brusquely. "We'll be here if you need us."

"Just a minute," she said. From a bureau, she produced a bulky sweater, one of his. It was a bit too small, not enough to cause any problems. They helped me get my head and arms into it. She tugged it down over my bandages.

I had no time to thank them. As soon as she stepped back, I started putting one foot in front of the other toward the door.

Sam held it open. I went out into the hall.

Headed for Joseph Hardhouse's room.

This time I made no effort to be quiet. Assuming that I could've done it, I had no reason to try. For a moment, I held the doorknob as if it were the last support I would ever get. Then I turned it and pushed the door open and lurched into the room.

They were done, at least for the time being. They sat in bed against the headboard, propped by pillows. Her neck rested on his arm. The tips of his fingers stroked the tip of her breast.

She went stiff when she saw me, blank and rigid—expressionless with surprise or anger. He jerked his head up, glowered furiously. Neither of them said anything.

I faced him because I couldn't bear to see her naked in his embrace. But I spoke to her.

"Tell him to get out."

"It's my room," he retorted. After the initial jolt, his glare looked happy, practically victorious. He liked to flaunt his conquests. "*You* get out."

I concentrated on Ginny. "Tell him. I need to talk to you."

His laugh sounded like bricks grinding together. But she pushed him away, swung herself out of bed, and began putting her clothes on. Jeans, a cotton chamois shirt. Her eyes never left me. They were gray and hard and blank, unreadable.

After a moment, Hardhouse shrugged and followed her example.

When he was dressed, he came over to me.

He could've knocked me down with one hand. But I had a grip on the .45 in my pocket. If he touched me, I was going to do my damnedest to shoot him before he got away. However, he intended a different kind of violence.

With a grin that bared his teeth, he nodded toward Ginny and said, "That claw's the sexiest thing I've ever seen."

Then he left. The door clicked shut behind him.

Just for a second after he was gone, she gaped at the door as if he'd stunned her. But then she regained her focus. Grimly she strode toward me.

In her claw, she held her purse by the strap, ready for

anything. Her crooked nose had gone white. The lines between her brows seemed deep enough to be part of her skull, and her gray eyes glinted at me. Her face betrayed nothing. Sounding almost neutral, almost willing to forgive me, she said, "This had better be good."

You have to tell the truth.

How? That smoke had nearly killed me. An infection raged in my guts. Lies were my only defense.

Carefully, so that I wouldn't make a mistake, I unknotted my fingers from the .45 and took my hand out of my pocket.

Then, with all the strength I could summon through the fever in my head and the glowing stimulant in my veins, I hit her.

The blow rocked her back on her heels. Her cheek went pale, then flamed red.

That was the best I could do.

So fast that I didn't see it happen, her .357 came out of her purse. The barrel lined up on my face. She'd shot a man in the face once, after he'd broken her nose. She'd already thumbed back the hammer. Her knuckles were white on the grip.

"Do that again," she rasped, a low snarl from the core of her bones. "Do it."

Tell the truth.

I could still feel the impact of hitting her like a tremor in my belly. The muzzle of her gun looked big enough to blast me out of existence. But I was full of hurt and loss and old rage, and we were finished with each other anyway. There was nothing worse that she could do to me.

I tried to hit her again.

My second blow was weaker than the first, and she saw it coming from miles away. She slipped it aside by twitching her head. With nightmare slowness, the .357 came back into line.

But she didn't shoot me. Instead she used her claw to jab at my stomach.

Red blossoms of pain burst behind my eyes. Gasping, I crumpled to my knees.

I couldn't move or think. Involuntarily I clamped my arms over my belly. They didn't do me any good. If Sam's new bandages hadn't protected me, I would've been torn open.

On the other hand, I didn't start to cry again. I was spared that indignity. I was too mad for tears.

Past flowers and explosions, I saw the .357 drop to the rug, saw Ginny fall to her knees. She took hold of my sweater, closed her fingers and her claw in the soft material. "Brew," she breathed, panting softly, "Brew, what're you doing? What the hell do you think you're doing?"

Telling the truth. "Giving you an excuse to ditch me." Pain and rage had left me half dead. I had no idea why I could still speak. "I won't put up with the way you treat me anymore."

"*Brew*." Red bloomed on her face, in her eyes. "What in *hell* are you talking about?"

"I'm your partner." That was the truth as well. I could say it because I had nothing left to lose. "Your partner. I won't let you ignore me.

"Cat was killed by accident. It should've been me."

I thought she would shout at me, but she didn't. "What do you mean? Brew, make sense."

"I love you. I've always gone about it wrong, but I love you."

She shook her head. "Not that. What about Cat? Why should it have been you?"

I didn't insist. I still needed her for this.

"He just tried again. In the den. He must've been trying to kill me when he shot Cat. He hit her by accident."

Her hand and her claw pulled at my sweater. "Who?"

"I don't know. Not Simon. He's locked up."

"Why?"

The truth.

I said it. "He works for el Señor."

"What?" Her demand for understanding was profound and passionate. "*What?*"

"Ginny." I said her name and looked into her eyes to anchor myself against a rising flood of anger. Oh, Ginny, please. "You never found out how we got this job."

Abruptly she shut up. Despite the white heat of her attention, she knew that she didn't need to question me. She knew that I would tell her the whole story.

"You never asked Rock or even Buffy how we got this job."

I remembered a voice. A voice that said, *Get out of there. He wants you. You're a sitting duck.*

"You never asked who had it before. You never asked where Rock heard about us.

"It wasn't a coincidence. It didn't just happen."

A voice that sounded muffled and familiar.

"It was Smithsonian. Lawrence Smithsonian."

Ginny opened her mouth, closed it again. Her eyes and her hand and her claw clung to me.

"He always did security for Murder on Cue. This time he pulled out at the last minute. Some kind of emergency, he said. But he gave Rock your name. He recommended you. And he was the one who called me. In the hospital. Threatening me. I knew the voice was familiar, but I couldn't place it. He was giving you a reason to take the job when Rock offered it.

"He set us up. Someone at this camp works for el Señor. He's a professional killer."

Ginny absorbed what I said as if she took it in through her pores. She didn't protest against it or argue with it or try to reinterpret it. She simply accepted it.

She trusted me that much, at least.

Slowly she said, "We used to think Smithsonian did business with that reptile. Now we know."

Then she was ready.

"What happened in the den? How did he try to kill you?"

I told her.

"How did you get out?"

I told her.

"Then what did you do?"

That was hard, but I told her.

The information should've pissed her off, but she didn't let it deflect her. "Does anybody else know about this?"

"They should by now. I told Ama to get help."

Without warning, she let go of me and surged to her feet. I nearly fell on my face, but she didn't notice. "We'll check on Simon," she announced. "Maybe whoever was on the roof left a trail. This damn snow has to be good for something. Then we'll get everybody together and warn them."

"Tell them"—I couldn't raise my head to look at her— "it's because of me. Cat's dead because of me. They're all in danger because of me. I brought it with me."

That hit a nerve. "God *damn* it, Brew!" Sometimes she was so strong it astonished me. Fiercely she reached down, grabbed hold of me, heaved me to my feet. As livid as a shout, she snapped, "Did you know that was Smithsonian's voice when we took this job?"

I shook my head weakly.

"Did you put it together when you found out how we got this job?"

No.

"How long ago did you recognize his voice?"

Rage and panic threatened to choke me. "A few minutes."

"Then," she said like the cut of a bucksaw, "stop blaming yourself. I'm *sick* of it. You aren't accountable for things you didn't know. *You* didn't kill Cat. And you sure as hell aren't the reason we're snowbound. We haven't got time for one of your culpability jags."

"Ginny." I could swallow my fear. Sam's injection helped with that, the same way it helped with the pain. But I couldn't force down my anger. She was right, we didn't have time, the situation was urgent. Nevertheless I needed an answer. If I had to, I'd hit her until she gave me one. "Why are you fucking Joseph Hardhouse?"

She may've been on the verge of saying, We haven't got time for *that* either. But something stopped her. Maybe it was the memory of his parting shot—of the surprise she'd felt when he said her claw was sexy. Or maybe it was just the extremity on my face. Maybe she could see that I'd come to the end of myself. Whatever the explanation, she didn't refuse me.

"You want to talk about whose fault this is?" The intensity of her outrage made her gulp for air. "Of course you do. You love it. It gives you an excuse to drink. Well, *I'm* responsible for getting you shot. That bullet in your stomach is *my* fault.

"You remember how it happened? You tried to warn me. You tried to tell me the truth. But I couldn't face it. I didn't listen. Instead I forced you to walk straight into Estobal's line of fire."

Well, in a manner of speaking. If you just assume that I hadn't moved my own feet—hadn't ignored my own judgment in order to do what she told me. But that was bullshit. On some level, I'd known that Estobal might come after us. I'd recognized the danger. I simply hadn't trusted myself enough to deny her.

Her anger didn't let her see the situation in those terms, however. "How do you expect me to feel now?" she went on. Except for the place where I'd hit her, her whole face was white and savage. "Do you think I *enjoy* seeing you limp around with all that pain on your face? I took this job to try to save your life, but the way you behave, you never let me forget I gave you this problem in the first place. And now you tell me I've helped set you up by not paying attention to my job.

"Christ, Brew, what am I supposed to do for self-respect? How am I supposed to start liking myself again? I'm a *cripple*. And I don't mean *this*." She jerked her claw past my face. "I'm so twisted inside I can't even pay attention to my *job*.

"I *hate* that.

"I need some reason to believe I'm worth having around. All I ever get from you is misery. Joseph is the only man I've met who acts like being crippled doesn't get in the way. He likes me the way I am. He *wants* me the way I am. Who he is doesn't even matter. I don't care if he's a shit, or cheats on his wife, or buggers his busboys. He makes me think my whole life doesn't have to be as twisted as my relationship with you.

"You say you're my partner." She had no time for transitions. "Are you coming, or do I have to deal with Cat's killer on my own?"

She didn't wait for an answer. Retrieving her .357, she shoved it back into her purse. Without so much as a pause in the doorway, she stormed out of Hardhouse's room and left me alone with my astonishment.

Her explanation wasn't what astonished me. It didn't exactly comfort me, but it made sense. I knew how she felt. No, the astonishing thing was that we weren't finished with each other. She still expected me to back her up.

I stayed where I was for a moment or two, swaying gently to myself, letting go of my grievances. Then I followed her.

15

The hall seemed long. What the hell, everything seemed long to me. But Sam's injection did its job. I was still ambulatory. I caught up with Ginny in the den.

Ama and Truchi had already gone to work. They'd opened the front door and several windows, and one of them, probably Truchi, had set up a big space fan to blow smoke out of the room. Smoke still curled out of the fireplace, but a bucket and puddles of water on the hearth indicated that the fire itself had been doused pretty thoroughly. I could smell a tang of acid, enough to make me think about gagging. The fan worked well, however, and the air was mostly breathable.

Judging by appearances, Ama hadn't suffered too much damage. Her eyes were red and puffy, but she looked solid on her feet, ready to do whatever was needed. Of course, smoke inhalation can kill anyone, but she probably hadn't been in as much danger as I was. She wasn't likely to bleed to death when she coughed.

Frowning slightly above his off-white mustache, Ama's husband tended the fan and watched the wisps from the fireplace with a gaze that managed to look innocent and doubtful at the same time. If he had an opinion about the situation, he kept it to himself.

"Do you know what caused this?" Ginny asked.

Petruchio shrugged. "Snow," he pronounced succinctly. "Chimney."

"I mean the smoke." Ginny's tone hinted at exasperation. "Wood doesn't make that kind of smoke."

My only encounter with Truchi, the first day of the camp, had been cryptic. I guess I didn't expect him to have much grasp on practical reality. So I was surprised when he pointed at the fireplace and said without hesitation, "Ratsbane."

Ratsbane? I thought.

"Ratsbane?" Ginny demanded.

Ama shrugged. As laconic as her husband, she pronounced. "Rat poison."

Ginny nodded once, sharp with recognition. "Trioxide of arsenic. That's what they make rat poison out of. Or they used to. It's been a long time since I looked it up."

Arsenic, I mused. Terrific.

She moved to the fireplace and peered inside. I did the same thing, except more slowly.

Back against the firewall, we saw the remains of a cardboard box big enough to hold a case of beer. Blackened powder spilled out of it. Powder had probably covered most of the wood, but water had washed it down into the ash.

"That," she commented, "is a hell of a lot of rat poison."

I thought Amalia would answer, but it was Truchi who said, "We got a hell of a lot of rats. Every year a new supply. We kill them every spring, and every spring they come back."

That made sense, I suppose. Deerskin Lodge must've been the best source of food in twenty miles.

But Ginny stuck to the point—which had nothing to do with the feeding habits of rats. "Where do you keep the stuff?"

Now Ama replied, "In the wine cellar. So we can lock the door."

I turned away from the fireplace so abruptly that I almost fell down.

The wine cellar. Shit.

Ginny had the same idea, only faster. Striding toward the kitchen, she told the Carbones in passing, "Get everybody together. Everybody. I don't care if you have to wake them up. If they can't stand the smoke, use the parlor. We'll be back in a couple of minutes."

"You need the key," Ama responded.

Ginny slapped her purse. "Art gave it to me."

Nearly running, she left the den.

I stumbled along behind her as best I could.

I didn't know where the wine cellar was—I'd missed the ritual of locking Simon up last night. But Reeson had called it "just a room off the kitchen," and that's what it was, easy to find. All I had to locate was a door with a padlock.

It stood between the drying pan of the Hobart and one of the walk-in refrigerators. Sharing a wall with appliances like that, the room had to be well insulated. They put out too much heat for wine.

Ginny fished the key from her purse. With characteristic ease, she found what she wanted in there without hunting for it. But she still had to clamp the lock steady with her claw so that she could insert the key. That gave me time to come up behind her and at least pretend that I was guarding her back.

Leaving the key in the padlock when it snicked open, she jerked out her .357, hooked her claw on the knob, and swung the door aside.

Over her shoulder, I saw that Simon had left the light on—a shaded bulb hanging on its wire to about the height of my forehead. But we didn't need its illumination.

Sunshine and cold poured in through a hole in the far wall.

Past the open space which held the card table and the chair and the cot stood four racks nearly as tall as I am— maybe two hundred bottles of wine. The room's interior insulation had simply been nailed to the studs in 4×4 sheets of dirty white asbestos or some related material. Apparently whoever had decided to convert this room to a wine cellar only cared about the wine itself, not about the decor.

One of the insulation sheets had been pulled down. It lay under the cot. And the exterior boards between the studs had been knocked or broken or pried out, leaving a gap to the outside. Ginny could've squirmed through it, even if I couldn't.

Simon certainly could have.

He must have. His sleeping bag was twisted on the cot. A half-eaten sandwich occupied a plate on the table. But he was gone. In the snow outside, we could see his trail. It headed away from the buildings up into the trees.

Ginny didn't bother swearing. The situation swore for itself.

Just trying to cushion the shock for myself, I muttered inanely, "I suppose you're sure this is the right room."

She nodded. "And I'm sure if we trace that trail we'll find where he got up and down from the roof.

"Also"—she hesitated, flashed a glance at me—"I'm sure that if we don't follow him right now we'll never catch him. The wind will blow his trail out. He'll be as good as vanished."

Sure. I understood. Parts of my brain had caught up with the circumstances. In fact, I understood too much. Panic crowded my throat. I had to force down bile to say, "Don't look at me. I'm in no condition to go hiking."

"I know," she replied softly. "I'll go." She hesitated again, longer this time. But she didn't look away. "You'll have to take charge here. Make sure nothing else happens."

I nodded. It was my job to keep the guests alive. Which meant that I'd have to let them know what the real dangers were.

"That," I said in a voice like a saw blade with broken teeth, "is why they pay me the big bucks."

For a second, I saw a gleam of appreciation in her eyes. "Do it," she said. "I need boots and a coat. Then I'm gone."

Good luck, I might've responded. But I was already alone. I could hear her heels on the kitchen tile, running.

Pure craziness, of course. I had a high fever and damaged sutures. She had no business leaving me in charge. I had no business accepting the responsibility.

But it was my *job*, and I knew how to do it. I sure as hell had the background for it— A little while ago, I'd accused Ginny of professional sloppiness. The time had come for me to put up or shut up.

The bare idea left me so weak that I could hardly move without leaning myself against the walls and countertops. Nevertheless I propped myself across the kitchen and through the dining room back to the den.

Everyone was there except Faith Jerrick and Sue-Rose Altar.

Truchi had turned off the fan, closed the den again. I could still smell arsenic smoke. I'd probably be able to smell it for days. But I couldn't do anything about that.

While the door and windows were open, the room had gone cold. Looking for warmth, Murder on Cue's guests had pulled their chairs and a couch or two close to one of the other fireplaces. Truchi knelt there under the trophies, stoking a few small flames.

Mac Westward and Lara Hardhouse sat together. Although they didn't look at each other, they held hands grimly, almost desperately, as if that were their only comfort. They both seemed oblivious to the dark and strangely fond way her husband regarded them.

Constance Bebb had a seat beside Hardhouse. Apparently she wanted to distract him from Lara's flagrant behavior—which I thought was unusually courageous of her. But she didn't have much success.

Somehow Maryanne had enticed Mile into a reconciliation. She sat practically in his lap, her arms entwined in his fat. No doubt because his fingers were cold, he kept one hand inside her blouse.

With their chairs so close together, Rock, Queenie, and Sam seemed to be keeping each other company. Rock ignored his companions, however. His eyes were fixed on Truchi, but he didn't really see the handyman. Instead he seemed to be watching his life curdle.

Sam and Queenie, of course, didn't need company. Nevertheless they were the most alert people in the room. They noticed me as soon as I appeared.

"Brew!" Sam jumped up and came over to me. "Where's Ginny? What's going on?" That may not have been exactly what he meant.

I ignored him for a moment. I didn't have much energy to spare, and I needed all my concentration.

Amalia stood against one of the walls nearby with her strong forearms folded over her apron. As she faced in my direction, I asked as if I had the right to make demands, "Where's Faith?"

Her eyes looked less puffy, but they remained red, and they leaked at the corners. She turned her head toward Truchi.

Without shifting his gaze from the fire, he answered, "I forgot."

"Where's Buffy?" I asked Sam.

He studied me carefully. "She isn't handling the shock well. I gave her a sedative this morning. She won't wake up for a while yet."

Which presented an interesting problem. I had no reason to assume that Simon would try to get away. More likely he'd stopped under cover of the trees to watch the lodge, see what happened after he plugged the chimney. If so, he'd known for a while now that I was still alive. And he could see Ginny coming, he could pick her off whenever he wanted, he still had plenty of guns. No, don't think about that, you can't do anything about it. He might double back, come after me again. And Faith and Buffy were alone. If he wanted hostages—or just more victims—

I didn't have much choice. I had to trust one or two people and take my chances.

In order, as you might say, to establish my credentials, I took the .45 out of my pocket, worked the slide with a vehement clack, held it up in front of me. Then I started talking.

"They aren't safe. Simon broke out of the wine cellar." Several people gasped at this announcement, but I ignored them. "We have to assume that he still has those missing guns. Truchi, go find Faith. Bring her here. If she won't come, stay with her. He probably isn't after her. But he might want a hostage."

Without argument, Truchi rose to his feet and left.

I didn't watch him go. I had other things to think about.

"Sam, can you lift Buffy?"

His eyes wide, he nodded.

"Go get her. Bring her here. She can sleep on a couch for a while."

Queenie rose to help him. He stopped her with a glare and strode out of the den.

Biting her lower lip, she sat down again.

Inadvertently she steadied me. She was troubled, deeply concerned, but she wasn't terrified. She could still do what she was told. I needed that.

"Now." I waggled the .45, more to remind myself why I was here than to keep anyone's attention. "I'll tell you what I know." My weakness hadn't receded any. Looking for support, I lumbered over to the fireplace and braced myself on the hearth. "It isn't much, but you're entitled to it." The stonework hadn't had time to heat up yet, so I wasn't uncomfortable. And I could put the .45 down on the mantel in easy reach. That way I wouldn't have to waste strength holding a gun.

Everyone stared at me—even Rock. I didn't particularly enjoy being the center of so much fixed horror, but there was nothing I could do about that. I tried to tune it out.

"Simon broke out of the wine cellar," I began. "Right through the wall. I have no idea how. That isn't critical right now." Actually, it might very well be critical, but at the moment I didn't have time to think about it. "What matters is that he's gone.

"Ginny went after him. She'll stop him if she can. If she can't"—I mustered an awkward shrug—"she'll do her best to slow him down."

The rest of the idea I left hanging.

Knees bent under the weight, Sam returned with Buffy. He was breathing hard, but he kept the strain to himself. I waited until he set her gently down on a couch beside the tree trunk and took his seat with Queenie. Then I went on.

"We think we know what he wants." The medication in my veins and the support of the hearth helped me say it. "He's after me."

"Oh, Brew," Queenie breathed.

Sure, everyone stared at me—but not the way Joseph and Lara did. They concentrated as if their eyes were on fire.

"Cat was an accident. He wanted to hit me, but we were standing too close together. That's why he came back. I'm still alive. Maybe he didn't realize how guilty he would look. After all, he couldn't know how many of us might have alibis. Or maybe he just didn't expect us to lock him up. Maybe he thought he could bluff his way past us. The point is that he *did* come back, and he got locked up."

Truchi reentered the den with Faith Jerrick. Neither of them made a sound. I felt a lunatic desire to congratulate the man who laid the floorboards. They didn't squeak for anyone.

At least now I could stop worrying about hostages.

I went on.

"So this morning he broke out and climbed up on the roof, lugging a box of rat poison he found in the wine cellar. While the rest of you were in your rooms, I fell asleep here. Alone. He dropped his box down the chimney, packed it with snow. Then he headed out of the valley. His trail is pretty obvious.

"I don't think he went far. If it were me, I'd stop up among the trees and watch for results. Rat poison is arsenic—or something worse. That smoke could kill me easily enough. But he'd want to be sure nothing went wrong. He probably stopped.

"And something did go wrong. Ama rescued me." I nodded in her direction. "I escaped outside. If he was watching, he knows I'm still alive.

"I figure being an actor is just cover. He's a professional killer. He won't leave until he gets me. And he won't care how many of you he has to eliminate in the process.

"It's too bad he shot Cat," I concluded, mostly to myself. "She probably knew enough about Simon to help us out. At least she could've answered some questions."

No one said anything. They were all too shocked. Maryanne looked as pale as an extension of Mile's fat. Houston himself was so upset that he took his hand out of her blouse. Connie concentrated fiercely on my face. Mac and Lara clung to each other.

But then Queenie found her voice. "*Why* does he want to kill you?"

I did my best to face it. "Ginny and I were working on a case. The one where I got shot. I killed a man named Muy Estobal. He was a bodyguard for what you might consider a 'crime lord' in Puerta del Sol. People call him 'el Señor.' Now el Señor wants me dead. He has his reputation to protect. Not to mention the people who work for him. He can't afford to let them be knocked off with impunity." I shrugged. "But he doesn't do his own killing. He hires pros for that."

"How do you know this, Mr. Axbrewder?" Connie put in. "How do you know Simon is working for this el Señor? You made no mention of it last night. What have you learned since then?"

Now for the hard part. My vision had gone gray around the edges, which made me think that Sam's injection wouldn't last much longer. I was weak and sick, and I'd spent my life loathing helplessness. Which was why I liked alcohol. It gave me something to blame my helplessness on.

But Ginny knew all that, and she'd still left me to deal with the situation here while she went after Abel. No matter how helpless I felt, I was still her partner.

"There's a private investigator in Puerta del Sol," I answered harshly, "Ginny and I think works for el Señor. And we know he hates us. We think he set us up.

"When I was in the hospital, he called me several times, threatened me. But he disguised his voice. I didn't recognize it. He was giving us a reason to get out of town for a while. At the same time, he arranged for the Altars to hire us, so that we'd have a convenient place to go. Somewhere isolated enough to suit a hit man."

Rock's lips moved. Despite the jolt I'd given him, his brain still functioned. Softly he said, "Lawrence Smithsonian."

Several other guests tried to ask questions. I didn't give them a chance. "He always did security for Murder on Cue. Isn't that right, Rock?" A rhetorical question. "But this time he pulled out at the last minute. And he gave Rock Ginny's name. He persuaded Rock to hire us, in spite of the fact that I can scarcely stay on my feet. He set us up."

Unfortunately that wasn't enough. I had to say it all. "Cat is dead," I pronounced as if someone really should've been swinging a scourge at me, "because I made an irresponsible decision. When Rock told me how we got this job, I still hadn't figured out that it was Smithsonian who called me in the hospital. I didn't recognize his voice until a little while ago. So I decided not to tell Ginny what Rock told me.

"If I'd told her, she would've known there was something wrong here. She could've done everything differently. Made you all be more careful. Insisted on locking up the guns earlier. Cat might still be alive."

"Jesus, Axbrewder!" Hardhouse swore, "that was bright. What do you use for brains?"

Talking at the same time, Mile made a reference to "criminal negligence."

I didn't listen to them. I was listening to Queenie.

"In God's name, why, Brew?" she protested. "Why didn't you tell her?"

Momentum is a wonderful thing. Since I'd already started, I found it almost easy to keep going.

"I was angry." A pitiful excuse, but there it was. "I was tired of being treated like the team cripple—like the only difference between being shot and being drunk was how much blood I lost. And," I insisted, "I hadn't recognized Smithsonian's voice yet. I didn't realize"—a small understatement—"the scale of the problem. I thought I could take care of it myself."

Hardhouse sniggered quietly.

"Do you hear me, Axbrewder?" Mile shouted. His face had gone an apoplectic red. "Ah'll break you for this! Ah'll have you up on charges, criminal charges! You'll lose your license. Ah'll make sure you never work again, goddamn sure!"

"If you get out of this alive, you're welcome to try." After what I'd just been through, I could face down a slob like him any day of the week. "But I should probably tell you that I haven't had a license for years." Deliberately I picked up the .45. "I killed one too many people."

"Until Ginny gets back"—if she got back—"I won't take any grief from you. You're going to do what I tell you. Exactly what I tell you. And you're going to keep that fat lump you call a mouth shut. I'm wounded and sick, and I haven't exactly covered myself with glory so far. But I'm a pro. Like Abel. I've been shot at, and I've killed people. I'm *familiar* with it.

"That makes me the best hope you've got."

To my astonishment, Westward spoke first. "You don't

need the gun, Axbrewder." The way Lara held his hand seemed to give him confidence. "Just tell us what you want. We'll do it."

I scanned the group. No one argued. Faith didn't raise her eyes, but she nodded as if she were thinking about something else.

So I told them.

16

What I told them wasn't anything special. Stay together. Lock your door if you absolutely have to be alone. Keep your windows covered and latched. If you see Simon, call for help. If he grabs you, don't resist. Dead hostages aren't worth much, so he won't hurt you unless you force him to.

Survive until Reeson gets back with help.

The one thing I didn't mention was weaponry, self-defense.

Mile noticed the omission right away. As soon as I stopped talking, he demanded, "What about them guns? We got to have 'em. We got to protect ourselves."

I let out a thin sigh. Some problems never go away. They just keep coming back, stupider each time.

"If by 'protect ourselves' you mean we got to start shooting at everythin' that moves, you're wrong. That's my job. I wouldn't give you a gun even if Simon wanted you personally. I don't trust you."

I guess circumstances had finally pushed him past the point of cowardice—or point of discretion, anyway. He bounced out of his chair and stood in front of me, jowls aquiver.

"Now you listen to me, Axbrewder. You've gone too far. Ah don't forget we're in this mess on account of you. Ah don't forget your negligence has already got one of us killed. There just ain't nothin' Ah can do about that right now. But if you think Ah'm goin' to sit here on mah hams and let you risk us some more, you best think again. It's your job to protect us? Fine. *Ah* don't trust *you*. You got a drinkin' problem, and a hole in your guts, and you admit bein' irresponsible. You ain't no protection at all.

"Ah mean to get me a gun, Axbrewder. *You* get it for me, or Ah'll get it mahself."

I shook my head. "No, you won't."

"Why not?" He did his best to bristle at me, which made him look like indignant Jell-o.

"Because if you do"—slowly I aimed the .45 at his face—"I'll blow your fucking head off. It's *me* Simon wants, and I'll be goddamned if I'm going to let a chicken-shit like you do his work for him."

Mile's features wobbled on their bones, and his skin went pale. Involuntarily he brought up his hands to ward me off. A step at a time, he retreated to his chair.

I held the .45 so that everyone could see me release the slide. "We're all scared." To myself, I sounded positively reasonable. "That's natural enough. But scared people are trigger-happy. Leave the guns to Ginny and me."

Assuming, of course, that we'd ever see Ginny again.

No doubt sensing that I needed the support, Sam got to his feet. "I'm willing," he said to the group. "Brew has made some mistakes, but he's still a professional. I'm ready to trust him."

"As I am," Connie seconded promptly. And Mac displayed his new initiative by agreeing with her.

Since no one else put in an objection, I was elected trust-worthy by default.

That was a relief of sorts, but I didn't dwell on it. "All right," I said, doing the best Ginny Fistoulari imitation I could muster. "Life goes on. That means we need lunch." I had no idea what time it was, and I didn't care. I just wanted to inject a note of normalcy into the situation. "Faith, how soon can you get us something to eat?"

Apparently Reeson's absence was the only fact that had any personal impact on her. "Half an hour," she murmured, just distinctly enough to be heard.

"Good." I put the .45 away. "In the meantime, let's make sure our windows are covered and latched. Truchi, I want the outside doors locked. No one goes out," I told the group. "You might not be able to get back in. And you don't want to risk being exposed."

Westward gave me a humorless smile. "That's what they do in all the novels. They turn the lodge into a fortress. Then they discover that they've locked the real killer in with them."

I was too tired to argue with him. Fortunately I didn't have to. "This isn't a novel," Hardhouse put in. "Right now, a fortress sounds like a good idea to me."

Maryanne, Sam, and Lara shared his opinion. Mile probably did, too, but he had guns on the brain and couldn't think about anything else.

I shrugged. Faith, Truchi, and Amalia left the den. Murder on Cue's guests stood up, too nervous to remain seated. Unexpectedly helpful, Hardhouse offered to carry Buffy back to her bed.

Sam and Queenie came over to me. In an undertone, he asked, "How are you doing?"

"Who knows? I'm relying on you to keep me on my feet."

"I'll do what I can. But I don't want to help you overdo it. That could turn into a perverse form of suicide." Then he asked, "Did you take your pills?"

"I've been busy."

"Queenie," Sam ordered, as if he were back in surgery, "go get Brew's pills."

His tone didn't bother her. "Where are they?"

"You'll find them," I said. The truth was that I couldn't remember where I'd left them.

When she walked away, Sam and I were alone—except

for Rock. Everyone else had gone to check on their windows.

Rock moved closer. Obviously, he wanted to talk to me. I looked at him wanly. "Yes?"

As if he feared eavesdroppers, he breathed, "I didn't want to say this in front of the group. But I think you're wrong."

Sam went rigid with attention. I didn't have the strength.

"What about?" I asked.

"About Simon."

Oh, good. Just what I needed.

But Rock didn't go on. I had to prod him. "Don't make me guess. I'm in no mood for it."

"It's the timing." He stared hard at my feet. "When did you kill this Muy Estobal?"

For some reason, I was vague on the details. "Last week."

"Is that the only reason el Señor wants you dead?"

"Far as I know."

"Then—" Rock hesitated, not as if he were unsure, but as if he wished he had the will to look me in the face. "It isn't Simon."

I held my breath.

"I signed a contract with him—Murder on Cue hired him and Cat—over a month ago."

Well, shit. Shit on everything.

I felt a sudden, overwhelming desire to sit down.

Simon, I'm sorry.

"In other words," Sam said in case I needed the explanation, "it would be an absolutely staggering coincidence if a professional killer who works for el Señor just happened to accept an acting job from you over a month ago and then turned out to be in the right place at the right time to attack Brew."

Rock nodded rather helplessly.

"Why didn't you want anybody else to know?" Sam pursued.

"Because it doesn't mean there isn't a killer after Brew. It just means the killer isn't Simon. Or any of us. Everyone here signed up weeks ago. You and Queenie were the last, and you sent in your money two weeks ago. Only Brew and Ginny got involved at the last minute.

"I don't know Lawrence Smithsonian well. We're acquainted, that's all. And I thought he had a good reputation. He always took our camps"—Rock swallowed—"about as seriously as I did. I have no way of knowing whether he works for el Señor.

"But Simon isn't the killer."

Sam accepted this. "That makes sense." He definitely liked mysteries.

"Come on." I lacked the courage to explain what I had in mind, but I knew what to do. "I don't want to go outside alone."

Before either of them could ask any questions, I lumbered off in the direction of the kitchen.

Faith Jerrick was there, stirring a pot of something. I ignored her. She'd locked the back door, but the dead bolt didn't need a key from the inside. I turned it and went out.

"Don't lock the door," Sam told Faith as he and Rock followed.

Outside. Down the steps. Around the corner of the building to the wall of the wine cellar.

The wind was blowing harder, but it hadn't completely filled in the marks outside the lodge—or Ginny's trail toward the trees. It still hadn't covered up the broken boards of the hole that let Simon out. I didn't have to dig for them.

"Brew," Sam kept asking, "what're you doing?"

I ignored him, too.

The stains of oil and weather made it easy to piece together the way the boards used to fit in the wall. And when I did that, what had happened became obvious.

Pressure notches marked the outer edges of the

boards—the kind of notches you get when you break boards out of a wall with a crowbar.

Simon hadn't escaped by himself. This hole had been made for him.

Wind curled around me, into my clothes, into my heart. I felt as bleak as the winter, chilled to the bone, dying for spring. Sam said something. Rock said something. I didn't hear them. I was exposed out here, an easy target, but I didn't care. Pieces of things that I should've thought of earlier fitted together like the boards, and they told the same story.

Sam took my arm, shook me to get my attention. "Brew?"

Like the wind, I said, "Simon is dead."

Then I said, "He was framed."

So that we wouldn't recognize the danger in time. And maybe so that Ginny could be lured away.

Sam forced me to hear him. "How do you know?"

I showed him the boards. "Someone broke into the wine cellar from the outside."

"Maybe he has an accomplice." The mystery lover talking.

"No. For the same reason we know he didn't do it."

And I could prove it.

How did I manage to be so goddamn *stupid*?

"You're all innocent. None of you came in at the last minute. He was framed."

Unless—

My head reeled. I wouldn't be able to keep my balance much longer. For some reason, I had the .45 in my hand again. Maybe that was why Sam held onto my arm. I jerked out of his grasp and jabbed the muzzle up under Rock's chin.

Sam could've stopped me. He was strong enough. But apparently he'd reached a decision about me days ago. He held back now for the same reason that he'd helped me earlier.

Despite the cold and the wind, Rock's face turned as white and gray as stale dough. He tried to back up, but I had my fist in the front of his shirt.

"No—" he gurgled.

"Listen to me, Rock." I dug into him with the sight of the .45. "This is your last chance to tell the truth and get away with it. After this, it's going to cost blood.

"You like messing up mysteries. You told me that yourself. You like helping the killer get away. If you're doing that now, say so. Before anyone else gets hurt." Even though it was too late for Ginny, far too late. "If you're lying about Simon—if you helped him escape—and I find out about it the hard way, I'll make *damn* sure some of the blood that gets spilled is yours."

"No. No." His voice cracked. "Are you crazy? I wouldn't do that. I mess up Buffy's mysteries. I change the clues. Yes. Those are *games*. The people who come to our camps are just *playing*. Nobody ever gets *hurt*. I wouldn't have anything to do with a real killer.

"Take me inside." He shivered with cold and urgency. "I have all the registrations and contracts in my briefcase. I'll show you when they were signed. Ask Buffy. She knows when I hired Simon. She interviewed him."

So much for that theory. I let him go. I hadn't actually believed that he was involved. But the alternatives were worse.

Much worse.

"'Mess up Buffy's mysteries'?" Sam asked in a strained tone. "'Change the clues'? What kind of camp is this?"

Rock wheeled on him. Appalled or angry, he yelled, "I don't like mysteries!" Almost immediately, however, his passion collapsed into chagrin. "Anyway, Buffy knows about it," he said like a shamefaced kid. "Houston told her."

I flapped a hand at him—I wanted them both to shut up.

Rock stumbled past Sam and leaned against the side of the lodge as if his heart were going bad on him. Sam moved toward me. I stared out along what was left of Ginny's trail. The trees looked too black to allow survival. If I were him—whoever he was—I wouldn't shoot her until she reached the trees. Then I could leave her body where it fell without being seen.

"You can't go after her," Sam said abruptly. "You aren't strong enough."

As if we were talking about the same thing, I replied, "He was framed. We locked him in that little room and left him to die."

"You can't stay out here," he added. "You're too visible. With the right rifle, he can pick you off whenever he wants."

"He didn't even have to follow us," I went on. "He knew we'd come here." A hit man I wouldn't recognize if he walked right up to me. "Smithsonian told him. For all we know, he was already here when we arrived."

"That doesn't change anything." Sam put as much bite as he could into his voice. "We still have a professional killer to worry about. We still need to take care of ourselves. If we want to stay alive."

"Cat is dead because I was irresponsible. Simon is dead because I was stupid."

At least that got his attention. "What? You mean you could have figured out he was in danger? You had some way of knowing he didn't shoot Cat?"

I sat down in the snow. I'd lost my balance anyway, and I needed rest. My whole body felt like it was on fire. Fever or guilt, I couldn't tell the difference. Sam hunkered in front of me, deliberately blocking the line of fire from the trees. I handed him the .45. Then I scooped up snow in both hands and rubbed it over my face.

Snow.

It wasn't cold enough, but it helped.

That was it. Snow. The snow on Simon's windowsill.

"Yes," I murmured to Sam. "It was right there in his room, but I didn't see it."

He'd said that he always kept his window latched.

"When we went into his room, we found the rifle in his closet. Which doesn't make sense in the first place. It's too obvious. But there was something else. His window was open. There was snow on the sill. Snow on the floor. But not a lot. An inch, maybe. And it was messed up. It showed that someone went in or out. Or both."

"So?" Sam asked.

"Let's go inside," Rock pleaded from the wall. "I'm freezing."

"So it doesn't fit. Suppose he unlatched his window before he went for his 'walk.' He'd have to leave it open at least a bit, or else he wouldn't be able to raise it from the outside. So he went out. Then he came back in through the window, got the rifle, and went out again. He located me and Cat in the parlor. He shot her. Then he returned through the window.

"At that point, he was in a hurry. But once he'd ditched the rifle he had plenty of time. He could've closed the window behind him when he left again. The snow might melt before we checked his room. Assuming he wanted to make us think he'd left the window open all along for fresh air, he should've closed it down to a crack. Then there would've been less snow. And he wouldn't have denied leaving the window open."

Sam nodded intently.

"But what if he was telling the truth?" I went on. "Then it fits."

"I'm going inside," Rock said in a miserable tone. I heard him slog away.

Wet cold soaked into my pants, but I didn't care. It helped me cool down.

"The killer was watching the lodge. He already had the rifle with him—he'd already taken the guns. He saw me and Cat in the parlor. He saw Simon go out. He went inside. In a hurry, so that he wouldn't miss his chance. He threw open Simon's window and jumped out. Ran around the lodge and shot Cat. Then he rushed back into Simon's room, ditched the rifle, and went out through the window again. Leaving the window open because he was still in a hurry. And because he wanted to draw attention to Simon. Now there's an inch or so of snow on the sill and floor, and it's messed up."

"Brew," Sam said. He sounded calm the way a doctor does when he doesn't want to scare you. "That's pretty thin."

I looked at him while water trickled through my whiskers.

"I think I understand what you're saying," he explained, "but it requires too many inferences. The amount of snow depends on how long *and* how wide the window was open. There are too many variables. You're jumping to conclusions you can't trust. The evidence is too ambiguous. You can't blame yourself for what's happened to Simon."

"That's not the point."

He watched me steadily. "Then what is?"

I did my best to be clear. "The point is that we had good reason to question Simon's guilt. But I didn't think it through. I ignored some of the possibilities. I didn't figure out that if he didn't do it, someone else did it to him. And if someone else did it to him, he was in danger. The real killer wouldn't want to take the chance that Simon might be able to prove his innocence somehow.

"I should've realized that if Simon didn't kill Cat he'd be a target himself."

"You did," Sam retorted. "You locked him in the wine cellar. By rights, that should have been the safest place in the lodge."

True enough. Ginny probably would've told me the same thing. In fact, she'd probably thought of all that last night and just hadn't mentioned it. But she wasn't the issue here.

I was. I was supposed to keep all these people alive, and I hadn't even figured out that Simon might be in danger.

There in the snow, with Sam studying me and cold everywhere, I decided to *get* the sonofabitch who did this. Just holding the fort until Ginny came back wasn't enough for me anymore. Somehow I intended to *get* the bastard.

As if I'd accepted Sam's reasoning, I said, "We can't stay out here. Let's go inside."

He approved. "Good idea. You're not due for another injection, but you could use some rest."

Something still bothered me, another detail I'd missed, like the evidence that Simon might be in danger. It had to do with this hole in the wall. But I decided not to nag at it. I had plenty of other things to think about. And it might come clear faster if I left it alone.

In any case, what I really wanted to do was go to my room and shave. I hated feeling this scruffy. It messed up my brain, and I couldn't afford that. If I wanted to catch Cat's killer, I needed to be able to *think*.

17

S tanding up was easier said than done, but Sam helped me. No one shot at us. He gave me the .45, and we returned to the kitchen.

The Carbones had joined Faith. With an air of impersonal weariness, as if his fatigue were metaphysical rather than practical, Truchi watched Ama help Faith with lunch.

Queenie and Rock stood there as well. As Sam and I clumped into the kitchen, shedding clots of snow, she approached us with a handful of pills and a glass of water.

Behind her, Rock wandered away like a man who had no idea where he was headed.

Sam let go of me. I braced myself on a countertop while he hugged Queenie.

"What's happening?" Her voice was softly intense. "I asked Rock, but he didn't make much sense."

With a tilt of his head, Sam referred the question to me.

"Sam's taking me to my room," I replied as if that were an answer. "I want to shave."

Queenie frowned. However, Sam's expression persuaded her to contain herself. "First your pills," he ordered me. "As long as you need a nurse as well as a doctor, you'd better do what we tell you."

She handed me the pills and the glass of water.

I took them. Then I let Sam and Queenie help me in the direction of my room.

Truchi observed our departure as if he wondered whether pain had any spiritual justification.

Maybe Sam's injection was wearing off. I reached my

room too tired to do anything as energetic as shaving. Ignoring my wet pants, I sat down on the bed, took as much air as I could into my cramped lungs, and tried to remember what strength felt like.

With an odd sense of dislocation, I noticed that I hadn't covered my window. In fact, I hadn't latched it. I'd told everyone else what to do, but I hadn't done it myself.

Brilliant, Axbrewder. I was off to a great start.

Fortunately Queenie had the presence of mind to latch and blind the window for me. At once the whole room went as dim as the inside of my head.

"All right," she said firmly. "Tell me."

Again Sam looked at me.

I nodded.

He told her.

She gnawed on the information for a minute or two. Then she asked, "Are you going to tell this to everybody else?"

I said flatly, "No."

"Why not?"

"Three reasons." It's amazing how clear you can be when you don't mean it. I was just stalling for time. "First, we can't be sure we're right. We haven't got enough facts. Second, nothing has changed. What we need to do until Reeson gets back," never mind Ginny, "remains the same, no matter who the killer is. Third, these people are scared enough already. If we start telling them stories about a faceless hit man, they may panic. That will make the situation even harder to control."

Fourth, my brain still didn't function worth a damn. I couldn't find the flaw in my own reasoning, the small detail I'd missed.

Queenie opened her mouth to ask another question, but the sound of Ama's chimes in the hallway interrupted her.

I didn't know which impressed me more—the lunacy of

playing lunch chimes or the determination to behave normally at a time like this.

Both Sam and Queenie considered me. I said, "You go ahead. I'll be along." To ease their obvious doubt, I added, "I have to learn to walk on my own sometime."

The way they consulted each other without speaking made them seem like the most married couple I knew. After a moment Sam gave me a nod. "But if you don't show up in ten minutes, I'm coming back."

I agreed. I was in no mood for an argument.

When they'd left, I spent a while mustering my resources. Then I got up off the bed. In the bathroom, I washed my face. Grimly I ground my electric razor over my whiskers like I wanted to eradicate my essential mortality, clean away the part of me that felt too grubby and human to cope.

In an effort to efface the clinging smell of port and blood and smoke, I slapped on so much aftershave that I reeked like a brothel. Mostly to prove that I could do it, I put on dry pants. Trying to warm my frozen feet, I put on socks. Somehow I remembered to transfer the .45 to my pocket.

At the same time, I tried to decide how to do my job.

From my perspective, that implied not trusting anything I'd come up with so far. I'd already demonstrated that my brain was ripe for a factory recall. And I had at least one nagging inarticulate, intuitive reason to believe that there was more to this mess than met the eye.

So I had several options. I could reverse my field like a running back and tell everyone my latest theory. That might elicit some interesting responses. Or I could play the mystery lover's detective and go around probing people like mad, seeing what came out.

Or I could make a concerted effort to convert my crippling disadvantages into strengths. I could use my weakness as a kind of camouflage to conceal what I really had in mind.

I liked that idea.

Before Sam had a chance to come back for me, I went to lunch.

When I'd succeeded at tottering to the dining room, I found everyone there ahead of me. Buffy and Rock sat at the ends of the table where they belonged, but they looked gloomy and beaten, like they'd been dispossessed. The guests had seated themselves in their proper pairs—Joseph and Lara, Mac and Connie, Houston and Maryanne, Sam and Queenie. Faith and Ama had just started to clear away bowls of vegetable stew.

They all stared at me. Except Faith, of course. And Amalia, who concentrated on her work.

For a moment I didn't sit down. Instead I blinked back at the group—mostly at the Hardhouses. The belligerent shape of his face never relaxed, but his flexible smile seemed almost affectionate. If I didn't know better, I would've thought that he was glad to see me. And the dark intensity in her eyes only made her beauty more poignant.

I couldn't figure them out. Why were they still together? Why did they look so much like they'd achieved a reconciliation after each time one or both of them got into bed with someone else?

Oh, well. My instincts told me nothing, and I had no other clues. Shrugging to myself, I sat down.

Like magic Faith appeared beside me with a bowl of stew. I sipped at it as if everyone weren't watching me.

By accident I sat across from Mac Westward and Constance Bebb. Over my spoon, I noticed that Mac had a bottle of wine at his place. He was the only one drinking, but he didn't let that slow him down. Every now and then, he aimed an oblique glance at Joseph or Lara. When he did that, his gaze conveyed an astonishing depth of venom and helplessness.

At his side, Connie was stiff with disapproval.

Maryanne's face gave a whole new meaning to *paleness*. This wasn't Faith's devout translucence. It was the kind of pale you get when you drain all the blood out of the heart. She looked like the victim of a vampire.

As for Mile, he kept chewing something even though he didn't have any food in front of him. The malice in his little eyes gave the impression that he'd acquired a taste for violent fantasies.

Of all the people at the table, only Sam and Queenie seemed to have kept their emotional balance.

Ama passed around a platter of bacon, lettuce, and tomato sandwiches. I waved them away—stew was as much as I could stomach. So did Buffy and Lara. But Hardhouse and Mile stocked up as if the prospect of murder made them ravenous.

By degrees the group stopped watching me so hard. On the other hand, no one had any conversation to offer. At intervals someone glanced up at the empty gun cases, then looked away.

Abruptly Hardhouse threw his napkin into the air. "You people," he said in a tone of humorous disgust, "act like we're all doomed. Don't you have any ideas? Can't you think of anything to say?"

Maryanne actively flinched. Sam raised his eyebrows.

Like soft acid, Connie articulated, "Perhaps you can, Mr. Hardhouse."

"Perhaps I can," he admitted. Rubbing his hands together, he scanned the table. "For example, here's an idea. Houston and Queenie had a bet, remember? They were trying to guess who the actors are—and the detectives." His grin included me. "They wrote down some names so that they couldn't cheat later by changing their minds.

"Let's settle the bet."

Both Buffy and Rock gaped at him like he'd suggested a gang rape. Sam started to object, but Mile got there first.

"Shee-it, boy," he snarled fatly. "You out of your mind? We got us a real killer on our hands, and about the only thing standin' between us and murder is Axbrewder's opinion of hisself." A subtle reference to my position on gun control. "This ain't no vacation. It stopped bein' a vacation when Cat Reverie took that slug. I ain't got time to play vacation games so you can be entertained."

Mile's outburst didn't daunt Hardhouse. "Shee-it, yourself, Houston," he drawled. "What I had in mind isn't a game. We know who the actors and detectives are. Nobody cares whether you win or lose that bet—although I would guess from your attitude that you were wrong on all four names.

"What interests me," he went on, "is your ability to think. You're right, we're not on vacation now. We're trying to survive. And we're up against a professional—a man who kills for money and gets away with it. As far as I can see, our best chance to survive is to play the mystery game for real. If you have it in you. If you can stop feeling sorry for yourself long enough to think."

"If that's what you want to know," Queenie put in without hesitation, "why didn't you just say so?" She sounded curious rather than irritated. "Why bring up that bet at all?"

Hardhouse shrugged. "It's a place to start. As I say, nobody cares what your guesses were—but I'm quite interested in your reasoning. From there, we might be able to work our way to an understanding of our situation. And that might save us."

"I don't have the papers," Buffy said unexpectedly. I'd thought that she was too shell-shocked to follow the conversation. "But I remember what they said."

"Houston said the detectives were Ginny and Brew. But he said he didn't think we'd hired any actors this time. He said Rock and I were going to do the crime ourselves."

"Shee-it," Mile repeated, ladling out disgust like rancid lard.

Buffy didn't stop. Maybe she didn't hear him.

"Queenie named Ginny and Brew, too. But she thought the actors were Houston and Maryanne."

At this Maryanne let out a little laugh like a glimpse of hysteria.

All the rest of us sat still with our brains going numb.

"In any case," Hardhouse concluded as if he hadn't been interrupted, "I doubt that we have anything better to do."

"But what is there to understand?" Maryanne asked. Her voice sounded like her pallor—like she'd used up all her courage a while ago. "Simon killed Cat. We know that because he's gone. He wants to kill Brew. We know that"— for a moment she seemed to lose the handle—"we know that because of Lawrence Smithsonian. What is there to understand?"

"Oh, I don't know," Hardhouse mused. "I'm just not sure the situation is that simple." He paused briefly. Then he explained, "For example, I'm not sure Simon shot Cat."

"Why not?" Connie interjected. The gleam in her eyes looked hard and unreconciled, like a threat.

He met her gaze and smiled. "His speech last night impressed me. One thing I think we can be sure of. When he shot at Brew and hit Cat, he knew he'd missed. He must have been able to see the wrong person go down. He knew he hadn't finished his job."

"So?" pursued Connie.

"So he knew he might need that rifle again. And we know he's a professional. So why did he hide the rifle in his own closet and then reenter the lodge in a way that forced us to suspect him? That doesn't sound very professional to me."

Westward burped up some wine. "He wanted to look so foolish that we wouldn't believe in his guilt."

Hardhouse was enjoying himself. "I doubt that. He couldn't be sure how we would react. For all he knew, we might do exactly what we did do—lock him up so that he couldn't kill anybody else. We forced him to reveal himself at a time when he needed to keep himself and his intentions secret.

"I don't know about you," he said to the rest of us, "but I find it easier to believe the killer is someone else."

Rock squirmed in his seat. He opened his mouth to say something, closed it again, looked at me.

Sam and Queenie looked at me as well.

What the hell. As long as Hardhouse wanted to do my thinking for me, I didn't see any reason to stand in his way. Indirectly, he was helping me keep a low profile.

"Tell them," I muttered.

Apparently Sam approved of my change of tactics. Without hesitation, he explained my theory about the killer and Simon.

"Christ Almighty!" Mile was so angry that he spattered saliva on the tablecloth. "Do you mean to say there's two of us dead now, *two of us dead,* and you want us to practice our *reasonin'*?" Ignoring Hardhouse, he aimed his ire at me. "You knew about this, you and Rock and them two"— he swung a hand at the Draytons—"but you wasn't goin' to tell the rest of us. You wasn't goin' to tell me because you *know* Ah won't put up with it!

"By God, Ah'm goin' to keep mahself alive if I got to kill ever' one of you to do it!"

Slamming down his napkin, he bounded to his feet. His chair clattered against the wall behind him. So hard that he nearly made the floorboards complain, he stamped out of the room.

Just for a second, the rest of us sat with our eyes wide and our mouths open, as if we actually believed him.

Then Hardhouse glanced at the ceiling. "For a fat guy, ol' Houston sure is temperamental."

Before she could stop herself, Maryanne let out another burst of laughter.

"But if you don't count him," Sam put in, making sure

everyone knew that I still had his support, "nothing has changed. Our problem remains the same." He nodded at Hardhouse. "If we want to survive, we need to think."

Connie nodded as well. Even Maryanne nodded, doing her best not to laugh—or wail. Mac took a long drink and refilled his glass. Lara studied me with her eyes on fire, as if I'd suddenly become wonderful.

Which was as good a reason as any for me to get out of there. After all, I had my own pose to maintain. "Speak for yourself," I muttered, levering my weight off my chair. "If I want to survive, I've got to get some rest."

"Good idea," Sam said. "I'll check on you in a few minutes."

No one took exception to the fact that I proposed to be alone, even though I was the killer's target—and in no shape to defend myself. Presumably we'd locked him out. Certainly we'd covered and latched our windows. The group let me go like it never crossed anyone's mind that I wasn't being sensible.

My withdrawal wasn't entirely a pose, however. My insides had a strange reaction to the stew—"digestion," possibly—and I feared that if I didn't lie down soon I would puke. With my guts gurgling like a worn-out sump, I returned to my room.

But I wasn't really sleepy, so I didn't take off my clothes. Instead I stretched out on the coverlet and let the room's dim quiet filter through my head. For a while I succeeded at what I needed most, which was to not think about Ginny. If I did, I might panic—which wouldn't do any of us any good.

Nevertheless when I heard a hand on the doorknob I thought it might be her. My heart jumped like I'd been poked with a cattle prod. I was half off the bed by the time Sam and Queenie entered.

"Brew?" Sam asked when he saw the distress on my face, "are you all right?"

I groaned vaguely and sagged back down.

He had his medical bag with him. At once he started to examine me. Took my pulse and temperature, listened to my stomach, checked my pupils. When he was done, he nodded approval.

"Considering how badly you care for yourself, you're pretty lucky. Your temperature is coming down, your bowels work, and your blood pressure is almost normal—for someone in your condition. I'm starting to believe that you haven't torn any sutures. If you stay right where you are for forty-eight hours, you'll be almost as healthy as you were when this camp started."

That good, huh?

Dully I said, "You know I can't do that."

He repacked his bag. "I know. Under the circumstances, you can only hope that you don't get any worse. I hate to say this, Brew, but you need to do some thinking ahead."

I frowned at him.

"Assuming you survive until Reeson brings help, you can't go back to Puerta del Sol like this. You won't be able to defend yourself. You'll have to go somewhere else. You'd better decide where while you can."

"Don't tell me," I muttered, "let me guess. The medical profession has determined that the best cure for a gunshot stomach is profound depression, and you're trying to help me recover. You want to make me as miserable as possible."

Sam didn't smile, but his eyes held a humorous glint. "You know, Axbrewder"—he snapped his bag shut—"you're a cantankerous sonofabitch. That's a good sign."

Queenie came to stand beside him. "There's something I want you to know," she told me. Her straight brave gaze raised my temperature at least a couple of degrees. "I think Rock made a better choice than he realized when he hired you and Ginny. I don't blame you for the danger. You couldn't possibly have known this would happen. But since it *is* happening, I'm glad you're here. I might not trust somebody else."

Sam put his arm around her waist and gave her a squeeze.

Sudden tears burned the backs of my eyes. Which made me feel incredibly foolish. Charming as ever, I said, "Get out of here. I'm supposed to rest, remember?"

Sam nodded. "Come on," he murmured to his wife. Apparently he knew when to leave his patients alone with their emotions.

Before she let him draw her away, however, Queenie bent over me quickly and kissed my forehead.

With their arms around each other, they headed toward the door—and nearly ran into Lara Hardhouse.

"I'm sorry," she breathed softly, seeming flustered by the encounter. "I knocked, but I guess you didn't hear me.

"How is he?"

"At the moment," Sam answered, sizing her up, "he's doing as well as can be expected. If he gets lots of sleep and plenty of antibiotics, he'll be all right."

"Good." Her hands made awkward little gestures, fluttered like a bird with a broken wing. "I'm glad. I've been worried about him." Then, as if she were summoning reserves of courage, she added unexpectedly, "He shouldn't be alone."

"He needs rest—" Sam began.

Lara broke in. "But he's in danger. More than the rest of us. How can he rest? If he sleeps, he'll be helpless." She took a deep breath. The mixture of determination and fear in her eyes made her extraordinarily beautiful. "I'll stay with him."

Studiously noncommittal, Sam referred the question to me.

What I thought was, No! Get that woman away from me. What I said was, "I don't mind."

If anything, the nameless panic Lara inspired in me had intensified. But that didn't seem like an adequate reason to avoid her. If I intended to turn my weakness to my own advantage, I couldn't afford to ignore the opportunities it created.

Sam shrugged and left with his wife.

Lara closed the door behind them—

—and quietly turned the lock.

Then she walked toward me like a hungry woman approaching her first and maybe her only chance for food.

As if I were helpless, I stared at her while she came to the bed and sat down and leaned over me. Her hair fell like abandonment on either side of her face as she kissed my mouth.

Her lips clung to mine, the kiss of a woman ready soul and body to be ravished by love. Despite its gentleness, she put everything she had into it. Her mouth held mine as if she fed on me.

I'd never been kissed like that. Not once in my whole life. Ginny wasn't a woman who let herself go that way.

For a moment, I forgot my weakness. As she kissed me, something that might as well have been strength filled my veins, and I ached to put my arms around her, wrap her into my heart until my loneliness burned away.

Which was probably why she scared me so badly.

So I didn't put my arms around her. After the first rush, I didn't kiss her back. Instead I lay there like I'd never had any use for love and waited for her to pull away.

Finally she did. "Oh, Brew, Brew." Trouble darkened her eyes, and she was unquestionably the most beautiful woman I'd ever seen. "What's the matter? What's wrong?"

I shrugged as well as I could while her hair hung over me and her beauty leaned so close to my face. A desire to weep choked my throat. Thickly I said, "I don't know why you're doing this."

"Isn't it obvious?"

"Not to me." The struggle to force words past my grief made me fierce. "You're married. Cat told me," poor Cat, all her loveliness and grace blown out of her, "your husband is pretty impressive in bed. You've already had one affair since you got here. Mac would kill for a woman like you." An unfortunate choice of words, but what the hell. "And I'm so damaged I can hardly stand.

"You don't need me. If you're looking for a way to get your husband's attention, use somebody else."

"Oh, Brew." If she kept saying my name like that, she'd break my heart. "You don't know. You don't understand.

"You're wrong about Joseph. Believe me, he isn't what you think. He doesn't want me. He wants"—she hunted for words—"women like Cat. Broken women. If he could break me, it would be different. But I can't let him do that. Can I? I have to keep myself from being broken somehow.

"Mac is sweet, but he doesn't mean anything to me. He's just"—she let me see all the pain in her eyes—"just a distraction. A way to protect myself because you won't let me near you. If you let me, I would sell my soul for you."

Which didn't make any sense, of course. What, sell her soul for a gut-shot and unreliable private investigator she hardly knew? Bullshit. Yet somehow she made me believe it. Just for a moment or two, she inspired me to believe that her passion ran so deep. Her eyes were moist, luminous with her particular vulnerability.

And I wanted to respond. I've always been a sucker for vulnerability.

Putting one hand on her shoulder, I moved her aside so that I could sit up. In response, she slid her arm across my shoulders as if she thought I wanted that. I lacked the will to resist, but I didn't encourage her, either.

Roughly I said, "You'll have to do better than that."

She avoided my gaze. Instead she watched my mouth, wanting it. Her lips parted. Gloss or moisture made them shine.

"What do you mean?"

"Look at me." My fierceness changed slowly, growing purer. "What do you see? I've been shot. A killer is after me. I brought him here because I couldn't get my brain out of the fog enough to recognize a voice over the phone. My life is a daily struggle with booze. If it weren't for Sam and his bag of tricks, I wouldn't even be able to sit up.

"What kind of woman wants a man like that?"

"Brew. Oh, Brew." She did it again. "You're wrong about yourself. You only think that way because you're surrounded by people who sneer at you. Your partner isn't any better than you are, but she acts like she is. Really, she's worse. She doesn't even know she's crippled.

"But it's false, Brew. It's false.

"Don't you know what you are?"

I held her gaze as if I wanted to fall into them and drown.

"You're a *man*. Compared to you, Joseph is only male. And Mac isn't even that. You're the only *man* here. You know everything there is to know about pain. Terrible things have happened to you, and you've been so hurt, so hurt— You've been lost in alcohol. Your partner doesn't care about you. You've been shot by a professional killer. Your enemies have torn at you until you can barely stay on your feet. But you aren't broken.

"That's what being a man *is*," she said as if she'd built her life on it. "You endure everything there is to endure, but you don't break.

"I don't know how any woman can look at you and not want you, not want to take every part of you inside herself, for comfort and healing and passion. If she did that—if you let her—she would be whole again."

Well, she was wrong about one thing, anyway. I didn't know everything there was to know about pain. She'd already taught me something new. I didn't know how to face it.

But I did. We can all be brave if we need courage badly enough.

I'd lost my ferocity. The naked heat of her confusion had burned away my anger. Gently, almost tenderly, as if she were a sore child I wanted to soothe, I said, "That has got to be one of the worst reasons for sex I've ever heard."

At last I'd succeeded at hurting her. Good for me. Her arm dropped from my shoulders, and her eyes seemed to go blank, almost opaque, as if she'd slammed the doors behind them shut. A hot spot of crimson appeared on her cheek.

"Maybe I was wrong," she retorted. "Maybe you *are* broken." Her tone held so much concentrated acid that I actually winced. "Broken in so many pieces that you can't tell you've been shattered. Maybe those bandages"—she poked a finger at my ribs, eliciting another wince—"are all that holds you together."

Before I could think of anything to say, we heard a scream.

More of a howl, really, a full-throated yell of rage and frustration and loss. A woman's howl, but doors and walls muffled it, I couldn't identify the voice. Nevertheless it had enough power to cut into me like the bite of a drill.

She screamed twice and then stopped.

My mind went blank with shock. But I'd already reached the door. I had the .45 in my fist.

The door refused to open. Lara had locked it.

Frantic to get out, I twisted the lock, hauled open the door, lurched into the hall.

I couldn't tell where the scream had came from. But Sam Drayton ran past me. I followed him.

Down the hall just a few doors. To Mac Westward's room.

By the time I got there, Lara and Queenie were right behind me. We found Connie standing beside the bed, Sam opposite her. She gasped for air in hard desperate chunks, the flush of her screams still on her face. She looked wild-eyed and extravagant, like a schoolteacher gone feral.

Sam examined Mac. But I didn't need a doctor to tell me that he was dead. People who lie with their heads at that angle are always dead. He must've been sleeping the sleep of the drunk when someone walked in and snapped his cervical vertebrae.

Queenie gave a little wail and hurried over to Connie. But Connie didn't react. She didn't want comfort. She stood rigid, panting hoarsely, like a woman who wanted blood.

The intensity of Lara's expression surpassed my capacity to interpret it.

We were the only ones in the room. No one else appeared. The other guests must've heard Connie's screams, but they didn't come to investigate. Apparently they'd already reached the same conclusion I had.

The killer wasn't outside where Ginny could hunt him down. He was in the lodge with us.

18

It didn't make any sense. I couldn't think. I could only stare at Mac. The angle of his neck made me want to throw up. Somehow I'd never clearly recognized the vulnerability of drunks.

And the insoluble simplicity of the problem appalled me. Anyone could've come into this room and done that to him, anyone. It didn't take strength. All it required was a working knowledge of how necks break. The killer could be anyone.

But what staggered me most, made my whole moral world stand on its head, was the certainty that Mac hadn't been killed by accident. Not like Cat.

Which implied—

I couldn't think.

Sam stood in front of me, glaring, his eyes hard—too hard. In a brittle voice, he said, "This changes everything, doesn't it." For the first time he sounded breakable. There were limits to what he could bear.

Like an echo in an empty room, I said, "Everything."

And Connie said, "Everything," contemplating murder.

"Any one of us," Sam went on, "could be next."

Come on, Axbrewder. Think, for God's sake!

"You found him like this?" Queenie asked Connie. "Did you scream right away? How long ago did this happen? Did you see anything? Why were you here?"

See, Axbrewder? She's thinking. Doing what people need to do when their lives are in danger—trying to get a grip on the problem.

Do it, you sonofabitch. Mac was dead. Killed deliberately, not by accident, killed for reasons that belonged to him and no one else. Which implied—

"Brew," Lara asked softly, urgently, "what're we going to do?"

Well, look on the bright side, I told myself. Simon might still be alive. The killer was here in the lodge, one of us. And none of us could possibly have killed him, lugged his corpse up into the hills, and then come back before the rest of us realized the danger. Ginny might well be safe. She was hunting a panic-stricken actor, not a professional hit man.

But that didn't matter, not to us, not now. I had a more immediate problem. The killer was *here*, and I was supposed to deal with him, I had no idea what was going on.

"What're we going to do?" Lara repeated.

"Survive." My voice shook. Hell, my entire body shook. "Which means that we're going to stay together. The whole group, everyone, in the same room. That way, whoever did this can't kill anyone else."

"Right!" San snapped. Somehow I'd said what he needed to hear. "I'll get them into the den. We can talk there."

He hurried out the door.

"Brew"—Queenie left Connie, came over to me—"is that safe? Should I go after him?"

Everything had happened too quickly. I couldn't think fast enough. She was right, I shouldn't have let Sam go alone. He might be the killer himself. Or the next victim. I should've sent Queenie and even Lara with him. But he'd left before I could get my brain in gear and my mouth open.

"No." I refused to risk Queenie, too. "He'll be all right. It's too soon for another murder." To keep her from arguing, I said, "Take Connie to the den. Stay with her. I'll be along in a minute."

Like her husband, she needed to move, to do something. She turned back to Connie.

Connie didn't budge. Rigid with strain and fury, she demanded, "Mr. Axbrewder, how are you going to catch Mac's killer?"

I wanted to yell at her, I don't know! Catching killers is Ginny's job! Don't you understand? I'm just the hired help! But that didn't seem particularly useful, so I swallowed it. Instead I faced her straight.

"I'll start by questioning you." Pay attention. This is a threat. "As far as I can tell, only two people here have a reason to want him dead, and you're one of them."

Queenie raised her hand to her mouth in shock, but she didn't interrupt. Lara studied me intensely, as if every nerve in her body were on fire.

Connie didn't flinch. She didn't even protest. But her face twisted and went pale, like I'd punched her in the stomach.

Well, I knew how that felt, but I didn't apologize. None of this made sense. That *was* Smithsonian's voice on the phone, I was sure now, and the shot that killed Cat could've been aimed at me, and someone had definitely tried to suffocate me with rat poison. No one except el Señor actively wanted me dead. But in that case Mac should still be alive. Mainly so that I wouldn't start to whimper in frustration, I ordered Queenie and Lara to get Connie out of the room.

They obeyed.

Connie didn't resist. I'd knocked the fury out of her. She walked with her arms folded over her stomach, protecting her pain.

Unfortunately I didn't have the vaguest notion what to do next.

Search for clues. Sure. What did I expect to find? Would I recognize a clue if I saw it? The only thing in the whole room—or the whole lodge—that mattered was the angle of Mac's neck. He hadn't been given a chance to defend himself. To understand his plight, or fear it. A useless death. As soon as he'd started pouring wine into himself at lunch, he was a goner.

He didn't deserve it.

Unless you believed that he deserved to die for screwing around with Lara Hardhouse.

I wanted to scream, but I didn't. Instead I studied the room for a while, trying to convince myself that I'd notice anything out of place, anything significant. I checked his windows. Behind their blinds, they remained latched. I checked his bathroom. The sink held a strand or two of hair that might've been Lara's. However, I wasn't really looking for clues. I just wanted time to calm my nerves.

Without this hole in my guts, I might've vacuumed the rug and dusted the chintz in an effort to restore my sense of moral order. But my wounds refused to go away.

As soon as I stopped shaking, I headed for the den.

Most of the group had assembled ahead of me. Comfortable fires had raised the room's temperature and cleared the last arsenic reek from the air. Nevertheless Murder on Cue's guests huddled in front of the hearths as if shock or fear had chilled them. But they didn't huddle together. Schisms of distrust separated them. Only Sam and Queenie clung to each other. Maryanne and Connie sat as far away from each other as possible on the same couch. Rock and Buffy had claimed opposite armchairs, facing different fires. And Joseph and Lara Hardhouse seemed to confront their marriage from either side of the tree trunk like a couple who couldn't choose between loathing and passion.

As self-effacing as ever in their distinct fashions, Amalia Carbone and Faith Jerrick stood back against the walls, out of the way. Of all the people there, only Faith didn't look suspicious of anyone. Even Ama glowered frankly at us all from her withdrawn position. But Faith had a friend in God, and that sufficed.

Which left—

I twisted against my bandages to scan the room. "Where's Mile?" I asked Maryanne. Facing Ama, I asked, "Where's Truchi?"

Maryanne gave a wan grimace. In a small forlorn voice, she said, "He didn't tell me. When we heard what happened—when Sam came and got us—Houston just left. He didn't say anything."

Ama was a good housekeeper. She knew her place. But she was also furious. In Italian she muttered something that sounded remarkably like, "That son of a goatfucker." Then she answered in bitter English, "He abuses my husband."

Somehow I knew exactly what that meant.

Riding the remains of my adrenaline, I headed out of the den. On my way, I commanded, "Wait here," as if I could take everyone's obedience for granted.

I found Mile and Petruchio Carbone in the kitchen. Which was a good thing, because otherwise I wouldn't have known where to look for them. Mile had his back to me; he didn't hear me coming. One fat fist gripped the front of Truchi's shirt. The other brandished a wad of bills. Must've been several hundred dollars.

"It's yours," he was saying. His voice sounded like what happens when you step on a stick of margarine. "It's all Ah have on me, but you'll get more. A lot more. No questions asked. All Ah want is a gun. The biggest cannon you got hidden. And ammunition. Ah mean to blow me away a killer."

Truchi didn't betray my arrival with any shift of his head or flick of his gaze. Under the droop of his mustache, lines of sadness shaped his mouth, and his eyes seemed to regard Mile with profound fatigue. Apparently his reaction didn't require words. He said nothing.

His silence didn't bring out the best in Mile's temper. Mile knew how to get what he wanted, and the name of that how was *money*. When money didn't work, he turned frantic. Or vicious. This time, it was vicious.

"You wop shit." He waved bills in Truchi's face like a club. "You listen to me, boy. You think you can say no to me, you got that wrong. Try it and you're dead meat. The minute Ah get to a phone, Ah'll buy me this lodge and everythin' on it. Then your job is mine. Your *ass* is mine, fucker. Ah'll make piss-sure you never work again. You and that thick slut you call your wife are goin' to be in the crapper 'til you *starve*. Where Ah come from, we eat you spick and wop bastards for breakfast. You get me a gun or you're *dead*."

Truchi looked all this in the eye without a flicker. Considering his strength, he probably could've beaten Mile to Jell-O with one elbow stuck in his ear. But maybe he figured that the owners of Deerskin Lodge wouldn't approve if he pounded the by-products out of a guest. Or maybe he was just impervious to abuse and had no use for violence. Either way, he didn't respond.

I had a different reaction.

Someone had already tried to kill me. Twice, maybe. I faced a series of crimes that I couldn't understand and didn't know how to handle. Ginny was gone, and the infection in my guts put up a good fight against the antibiotics, and too many things were my fault. On top of that, I smelled an insidious little reek of gas. Reeson hadn't done a particularly good job on the stove.

The odor reminded me of smoke and arsenic.

I picked my spot. I measured the distance.

Then I hit Mile in the back hard enough to rattle my teeth.

Afterward my pulse hammered like it was about to split open my skull. But I didn't care. There's no substitute for job satisfaction.

Mile slammed against Truchi and flopped to the floor like a bowl of overturned oatmeal. The way he arched his back and tried to crawl away from the pain worried me for a second. Maybe I'd broken something for him, or sent him into kidney shock. But I didn't worry much.

Truchi glanced down at Mile briefly. Then he looked at me and gave a sad shake of his head. No doubt Mile and I had confirmed his belief that everyone who ever came to the lodge was crazy.

I didn't worry about that, either. Stiffly I said, "Bring him," and turned away.

By the time I got to the den, I could feel the floorboards wobble under me, and my head hurt as if someone had buried an ax in my brain. Everyone watched me enter. Even Faith turned her head in my direction. But I didn't say anything at first. I went to the nearest hearth to prop myself in my familiar position against the mantel. I took the .45, the symbol of my authority, out of my pocket and set it handy. While my head pounded, I glared around the room.

"If anyone else wants to argue with me, do it now. You've got one minute." Anger and blood loss left me giddy. "If you give me any more grief after that, I'll turn my gun over to Mile and let the lot of you fend for yourselves."

They all stared at me.

As if on cue, Truchi came into the den with a coughing and defeated Houston Mile over his shoulder. He dropped Mile on the couch between Maryanne and Connie, then retreated to stand beside his wife. Mile's color suggested apoplexy or infarction. He didn't try to talk.

After that, no one said anything. No one dared. Maryanne studied Mile as if he nauseated her. She made no effort to comfort him.

"All right." Time to do my job. Now or never. "Sam probably told you what happened, but we're going to take it from the top anyway. This is just like playing mystery camp, except now everyone's life is on the line. Not just mine.

"You first, Connie."

"What?" Connie stared at me like I'd frightened her out of her outrage. Maybe I'd been too hard on her. I wanted information from her. And I wanted access to her professional expertise, the knowledge that she'd acquired being half of Thornton Foal.

But I didn't go easy. "Start with right after lunch." I

didn't plan to go easy on any of them. "Tell us what you did. Why you did it. Don't leave anything out.

"Then tell us why we shouldn't think you killed him."

At any rate, she wasn't in shock. And she wasn't the kind of woman who stayed frightened. She had too much fury in her.

"Mr. Axbrewder," she said in a congested voice, "you're treating me like a fool. I'm the one who discovered Mac's body. I'm the one who screamed. Any murderer with an ounce of sense would make absolutely certain she was somewhere else when the body was found.

"This is a small group, Mr. Axbrewder. For the most part, what we do here"—her gaze held my face—"is painfully transparent. I knew Mac was in trouble. How could I help it? For one thing, he doesn't drink like that. Not at lunch. Not in the middle of a mystery. And for another, he doesn't have affairs with married women."

In the background, Lara flushed. But no one made any comment.

"As far as I know," Connie continued, "he doesn't have affairs at all." She seemed unaware that she referred to Westward in the present tense. "He's an inward man, a writer, not an actor. What he does is *create*. And he is good at it." Outrage crowded her throat. "Our society doesn't take the mystery novel seriously as literature, but Mac should be taken seriously. His gifts—"

She gulped down emotion, tightened her grip on herself. The not focus of her eyes made them look almost crazy— as crazy as the flame tip of an acetylene torch.

"I knew he was in trouble."

Mile coughed once more, hard, possibly trying to spit up blood. Then he subsided.

"After lunch," Connie explained grimly, "he went to his room. He went alone, although you had instructed us to stay together. This worried me, Mr. Axbrewder. I could understand his desire to numb his troubles with alcohol. But alcohol isn't selective. Numbing his troubles, he also numbed himself to danger. For that reason, I decided to watch over him.

"A short time after lunch—no more than half an hour—I went to his room to be sure that he was all right. I intended to stay with him until he awoke. Or until Ms. Fistoulari returned.

"I found him as you saw him.

"I'm not acquainted with violent death, Mr. Axbrewder. I write about it, certainly, but I have no personal experience with murder. Catherine Reverie was the first *victim* I've seen.

"Nonetheless no one could mistake what had happened to Mac." Without warning her voice caught, clenched around a sob. Again she tightened her grip on herself. "And only a fool could fail to draw the obvious conclusions. I am not a fool. Clearly, our reasoning—*your* reasoning, Mr. Axbrewder—was predicated on a false premise. Clearly—"

I interrupted her. "Did you touch anything?" I had my own panic and outrage to deal with.

She shook her head. Judging by her expression, her estimation of me sank every time I opened my mouth. "Of course not."

"You didn't touch him? To see what he felt like?" What violent death felt like? "See if he was still warm?"

At least I succeeded at surprising her. "What would be the point?"

That got a reaction out of Hardhouse. "To find out how long he'd been dead. It might make a big difference if we knew when during that half hour he was killed."

I sighed to myself. One of the last things I wanted in life was to have Joseph Hardhouse on my side. But the issue had to be faced. I looked at Sam.

Sam shrugged. "I examined the body." He had his own brand of bitterness, which he made no effort to conceal.

"Without an autopsy, I can't be sure of much. I can't even be sure he was killed by a broken neck. For all I know, that was done to him after he died, just to confuse us.

"In addition, the gradient along which a body loses warmth—like the rate of rigor mortis—varies widely from one individual to the next, one situation to the next.

"If he was cold, we could've been reasonably sure he was killed early in that half hour. But he was still warm— warm enough. It could've happened anytime."

"Which brings us," Rock put in unexpectedly, "to the question of alibis."

I stared at him. So did Sam and Queenie and Hardhouse. Connie, Lara, and the rest kept their attention on me.

"We all know the killer is one of us." From his tone, you would've thought that we held guns to his head, forcing him to explain leveraged buyouts to morons. "Right? The doors are all locked. There is no one else to suspect. We all had the means to kill Mr. Westward. Who had the opportunity?"

He faced me. He still looked like ashes and defeat, but he'd been cursed with a brain that continued to function.

"I had the opportunity. I was here"—he indicated the den—"alone. And my wife had the opportunity. She was in our room, also alone."

Buffy bit her thin lips in distress.

Rock glanced around the room, mutely asking, Who else?

"But you didn't have any reason," Maryanne put in timidly. "Did you? You've run mystery camps for years now. Why would you suddenly start killing your guests? And Thornton Foal is famous. Once people find out Mac was killed here, they'll never come to another Murder on Cue camp."

"That's right," Buffy breathed from the bottom of her heart. "We don't have any motive. We don't—"

I stopped her. "One thing at a time. If we're going to make sense out of this, let's do it by the numbers.

"Buffy and Rock had opportunity. Connie had opportunity. Lara and I didn't. We were together." When I said that, Lara looked so grateful that I couldn't resist adding, "Unless she did it during the first ten minutes after lunch.

"Maryanne, what about you and Mile?" I would've loved to ask Mile himself, but he was in no condition to answer.

Maryanne's expression made me feel like a child molester. Her fear went right to the core. "I didn't do it." Her voice wobbled like a frail chair with too much weight in it.

"That isn't what I asked you."

Her fellow guests seemed to hold their collective breath while Maryanne groped for courage.

Thinly she replied, "Houston sent me to our room. I thought he wanted to look for those guns. But he didn't tell me that. He didn't say anything about it.

"He came back after fifteen or twenty minutes. I was alone that long." She shot me a pleading gaze and repeated, "I didn't do it."

I ignored her insistence. "Sam? Queenie?"

Queenie shrugged. "Sam and I were together the whole time."

"So if you did it," Hardhouse remarked like he was having fun, "you did it together. That's clever. I wonder how much easier it is to commit murder when you have a partner. You sure as hell don't have to worry about alibis, do you?"

"One thing at a time," I said again. I spoke harshly, mostly because I hated Hardhouse. "You're the only one left. What's *your* alibi?"

He faced me with fire in his eyes and a range of interesting emotions on his mouth. "What do you mean, I'm the only one left? What about them?" He indicated the Carbones and Faith Jerrick.

Amalia snorted in disgust. But she responded before I could prompt her. "Petruchio chose to prepare boards to repair the wall in the workshop. We were instructed to remain indoors, but then he cannot do his work. He left and returned through the kitchen. Faith and I saw him. We washed dishes together."

Which wasn't the best defense I'd ever heard. If anyone had keys to the doors, Truchi did. He could've gone out, let himself in another door, killed Mac, and retreated the way he came. But Reeson had already pointed out the absurdity of accusing the Carbones or Faith. Rock and Buffy were better candidates.

I returned to Hardhouse. "Like I say"—friendly as a hacksaw—"you're the only one left. Tell us why we should cross you off the list."

The Draytons, Rock, and Maryanne all turned to study him.

He spread his hands as if to show us how clean they were. Despite his animation, his artificially slick hair made him resemble one of the animal trophies. "I was alone, too. No alibi. I was in my room, trying to get some sleep. After all the exercise I've had"—I couldn't mistake his point—"I need rest."

Lara bit her lips and scrutinized the floorboards.

Silence answered him. The only sound was the soft rush of the wind past the chimneys and the faint crackle of the fires.

"Which brings us," Sam said suddenly, in the hard, brittle voice I'd heard earlier, "to the question of motive."

"Why look at me?" Hardhouse retorted, facing Sam now.

Sam didn't hesitate. "Because I think you killed him."

Hardhouse widened his eyes as if he were actively surprised. "Me? Why me?" A second later he added, "What about Connie?"

No one so much as glanced at Connie. Stiffly Sam said, "You killed him because he had an affair with your wife."

Lara did her best to melt into the floor or the tree trunk, but neither of them accepted her.

Hardhouse laughed confidently. "Don't be absurd." His tone mocked Sam's accusation. "She's had dozens of affairs. So have I. That's how we keep our marriage fresh. It turns us on. It makes us excited about each other.

"Isn't that right, Lara?"

His wife went on trying to melt. She didn't respond.

"Lara?" he asked again. He had so much confidence that he didn't need to threaten her.

For another moment she didn't reply. Then she said in a muffled voice, "Joseph is right. We've done it for years. If he wanted to kill my lovers, he should have started a long time ago."

"But that's *sick*," Buffy protested.

Lara looked up. Sudden fire showed in her eyes. She may've been uncomfortable about being exposed, but her behavior didn't embarrass her. "How do you know? Have you ever tried it?"

"If it works," Hardhouse put in, "it isn't sick. What gives you the right to judge? Look at you, sitting there half dead. You and Rock"—he sneered the name—"probably haven't touched each other for decades. But whenever Lara goes to bed with another man, I know I'm being tested. Before and after. I'm being given the chance to prove I'm the best she's ever had.

"That doesn't scare me. It doesn't intimidate me. I *like* a challenge. The rest of you talk about it, but you don't mean it. The kind of challenge you like is a mystery camp, where everyone *pretends* the issues are serious. There's no pretense about what Lara and I do. Every time we have sex, we're on the line with each other, we're being tested, we have to prove ourselves in the most intimate way there is.

"You only think it's sick," he finished almost triumphantly, "because you couldn't handle it."

"No," Connie said into the silence, as flat and sure as the blade of a knife, "that isn't the reason."

I couldn't think of an answer. Knowing the real reason that Lara had wanted sex with me made me feel demeaned and helpless. Ultimately I was irrelevant to her. I'd endured the distress of her attempted seduction for nothing. But Connie didn't have that problem.

I hadn't seen her stand. Nevertheless, she was on her feet, facing Hardhouse as if this were a contest between the two of them and none of the rest of us mattered.

"You and I, Mr. Hardhouse," Connie said. "Only we have any apparent motive for killing Mac, you because he slept with your wife, I for essentially the same reason, because he was my partner, perhaps my lover, and he was unfaithful. I'm the one who says it, Mr. Hardhouse—I who have the right. What you and Lara do is sick."

Hardhouse probably wanted to retort. But Connie had too much dignity. Her controlled indignation kept him quiet.

"Mac was a *writer,* Mr. Hardhouse. He understood, as every artist must, that there is no such thing as a contest between persons. Oh, competitions exist, competitions for jobs or advancement, athletic competitions. A murder mystery is a competition. But the *writer* of the mystery must know better.

"It is impossible to *create,* Mr. Hardhouse—ultimately it is impossible to *live*—on the assumption that any contest can exist between persons. All characters must have the same distinctive worth, the same individual value, the same right to life, or else they have been poorly created, and the artist has failed.

"Mac understood this, I say." She spoke as if tremors rose in her bones. "I consider him a *writer* in the best sense, a good writer. We didn't work together because we were weak apart, but because we were stronger together. And I tell you plainly that he did not have sex with your wife in order to measure himself against you. Nor did he have sex with her in order to measure her against me.

"*That* is why I have no motive. There was no contest between Lara and me—or between Mac himself and me. Nothing that either of them did reduced me in any way. But *you*, Mr. Hardhouse—you perceive a contest. Any motive here is yours, just as any failure is yours."

I wanted to applaud. It was a wonderful speech. Queenie's eyes shone with appreciation, and Sam nodded approval. Maryanne's face had gone all soft and childlike, and even Rock and Buffy looked like they'd felt the brief butterfly kiss of grace. But you had to give Hardhouse credit. He wasn't an easy man to get around.

He didn't try to argue. Instead he simply bowed to Connie and grinned. "I surrender," he said humorously. Then he looked across at me. "Since I'm the only one with means, opportunity, *and* motive, you'd better lock me up. In fact, you'd better put handcuffs on me. That way I'll be safe." His eyes flashed. "Just like Simon."

Just like that, he paralyzed me. With one insidious little remark, he made me realize what was wrong with my theory about Simon being alive.

Who broke Simon out of the wine cellar? Mac's killer, presumably. Why? To make Simon look guilty. And to get at the rat poison. But if Mac's killer did all that, he couldn't afford to let Simon live. Simon knew who he was. So if the killer was still outside, being chased by Ginny—which was impossible, how could he have killed Mac?—Simon was dead. And if the killer was here—which was also impossible, who else could've left that trail into the hills?—Simon was still dead.

If I did anything to imprison Hardhouse and turned out to be wrong, he might become the next victim.

None of this made any *sense*.

I didn't turn away from the problem. I didn't even wince. But in the back of my brain, panic began to gibber.

I was out of my depth.

I needed Ginny.

19

What are we going to do?" Buffy asked.

She spoke to Rock, not to me. That was a good thing, because I had no idea. The effect of Sam's miracle drugs faded by the moment, and fever left my brain flopping around loose in my skull. Simon was dead, innocent Simon, and Hardhouse couldn't have killed Cat because he was with Ginny at the time, yet he was the only obvious candidate for Mac's murderer.

"I don't know," Rock said like a shrug. "It's up to Axbrewder."

I should've paid attention, but I didn't. I didn't hear the threat gathering in the room. Instead I made a positively heroic effort to face Hardhouse's grin.

He could only be the killer if he and Ginny worked together.

Wonderful. The perfect solution. It all fit. Together they could've shot Cat and planted the rifle and broken Simon out of the wine cellar and hidden his body and stuffed rat poison down the chimney and killed Mac. People can do amazing things when they work together.

Without her I wasn't even a whole person.

"Brew"—Queenie echoed Buffy's question—"what're we going to do?"

"All of a sudden," Mile growled, "you don't look so good, do you, boy?"

That brought me back. Until then I hadn't grasped how much my credibility depended on the idea that I was the intended victim. But if I were irrelevant to Cat's death—a deduction which followed logically from the angle of Mac's neck—I was irrelevant to everything. My relationship to the whole group changed. And Houston Mile, for one, had no more use for me.

"You like to strut, don't you?" he continued. He didn't appear to notice as Maryanne shifted away from him. Pain still marked his face, leaving hints of congested crimson around his bad teeth, but he'd had enough time to recover his natural charm. "You like to wave that cannon around, and punch innocent folks in the back when they ain't lookin', and carry on like the almighty law of God. But you been wrong about everythin' so far, ain't you, boy?

"You and that fuckin' partner of yours, issuin' orders, thinks she a man, and she ain't got better sense than to go off huntin' a boy who ain't killed his first horsefly yet, never mind an actual woman. Unless she's on the run herself, leavin' us to get picked off one at a time while you stand there refusin' to let us defend ourself."

Rock nodded as if he agreed with all this.

"You're a pitiful excuse for a detective, boy, and you're finished." Mile's anger gave him confidence. "Ah ain't takin' your orders no more, and the rest of us ain't either." He waggled a pudgy hand at me. "You pass over that cannon before anybody else gets killed, and Ah'll show you how to do your job."

"What would you do with it, Houston?" Sam put in, at the limit of his patience. "Shoot Joseph?"

"For a start," Mile retorted. "The way Ah got this thin' figured, there's only two possibilities, and givin' him a little ol' third eye in the middle of that nice face eliminates one of 'em."

Lara made a small noise that might've been a giggle before she swallowed it.

Hardhouse glanced at her, back at me. "In that case," he said equably, "I think I'll vote to leave Brew in charge."

Mile ignored him. "After that, pretty boy," he snarled at

Sam, "Ah'll make you and this flouncin' bitch"—he meant
Queenie—"tell us what you're really doin' here."

Just for a second, I thought Sam might haul off and deck
Mile. Or maybe that was just wishful thinking. In any case,
he didn't do it. Instead he tightened his grip on his wife. "I
think," he said between his teeth, "you had better explain
that before I make you eat it."

No. Absolutely not. I felt sure that I knew what Mile was
about to say, and I didn't want to hear it. Deliberately I
picked up the .45. I meant to cock it—I meant to fire it, if I
had to, to shut him up.

Unfortunately, I couldn't. I lacked the strength to work
the slide. The room had started into a lazy spin, and there
wasn't enough air, and as soon as Mile said anything about
Ginny and Hardhouse working together I'd cackle my
brains out.

Fortunately something else interrupted him.

A muffled pounding.

A distant sound like a doorknob being rattled.

More pounding.

Maybe a voice. I couldn't be sure.

But everyone else heard it, too. The whole room went
still, as stiff as a corpse. Maryanne covered her mouth.
Buffy's face turned as pale as her eyes. Sam and Mile cut
off their argument. Lara jerked around.

The sound seemed to come from one of the bedroom
wings.

"Somebody is at the back door," Hardhouse said clearly.
He was already on his way to answer the pounding.

From somewhere I dredged up the energy to shout at
him. "*No!*" When he paused and turned, he saw the .45 in
my fist, aimed right at him.

No one else moved a muscle.

I pushed away from the mantel, leaned into motion.
Locking my knees so that I wouldn't fall, I went around the
furniture and the tree to Hardhouse. He studied me in an

intense but noncommittal way, almost disinterested, as if for purely scientific reasons he wanted to know how much farther I could go.

"It's still *my* job," I said past the muzzle of the gun. "The rest of you, stay here. If you want something to do, watch each other. You're all safe as long as you watch each other."

I waited for a reaction, not from anyone else, but from Hardhouse.

"Don't worry," he said in a friendly tone. "I'll make sure they don't hurt themselves."

Instead of jamming the .45 up one of his nostrils, I stumbled away into the hall.

I couldn't actually tell which hall the pounding came from. But I'd entered the one Hardhouse had headed toward. Down an aisle of tight floorboards padded by an expensive runner. Past bedrooms and the parlor. If I'd been in better shape, I would've seen immediately that this was the right hall. A shape showed through the panes of the door ahead, and the knob rattled again. I was halfway there, however, before I registered any of this information. And I'd nearly reached the door before I recognized Ginny's coat under its camouflage of snow.

I didn't hurry. The gibber of panic in my head had grown louder. Manic and lucid, it informed me that anyone could wear a coat.

Shattered by alarm and fever, I had to brace the .45 against my leg to cock it. Then, as if this were the scariest moment of my whole life, I twisted the dead bolt and let the door open.

Ginny staggered inside.

Details which I didn't notice immediately slipped past me. She'd obviously spent a fair amount of time stretched out in the snow. It still clung to her coat and hair. Clots of it packed the prongs of her claw. Her face had the particular pallor underlined with blue that comes from intense cold.

She seemed too frozen to shiver. Her eyes were glazed, almost blind.

But all of that was secondary. Instead my attention jumped into focus on the wound on her left temple.

Snow and hair and coagulated blood disguised the injury, but it looked like a bullet mark—the kind of furrow a slug leaves in your skin as it skims past you.

Oh, Ginny. My gun weighed too much. Ginny. I managed to uncock it. Then I left it dangling from the end of my arm and leaned my weight against the wall. I couldn't speak. Even simple words refused to come out.

"Brew," she breathed in a soft, empty voice, as if all her blood had gone to ice. "He almost got me."

It was like magic. As soon as I heard the need in her voice, I forgot about being weak. Quickly I picked myself off the wall, put the .45 away. Wrapping an arm around her, I drew her back from the door.

"Sam!" I called. "Queenie!"

We only went as far as the parlor. A fire crackled in the hearth, so I steered Ginny inside, toward the nearest heat.

At the same time everyone from the den poured into the hallway like I'd uncorked a bottle.

Hardhouse led the way, of course, but Sam and Queenie followed close behind. While I fumbled at the sash of Ginny's coat, they rushed into the parlor. One glance at Ginny, and Sam wheeled away, fighting the press of people to go get his medical bag. I didn't see Hardhouse's reaction, Ginny's coat gave me too much trouble. Fortunately Queenie came straight over and helped. In a moment Rock and Buffy, with Connie and Maryanne and Lara, reached the parlor, and Mile filled the door, and the Carbones and Faith stood outside. Queenie shoved Ginny's coat off, urged her closer to the hearth.

A faint aftersmell of port and blood tinged the air. They'd soaked into the rug, marking the place where Cat died. Luckily Truchi or Reeson had moved her body some-where. And the fireplace sucked most of the odor away.

I looked around for something to warm Ginny. The de-canter of port still stood on the wet bar, but I knew she hated port, so I opened the liquor cabinet. Like everything else in Deerskin Lodge, it was well stocked. I spotted a bottle of Black Bush, but I didn't touch it—I didn't think I could stand the smell of that much heaven. Instead I grabbed some vodka and a glass, poured a healthy shot, and took it to her.

Sam had already returned, shouldering Mile aside to reenter the parlor. When he saw the glass in my hand, he snapped, "That's not a good idea.

"Get her something hot," he instructed Faith or Ama, "tea, coffee, cocoa, I don't care, something with sugar in it." Then he hurried to examine Ginny.

Faith and Ama left together. Truchi stayed behind Mile, guarding all of us.

Now I had time to remember vodka. My stomach knot-ted, and I nearly dropped the glass. With an effort I put it down beside the port.

Sam poked a thermometer into Ginny's mouth, checked her pulse and blood pressure. Then he tore open a Betadine swab and started on her forehead. "What happened?"

Around the thermometer, she mumbled, "I got shot."

I could hardly hear myself think through the gabble of panic in my head. Apparently she'd been shot at approxi-mately the same time that Mac got killed.

Hardhouse noticed the same problem. "You know," he said conversationally, "this is as good as one of those 'locked room' puzzles. The facts are impossible. The killer must be outside, but he can't be because he's in here with us. He must be in here with us, but he can't be because he's outside.

"Congratulations." He bowed to Buffy and Rock. "This has to be the best mystery you've ever put on."

Lara gazed at him as if she contemplated eviscerating him in his sleep.

Maybe Ginny wasn't as close to hypothermia as she looked. Or maybe she was too stubborn to quit. Something in Hardhouse's tone or words snagged her attention. She looked around the room, then took the thermometer out of her mouth and asked harshly, "Where's Mac?"

Sam took the thermometer and studied it, frowning hard. He didn't answer her question. Instead he said, "You and Brew have one thing in common anyway. You're both lucky as hell. Whatever hit your head doesn't appear to have done any structural damage, and your temperature is only a little low. What you have to worry about now is shock. You need fluids. Force down as much as you can stand. And stay awake. Let me know if you feel drowsy.

"How long were you down in the snow? Do you know? Did you lose consciousness?"

Ginny was in no mood for medical details, however. Already I could see the difference in her, the recovered snap and fire. That more than anything else helped me believe her wound wasn't serious. Stiffly she repeated, "Where's Mac?"

"Sit down," Sam commanded as if he wanted to hit her. "Head injuries are always dangerous. You can make this worse than it has to be if you don't take care of yourself."

"*Brew.*" Ginny caught me with her gray gaze so hard that I almost saluted. "*Where's Mac?*"

Panic suddenly filled my throat. I forced out one word, "Dead," and stopped.

"He was killed," Sam rasped in a kind of fury. "Someone broke his neck. Sit *down.*"

She sat down.

Obediently Lara, Connie, and Maryanne sat down as well.

Ama and Faith had returned, but Mile didn't move to let them in. Truchi solved this problem with a gentle nudge that shifted Mile's position by several feet. At once Faith carried a steaming electric coffeepot and some cups into the parlor. She probably kept coffee for the guests ready all the time.

Promptly, but without any obvious hurry or concern, she filled a cup, stirred in some sugar, and handed it to Sam in its saucer.

He pushed it at Ginny. "Drink this."

One thing a prosthetic device doesn't do well is hold a cup and saucer. Just for a second, a look of naked helplessness crossed Ginny's face. Then Queenie saw the problem and intervened. She took the cup and saucer from Sam, kept the saucer, and turned the handle of the cup toward Ginny.

Ginny accepted it and hid her face over the coffee to recover her balance.

Calm as a saint, Faith put the coffeepot down on the wet bar and plugged it into an outlet.

"I don't understand," Maryanne said as if she thought everyone else did. "How could the same person shoot Ginny and kill Mac?"

Rock had been watching Sam and Ginny with a blank look that resembled catatonia. Now, however, he roused himself enough to murmur, "Depends on how long ago she was shot. He could've hidden a hundred yards away. It's less than that up into the trees. He could've shot her and come back inside while we ate lunch. Then he could've hidden in Mac's room and waited." Dully he finished, "He could still be here."

This novel idea made the guests flinch.

"Let me see if I understand you," Hardhouse said. "You think the killer *isn't* one of us. You're back to Axbrewder's theory about a hired gun—an outsider who wants to get rid of one or all of us for some unknown reason."

Rock accepted this interpretation without blinking.

"There's only one problem," Hardhouse continued. "We locked all the doors from the inside. If our killer did what you're suggesting, he would have to have a key."

Unless he came in through my window. I hadn't latched it. Queenie did that for me some time after Ginny left—after Sam and I returned from looking at the wine cellar.

In which case, why wasn't I dead?

So what other possibilities were there? Who had keys?

By the time I thought of an answer, Sam, Lara, and Connie had all turned to stare at Ama's husband like they feared he carried an Uzi under his shirt.

Ama may've grasped what this was about. Truchi didn't appear to. If anything, his general stoicism seemed less weary than usual, more bemused. She looked disgusted on his behalf.

"I don't believe it," Connie pronounced as if no one else's opinion mattered.

"Tell me what happened," Ginny demanded.

Sam dragged his attention back to her. "You first. It's good for you to talk. It'll help you stay alert."

Ginny looked at me. Maybe she wanted me to ignore Sam and answer her. Hell, maybe she wanted me to tell her what to do. At the moment, I didn't know, and I didn't care. I needed to sit down. My efforts to take charge of this situation had ended in panic, and I didn't feel able to continue functioning.

I had to do better.

The two armchairs and the love seat were already occupied, so I retreated to the wall beside the wet bar and lowered myself to the floor. The rug was almost as thick as a cushion, but comfort wasn't exactly uppermost in my mind. Fighting the confusion of fever and the slow erosion of the artificial energy Sam had given me, I tried to make my brain work.

I needed to figure out what was wrong with that hole in the wall. It meant something—something I hadn't seen yet. Unfortunately reason and deduction weren't my best skills. As a rule, I lived on intuition. And at the moment I felt so hampered, so incomplete, that I couldn't think about anything except the night I got shot.

That night, when I was supposed to be in my hospital bed, I went hunting for a killer, armed only with my instincts and the .45. I found him. Naturally he insisted that he was innocent. But he'd left a window open because he couldn't afford the time to close it. That small detail should've given me the hint I needed. It should've told me that I was right, warned me to trust myself. Too bad I didn't pay attention. Instead I let him give me a glass of vodka, thinking it was water.

That mistake had nearly killed me and Ginny both.

Simon's open window was another hint. And Queenie had given me a glass of water that wasn't vodka. That felt like a hint as well, a trigger for intuition.

But why? What did either of those details have to do with the hole in the wine cellar wall?

Ginny was saying, "Brew must've told you what I was doing." She spoke coldly, without emotion—thinking hard, sifting information, organizing facts. "After he warned me about Smithsonian, we discovered Simon was gone. I went after him.

"I started out assuming he was a hired gun who worked for el Señor, here to kill Brew. But once I had time to think, I realized there were other possibilities. He might be innocent. The real killer might've broken him out to get at the rat poison. In that case, he was probably dead. The killer couldn't afford to leave him alive. So I had two reasons to catch up with him. To stop him, if he was the killer. Or to save him, if he was still alive.

"I didn't see anybody." In this kind of mood, she wasted no time on bitterness or frustration. "I still don't know who I was after. He hit me as soon as I reached the trees. Must've been less than half an hour after I left Brew, probably no more than twenty minutes." She wasn't digressing, just making connections. "He had plenty of time to come back here while you were having lunch.

"He nearly finished me. I went down, and for a minute or two I hurt so bad I thought the slug was somewhere in my head. But I don't think I passed out. Instead I waited for him for him to check on me, see if I was still alive. The snow covered me pretty well, and I was sure I'd hear him coming."

Ordinarily this sort of thing made me want to yell at her. Damn woman, who did she think she was, lying there in the snow with a head wound trying to spring an ambush on the goon who shot her? But now I couldn't muster my usual indignation. My mind kept sliding away.

El Señor's hit man could have entered the lodge through my window. He could be here right now.

In which case, why wasn't I dead?

The back of my brain wanted to tell me something about glasses of water—or glasses of vodka—but I couldn't hear it.

"I waited a long time," Ginny went on. "He didn't come. When I stopped shivering and got sleepy, I knew I had to take a chance on standing up and coming back here."

Sam muttered some sort of medical curse that had to do with drunks and idiots, but she didn't stop.

"It was harder than I thought it would be. I couldn't tell if I'd lost blood or was just frozen, but I kept falling down. That's how I know he wasn't watching the lodge from my side. Otherwise he would've seen me and tried again. Which was a comfort." For a moment she let a little of her anger out. "It helped me concentrate on getting up and going on."

But she didn't dwell on that. "Eventually," she concluded, "I got here. Now you know as much as I do. It's your turn."

Sam scanned the group, apparently looking for volunteers. I guess he didn't feel up to providing a summary of recent events. But no one else seemed to want the job either. Lara sat in one of the armchairs, chewing on her lips so hard that I thought she might draw blood. Her husband frowned studiously to himself like an entrepreneur deciding how to take advantage of a competitor's mistakes. Beside Connie on the love seat, Maryanne looked too frightened to explain anything to anyone. To my surprise, Rock and Buffy stood together with their arms actually around each other, as gray as two halves of one lost soul. Mile's eyes flicked piggy malice all around the parlor, but he didn't speak.

"Somebody?" Ginny asked acerbically. "Anybody?"

I didn't offer. In my struggle for insight, I was trying to be logical, even methodical. Which doesn't usually work with intuition—but what the hell, I had to try something.

Abruptly Connie said, "I'll do it."

Scrutinizing the stained rug as if she needed to understand its pattern, Mac's collaborator gave a clear, accurate, and concise account of events since Ginny went after Simon.

I suppose I should've been impressed, considering the fact that Connie herself was one of the chief suspects, but most of the time I couldn't make myself listen.

Ginny absorbed the information intensely. When she asked a question, it amplified Connie's explanation without distracting her. Then she thought for a while, scowling into the air.

Everyone waited for her. The atmosphere in the parlor was tense with expectation or dread, but no one wanted to interrupt the professional investigator at work.

"So," she said finally, "we need to reconcile two apparently irreconcilable crimes. We have somebody with a gun outside, and somebody with strong fingers inside, and we don't know how they fit together." She emptied her cup and handed it to Queenie. "First we need to consider timing and access."

Rock and the Hardhouses nodded sharply. Even Connie nodded. To himself, Mile growled something I couldn't make out.

Queenie moved across the room to get more coffee. I followed her with my eyes simply because she was moving. When she picked up the coffeepot, I saw the decanter of port on the wet bar.

A shiver ran through my head. Queenie had given me a glass of water. Which had reminded me of drinking vodka. Which now felt like a hint.

A hint of what?

What else, I thought because I'd just noticed it on the wet bar, what else besides Cat's port?

"Timing." Ginny clicked her claw experimentally. "As far as I can tell, Mac could've been killed as much as half an hour after lunch. And you didn't go to lunch right after I left. You talked in the den for a while. Whoever shot me obviously had time to come back here and kill Mac.

"Another point. If we start from the assumption that one of you killed Mac, we'll have a terrible time figuring out who was able to get away long enough to put rat poison in the fire, break Simon out of the wine cellar, leave that trail up into the hills, dispose of the body, shoot me, and come back without being missed. That doesn't sound possible. If we assume the killer is an outsider, we're at least dealing with things that are possible."

This made a certain amount of sense. Rock regained a bit of color, and Maryanne's eyes brightened. With an air of concentration, Queenie took a fresh cup of coffee to Ginny, then stepped out of the way. Sam's frown relaxed slightly. The idea of an unknown killer was bad enough, but it was better than the possibility that one of us, *someone in this room,* did it.

For the time being, however, I left that stuff to Ginny. A completely different question troubled me. On what conceivable basis did a decanter of port accidentally left on a wet bar constitute a hint?

Because Catherine Reverie, rest her poor lonely soul, had made such a point out of it. She was an actress, and she'd been downright ostentatious about her taste for port.

Why would she do such a thing? What did it imply?

"But," Hardhouse said to Ginny, "that brings us back to the question of access. Your hypothetical outsider had to get into the lodge somehow. He had to have a key. Or help."

For a moment, Ginny seemed to accept this assertion. Once again, heads turned toward Truchi. But then she said, "Wait a minute. Did anybody relock the wine cellar after I left?"

Considering his air of vagueness, Truchi's prompt reply came as a surprise. "Me," he said distantly. "The key was in the lock." He rummaged in his pocket and produced a key. "The kitchen was cold, and we were told to lock all the doors."

"Shee-it," Mile pronounced profoundly.

So what, I asked myself, did Cat's display of fondness for port suggest? For one thing, anyone who wanted her dead didn't need to shoot her. All he had to do was spike her port. No one else drank the stuff.

"Anything else?" Ginny asked the group. "Can you think of any way somebody could get in here without a key?"

Abruptly Queenie gave a low gasp. "Brew's window."

I should've expected this. Failing that, I should've reacted to it. But I was obsessed by nameless possibilities, and I wanted to talk to Rock. Or Buffy.

I wanted to ask them how Simon was supposed to kill Cat.

Heads swiveled from Truchi to Queenie. In a startled voice, Sam said, "That's right."

Everyone waited for Queenie to explain.

"It wasn't latched," she said awkwardly. She looked at

me with misery in her eyes. She may've been asking me to forgive her. "I guess he forgot. I latched it for him."

"When was this?" Ginny demanded.

"Right before lunch. Brew talked to us in the den. He asked Faith and Ama to get lunch ready. Then he and Sam and Rock went to look at the wine cellar from the outside. When they came back in, we went to his room. That's when I noticed the window."

Ginny made a musing noise. "That complicates things. If the man who shot me got in through Brew's window, he had to do it well before lunch. Was there enough time? Did any of you happen to see the time? How long did Brew talk?"

Unfortunately that distracted me. It was too implausible. I simply couldn't imagine a killer, presumably a professional, shooting Ginny and then running back along his trail to the lodge in plain daylight, risking being seen, encountering someone, all for the unlikely chance that he'd find a door or window unlocked.

I shouldn't have let my attention shift. I should've finished thinking about port.

No one answered Ginny's question. No one said anything. Except Queenie. In a worried tone, she murmured, "I need a drink."

For the second time, she crossed the parlor to the wet bar. I'd left a glass of vodka handy, but she ignored it. Instead she picked up the decanter and poured herself a hefty slug of port. Holding the decanter in one hand and her glass in the other, she turned back to the group.

"Anyone else want anything?"

Too late, I caught up with myself. I didn't believe that Truchi had killed anyone. And I didn't believe that he'd given his keys to a killer. Therefore—

If the outsider theory were true, the killer must've entered the lodge through my window. And I sure as hell didn't believe *that*. No one who knew what he was doing would take that risk.

Therefore the killer was one of us. Someone who wanted a random assortment of us dead. Cat, me, Simon, Mac—

—and who else? Surely he wouldn't stop there?

"No," I choked out, "don't." But Queenie didn't hear me. Or she didn't know I meant her. Before I could stop her, she lifted her glass and took a deep swig.

I'd nearly reached my feet when she started gagging.

The sound she made was horrible to hear. Her own muscles strangled her. As she went into convulsions, she dropped her glass and the decanter. Sweet purple splashed the rug like blood. I tried to catch her, but she was too far away, I had too much of my weight braced on the wall. Flailing wildly, she went down in a pile of limbs and spasms.

"*Queenie!*" Sam cried, a hoarse wail from the depths of his heart. Then he vaulted past Ginny's chair and dove at his wife.

For some reason, I noticed that a blue marble rolled out of the decanter into the middle of the puddle on the rug.

20

The puddle soaked in slowly, staining the rug a nauseating color, blurring the ambiguous design, while Sam fought to save Queenie's life.

Ginny took his bag to him before he called for it—before he finished his first quick check of Queenie's vital signs. Then she knelt to help hold Queenie still while he worked.

The way Ginny moved made her look like she'd never needed help in her life.

Strain mottled Queenie's face. The seizure closed her throat, sealed her chest, she wasn't breathing. Spasms fired in her muscles. She thrashed like a madwoman. Ginny couldn't control her. Sam needed someone to clamp down Queenie's legs.

It should've been me, but Joseph Hardhouse and Amalia Carbone got there ahead of me. They reached Queenie at the same moment and put their weight on her legs.

Instead of pushing either of them aside, I lowered myself back down the wall and crawled on my hands and knees after the marble.

Sam tore open a disposable needle, fixed it to a syringe. He snapped the top off an ampoule and filled the syringe. Every line of his face and arms focused on the necessity of keeping his hands steady.

As soon as he had the injection ready, he snapped, "I need a vein!"

Ginny didn't seem to understand.

No, that wasn't it. She simply couldn't pull either of Queenie's arms away from her chest.

She released Queenie's shoulders to work on one arm. But when she did that, the convulsive wrenching of Queenie's body went wild.

I picked up the marble, closed it in my fist. My hands were sticky with port from the damp rug. At this rate, I'd smell like port for the rest of my days.

In tandem, Hardhouse and Ama moved. He shifted himself onto Queenie's legs while she leaned against Queenie's shoulders. That enabled Ginny to concentrate on freeing one arm so that Sam could reach a vein.

Ginny still wasn't strong enough. She had only one useful hand. And the seizure gripped Queenie like iron, inhuman and unbreakable.

But she wasn't breathing, she couldn't breathe, and oxygen starvation eroded her strength. As she lost consciousness, her muscles weakened.

Sam helped as much as he could with his free hand. An inch at a time, Ginny broke the clench of Queenie's arm.

"Brew!" she panted. "Get them out of here. Give us room."

I knew that tone. It compelled me, in spite of all my mistakes and obsessions. The blue marble I followed in my mind would have to wait. With a heave, I got my legs under me and pitched upright. "Come on!" I barked at the group. "Everyone out! Back to the den!"

I didn't have Ginny's talent for command. No one reacted. Matched like twins, Rock and Buffy looked like they might faint. Connie had her hands up over her mouth, uncharacteristically aghast. Maryanne's whole face stretched for a scream that refused to come out, paralyzed by terror. Mile muttered to himself, words I couldn't hear and didn't want to. Only Lara glanced at me. The light in her gaze had the shining intensity of an orgasm.

Without hesitation I pulled the .45 out of my pocket, worked the slide, and fired at the ceiling.

That got everyone's attention, no question about it. Even Ginny gaped for a second as if she thought I'd lost my mind. But she didn't loosen her grip. Sam concentrated on his syringe as if the .45 and I didn't exist.

"I'm only going to say this one more time," I remarked. "Everyone out. Back to the den."

This time people moved. Taking Maryanne by the hand like a frightened schoolgirl, Connie stood up and started for the door. For reasons of his own, Truchi put a hand on Mile's arm and tugged him in the same direction.

Then everyone else complied—the Altars, Lara, Faith Jerrick. To Ama, Ginny panted, "Joseph can do it." Ama seemed to know that tone as well as I did. Without hesitation she joined her husband. At once Hardhouse stretched out across most of Queenie's torso.

Still clinging to the .45, I herded the depleted group back to the den.

Queenie's plight seemed to claw at my back as I left. I still hadn't heard her breathe. How long could she go without air? How long before she suffered brain damage? Or died?

It would be my fault. Another failure, like my failure with Simon. I couldn't have known the port was poisoned, of course. But once again I'd recognized the potential danger too late. If I'd been faster, I could've saved her.

To make matters worse, Mile was waiting for me in the den.

Buffy and Rock had collapsed on one of the couches, and Connie and Maryanne sat as well, holding onto each other as if one of them, anyway, couldn't go on without the other. Too tense for anything as helpless as sitting, Lara had begun to pace around the tree, repeating the circle to calm herself. Truchi had moved to the nearest hearth to build up the fire. His wife and Faith stood together, their arms folded across their bellies at exactly the same angle, but with very different effects. Ama looked like she was restraining a visceral outrage. Faith seemed to cradle her trust in salvation, using it to warm her heart.

In contrast, Houston Mile confronted me with his fists braced on his hips and a flush of fat anger on his face.

"This is your doin', Axbrewder," he rasped. "You know that? She's goin' to die. You know why? You didn't listen to me. Ah tried to tell you, and you wouldn't listen. You wouldn't even *listen*, never mind give me a gun and let me try to save us. How many more of us got to become corpses before you *wake up?*"

I glared at him and didn't say anything.

"Sam is a doctor," Connie put in as if she'd taken on the job of reassuring everyone. "I expect he's a good doctor. He may be able to treat her. Especially if he can guess what kind of poison it is."

"No," Mile snarled. "You left the wrong people with him. They'll make damn sure she dies."

There it was in a nutshell—Mile's solution to the mystery. After all, he had his reputation to maintain—the one who always solved the crime, the best player at Murder on Cue's camps. Now he intended to explain it to us. Judging by appearances, he didn't plan on letting anybody stop him.

I didn't give a shit. In my own way, I was as lost as Queenie, as far gone. If I didn't do something to treat myself soon, I'd never recover.

I followed the blue marble.

Ignoring Mile, I moved to the couch and stopped in front of Rock and Buffy. They didn't notice me at first, but I stood there until they both raised their heads and looked at me.

"Tell me something," I said. I wanted to sound casual, detached, I wanted to sound like I had everything under control, but my voice twitched. "How was Simon supposed to kill Cat?"

In unison Buffy and Rock blinked at me. Their mouths hung open.

"You're stallin', boy," Mile put in. "This ain't no mystery camp now. We ain't in no mood to waste our time figurin' out a pretend crime that never had no chance to happen anyway."

I still ignored him. I ignored Connie and Maryanne and the Carbones and Faith and Lara. And I ignored common sense, too. Common sense suggested that I wasn't in a particularly good position to make promises or bank on my credibility.

I did it anyway.

"Trust me," I told the Altars. "This isn't irrelevant."

Rock closed his mouth and cleared his throat. Buffy answered me.

"We aren't sure."

That wasn't what I wanted to hear. "What do you mean, you aren't sure? This is your camp. You hired Simon and Cat. You designed this whole experience. How could you not know what they had planned?"

Buffy nodded. "We designed it, yes. But only in a general way. We couldn't know what the rest of you would do, so we couldn't be too rigid. Otherwise the actors couldn't adjust it to fit the circumstances. It might go wrong. You might say we"—she glanced at her husband—"I designed the theory, but Simon and Cat were responsible for the application."

"Tell him the truth," Rock murmured heavily. "You're just confusing him."

Buffy ducked her head. As if she were ashamed of something, she admitted, "I used to plan out the whole thing. I liked doing that. It was like writing a mystery novel myself, except better. I had live characters to work with.

"But then"—her voice was so gray and small that I could hardly hear her—"Rock started tampering with the clues. After that, the camps didn't go the way I planned.

"So I stopped planning them. All the details, I mean. I wanted to make it harder for him to interfere." Now she looked up at me, almost gallantly daring me to doubt her. "And when I didn't plan everything, I could be surprised myself. That made our camps fun in a different way. Instead of being like a writer, I was more of a participant. And Rock had to work harder if he wanted to tamper. He had to pay more attention. I liked that, too."

For some reason, she needed to make me understand that she didn't resent her husband.

But that wasn't the point. Clinging to my reasons for asking the question, I pursued, "So you had no idea what Simon and Cat cooked up between them? Her taste for port wasn't your idea?"

Again Rock cleared his throat. "Actually, it was my idea."

Huh?

"Part of the planning," he explained, "involved creating opportunities for a murder. We didn't tell Simon what to do, but we did help invent circumstances he could use. And I still wanted to interfere. I thought if I planted a suggestion, and Simon used it, I'd have the upper hand. So I suggested the port. And I told Cat it would be clever to get herself poisoned at a time when it would be hard to connect the port and Simon." For instance, while Cat and I were alone—and Simon had gone out for a walk. "I meant to smuggle the marble out of the port after she collapsed. Then no one would know how she was killed." He shrugged limply. "But when she was shot I forgot all about it."

"You done yet, Axbrewder?" Mile demanded. "You ready to start facin' some facts for a change?"

With an effort, I pulled myself away from the Altars. In an odd way, I was ready for Mile now. What Buffy and Rock said changed nothing, at least as far as Cat's murder, and Simon's, and Mac's were concerned. But it affected the tissue of hints inside my head. Hints don't kill anybody. They don't prove anything. But they help make intuitive connections. And on that level Cat's port told me as much as any fact.

"Oh, sure," I said across the den at Mile. "If you have some facts that need facing, you might as well mention them now."

"Fine," he growled, "fine," trying for assurance. If nothing else, my attention to the marble question unsettled him. He didn't know what I had in mind.

"Take your time," I retorted harshly. "We've got all day."

Lara had stopped pacing. She stood opposite Mile, facing me. Her burning eyes gave the impression that she'd remembered why she wanted to go to bed with me.

Truchi finished with the fires and moved to stand beside his wife. Both of them watched me, too. But Connie and Maryanne had turned in their seats to look at Mile. Maryanne concentrated on him as if he hypnotized her the way a snake does a bird.

"What you all ain't thinkin' about," he began, "what you been refusin' to listen to, Axbrewder, is that we ain't got one killer here. We got two."

I nodded, trying to project a confidence I didn't feel.

"You been workin' too hard to figure out how one man shoots Cat and plants that gun on Abel and gets him out of the wine cellar and breaks Westward's neck and still has an alibi. It don't wash. There ain't enough leeway. There ain't no way one of us could do all that.

"But if you're goin' to claim we got us an outside killer, you got the same problem. There ain't no way the man who shot Fistoulari is goin' to come back here to snuff Westward 'less he knows he got a way in he can count on. He ain't goin' to sneak around here in broad daylight just *hopin'* there's a window open. He's got to have him an accomplice. Just like any one of us got to have an alibi.

"That means there's two of 'em.

"But if there's two of 'em, we don't need to take no notice of this outside killer idea. Ain't none of us here got that kind of enemies 'cept you, Axbrewder—and you ain't dead. All we got to do is look for two of us who always got the same alibi. They're the ones lyin'."

"That don't include none of us." He waved a fat hand around the room. "Sometimes we got alibis, sometimes we don't." He indicated Connie pointedly. "When we got more than one, they ain't the same." This may've been a reference to Lara Hardhouse, or to me—or to himself. "But you can't say that about good ol' Dr. Sam Drayton, or his floozy wife neither."

"On the other hand," Connie put in with the kind of sarcasm that wilts house plants, "Queenie Drayton is the one dying right now."

"So that lets 'em out," Mile went on fiercely. "But it don't let out Joseph Hardhouse"—he faced me with his teeth bared—"and that bitch you call your partner."

Before I could protest, he snapped, "They say they was together when Cat got shot. We know they was together when that rat poison went down the chimney. He got no alibi for killing Westward, he admitted that. She don't either. And for all we know she went after Abel so she could kill him. Maybe she and Hardhouse didn't have time when they broke him out. Then she clubbed herself over the head—or she got Abel to do it for her before she killed him—so she could look innocent.

"Queenie Drayton is goin' to end up dead"—his teeth resembled the fangs on a dog with distemper—"because you let two killers help her husband save her."

Lara wanted to say something. Once again, however, Connie was the first to speak.

"Houston Mile," she pronounced firmly, "you are out of your mind."

"Why would they do that?" Maryanne's question came out like a little wail. "People don't just kill for no reason. Joseph and Ginny didn't even know each other before we came here. Why do they want Cat and Mac dead? Why did they try to kill Brew? They must have had a *reason*."

"How the hell should Ah know?" Mile shouted back at her. "Ah ain't God! Ah don't see inside their heads. There just ain't nobody else got the means and the opportunity to kill us like this!"

Out of the empty air, Rock mumbled, "It's possible, I suppose."

In an incredulous tone, I demanded, "Say what?"

"Well," he replied without focusing on any of us, "suppose there's an investor who wants to buy Deerskin Lodge, but the owners don't want to sell. One way to get a property under those conditions is to devalue it in some way. Perhaps by making it the site of multiple murders. So the investor hires Ms. Fistoulari. But she can't rely on her partner due to his injuries, so she turns to Joseph for help. Perhaps they were already lovers. Or perhaps he's the investor. Together they come here and begin killing the rest of us.

"Of course, this won't work unless they appear innocent at the end. Otherwise they wouldn't escape arrest. That may be your role, Mr. Axbrewder. You'll vouch for Ms. Fistoulari. You'll explain about el Señor. But it's possible." He glanced, not at me, but at Buffy. "Isn't it?"

His theory must've sounded plausible to Connie. Turning to Lara, she asked, "Is your husband capable of such a thing, Mrs. Hardhouse?"

Whatever Lara thought about the situation, she thought it intensely. She kept it to herself, however. Instead she flared, "Anything is possible. Joseph is capable of anything. But he isn't the only possibility here." Facing Rock and Buffy, she demanded, "You're an investor yourself, aren't you, Mr. Altar? Who would be better placed than you are to set up such a scheme?"

Rock didn't react, but Buffy seemed to gag on something horrible. When she could get words out, she admitted thinly, "That's one of the scenarios we considered. A series of murders to lower the value of the lodge. I rejected it because it was too—too abstract. The murderer would be too difficult to catch because the motive was so impersonal." In a sickened tone, she added, "It was Rock's idea."

Rock nodded dully.

"You *see*?" Lara insisted, facing Mile now. "You can't pin this on Joseph. There are other possibilities."

"No." Mile didn't waver. "*You* care about *reasons*. Ah don't. All Ah want is to stay alive. All this couldn't happen 'less two people did it. And the only two people could've done it are your husband and Fistoulari. You want a reason, try holdin' a gun to one of 'em's *head*. Maybe that'll make 'em talk."

"No," I said myself. This had gone on long enough. "You weren't listening, Mile. You missed the point."

"The point?" he rasped. "What point?"

"Catherine Reverie was the only one who drank port. We all knew that. She made an issue out of it, she made sure we all knew. And Ginny *is* my partner. She doesn't want me dead. If she did, she could've left me in the hospital, come on this case alone. I would've been too vulnerable to defend myself. Her only reason to bring me along was to keep me alive.

"But if you're right, her reason was to make the idea of an outside killer believable. Because el Señor really does want me dead. So she still can't afford to kill me. If someone else gets killed after I'm dead, the whole plan goes out the window. Therefore whoever shot Cat was *not* aiming at me. She was the intended victim all along.

"That pretty well destroys your accomplice theory, doesn't it."

I was too far ahead of him. His lips flapped on his teeth before he managed to ask, "How?"

"Because"—I wanted to shout at him, but my stomach hurt too much—"Cat didn't need to be shot." I was *goddamned* if I'd let anyone else die because I didn't think fast enough. "The port was already poisoned. Why would

Ginny and Hardhouse—or anyone with an accomplice—bother shooting a woman who was already as good as dead?"

That did it. I'd finally said something effective against Houston Mile. In fact, I'd scared him down to his socks. His attack on Ginny was his way of fighting off his fear. Without it, he looked suddenly defenseless—as frightened as Maryanne.

"Axbrewder," he murmured thickly, "give me a gun. Ah got to have me a gun."

Everyone ignored him. He might as well have made himself irrelevant. Even Maryanne turned away.

"So what you're saying," Lara proposed in a thoughtful tone, "is that none of our theories is any good. These crimes must have been committed by someone working alone—but they couldn't have been committed by anyone working alone. Nothing makes any sense."

"Not quite. All I'm really saying is that Cat must've been killed by accident. That shot was aimed at me. Which lets Ginny out." And Hardhouse as well, since he'd been with her when Cat died. "Everything else is still open to question."

"Axbrewder," Mile begged, nearly blubbering. "Ah *got* to have a gun."

"Perhaps we're going about this in the wrong way," Connie offered. "We're attempting to reason from opportunity or motive to guilt. That's the method of most novels. It's easier. But perhaps we should try to reason from *capacity* to guilt. Certainly those of us who are *incapable* of committing any of these crimes can be dismissed from consideration." She made this sound like a reference to Maryanne. "We may be able to go further, however. We're intelligent people, and we've spent some rather concentrated time together. We may be able to evaluate who among us is sufficiently determined, desperate, or unscrupulous to have done these things."

"But how can we do that?" Buffy protested plaintively. "You want us to figure out who *isn't* capable of murder. Until now, I would have said I've never met anyone who *is*."

"*Axbrewder!*" Mile came at me before I noticed the white craziness in his eyes, the frenzy in his movements. "*Ah got to have a GUN.*"

He was fast when he thought his life depended on it. And my own special brand of desperation clogged my reflexes. He came past the couches at a run and threw himself at me before I could do anything more than gape at him.

I went down hard.

Which was just what I needed, a fall like that, with him on top. I didn't even know whether he knocked the air out of me. Too many other kinds of pain happened at once. The impact and his weight lit napalm in my guts, sudden flame splashed along my nerves, I blazed from head to foot. The way he scrabbled at the .45 in my pocket felt like he'd cut into me with a welding torch. The walls and the tree crackled like the hearth, and the ceiling blurred.

Somehow I remained conscious. Distinctly I heard Ginny yell, *"Stop it or I'll blow your fucking head off!"*

Now I could see her. She crouched over me with her .357 jammed into Mile's ear. Sam hadn't bandaged her forehead yet. Blood oozed from her wound, staining her pale skin. But the wound itself didn't look especially deep or dangerous.

Hardhouse must've come in with her. When Mile froze, Hardhouse heaved him off me.

I still had the gun.

Mile sounded like he was whimpering for his life, but it didn't come out in sentences.

As soon as his weight left, I began to take fractured little gasps, trying to sneak pieces of air past the voiceless howl of the fire.

"Brew." Ginny knelt beside me. "Are you all right? Can you stand?"

I croaked, "Sam."

What I meant was, I need Sam. But that wasn't what she heard, so she said, "He's taken Queenie to their room. He doesn't know yet whether she'll make it. He finally got enough IV Valium into her to ease the seizure. But by then she'd been unconscious for a while. She may be in a coma. And she could have another attack anytime. Her heart could stop. He's doing what he can to stabilize her. But he can't tell how much poison she swallowed, or how powerful it is, or whether she'll ever wake up.

"Can you stand?"

Fire filled my chest. I had too many things to say, but the words had been burned away.

"Help me," I croaked.

"Sure." She braced her arm under my shoulders.

Hardhouse didn't help her. Maybe he was still busy with Mile. But Rock seemed to appear out of the air at Ginny's side. The two of them got me onto my feet.

The difference between up and down confused me. And I couldn't hear anyone except Ginny. Only her voice penetrated my distress.

"I'll get you to Sam's room," she told me. "He can take care of you there. Maybe the distraction will do him good. Then I'll organize a search. If we have a killer hiding here, we'd better find him. Anybody who doesn't want to help I'll send to you."

Did that make sense? I had no way of knowing. As far as I could tell, I was being taken in the direction of Sam's room. At the moment, nothing else felt important.

One step at a time. Across the den to the hallway. The people behind me seemed to do too much moving around. General panic? Struggling to control Mile? Whatever it was, I couldn't do anything about it.

Ginny knocked on Sam's door before we went in. A wasted precaution. He sat on the bed beside his wife without turning his head to see who we were. Instead he

gripped both her hands as if he wanted to anchor her somehow. The strain left his knuckles white. From time to time,
a tremor ran down his shoulders. If he kept holding her like
that, he might crush her fingers.

Her pallor made her look like she'd lost blood somehow, and her limbs sprawled, limp as a corpse's. Her eyes
were closed. Her breathing seemed too shallow to sustain
her life.

Ginny steered me to a chair and propped me there. She
didn't try to talk to Sam. Instead she asked Rock if he
wanted to stay with me.

He took a deep breath. Without looking at her, he said,
"This is your job. You're being paid for it. But you're here
because of me. I'm responsible for this whole camp. Buffy
and I. And I'm the one who didn't mention Lawrence
Smithsonian. I won't let you risk searching the lodge without help."

She didn't comment on his unexpected determination.
She just accepted it with a nod and turned to me.

I managed a nod of my own.

A moment later, she and Rock left me alone with the
Draytons.

Sam still didn't glance in my direction. After a minute or
two, I realized that I'd better attract his attention somehow,
so I wheezed his name.

That made him turn his head. He couldn't refuse the
sound of need. Slowly he focused on me. "Brew," he said
dully, almost like he'd become stupid. "What happened
to you?"

This didn't seem like a good time to go into detail. "Mile
jumped me," I answered weakly.

To my surprise, he released Queenie's hands and got to
his feet. At once he came over to me, began checking
my pulse and respiration. If I'd only watched the way he
moved and hadn't looked at the darkness on his face or
the hollow helplessness in his eyes, I would've thought he

knew what he was doing. But as he went through the motions of examining me—a thermometer in my mouth, a blood-pressure cuff on my arm, a flashlight at my pupils—he asked me nothing about my condition.

"Do you know how long we've been married?" He sounded like he'd worn out his voice shouting for help in a wasteland. "A year." He checked the gauge on the blood-pressure cuff as if he had no idea what it indicated. "That's all. A year."

Next the thermometer. Maybe he never actually saw it.

"You may not realize it, but doctors have a hard time meeting eligible women. Oh, we meet lots of nurses. But they're deadly to marry. They can't forget we're doctors, and then the marriage doesn't work. Or they forget too easily, and then the profession doesn't work. And who else is there? Secretaries? Most of them work in billing. They can't afford to remember that the patients who have no money are still people. Or in personnel. If you work in personnel, you aren't allowed to use your brain. Or in publicity. If you work in publicity, you don't have a brain.

"I have no *time* for singles bars."

Out of habit, he put the thermometer and blood-pressure cuff and flashlight away in his bag.

"But the one thing a doctor should absolutely never do is marry a patient. It's better if we don't even know their names. That sounds callous, but it isn't. It avoids confusing the illness and the person. When you know your patient is a scuzzball, you have a hard time treating him. It's hard to make painful decisions about an illness when the woman who has it is someone you love.

"And patients make lousy wives. They think you're magic. They think you can save them from their problems for the rest of their lives. They confuse the treatment and the person."

Next he filled a syringe. I didn't know what was in it, and maybe he didn't either. But I didn't care. I was listening too hard. His wasted face and worn-out voice made everything he said personal, poignant.

"Queenie was a patient."

Sudden fury bared his teeth. Nevertheless he slid his needle into me as gently as a caress. Almost at once, a soothing sensation eased along my veins.

"She should've died. Pure neglect. She's as bad as a drunk when it comes to her own health. She didn't think those lumps and all that discomfort were worth worrying about. We did a radical mastectomy on both sides and pumped her full of enough chemo to fry her brains, and she still should've died. But she didn't.

"In the middle of all that, during one of her lucid moments, I had to tell her her breasts were gone." Tears streamed down his face. He could only talk by biting down on the words and snarling. Yet his movements were pure calm as he put down the first syringe and filled another one. "When she understood what I'd said, she gave me such a smile—I wanted to die for that smile. And she said—"

For a moment, his throat and chest locked. He couldn't breathe or talk. But he kept on filling the syringe. Then he held it up to the light and cleared out the air. Like a farewell kiss, he planted the needle's little pain in my arm.

"She said, 'Thanks, Sam. That helps.'

"I think she was trying to do me a favor when she let me talk her into plastic surgery—implants and so on to give her a normal figure. She wasn't confused about me. She wasn't in love with my power or wisdom. She just wanted to let me help her again if I felt like it. If helping her felt good to me. She didn't need it. She didn't need breasts. She didn't even need me to save her. She loved being alive too much to need that. But she had room in her heart for everything I wanted to give."

Then he was done. Without another glance at me, he repacked his bag and closed it. Returned to the bed. Sat down again. Took hold of Queenie's hands.

At the same time, I felt an artificial strength returning. Any minute now I'd be able to stand up and go do something about my rage and grief and guilt.

"Why was she poisoned, Brew?" he asked as if he'd given me all the strength he had—as if that worn-out whisper was the only cry for help he could manage. "Who wants her dead?"

"No one." If he'd been more alert, he could've heard black murder in my voice. "It was an accident. That stuff was aimed at Cat. It was put in the port before she was shot. She just never got a chance to drink it.

"That bullet was aimed at me."

He didn't react. Maybe he didn't hear me. Or maybe he knew there was nothing I could say that would change anything.

"Sam," I asked unsteadily, "is she going to make it?"

I barely heard his answer. "I'm not magic, Brew. I don't know."

I sat with him for a while longer. But he didn't move or speak again. Every ounce of him concentrated on Queenie. Eventually I knew that I had to go.

Leaving the room quietly, I went back to the den.

21

In the den, the situation hadn't improved any. Only four people remained, Faith Jerrick, Sue-Rose Altar, Maryanne Green—and Houston Mile. None of them noticed my arrival. Buffy sat on one of the couches with her hands over her face and her shoulders shaking noiselessly, gripped by revulsion or grief. Beside her knelt Faith. Art Reeson's girlfriend held her crucifix and moved her lips like a woman in prayer, but she didn't make a sound. I couldn't tell whether she prayed for herself or for Buffy.

In fact, Maryanne was the only one talking.

She'd pulled a chair so close to Mile that their knees touched. Leaning forward with her weight braced on her elbows, she spoke softly, urgently, almost pleading with him.

"You have to understand, Houston, dear." She seemed to be repeating herself, not for the first time. "This is for your own good. You've had a breakdown—like a nervous breakdown. You're more sensitive than anyone realizes. All this violence has upset you, and you want to defend yourself. You want to defend me. That's why you attacked Brew. But we can't let you do that. I can't. If Brew is honest, we need him. He's used to violence. He doesn't have your sensitive nature. And if he isn't honest, he might kill you. I couldn't bear that. Dear Houston, it's for your own good."

For some reason, a moment or two passed before I noticed that Mile had been tied to his chair, trussed like a turkey. He even had a gag between his teeth. He struggled to spit it out so that he could yell something—hell, he looked like he wanted to froth at the mouth—but whenever he worked the wad of cloth loose, Maryanne pushed it back into place. Behind her gentle, pleading tone, I heard an edge that sounded, not like hysteria or fear, but like retribution. No matter what else happened, she meant to keep him tied and gagged just as long as she could.

I approved.

I didn't want to listen to it, however. I needed something more direct and bloody, more like a bullet in the head than poison masked by sweet port. Roughly I demanded, "Where's everyone else? What happened here?"

Buffy and Faith ignored me. Maryanne glanced up, a bit startled, but she didn't answer right away. Instead she whispered to her prisoner, "It's Brew, Houston, dear. He's right behind you. He has his gun. Please sit still. Don't provoke him. I'll try to protect you."

When she stood up, I saw triumph in her eyes, plain as a placard.

She drew me a few steps away. "We couldn't get him to stop," she told me softly. "Ginny sent Truchi for some rope. She wanted us to join you with Sam, so you could guard us. But Houston wouldn't stop, and Joseph said it wasn't a good idea to put him in with Queenie. So Ginny told us to stay here. Stay together. The others are searching the lodge.

"Buffy didn't want Rock to go, but he insisted." Maryanne grimaced sympathetically. "She got a little frantic, so Faith offered to stay with her. And I wouldn't be any good at searching. I'm too timid." She did her best to look timid, but at the moment she was enjoying herself too much. "Ginny said I could keep an eye on Houston."

That made sense. Unfortunately it didn't shed any light on what I should do next. I had to ask, "Did anyone tell her what he said about her?"

Maryanne looked blank for a second, then shook her head. "I don't think anybody believed it."

So Ginny still believed that we had an outsider on our hands. Someone hidden in the building. She'd gone looking for him with the remaining survivors—the Hardhouses and the Carbones, Connie and Rock. She hadn't heard Mile's reasons for thinking that no one killer could've done all this alone.

I liked the outsider theory myself. It explained Smithsonian's phone calls. But it had problems. For one thing, Mile was right. The murders would be easier to explain if the killer had an accomplice. For another, I simply couldn't imagine why the same killer would want me and Cat and Mac and Simon all dead. Which in turn suggested that the murders had nothing to do with any one of us personally— which made nonsense out of those calls from Smithsonian.

And for another—for another—

There was definitely another problem, but at the moment I couldn't put my finger on it.

But the insider theory was just as bad. According to Mile, it required two insiders. And I had only ten candidates, leaving out the Draytons. Seven, if I ignored the Carbones and Faith Jerrick. Five, if I crossed Mile and Maryanne off the list. Four discounting Buffy.

That left the Hardhouses, Rock, and Connie.

The same people helping Ginny with her search.

When I made that connection, apprehension tingled down my back, and the skin of my scrotum tightened. Now I knew what I should be doing.

Ginny needed backup, in case she opened a closet or turned a corner and found herself facing the missing guns.

"Which way did she go?" I asked Maryanne.

Apparently she hadn't expected that question. "What do you mean?"

I made an effort to control my sudden impatience. "How did Ginny organize the search? Where was she going?"

"Oh." Now Maryanne understood. "She paired the Hardhouses together. Lara didn't kill Mac, and Joseph didn't kill Cat, so she said they were safe. She told them to search Rock and Buffy's room, and Connie's, and Mac's. And she put Connie and Rock together. To keep an eye on each other. They're supposed to search Simon's and Cat's rooms, and yours, and hers. She's going to start with Mile's and my room. Then she's going to do the Hard-houses'. And the Draytons'.

"She sent Truchi and Ama to check the dining room and kitchen, the storerooms. When they're all done, they're supposed to come back here. Then they'll tackle the attic."

I didn't have time to be impressed by the clarity of Maryanne's grasp on these details. "Ginny's working alone?"

"Yes."

Great. Wonderful. Over my shoulder, I said, "I'll go help her." I was already on my way.

Faith stopped me. She must've been paying attention after all. As I left Maryanne, she rose from Buffy's side.

"Mr. Axbrewder."

I wanted to brush past her. Alarms of all kinds sounded in my head. Some of them started quietly, but they were turning into klaxons, inarticulate squalls of warning.

Nevertheless Faith's assertiveness held me. She looked pale and determined, as if God had instructed her to prevent me from leaving the den until she'd made one last effort to save my soul.

I didn't understand why she hadn't joined the search. Ginny would've been a hell of a lot safer with a companion, any companion.

"What do you want?" I demanded harshly. "I'm in a hurry."

"Murder is offensive to God," she said with soft intensity. "It is a crime against the souls of those who die. If they are not among the redeemed, they are deprived of their hope of heaven. And it is a crime against the souls of those who kill. Life and death and hope belong to the Lord, not to men. A man who kills damns himself by claiming powers which belong to God.

"When will these crimes stop?"

I heard an implied accusation which may or may not have been intended—and I was in no mood for it. "If you're so eager to see them stop," I growled, "why aren't you helping Ginny?"

No, Faith hadn't intended any accusation. She wasn't thinking about me or my competence—or my culpability. She had a dilemma of her own. Just for a second, her gaze flicked across my face, almost met my eyes. Then she said simply, "Because I'm afraid.

"I have a horror of violence, Mr. Axbrewder. It is true, certainly, that the Lord does not ask violence of me. But at need He asks all who serve Him to enter the presence of violence, to accept the sight and the risk of bloodshed. We are asked to love others as He loves them—and if we love them we must serve them as well as we can. It may be necessary to serve them by standing between them and murder.

"You have done that, Mr. Axbrewder. But I cannot. God's will is plain, yet I cannot obey it. I can only pray that He will pity me and forgive."

Without transition, my irritation evaporated. Instead of the contempt she probably expected me to feel, she forced me to respect her. She may've been a religious fanatic, deaf and blind with thoughts of God, but she didn't make excuses. Which made her braver than I was. Like her, I'd been deaf and blind for a good part of my adult life, but I'd never hesitated to use my drinking as an excuse.

"Don't worry about it," I muttered. "We're all scared. If God doesn't understand that, He doesn't deserve to be worshiped anyway."

Driven by klaxons, I headed past Faith toward the bedrooms.

Too late. As usual. Before I reached the nearest doorway, I heard Lara Hardhouse cry out, "Ginny! Oh, my God!"

I forgot Faith and Buffy, Maryanne and Mile. I forgot

pain and fever and weakness. And my gun. Empty-handed, I jumped at the door and hauled it open.

Gloom filled the hall. Bulbs had burned out—or someone had switched them off. For an instant, I saw only the dim air, the condensed darkness of wooden doors, the black stretch of the carpet—

—and a couple of shapes where the gloom solidified.

As I ran toward them, they turned into Lara and Ginny.

Lara stood against the wall with her hands over her mouth, braced to scream again. The dimness hid her features, but her whole body looked like panic.

"*Brew!*" she cried. "Oh, my God! *Come quick.*"

Ginny sprawled almost at Lara's feet. She might've been trying to bury her face in the carpet. I couldn't see her move. The rug under her looked dark as blood, and she lay motionless, as if she'd been nailed there.

Another fraction of a second passed before I made out the shape jutting from her right shoulder.

A knife.

I slammed to my knees beside her. But then I froze. She had a knife in her back—down in her right shoulder at an angle toward her heart. I couldn't decide what to do. Turn her over to see if she was still breathing? Just pull the knife out? How deeply had she been stabbed? The knife didn't look particularly long. A couple of inches of the blade hadn't gone in. How badly would she bleed if I pulled it out?

While I dithered, she lifted the stump of her left arm and thumped her claw sideways against the wall. In a voice muffled by pain and fury, she started cursing.

"Ginny," I panted, "Ginny, don't move. You've got a knife in your back." As if she couldn't tell what had happened to her. "I don't know how deep it goes."

"Brew," she gasped. "Christ! Get that thing out of me."

"Wait," I insisted, "wait, we need Sam, I don't know

how bad it is, when it comes out you're going to lose blood."

Her claw hit the wall again. Squirming against the pain, she twisted her head up. "*Get that thing out of me.*"

I looked around. No one appeared. Where were they all when I needed them? Surely everyone in the lodge had heard Lara's yell? But Maryanne and Faith and Buffy kept to the illusory safety of the den. The Carbones might not have heard Lara from the distance of the kitchen. Sam probably wouldn't leave Queenie for anything. Connie and Rock and Hardhouse—

When Ginny gave me orders, I was supposed to obey.

"*Damn* it, woman!" I snapped, "hold still! You need a *doctor*. I don't want to make a mistake about this."

Then Hardhouse materialized out of the gloom, soundless on the tight floorboards. Practically skidding to his knees opposite me, he barked, "Have you lost your mind? Pull it out!"

Before I could react, he tugged the blade loose, slapped it into my hands, and immediately jammed the heel of his palm onto the wound to stanch the bleeding.

Over Ginny's cursing, he commanded, "Get moving, Axbrewder! We need Sam."

The knife was slick and warm with blood—it felt almost hot on my shocked fingers. No one would've called it long, a five-inch blade at most. And it hadn't gone all the way in. Her attacker hadn't been very strong. Or the blade had struck on her scapula and skidded aside.

I had enough experience with knives and wounds to see that Ginny wasn't about to die.

Dumbly I got to my feet. The warmth of her blood seemed to burn into me like a splash of acid. Every beat of my heart carried concentrated sulfuric. I didn't care whether I was on my knees or standing or stark mad. I had the knife in my right hand, the handle wedged into my palm. With my left, I grabbed at Lara's blouse so hard that her head flopped against the wall.

Aiming the knife at her face, I demanded, "*Who did it?*"

Unmistakable panic glistened in her eyes. As soon as she saw the knife she started to babble.

"Brew, no, don't hurt me, I didn't do it, *I didn't do it*, I swear it, she was like that when I found her, don't hurt me!"

I shifted my left hand from her blouse to her chin. Hunching over her, I forced her head up. Almost softly, as if I weren't too savage to care what I did next, I repeated, "*Who did it?*"

"I didn't see." Her eyes were about to melt with fear. Nevertheless she stopped babbling. "Honest to God, Brew, I didn't see. I didn't see it happen. The hall's too dark. She was like that when I found her.

"Joseph and I finished the rooms—the ones she told us to search. We didn't find anything. He sent me to tell her we were done. He went to help Rock and Connie.

"I heard her fall. The way she groaned—God, I thought she was dead! But I didn't see it happen. He was gone when I got here. I didn't see anyone. There isn't enough light."

That left Connie and Rock.

Constance Bebb, who might not be able to drive a five-inch blade hard enough.

Roderick Altar, who might not know how to drive it at all.

"Whose is it?" Hardhouse put in tightly. "If we knew that, we might be able to figure out who did it."

Ginny coughed something that sounded like, "How?"

The pressure he put on her shoulder showed in his voice. "Whoever searched the room where that knife was is probably the killer. If we find out whose knife it is, we'll know who searched that room."

Which made sense, but I didn't care. I had other priorities. Another hint—

Just to be on the safe side, I waggled the knife and asked Lara, "Is this yours?"

She didn't look at it. "I've never seen it before. I don't like knives. I don't know whose it is."

I let her go. "All right," I grated. "Go get Sam. Make him come. Tell him to bring his bag. Hit him if you have to."

She glanced at her husband for confirmation. When he nodded sharply, she moved away.

Another hint. Not a piece of evidence, just an idea. Imagine someone—Connie, Rock, I didn't know who—searching rooms. Pretending to hunt for a killer, but really on the skulk for some way to attack Ginny without getting caught. Would this someone be willing to wing it—to take a chance on a random knife and unpredictable hallway lighting? Or would he require a more reliable combination of means and opportunity?

Would whoever had shot Ginny come back to the lodge without being sure that he could get in?

One interesting difference between professional and amateur killers is that professionals don't like chance.

I didn't get to pursue the question, however. Before Lara reached the doorway, Sam came into the hall from the den.

He had his bag with him.

Connie held him by one arm as if she were leading him along.

As soon as I saw him, I forgot knives and hints. Suddenly I cared about nothing except what Sam could do for Ginny.

He came forward with the unsteady gait and aimless movements of a man who'd lost his essential balance. In some way, he seemed dependent on Connie's grip. But none of us had to tell him what Ginny needed. As he reached her, he said in a husky voice, "Get some light." Then he pushed Hardhouse aside to kneel beside her.

No one else moved, so Hardhouse went looking for a light switch.

To no one in particular, Connie said, "Mr. Altar and I heard Mrs. Hardhouse cry out. We didn't know what had happened, of course, but we could guess that Dr. Drayton would be required. It was difficult to persuade him to leave his wife. But Mr. Altar volunteered to stay with her while I brought Dr. Drayton here. He's there now."

Alibis again. Connie and Rock could vouch for each other. If they weren't both guilty, they were both innocent.

At the end of the hall, Hardhouse found a switch. When he flipped it, the lights came on. The gloom disappeared so fast that the hallway seemed to blaze.

No burned-out bulbs. Someone had deliberately ditched the lights.

Sam inspected Ginny's back. To improve his view, he stuck two fingers through the cut in her shirt and ripped the material away. Because of Hardhouse's pressure—or because the knife hadn't hit anything vital—she'd stopped bleeding, and her shirt had soaked up the blood. I had a good view of the wound. It looked minor and insidious, too small to be dangerous, too ugly to be ignored.

It pulled me down to the floor again, on my knees across from Sam, as if I might see what it meant if I looked at it hard enough.

Whoever had tried to kill her was definitely an amateur.

Tearing open swabs and syringes, Sam asked, "Is that the knife?"

I still had it in my hand. Instead of answering, I showed it to him.

His eyes were dull, pulled down at the corners by anguish, and his skin had a cheesy color that didn't suit his handsome features. But he was still a doctor. After a glance at the knife, he muttered, "Doesn't look like it went in deep enough," and began to work.

"Don't you want to know what I think?" Ginny rasped. "I think it went in fucking far enough."

Sam ignored her. She swore under her breath for a moment. Then he used a syringe to squeeze antiseptic down into the cut, and she flinched involuntarily. But she didn't protest.

"Ginny." I knew she was in no position to answer questions, but I had to try. "Did you see anything? Hear anything? When did the lights go off? Do you know who stabbed you?"

"No!" she gasped as Sam probed at her shoulder. "The light was out the whole time. I didn't mind. I thought I could use the cover. But that sonofabitch got me easy. Like I was one of the Ladies Auxiliary. All I had to do was turn around, and this damn case would be over."

"If you'd turned around," Sam retorted with unexpected vehemence, "the knife might've gone straight into your heart. You're already luckier than you deserve."

"So that proves it," Hardhouse commented as if we were all talking to him. "The killer isn't one of us. It has to be someone we don't know—someone still hiding in the lodge."

"Perhaps you would care to explain yourself, Mr. Hardhouse." Connie's tone didn't express confidence. Her own anger ran deep, and she made it clear that she meant to draw her own conclusions. "How do you arrive at that deduction?"

"Simple." The worse the situation got, the more assurance he seemed to feel. "We don't need to consider the Carbones or Faith Jerrick. Reeson explained why we can trust them. That leaves the rest of us. In fact, it only leaves those of us right here. Maryanne, Houston, and Buffy are together in the den—with Faith. None of them could have stabbed Ginny.

"And Brew was in the den as well. Weren't you, Brew?"

He didn't wait for an answer. "Sam's an unlikely candidate in any case," he continued. "And you and Rock can vouch for him. He was in his room when you went to get him. Similarly, the rest of us can vouch for you. Assuming you attacked Ginny, there are only two ways you could have reached Sam's room from here—the two exits from the hall. One would take you through the den. Past Brew. The other would take you outside. You didn't have time for that.

"As for Lara and me—neither of us could have committed the other murders. And we were together until just moments before she found Ginny. I can tell you she didn't have time to stab Ginny. In fact, I can tell you she didn't have a knife with her.

"That's everybody." Hardhouse spread his hands. "We're all accounted for. The killer isn't one of us." He paused suggestively. "He must be hiding in one of the rooms in this wing. Unless he's opened a window and gone outside."

His explanation sounded too persuasive—so persuasive that I dismissed it completely. But I didn't have time to react. Before I could take hold of what the back of my brain was trying to tell me, we all heard a pounding noise. Again.

A noise like someone knocking on a door.

Knocking hard.

It came from the direction of the den.

At the same instant, Buffy let out a squeal of fright.

Connie and Lara turned to the sound. Growling, "Now what?" Hardhouse started toward the den. Even Sam raised his head. He looked confused, as if he'd forgotten what he was doing.

Ginny twisted over onto her side. "Brew." Her right hand clamped onto my wrist. "Stay close," she whispered. "I need to talk to you."

Then she added, "Find my gun. I dropped it."

Somehow I hadn't realized that I was kneeling virtually on top of her .357.

I picked it up. With her hand on my wrist and my arm across her back, we climbed to our feet. I wanted to stop there, put both arms around her, let the acid burn through me. But my fists were full of weapons, and the pounding hadn't stopped.

Leaning on each other, we stumbled into motion.

"I'm not done," Sam remarked as if he didn't expect either of us to care.

"Come on," I told him over my shoulder. I didn't want him left alone. But Ginny and I kept moving.

By the time we reached the den, Hardhouse had already taken it on himself to open the door.

Arthur Reeson stood outside.

He looked like he'd just completed a forty-mile trek through four feet of snow.

22

He didn't come in. When he saw me with the .357 in one hand and a bloody knife in the other, he stopped on the doorsill.

All in all, we must've presented an interesting picture. Ginny was obviously injured. Sam did a pretty convincing imitation of a derelict. Mile hadn't stopped struggling against his bonds. The gag made him look apoplectic. Maryanne was obviously delighted to see Reeson, who represented rescue, but Buffy gaped at him as if she didn't know if he came from heaven or hell. And I couldn't manage anything more intelligent than to drop my jaw and stare. Only Connie, Lara, and Joseph didn't appear to have been traumatized during Reeson's absence.

"Art!" Faith cried. She ran to him, flung herself into his arms, and kissed him ravenously.

"Did you get through?" Hardhouse demanded with aggressive good cheer. "Is help on the way? We're dropping like flies around here."

Reeson eyed me past Faith's shoulder. Still hugging her, he opened his hands to show me they were empty. As soon as she finished kissing him, he gave me a quizzical smile—which reminded me I'd never liked his smile.

"May I come in?"

Behind him wind blew across the valley. The sky had stayed clear, but the light was fading. Dusk cast Deerskin Lodge into shadow. He'd been gone for less than a day.

Like Hardhouse, I wondered if he'd summoned help.

"If you don't"—Ginny's voice was almost as hoarse as Reeson's—"we'll all freeze to death."

Hell, I'd freeze to death if I just had to look at Reeson's smile much longer.

He nodded. Disentangling himself from Faith, he shrugged the pack off his shoulders and dropped it on the porch. Still watching Ginny and me, he dusted most of the snow off his legs.

Then he came in.

Faith closed the door for him. With tears bright in her eyes and an uncharacteristic flush on her cheeks, she hung at his side.

He unbuttoned his coat smoothly. "Maybe," he said, trying to be helpful, "you'd better tell me what's happened."

"Maybe," Ginny retorted harshly, "you'd better tell us if you got through. You're back early."

His smile had a faintly maniacal twist, but his voice remained steady. "If you think I'd come back without doing what I said I would, you don't know me very well. Ordinarily, I'd take offense. But I can see you haven't been having an easy time.

"Yes, I got through. There's a cabin five miles from here. Some city guy—an artist, I think—uses it in the summer." He shrugged. "I broke in to check the phone. It worked. The sheriff is on his way. He'll be here as soon as a plow opens the road."

Buffy gasped a sob of relief. Maryanne sat down suddenly, as if the strings of fear which kept her on her feet had been cut. Staring like he couldn't believe his ears, Mile stopped trying to work the gag loose.

"Thank God," Connie said succinctly.

"There's a lot of road to clear," Reeson warned. "Help won't arrive until sometime tomorrow."

We were still in trouble.

Apparently. Hardhouse didn't realize that. Hurrying for

some other reason, he took Lara by the arm and drew her away from the door. "We'll go tell Rock and Queenie the good news." Without any sign of protest from his wife, he swept her out of the den.

"Are they—?" Sam had to struggle to clear his throat. "Are they bringing an ambulance? Paramedics? I need more IV Valium. She's still in a coma."

Reeson started to ask a question, but he thought better of it when he looked at Sam. "An ambulance, yes," he answered, "for the woman who got shot. Catherine Reverie. I don't know about paramedics."

Then he added, "The sheriff has a radio. So do the plows. When they arrive, the road will be open. They can get what you need up here in an hour."

Faith gripped his arm so tightly that the cords in the backs of her hands showed. She seemed to consider him a better anchor than her religion.

"I need them today." Sam didn't look at any of us. "By tomorrow she might be dead."

That was too much for Reeson. "Who?" he demanded. "What's happened? I can't do anything about it if you don't tell me what's going on."

Out of the corner of my eye, I saw Mile's gag drop free.

"*God,* Reeson!" he spat at once, "you took your sweet time gettin' here. We got us a killer on the loose. Broke Westward's neck, ditched Abel somewhere, took a shot at Fistoulari, poisoned Drayton's wife. And these sons a bitches won't let me defend mahself. Get these ropes off me! Tomorrow ain't near fast enough. We need *guns.* Before he tries again."

Reflexively we all watched Reeson. He had that kind of effect on people—he made us want to see what he would do.

He was surprised, I'll give him that. He couldn't have known what had happened to us, and he showed it. At least we got his frown back, which relieved my sense that he was about to explode. His eyebrows did a quirky little dance, up and down, up and down. "My, my." His voice sounded like someone had tried to strangle him a while back, and he hadn't fully recovered. "We do live in interesting times, don't we?"

"And you don't have any idea who did all this?"

For some reason, Mile let the question pass. In unison, Buffy and Maryanne shook their heads. But Ginny's face was blank—studiously blank, like a mask—and I kept my thoughts to myself.

"Offhand," Reeson commented to me, "I'd say the ghouls and beasties are coming out of the woodwork." Like an acknowledgment of Buffy's distress and Sam's shock, he added, "With a vengeance."

Vengeance. Another unexpected hint. Not that Reeson meant to hint at anything, of course. He was just talking. Nevertheless a little shiver of recognition ran through my brain.

As far as I knew, no one here had anything to do with vengeance. Except me.

El Señor's revenge.

Reeson scanned the room again. "Where are the Carbones?"

Faith started to answer, but right on cue Ama and Truchi appeared from the dining room. Neither of them indicated any surprise at Reeson's arrival. Truchi simply nodded. Ama muttered quietly, "It's about time," and folded her arms under her bosom. Together, she and her husband took up their deferential stations against one of the walls.

"We need to talk about this," Ginny told Reeson abruptly. As if she'd reached a decision, she stopped leaning on me. "I'm in no mood for an audience. Let's go to the office."

Deliberately, so that everyone could see her, she took her .357 from me. Ignoring the pain in her shoulder—never mind the fact that Sam wasn't done with her—she hefted the gun, checked to be sure it was loaded.

Just for a second, Reeson's frown flicked into a smile. Then he resumed his dark, contented scowl and nodded. "Sure."

To Faith, he said, "These people want supper. They just don't know it yet. Maybe you'd better get started."

He and I both knew she wouldn't argue with him. A woman who looked at him like that wasn't about to argue.

"Let's go," he said to Ginny.

"Good." Without hesitation, she headed across the den toward the office.

I followed. The shiver in my brain grew stronger. It seemed to feed on anger and medication.

After two steps, however, Ginny turned back. Pointing her claw at Mile, she commanded Maryanne, "Don't untie him. I don't want him loose. If he drives you crazy, gag him again."

Then she left the den.

Reeson and I didn't hang around to hear Mile's response.

To all appearances, no one had been in the office since Rock and I sat there the first night of the camp—except, of course, to latch and cover the window. I raised the blind for confirmation, saw that the latch remained securely shut. I didn't know where the light switches were, so I left the blind up for a little extra illumination.

The room itself smelled vaguely musty, disused. When Reeson snapped on the lights, we could see that nothing had been disturbed—no covert ransacking of the filing cabinets, no scrabbling through the desk. Apparently none of our murderers needed to know the things they could've learned here.

The artificial light emphasized the mismatch between the dark desk and chairs and the blond paneling and floorboards. That discrepancy reminded me of my strange conversation here with Rock—listening to him tell me that he didn't want to stir up trouble about the guns—hearing him talk about Smithsonian.

The back of my brain churned, bitter as bile. I wanted something to hit.

I should've pulled the blind down again, but I forgot.

Emphasizing her authority, Ginny went around the desk and sat in the big armchair. That left Reeson and me to argue over the less comfortable seating arrangements.

He pulled up a chair in front of the desk. I thought about doing the same, but the pressure of Sam's injection kept me on my feet. Instead of sitting, I went to the wall behind Ginny, beside the window, and propped myself there. Reminding Reeson that I was on her side.

Reeson still wore his coat. Under it he had on a bulky insulated vest that all by itself looked warm enough to keep out a blizzard. Facing Ginny, he unpopped several of the snaps. His hands seemed to function independent of his attention.

"So," he said, "this Houston Mile had something to do with it."

Ginny rolled her chair forward so that she could lean her arms on the desktop. With that wound in her shoulder, she must have found it hard to hold the gun. As if to let Reeson know that the .357 wasn't intended for him, she put it down on the big blotter that covered half the desk.

"No." She did her best to sound clear, but I heard the strain in her voice. "If anything, I'm sure he *isn't* involved. He's just dangerous. He's a coward. He wants to blow people away before they get a chance to threaten him."

"Does that mean you don't know anything?" Reeson asked. Somehow he managed not to sound critical. "You don't have any ideas? You haven't found any"—despite his careful tone, his pause gave the word a little sneer—"clues?"

"Oh, we have enough evidence to convict a truckload of murderers." From where I stood, I couldn't see Ginny's face, but her tense posture made her look like she was engaged in some kind of contest with Reeson. "We just don't know what it all means."

He lifted his shoulders in a small shrug. "I can't help if you don't tell me about it."

She nodded curtly. "I'll give you the short form."

Outside night came down fast as the mountains cut off the light.

"A while after you left, Brew took a nap in the den. Someone dropped rat poison in the fireplace. Nearly asphyxiated him."

The world was growing as dark as when Cat was shot. The lights in the office seemed unnatural, fragile somehow, like you couldn't trust them.

"When we checked the wine cellar, Simon Abel was gone. Someone broke him out through the wall. We haven't seen him since. But he left a trail in the snow, so I followed it. Got shot for my trouble." She pointed at her temple.

"While I was gone, Mac Westward had too much to drink at lunch. He went to his room to sleep it off. Someone went into his room and broke his neck. When I—"

"Wait a minute," Reeson interrupted. "*While* you were gone? How could somebody shoot you outside and still be inside breaking Westward's neck?"

"Interesting question," Ginny drawled acerbically. "If you think of an answer, let me know."

Soon the light inside and the dark outside blinded the window. The glass looked opaque, like the surface of a black pool. Anything could happen out there now, and we wouldn't be able to do anything about it.

"When I got back," she continued, "Queenie Drayton decided she needed a drink. It was poisoned. She went into a seizure."

Obliquely I noticed that Ginny didn't identify the drink. Her caution may've been unnecessary, but I approved anyway.

"We thought the killer had to be somewhere in the lodge, so we organized a search. While we were doing that, someone came up behind me and stuck a knife in my shoulder.

"So far we've lost Cat, Simon, and Mac, and Queenie may die."

Ginny stopped.

Reeson's eyebrows did their dance on his forehead. The moral equivalent of whistling in surprise. First he said, "None of this makes sense." Then he asked, "What's your 'evidence'?"

"I'll give you an example." Shock and loss of blood frayed her voice. She sounded like she had the same fever I did. "Brew, this is what I wanted to talk to you about." She didn't glance at me. "I think I know how Queenie was poisoned."

Reeson and I both listened. Judging by appearances, however, he paid more attention than I did. Fury and chemicals made a witch's brew in my blood, and the cauldron's seething consumed most of my brain. I'd already missed my chance to save Queenie. If I didn't start to think effectively, I'd continue missing vital connections and clues until we all died for it.

"Before I was stabbed, I had time to search two rooms, Mile's and Lara's. I didn't find anything useful in his. But in hers"—she paused to focus her anger—"I found cocaine. A lot of it."

The cauldron bubbled and spat. Coke might explain a lot of Lara Hardhouse's behavior.

"Do you know what happens," Ginny demanded, "when you get a massive overdose of cocaine? You go into seizure. Every one of your muscles locks up. You can't even breathe. Even if your heart doesn't fail from shock, you die because you get no air. Or you collapse into a coma because of the brain damage."

She sounded quietly savage, too angry to suffer her own despair. "But we know Lara isn't the killer. Brew was with her when Mac died."

I couldn't suffer it myself. My heart felt as black and blind as the window, and I'd come to the end of what I could endure. Window latches and port. Vengeance and wine cellars. And something else that might boil to the surface any second now.

"I'll give you another example," I said harshly. "Another useful bit of 'evidence.' We know that shot wasn't aimed at Cat. It was aimed at me."

Reeson cocked his head. His scowl flickered on the edge of a smile.

"A goon called el Señor wants me dead. And he's got his hooks into a private investigator named Lawrence Smithsonian. You've heard of Smithsonian. He arranged this job for us. He even called me while I was in the hospital, trying to scare us into taking this job.

"Why do you suppose he did that? I think he wanted to set us up. He knew el Señor could have me killed when I got here."

"I wouldn't know anything about that," Reeson answered noncommittally. "But it doesn't make sense. It doesn't explain why Westward was killed, or why Mrs. Drayton was poisoned."

He didn't mention Simon. I noticed that.

"Because," I said.

Window latches and port. Vengeance and wine cellars. Coke aimed at Cat had poisoned Queenie, I couldn't argue with that. And Lara Hardhouse had cocaine. But it was an amateur job, dependent on chance. The dose had to be enough, or the treatment had to be wrong, or the treatment had to come too late. And Mac's murder relied on chance. Connie could've walked into the room at any moment. And the knife in Ginny's back was another amateur job, rank with chance and luck.

But—

Any killer hired by el Señor wouldn't trust chance. He

wouldn't shoot Ginny and then run down to the lodge in broad daylight just *hoping* that someone had left a window unlatched. Too many things could go wrong. First he'd make sure Ginny was dead. If she hadn't played dead trying to trap him, he would've finished her. Then he'd take all the time he needed to come back carefully.

"Because," I said, "we have more than one killer."

Instinctively Ginny twisted in her chair to stare at me.

A smile twitched Reeson's mouth, and his eyebrows worked.

"One of them is el Señor's hit man," I told her. "He shot Cat and you, broke Simon out of the wine cellar, put rat poison down the chimney. The other killed Mac and doped Cat's drink and stabbed you."

Out of an obscure sympathy for vulnerable women, I added, "It doesn't have to be Lara. Anyone who searched her room could've found that coke and used it. Or someone could've planted it in her room. Like the rifle in Simon's closet.

"But there have to be two of them. Mile is right about that. An amateur and a professional. The pro wants me. The amateur is just trying to take advantage of the confusion."

Then I had it. The cauldron spat in my face so hard that I nearly went blind, and the room started turning on its axis, changing the meaning of everything. But I had it.

Facing Reeson with blood in my throat and no strength left, I said, "You never went for help. There's no help coming. After you tried to shoot me and hit Cat, you decided to get away from the scene so that we wouldn't connect you with whatever happened next. And you wanted to keep your freedom of movement. But you didn't go anywhere. You freed Simon from the wine cellar and ditched his body and shot Ginny, and now you're back to finish the job."

Until I saw Ginny's stunned expression, I didn't understand how much trouble—personal trouble—she'd had with this case. It wasn't just a matter of being shot and stabbed. Or of having her wounded partner wander around like the universal victim. Her fear of el Señor and her involvement with Hardhouse got in her way. She actually didn't seem to grasp the implications of what I said.

"Axbrewder," Reeson murmured gently, "the ghouls and beasties are getting the better of you. You'll look pretty foolish when the sheriff gets here."

Ginny swiveled slowly to face him. He didn't take his eyes off me, however, and a moment later she swiveled back. Her gaze was fractured and uncertain. It reminded me of the way she'd looked after she first lost her hand. Uneasily she asked, "How do you know all that?"

Pain throbbed through my stomach. I wanted to jump Reeson, but I knew I couldn't. I didn't let myself meet his gaze.

"The killer has to be someone who works here. Someone with inside information about the lodge. That's obvious." So obvious that it hadn't occurred to me until a moment ago. "But the Carbones and Faith never go anywhere. El Señor couldn't use a hired killer who lived up here all the time. That leaves Reeson. He takes vacations and doesn't even tell Faith where he's going."

Ginny shook her head. "Slow down. Back up. Why is it obvious? Even if you're right about two killers, why does either of them need inside information?"

The throb expanded. I heard an odd rushing noise like a gale chewing on the trees around Deerskin Lodge. Too much pain and infection and anger—too much medication. The gale seemed to crowd the edges of my vision, contracting my field of view.

"Because of the rat poison."

Ginny's mouth shaped the words, *rat poison,* but no sound came out.

"No one knew it was there except the people who work

here. Anyone who wasn't personally familiar with Deer-skin Lodge on a day-to-day basis wouldn't have known there was rat poison available. Or known where to find it.

"Reeson is the only candidate."

Darkness tightened around my vision like a noose, but I still saw Reeson get to his feet. Ginny flung her chair back to face him, but she was too slow. He picked up her revolver. Just for a second, he smiled at it disapprovingly, as if it weren't good enough for him. Then he reached into his vest and brought out his own gun.

I recognized it right away. It was one of the guns missing from the dining room, a Ruger .357 Magnum. The kind of weapon that can powder your bones and spray your blood for ten yards in all directions.

When he pointed it at her, Ginny froze. I would've frozen myself, but I was already immobilized. If I took my weight off the wall, I'd crumble.

"You don't think very highly of my intelligence, Axbrewder," he commented amiably. "I'm the one who first suggested the wine cellar. Why did I do that, if I wanted something out of it? Why didn't I get the rat poison before I let you put Abel in there?"

"You didn't know you'd need it." My voice came out of the wind. "But that's not the main reason. Mostly you wanted to frame Simon—make him look guilty when he broke out, so that we wouldn't think of anything else. And if we hadn't already locked him up, you couldn't have broken through the wall to get the poison. That would've been too obvious.

"Professionals don't usually take chances, but of course that isn't always true." Now that I'd started talking, I couldn't stop, even if I wanted to. Once the room began to turn, I had to ride the spin until it ended. "They need opportunity, just like the rest of us. When you saw Simon go out for a walk, you grabbed an opportunity.

"You were already outside with that rifle, watching the

lodge for a shot at me. You'd already taken the guns, mostly to create confusion, make everyone look guilty— but also so that your weapon couldn't be traced to you. The random assortment was a smoke screen. You wanted the killer to look like someone who didn't really know what he was doing, an amateur.

"Simon gave you part of your chance. You knew he was one of the actors—you handled the reservations for Murder on Cue. Once you saw Cat and me in the parlor, you had everything you needed."

With every angle and muscle, Ginny focused on Reeson.

"But Simon's window was latched," I continued. "That didn't leave you much time. You had to run inside by one of the back doors and go out through his window. Then you shot at me and hit Cat instead. So you dumped the rifle in Simon's closet and left again, leaving the window open— another ploy to make him look guilty. And you didn't have time to do anything else.

"So you took a chance. That's OK. You're smart—you took a smart chance. You're just not a very good shot. So now you had to arrange another opportunity.

"That's why you pulled down the phone line, disabled the vehicles. To give yourself an excuse to go for help. Only you didn't go anywhere. You hiked out of sight and then sneaked back. When you were sure the way was clear, you reached the lodge and got up on the roof. From the roof, there's probably a way into the attic—and from the attic there are probably knotholes and gaps that let you watch some of the rooms. The den, anyway.

"The way this place is built, nothing creaks. We wouldn't hear you up there."

Reeson did me the courtesy of looking mildly impressed.

"My nap in the den gave you another opportunity. You broke Simon out of the wine cellar, killed him, and took the rat poison. You dropped the box down the chimney and packed it with snow. Then you carried Simon up into the hills, leaving a nice plain trail to make us think he was on the run. After that, you waited to see if you were followed. You wanted me, of course, but you didn't mind getting Ginny out of the way while you had the chance. El Señor sure as hell wouldn't object.

"Unfortunately after you shot her you didn't get any more opportunities. You were out in the hills, and I was here. You waited for a while in case you got lucky again, like you did with Simon, but when the day was almost over and nothing solved your problem for you, you came back to tell us that we were about to be rescued. That way, you could be sure that you'd get another chance at me."

Then I was finished. I'd come to the end of words. And I had no other weapons. The gale rushed closer, stalking me by increments, and I knew that I wouldn't be on my feet much longer.

Fortunately Ginny took up the struggle. I'd given her time to recover her grasp of the situation. "Too bad you're stuck now," she put in grimly. "Everybody knows where you are. When you shoot us, they won't need to guess who did it. Then you'll have to kill them all. Or go on the run. And a hit man on the run won't be much use to el Señor. In fact, he may decide to have *you* killed, just in case you think the cops might trade immunity for testimony.

"You're out of opportunities, Reeson. Put the guns down. Give it up while you still can."

"Oh, I don't think so." His frown looked as secure as his grip on the guns. "After I shoot you, I'll just yell for help. I'll say you were shot through the window. Luckily Axbrewder was kind enough to pull up the blind. Before anybody questions me, I'll go after the killer. When I come back with Abel's body—not to mention his fingerprints on this gun"—he indicated the Ruger—"there won't be any-one around to contradict me.

"Look at it this way. After wrestling for all these years with the things that haunt you, and not doing very well at it, you'll finally be at peace."

He had a point. I couldn't deny that. If he gave a shout and then jumped out through the window, no one would ever know that the glass had no bullet holes. The rest would be easy.

I had to do something. This was my job, the work Ginny paid me for—this was why she had a partner in the first place. Whether she still loved me or not didn't matter anymore. I was sick of all the things I blamed myself for, sick of being pushed around by circumstances, sick of making excuses. And I'd made a promise to myself.

I'd promised that I would *get* this bastard.

I had to do *something*.

Nevertheless I was helpless—which nearly broke my heart. At my best, I couldn't have pulled out the .45 and shot Reeson before he killed both of us. On top of that, I didn't have the strength to fight him, even if I could've reached him before he fired. The gale gathered in the room, and darkness squeezed my vision down to a tunnel barely big enough to include both Reeson and Ginny, and I was helpless.

Ginny was about to die because of me.

At that moment, I stopped being angry. The spin of the room carried all the fury out of my bones. El Señor and Smithsonian and Reeson no longer enraged me. I wasn't even angry at myself.

I simply couldn't endure letting Ginny die.

She slid her hand and her claw off the desktop into her lap and bowed forward as if she were beaten and couldn't hide it anymore, I did the only thing I could think of.

I collapsed.

Rolling my eyes, I toppled toward the corner of the desk like a man in a dead faint.

It worked.

Damn near got us both blown away.

My tumble caught Reeson's attention, snagged his eyes away from Ginny. Instinctively he lined up both guns on me. If I hadn't been falling, he would've shot me then.

I only distracted him for an instant. But during that instant Ginny reached under the desk, found the Smith & Wesson .44 I'd discovered four days ago, and hauled it out.

In a voice like a gunshot, she yelled, *"Stop!"*

Reeson stopped. His weapons were directed at me, and she had an absolutely unobstructed shot at the center of his chest. That .44 was no Magnum, but at this range it had the power to drive his heart out through his back.

He didn't know what I knew.

Too bad she didn't, either. I hadn't told her that the gun was empty—that I'd taken out the shells.

But *he* didn't know, that was the crucial thing. With any luck at all, he might take five or ten seconds to figure it out. The .44 was a revolver. As soon as he got a good look at it, he would see that the cylinder held no shells.

Ginny and I had that long to live.

Fortunately I was moving faster than I could think.

Snatching up my hands, I caught myself on the corner of the desk. But from there I didn't go around the desk at Reeson. If I tried that, he'd shoot me, no matter what Ginny did. A survival reflex. And then he'd be safe.

Instead I shoved my weight backward with every atom of stubbornness and need I could muster.

Whirling, I dove headfirst through the window.

Out into the dark and the deep snow.

23

I landed in a shower of shattered glass and a splash of cold, but I didn't notice either of them. The impact drove the air out of my lungs and turned my guts into a howling blast of pain.

Would've been worse if the snow hadn't been so thick.

Familiar, all of it. Just a few days ago, I'd gone through a window into snow to get at Muy Estobal—and I'd done it so that I could save Ginny. Even the gale exploding inside me, raking my nerves with agony, was the same.

And we were up against more than one killer. That was similar, too.

Everything else had changed.

For one thing, Reeson probably wouldn't let me sneak up behind him and crush his larynx.

For another—

Any second now, he'd lean out the window and blow my head off. I had to get moving right now, *right now.*

I scrabbled my legs and arms under me. Shedding clumps of snow as if I'd climbed out of a winter grave, I heaved myself upright. I still couldn't breathe, but I didn't have time to worry about that. *Get out of the light.* The glow from the window seemed to etch me where I stood—a dummy set out for target practice. Stumbling frantically, I flung myself at the wall and collided my way along it as fast as I could go.

Toward the front of the lodge.

"Axbrewder!"

Reeson's shout hit me hard. I almost stopped.

If I'd stopped, he would've gotten me. He must've known where I was. He could see my trail—he could probably hear me against the wall.

But the light of the office and the dark outside blinded him temporarily, just for a couple of heartbeats.

I plunged ahead.

Then I dropped back into the snow around the corner of the porch and lay there gasping for breath, retching at the pain.

He hadn't fired.

"Axbrewder!" His hoarse shout sounded like a cry of despair. *"Come back! I've got her! Come back or I'll kill her!"*

Ginny—

Wait your fucking turn, you sonofabitch!

I got up again. Supporting myself on the edge of the porch, I went for the front door.

I knew exactly what I had to do. You've got to draw the line somewhere. I drew it at letting him shoot Ginny.

Which might not be under my control, of course. I'd killed Muy Estobal. I'd brought el Señor's vengeance here without understanding it. Those things had consequences.

But Reeson's real violence was directed at me, not Ginny. He held her hostage to get at me.

While he did that, I had a chance.

He could kill her at any time. Under the circumstances, he might decide to do his job by eliminating the survivors, the witnesses. Naturally he'd start with her.

I had to get to him before he made that decision.

And I had one advantage that he probably didn't realize.

He knew I was hurt, but he didn't know *me*. He couldn't begin to guess how far I was willing to go.

He might let Ginny live a little longer because he wasn't afraid of me.

Your turn is coming, Reeson. Just wait for it.

I reached the front steps. The way I went up them should've made a racket, but the snow muffled my feet.

Ginny needed to do a hell of a balancing act. She had to convince Reeson that he needed a hostage. Make him think that I still had the strength to threaten him. If I were unconscious out in the snow somewhere, he could afford to kill her. At the same time, however, she didn't want to rush him into a decision—which meant she had to give him the impression that I was too stupid, or too crazy, to surprise him. If she could find that balance, she might buy herself a little time.

I skidded gracelessly across the porch and hauled at the front door.

Thank God and all His Angels, no one had thought to relock the door after Reeson came in.

A rush of heat nearly dropped me to my knees. Maybe because he didn't know what else to do with himself while his wife and Faith prepared supper, Truchi had built up the fires to a roar. Compared to the cold outside, the den felt like an oven.

But I didn't have time for warmth. Swinging the door shut hard to preserve my momentum, I headed through the den as fast as I could, approximately running.

The place seemed unusually empty. Only Carbone and Mile and Maryanne were there. I didn't try to guess where everyone else was, but I could see why Houston Mile and his "filly" had remained. No one had untied him. And Maryanne had shoved the gag back in his mouth. She'd resumed talking to him, sitting knee to knee with him as if this were an insidious form of torture.

Now, however, what she said brought an entirely different expression to his piggy eyes. Her hands were on his thighs, and her fingers seemed to be probing his crotch.

Apparently she was trying to get back into his good graces the only way she knew how.

I'd already passed the tree and had almost reached the dining room hallway when I heard her cry, "Brew?" Not scared yet, not the way she used to be. Nevertheless a little lift of panic in her voice betrayed her fragility. "Why did you come in that way? What's going on?"

"Later."

I didn't wait to see how she took my rebuff. The last thing I needed right then was people following me, asking frightened questions.

The hallway. The dining room. Both empty.

The hall to the kitchen.

There I found Faith Jerrick.

Alone.

She stood at the cooktop, stirring a big four-quart soup kettle. The air held a persistent suggestion of gas. I'd expected to find Amalia as well, but apparently she had other duties. Desperately I hoped that she and Truchi would stay out of my way. I needed people out of my way. Especially the Carbones, who were probably sane. Anyone who retained a substantial amount of sanity wouldn't like what I had in mind.

Faith absolutely wouldn't like it.

I did it anyway.

The fluorescent lighting made the countertops and appliances gleam feverishly, like a hallucination. All the utensils looked sharp as knives, and the huge Hobart resembled a gas chamber for roasting martyrs. Bracing myself from surface to surface, I advanced around the counters toward Faith.

She raised a brief glance as high as my chin, then returned her gaze to her soup. Cream of tomato. It had the sickly reddish shade you get when you don't put in enough milk.

"Mr. Axbrewder," she said, "where's Art?" Only her voice betrayed the fact that she didn't give a damn about the soup. Her real attention was fixed on me. "I thought you would be done talking by now. I've made some soup." The pot steamed, full of simmering. "I can make sandwiches in a minute. What is Art doing?"

Her appearance—the deferential and passionate line of her neck, the clarity of her skin, the self-contained extravagance in her eyes—made me think that what I had in mind just might be terrible enough to succeed.

"Faith."

In an odd way, she daunted me. Just for a second, I couldn't go on. She was one of the innocent. She didn't deserve the kind of damage I intended.

But I had no choice. I needed help. Too many people had already died, most of them innocent. And more might follow.

"Yes?" she offered.

Groping for a way to approach her, I asked the first question that came into my head. "Do you ever talk to Art about the guests? Did you tell him that Catherine Reverie liked port?"

"No." She allowed herself to look mildly startled. "Why would I? He has his own concerns. And the guests have a right to their privacy. Ama feels the same way. We haven't discussed Miss Reverie's habits with anyone."

So. Arthur Reeson hadn't poisoned Queenie. He hadn't killed Mac or stabbed Ginny. At some point—if I lived long enough—I'd have to face that problem. But not now. First things first.

Ginny always said that. She believed in tackling crises in some kind of logical order.

"You told me once," I floundered on as if I weren't changing the subject, "that Art doesn't take you when he goes on vacation. And you don't know what he does when he's away."

Well, at least we were talking about Art. That relieved her chagrin at my strange manner. Softly she said, "That's right."

"How often does he go? How many vacations does he take a year?"

For a woman who had God's company during Reeson's

absences, she was remarkably prompt with the answer. "Never more than eight. Usually five or six." Then she let her curiosity get the better of her. "Why do you ask?"

Five or six *vacations* a year. Christ! How many people had he hit?

"Faith," I repeated. I didn't falter now—but I didn't attack her either. I was as gentle as my pain, and my fear that I'd hear shots, allowed. "Arthur Reeson shot Cat. He tried to kill me. He tried to kill Ginny. Now he's holding her hostage in the office. He's been hired to kill me. If I don't go back in there, he'll kill her.

"I want you to come talk to him."

Be *my* hostage, Faith. Give me something I can trade for Ginny's life.

She didn't flush. She had blood and passion in her, but not for that. And she didn't turn pale. She was already about as pale as she could get. And she didn't look at me. She had no need to see who I was. She just went completely still, like a small animal in a corner. Her hand stopped stirring the soup. As far as I could tell, she stopped breathing.

"You never asked him what he does with his vacations. Or why he needs so *many* of them." Urgently I pleaded with her. "You never asked him why he's content with a job like this—a man like him isolated out here, with so much competence and so little need for it.

"I'll tell you why. He's a professional killer. When he goes on vacation, he kills people. And then he comes back here because it's isolated and safe, and no one questions him.

"I told you about el Señor. You were there when I talked about him. He wants me dead, I told you why. He hired Art to kill me." I wasn't on a first-name basis with Reeson. I faked it for her. "When he shot Cat, he was trying to hit me. She got in the way.

"He doesn't want Ginny. She's not his target. But he'll gladly kill her to get at me."

Would Faith ever breathe again? I couldn't tell. In her shocked stillness, she might've been transformed to alabaster, or a pillar of salt, or whatever it is you turn into when you look back on degradation and ruin. She should've prayed, clutched her crucifix and beseeched God. Or at least called me a liar, yelled at me somehow. But she didn't. The soup under her ladle seethed in spots. Before long, it would boil, and if she didn't stir it it would scald. Without moving a muscle, she gave the impression that I'd kicked out the bottom of her heart.

"I need your help." I didn't raise my voice, despite my desperation. I feared that I'd miss the sound of his Ruger. And I didn't want to treat Faith like an enemy, responsible in some way for Reeson's violence. I drew the line at letting Ginny get killed—but I drew it here, too. "I want you to talk to him. If he knows that you know what he's doing, he might stop."

No, that wasn't enough, it wasn't the truth. And she deserved the truth. Now more than ever before in her life she deserved it.

"You're the only one here he cares about. I want to use you to save Ginny. I want to trade you for her."

A quiver plucked at the corner of her mouth. She couldn't accuse me of lying about her lover. She didn't know *how*. Lies had no place in her life with God. To me the little spasm in her cheek looked like the first faint tremor of an earthquake, a shattering upheaval. She was so still, so needy— That minor vibration would be enough to break her.

I fought for quietness, kept my voice gentle. I didn't intend to browbeat her with my own need.

"If you can't help me," I said, "I don't know what else to do. He's only keeping Ginny alive so that he can use her against me. If I don't give him what he wants, he'll kill her. But even if I let him have me, he'll kill her. She's a witness. He can't let her go.

"And that isn't the end of it. He'll have to kill everyone. When I escaped from the office, I doomed you all. He doesn't know where I've been, who I've talked to. He can't trust anyone now. Not even Truchi and Ama." I choked convulsively. "Not even you."

Abruptly the quiver spread across her cheek, ran down her neck to her shoulders. Her hands began to shake. Twitching, she let go of the ladle. It clattered dully against the side of the kettle—her distress only made that one sound, and most of it was muffled by the soup.

With the least amount of movement possible, using only the parts of her that were absolutely necessary, she turned away.

Between the counters, she headed for the back door.

Away from the office.

Toward her cottage.

Oh, Ginny.

If I were sane, I wouldn't have told Faith anything. I would've simply said that Reeson wanted to see her in the office. But if I were sane, I wouldn't have been here in the first place. I would've found a better answer to my life, one that didn't involve asking the innocent to pay for my mistakes. Turning her back on me, Faith abandoned Ginny as well, but I had no right to complain. I had nothing to complain about.

She went slowly toward the door. For a moment, I couldn't move. Darkness filled my head, and pain cramped my heart, and walking away she used up all the movement in the room, all the decision.

Reeson might shoot Ginny any time now.

I stumbled after Faith.

Distress clogged her steps, held her back. I caught her several paces from the door. When I put my hand on her shoulder, she flinched so hard that her own dismay turned her around. Tears pouring from her eyes, she faced me, and her lips quivered.

"I can't endure violence." Her voice trembled like her lips. "You know that. I can't."

"Faith," I murmured softly, as if I were her friend and counselor instead of her doom, "you love God. You love Art. You don't want him to kill Ginny. Not at the cost of his soul.

"I need to save her, but I can't let him kill the rest of you. If you won't help me, I'll have to let her die. So that I can hunt him down before he kills anyone else."

I didn't mention the obvious fact that I couldn't hope to outhunt Reeson. There didn't seem to be any point.

"Please help me."

"Brew." Lara spoke quietly, but her voice hit me between the shoulder blades like an ice pick. "I need to talk to you."

Oh God, not now. Not *now*.

Ignoring the woman behind me, I concentrated everything I had left on Faith. "Please," I repeated as if that were my last argument, and my best. "Please."

"You're the only one who can help me, Brew," Lara insisted.

I felt so close to the edge that I nearly whimpered. What was that damn woman doing here now anyway? And how had she chosen *this* moment for whatever she had in mind? Couldn't she see that I was fighting for Ginny's life?

Faith watched me. Her eyes spilled water like wells, but she watched me. Her gaze seemed to study me, measuring me by the way I responded to Lara.

"Later," I coughed against a mounting wave of panic. "Ask me later."

"*Brew*."

Lara's tone cut through my alarm. Suddenly I heard something like hysteria in it—and something like glee. She may've been a coke addict after all, submerged in so many artificial substances that her brain had gone to mush and wildness. She sounded on the verge of ecstasy or a break-down, whichever came first.

"What did Ginny find in my room?"

I snapped, staggering like a ship in a long wind when the cables that tied it to its the berth parted. With a howl rising from my torn-up guts, I wheeled on Lara Hardhouse—

—and froze. Stricken, my howl came out as a strangled groan.

Lara held a gun.

She pointed it at my sternum from a distance of less than ten yards. Her finger curled on the trigger. She'd already advanced past the stove where Faith's soup steamed. At this range she was never going to miss.

Her eyes glittered intensely. Exaltation limned her face. Quietly now because she knew she didn't need to shout, she repeated, "What did Ginny find in my room?"

My head felt like a discus. Some great mother of an ath-lete whirled me around and around, and any second now he would let me go, send me sailing into the empty air and the dark. I couldn't tell whether Faith pulled away from me, headed for the door again. She found coke in your room, the coke you used to poison Cat. You didn't know Queenie would drink it instead. None of this makes sense. Who killed Mac?

I wanted to turn my head, catch some sign of Faith, but if I looked around at all, released my focus on Lara's gun, the spin would carry me away. It was a little .22, a plinking gun you could hide in a clutch purse. But it was as good as artillery from this distance.

"Ask her yourself," I croaked. "She's in the office. With Reeson."

Lara shook her head. "I don't want to ask her, Brew. I want to ask you." She sounded strangely sure of herself. "And you're going to tell me.

"Do you know why? Have you figured out why I come to

you? Why I'm attracted to you? Why I want you to go to bed with me?

"It's because you're a *cripple*, because you're *flawed*. You're only half a human being, Brew—and I like that. I like having sex with crippled men."

She seemed to expand in front of me, her underlying passion made her tower over me. Or maybe it just made me shrink.

"Sex with me would make you feel like you aren't crippled. Like you aren't as pathetic as you look and feel. I like having that much power, Brew.

"And I like knowing it won't make any difference. When you fuck me, you feel like a man again, you feel alive again—and it doesn't make any difference. Because I know as soon as you start to feel that way you're going to die. I can take you to the top of the mountain, Brew, and I enjoy it because I know you'll fall off. You're going to end up dead."

I saw movement behind her. For a moment I couldn't fix on it. I couldn't do anything except watch the .22 and shrink. If I took my eyes off the gun, I might warn her—

Then the background clarified, and I saw Connie.

She eased forward carefully, so carefully that she hardly seemed to move. Her gaze flicked back and forth between Lara and me, hunting for some hint of what was going on.

Lara didn't know Connie was there. "That's *power,* Brew," she said. "You can't say no to me, you really can't. You're a cripple, and cripples can't say no. They never can.

"What did Ginny find in my room?"

"You can't shoot me," I replied thinly. "You poisoned Queenie. I figured that out." I spoke for Connie's benefit, explaining to her, giving her time. But I couldn't answer Lara's question. If I did, she wouldn't have any reason left to hold back. "And you probably stabbed Ginny. But who killed Mac?"

Lara's finger clenched on the trigger. "Brew," she warned, "I asked you a question."

Connie hadn't advanced far enough. Her features were pure and hard. She didn't intend to let anything stop her. The anger which had held her since Mac's death impelled her. But she'd never reach Lara in time.

"No. You can't shoot me." I wanted to sound casual, but my voice twanged like a snapping rubber band. "Don't you smell it?"

Lara frowned. "Smell what?"

"Gas." Personally I couldn't smell it at all now. Just soup. "There's a leak in here somewhere. I first caught a whiff of it a couple of days ago, but it's getting stronger.

"If you shoot me, the muzzle flash will set it off. This entire kitchen will blow. Do you know what that kind of fire does to you? Even if you live, it'll char the skin from your bones."

Lara hesitated. "You're lying." Just a small falter—a tiny decrease of pressure in the trigger—but it sufficed. "I don't smell any gas."

You're going to end up dead.

In that instant, a wild and unholy look like a glimpse of the abyss crossed Connie's face. With both hands she picked up the kettle and poured soup onto Lara's head.

The shock saved me. Lara didn't shoot. She didn't manage to fire at all. The .22 flipped out of her grasp as she screamed and clutched at her scalded flesh.

Still screaming in short mad bursts, she dropped to the floor. Her hands clawed at the back of her dress, fighting to tear the burn away, but she couldn't rip the fabric.

"Oh, my Lord," Faith moaned. "God help me."

Connie looked stricken, as if she'd terrified herself unexpectedly, but she went and retrieved the .22. She'd written enough novels about violence. She knew what to do. When she had the gun, she met my gaze. Shadows shifted like ghosts across the depths of her eyes. "Second degree burns," she announced as if she were sure. "She'll live."

I didn't thank her. I didn't have time. Quickly I said,

"Reeson killed Cat and Simon. He wants to kill me. He's holding Ginny hostage in the office."

Then I said, "Faith is going to help me rescue her."

Both Connie and I turned toward Faith.

"You can't get away from it," I said softly, gently. "No one ever gets away from violence. No one is ever safe. That isn't the way God works. If you want these murders to stop, you have to make that happen yourself."

She didn't respond. Her eyes were riveted on Lara. But her hands were where they belonged, holding her crucifix, and her mouth shaped prayers I couldn't hear.

When I took hold of her arm, she didn't resist. Clinging to the delicate silver remnant of her beliefs, she let me steer her in the direction of the office.

None of us tried to help Lara.

As we left I told Connie, "Get everyone together in Sam's room. Even Mile. But don't let him have the gun."

The way she said, "Leave it to me," was good enough.

Faith and I moved along the halls like martyrs on their way to the stake. Although she didn't know it, she actually kept me on my feet, supporting me through my grip on her arm. Under her breath she murmured prayers that went nowhere.

Dazed by our separate fears, we reached the office.

I couldn't hear voices, which scared me so badly that I nearly let everything else go and charged inside by myself.

But I still hadn't heard a shot. I clutched that fact the same way Faith clutched her crucifix.

Trying not to shake like a drunk with the DTs, I took out the .45 for the first time in what seemed like forever. Bracing my arm, I worked the slide.

As a kind of apology, I muttered to Faith, "I have to make this look good." Then I put the gun behind her and pointed the muzzle at the back of her skull.

God help me.

"*Reeson!*"

My voice cracked. I swallowed, nearly choking. The silence from the office was absolute.

"I've got Faith!"

Absolute.

"I'll trade you! Her for Ginny!"

Not a sound. Nothing. Reeson had already killed Ginny. He'd gone out through the window. By now he'd probably positioned himself right behind me.

"I have a gun on her! You've got five seconds! Then I'm going to blow her head off!"

From somewhere I heard an odd thunk. It sounded like Ginny's claw hitting the desktop.

"*Faith.*" Reeson didn't shout, but his hoarse whisper carried like a cry. "Get away from him. He won't shoot you."

An inarticulate sob burst from Faith's throat.

Praying as hard as she did, I reached past her to the doorknob, turned it, pushed the door open. While it swung aside, I pulled her in front of me, giving Reeson a blocked target if he decided to fire.

He stood at one end of the desk. His hands knew what to do without help. One held the Ruger on Ginny, steady as death. The other aimed her .357 at Faith and me.

Directly at Faith's heart.

Ginny's face was pale iron, as stiff as a mask. She didn't so much as nod at me. She held both arms braced on the desktop where Reeson could watch them—where they were helpless. She loathed helplessness as much as I did, but she didn't excuse it with alcohol. When she accepted her claw, she'd given up excuses. Nevertheless her grim mask kept her loathing secret, away from Reeson. She'd given him nothing of herself, nothing he could use.

"Art," Faith murmured brokenly, "oh, Art." Now she saw that I'd told the truth. Reeson didn't try to hide it. He had nowhere to go. "Don't do this."

"Get away from him." Reeson's face looked like it was about to crack, split open by murder and love. Seeing Faith brought him face to face with his own ghouls and beasties. He knew too much about death. He shouldn't have allowed himself to care for her. "I'll shoot you if I have to. Don't make me do it."

Faith moved—but not away. Instead she took a step toward him. As if she thought that she might still be able to convince him, she said, "Oh, Art, killing is evil. Life and death belong to the Lord."

"*Stop*. Don't." Despair ached unmistakably in Reeson's voice. "I don't want to kill you."

She took another step. "This has to end. Don't you see that? Everybody knows what you've done. God knows. This is a crime against your own soul."

Another step.

"Art, please."

Reeson actually backed away from the desk, retreated to the wall. He no longer covered Ginny. Instead he held both guns aligned on Faith, and his fingers hugged the triggers.

Ginny still didn't move, however. She knew better. Anything sudden might set him off.

"No," he rasped. "No."

Yes.

Maybe he wasn't that desperate. Maybe he wouldn't shoot her. I didn't know how much power his demons had with him. But I couldn't take the risk. She was worth too much.

As soon as I had a clear shot past her shoulder, I raised the .45 and fired.

For once in my life, I hit my target. The .45 made a sound like a stick of dynamite in the enclosed space, and bright red burst from the center of Reeson's chest.

When she saw him fall, Faith lifted her voice and began wailing.

24

An hour or so later, the rest of the group gathered in the Draytons' room, those of us who were still alive, or functional, or who didn't have better things to do.

My own ability to function was open to question. Sam's second injection, the jolt of artificial energy, didn't last as long as the first. The blood had gone leaden in my veins, which forced my heart to beat overtime, and fever filled my head again. To keep myself out of everyone's way—out of trouble—I sat on the floor beside the window with my back against the wall and my face toward the door. In that position, I did what I could to prevent my mind from merging with the woodwork.

Just to be on the safe side, I had the .45 on the floor between my legs, in easy reach. But I didn't believe that I'd ever be able to shoot straight again.

Nevertheless I was in a hell of a lot better shape than Queenie. As far as I could tell, she hadn't moved a muscle for hours. Her coma had shut down on her like the lid of a coffin.

But I would've given several of my remaining body parts to see her smile again.

Sam sat on the bed beside her, clenching her hand as if he'd never left. Now he faced in the opposite direction, however, out toward the rest of us rather than down at Queenie. In that position I could see his face too well. He looked altogether haunted and fragile, as if he had all Art Reeson's ghouls and beasties caterwauling loose inside his head. The fact that we'd caught the woman who poisoned his wife didn't give him any noticeable relief.

Lara Hardhouse wasn't among us, naturally. We'd left her in her room, handcuffed facedown to her bed so that she wouldn't get away. Sam had wrapped her burns in damp gauze. The cracks and blisters punctuating her red skin he'd treated with Silvadene. Then he'd given her a sedative against the shock—a gesture which I considered remarkably charitable under the circumstances. Like Connie, he thought that she had only second degree burns.

Like Connie, he didn't seem to care.

Faith Jerrick was absent as well. Sam had sedated her, too, and she slept a frail heartbreaking sleep in Cat's bed. I didn't trust this. I doubted that any mere sedative could contain her distress for long. When she woke up, she'd be more alone than she'd ever been in her life. So I was glad that Amalia had decided to stay with her.

Meanwhile Truchi had gone to search Reeson's cottage for the missing rotors, at Ginny's suggestion. Like me, she found it impossible to imagine the Carbones guilty of anything.

As for the rest—

Counting Queenie, there were ten of us. More than half of the fourteen we'd started with—which was a pretty good survival rate for a guerrilla war, but just plain shitty for a mystery camp. In a characteristic display of Texas chivalry, Mile had commandeered one of the two original chairs. Buffy creaked away in the other, rocking herself determinedly for comfort. But Rock had brought two more chairs from some other room. With more weakness than she usually let herself show, Ginny accepted one of them. When Connie refused the other, Maryanne sat down beside Mile. They'd resumed holding hands. From my angle, I couldn't tell whether that was her idea or his.

Rock, Connie, and Hardhouse remained standing. Rock occupied the corner of the room closest to Buffy. Apparently, he wanted to keep an eye on all of us—but especially on her. Connie stood at the head of Queenie's bed across from Sam. I didn't see any sign of the .22. She'd put it out of sight somewhere.

Against the wall near the door, Hardhouse lounged with his arms folded over his chest and his aggressive chin jutting. He didn't look exactly chipper, but his eyes were bright and clear, and his attention remained sharp, as if he had unlimited resources of adrenaline to call on.

I couldn't say the same for the rest of the group.

After what Ginny had endured, her exhaustion showed in the blurred color of her eyes and the deep lines on either side of her pale nose. At odd moments she shook her head and scowled angrily, as if she couldn't forgive herself for failing to recognize Reeson's guilt earlier.

Superficially, at least, Mile and Maryanne concentrated on each other. But his gaze when he glanced at her was strangely baleful and lost, confused by lust or loathing. And her relief at Reeson's death and Lara's capture only made her seem morose. Maybe she'd had a taste of power, of her own kind of vengeance, and didn't want to resume her familiar role with Mile. On the other hand, she had no idea what else to do.

If they felt any relief, Buffy and Rock didn't show it. For better or worse, they both knew too much about murder. Rocking hard looked like her only defense against hysteria. By degrees, he inched deeper into the corner like a man who stood there because he wanted to escape his responsibilities.

As for Connie, nothing in her face or posture suggested anything except vigilance and unrelenting anger. Nevertheless I had the impression that she'd come to some kind of limit inside herself. More than most of the people here, she knew what she was doing. She thought clearly, she understood the consequences of her actions. And she was a novelist who preached the importance of sympathizing with all her characters, even the criminals. Scalding Lara was probably the most hurtful thing she'd ever done. It may've been the most hurtful thing she could ever do.

For a while no one spoke. Our own thoughts occupied our attention. Murder does that to you. It forces you to look at your life. And most of the time you can't honestly say that you like what you see. But eventually Buffy gave her rocker a vehement swing and protested in a frayed voice, "I don't understand."

"What is there to understand?" Maryanne asked plaintively. "Houston was right all along. There were two killers—and now they've both been caught. We're safe at last." She looked around the room for confirmation. "Aren't we?"

Connie shook her head. "Mrs. Altar is right." She sounded unkind, but she was only angry. "The pieces don't add up. Who killed Mac?"

Even though I'd been doing my best to meditate on that question, I still felt a chill to hear it stated. As long as we didn't know the answer, we could be wrong about any number of other things as well. Lara Hardhouse, for instance.

"Why, Art Reeson, of course," Maryanne countered a shade frantically. "Didn't he? He and Lara were working together, just like Houston said. She opened a window for him, and he came in and killed Mac. Then he went out again and pretended to come back for the first time." She turned to Mile. "Isn't that right?"

He glared at her without answering. However, he didn't make her let go of his fingers.

"But *why?*" Buffy insisted. "*Why* were they working together? *Why* would they kill Mac? *Why* did they want to kill Cat?" Too much weeping had tattered her voice, but now she'd used up all her tears. "I don't understand."

"All right," Ginny said heavily. This was her job. For some reason she didn't want to do it. But she did it anyway. "We'll start with what we know.

"The idea that Lara and Reeson are in this together has too many practical problems. According to your theory, he would've had to return here while I was playing dead outside. If he did that, I probably would've heard him. He didn't have time to go around the hills to the other side of the lodge. He would've had to pass fairly close to me.

"According to your theory again, he must've been the one who stabbed me. As Joseph pointed out, Lara was the only other possibility—and she didn't have a knife. So Reeson was still in the building. He stabbed me and then went out through a window. Maybe she closed it after him to cover his trail.

"But he's a professional killer. If *he* stabbed me, I wouldn't be here talking about it.

"What we do know about him is *why*." He was in the business of death. That's how he proved himself against his demons. "He worked for el Señor—and el Señor wanted him to kill Brew. We know that. Otherwise he would've shot me while he had the chance, instead of holding me to use against Brew.

"That means he had no reason to kill Mac.

"And," she asserted, "he couldn't have poisoned Cat if he'd wanted to." I'd explained this detail to her before we gathered in Sam's room. "Faith never told him about her taste for port.

"Another thing," she continued. "I can't really believe that a man like Reeson would work with a woman like Lara. He was a professional. She's too unreliable for him.

"And he loved Faith. Otherwise Brew and I'd both be dead."

"So Mrs. Hardhouse acted on her own," Connie said flatly. "And she must've intended murder almost from the first. The port was poisoned before Cat was shot. If she didn't arrive here meaning to kill, she conceived the idea soon after we settled in.

"She put cocaine in the port because she had some rea-

son for wanting Cat dead. And she stabbed you"—Ginny—
"for the same reason.

"What reason, I wonder?"

The way she asked the question brought back an odd
memory. When Lara had entered the parlor with Mac right
after Cat's murder, her first words had been directed at her
husband.

Joseph. What have you done?

She hadn't just jumped to the conclusion that he was responsible. She'd been offended by it.

And he'd answered, *I didn't do it.* As if he owed her that
particular reassurance.

And I'd seen them kissing like lovers at a time when
they were both busy fucking everyone they could get their
hands on.

You're going to end up dead.

In a tone of exhaustion, Ginny said, "Maybe it was the
same reason for both of us."

"You're scaring me," Maryanne protested. "What are
you talking about?"

"Maybe Lara wanted Cat and me dead because we both
had sex with her husband."

That was it, of course—the only possible connection between Catherine Reverie and Ginny Fistoulari, the only
thing they had in common.

Suddenly everyone in the room stared at Hardhouse.

He unfolded his arms, shoved his hands deep into his
pockets. Apparently making an effort of self-control. His
gaze flicked around at us as if we'd all accused him of
something and he didn't know who to defend himself
against first.

"Is that possible, Mr. Hardhouse?" Connie sounded
like she'd already made up her mind. "Is your wife that
possessive?

"Why does she kill your lovers instead of you?"

He opened his mouth, closed it again. His hands started

up out of his pockets, then went down again. Whatever he saw when he looked at us steadied him.

"It's the damn coke," he said harshly. "She wasn't like that when I married her. But the coke changed her. It made her paranoid. After that I couldn't stand her. Our marriage was effectively over. But she didn't want a divorce. And I couldn't divorce her. She owned most of the business—it was her money in the first place. I couldn't afford to divorce her."

Sam followed this with a hollow expression, as if he didn't understand a word of it.

"She had the idea," Hardhouse growled, "that if she got rid of every woman I went to bed with, I'd come back to her. I'd have to. That was her delusion.

"But she never killed anybody. Not until now." His voice was a snarl of sincerity or violence. "I would've turned her over to the police if she did. But until now she just drove my women away. As soon as I found someone I liked, she made her leave.

"It's a tragedy, really. She was a wonderful wife before she started on coke."

He watched all of us for our reaction.

Ginny answered him. She sounded tired to the bone, worn down to her marrow. But she didn't back away.

"I don't think so."

He gauged her with his eyes. "What do you mean?"

"Your wife had no reason to kill Mac. He was her lover, not yours. And anyway she couldn't have done it. She was with Brew. Trying to seduce him. Which doesn't make her sound like a possessive lunatic."

"I agree," Connie put in, as stiff as a teacher's paddle.

Buffy continued rocking as if she wanted to achieve escape velocity. Rock had shrunk so far into the corner that he nearly disappeared. Mile and Maryanne held onto each other. Neither of them moved a muscle.

Ginny shifted her weight in the chair. Her purse lay on

the floor beside her, close to her right hand. "On top of that," she sighed, "you said she didn't have a knife. But she must've had one. How else could she stab me? Either she had it when she was with you. Or else you weren't together. In either case, you're lying. You must've known what she was doing."

Hardhouse's gaze burned. "You'd better say what you mean." His hands fisted in his pockets, holding onto his self-control. His voice was as hard as a hammer, but he used it carefully. "I can't answer you until I know what you're accusing me of."

"I'm accusing you," Ginny replied with a hint of her old ferocity, "of murdering Mac."

Maryanne choked. No one else made a sound.

"I'm accusing you and Lara of plotting together to murder Mac and Cat and me." Ginny's voice held more than just weariness and anger. I heard something else as well—something that sounded like loss. "That's what you do, both of you. You have affairs with as many different people as you can manage. Then you kill each other's lovers. That's what holds your marriage together. That's how you get your kicks. It isn't cocaine. It's blood."

You're going to end up dead.

Hoping that Hardhouse couldn't see me, I reached between my legs and closed my hand around the butt of the .45.

"That's crazy," he murmured as if he were honestly astonished. "You think I'm crazy."

Ginny didn't hesitate. She was prepared to pay the price of her mistakes. "I've been in bed with you. I know what turns you on. At the time I thought something was strange, but I couldn't identify it. I didn't realize what it was until you told Brew my claw was sexy. I *know* you're crazy.

"How long have you been doing this? How many"—she snarled the word—"*damaged* women have you fucked so Lara could kill them?"

I like having sex with crippled men.

"How many of her lovers have you killed?"

In a sane world, Hardhouse would've panicked. He would've realized that he was caught, trapped, he would've broken. But the world wasn't sane—or he wasn't. Instead of panicking, he threw back his head and laughed.

The sheer unexpectedness of his reaction paralyzed all of us.

Connie hesitated a fraction of a second too long. His laugh disrupted her concentration. And she asked too much of herself. After scalding Lara she didn't know how to make herself go farther.

For that fraction of a second, she faltered. Then she drove her hand under Queenie's pillow and came out with the .22.

Too late.

Maryanne screamed as Hardhouse snatched a gun out of his pocket.

A flat automatic of some kind, I didn't have time to recognize it. He aimed it right into Ginny's face and yelled at Connie, "*Drop it!*"

Pandemonium.

Connie's desperation to get rid of the .22 before he fired flung it from her. It bounced away across the carpet and skidded against the wall.

Instinctively she crouched behind the bed.

At the same time, I hauled up the .45. I'd already started squeezing the trigger.

Before I could get a bead on Hardhouse, Mile and Maryanne jumped in front of me. He bounded out of his chair, scrambled for escape. Still screaming, she clung to him as if even now she thought he might protect her. They collided and grappled with each other frantically, blocked my shot.

Simultaneously, Rock burst out of the corner. In a wild rush he grabbed Buffy, heaved her and her rocker to the floor. Then he dove on top of her, covering her body, muffling her wails.

"You, too, Axbrewder!" Hardhouse roared. *"Drop it!"*

Ginny hadn't moved a muscle. He'd never miss her at that range. No matter what else happened, she'd be shot. And her .357 was in her purse, out of reach.

Somehow I managed to catch myself before I made a mistake.

"Don't shoot!" I shouted back urgently. "I'll drop it!"

Trying to be obvious about it, I tossed the .45 away.

Damn near brained Rock with it, but Hardhouse didn't seem to notice.

"All of you, *stop!*" His aim at Ginny never wavered. I recognized the gun now—a lightweight Star BKM 9mm. Not part of the lodge collection, as far as I knew. Hardhouse must've brought it with him. It held nine rounds. He had nine of us to kill. *"Hold still!"*

Even Mile and Maryanne froze. Rock held Buffy down. Connie shrank into her crouch behind the bed.

"Well, well." Hardhouse breathed heavily, mostly from adrenaline, but he still managed to sound conversational. "It looks like we'll get away with it after all. Lara always says anticipation is the best part. Knowing what's about to happen. Personally, I like this part best. Getting away with it."

"No, don't, Joseph," Maryanne pleaded in a whimper, "don't kill me, oh, my God, don't kill me."

"Rock," Buffy panted, a thin whisper, as if he were suffocating her. "Rock, please."

I distinctly heard him say, "All right."

A heavy shudder ran through him, and he sighed. As if he were surrendering her to be murdered, he rolled off her. Then he came up onto his knees with his back toward Hardhouse.

In both fists he clutched my .45.

He probably knew that he didn't stand a chance in hell of turning fast enough to fire at Hardhouse before Hardhouse shot Ginny. He didn't try—he was no hunter. Instead he did what he could to make himself the target.

Concealing the .45 with his pudgy frame, he jerked one heavy slug into the wall. For the second time in less than two hours, my gun went off like gelignite.

Hardhouse flinched.

In that instant, Sam moved. With a shout of recognition, as if he'd finally identified an outlet for his anguish, he hurled himself at Hardhouse.

I couldn't see clearly, Mile and Maryanne were in my way. A shot went off as Sam dove into Hardhouse. Ginny recoiled like she'd been hit. Galvanized by panic, I pitched to the side, got my legs under me, came to my feet almost on top of Buffy. Practically in the same movement, I ripped the .45 out of Rock's fists and fumbled the butt into my palm.

Sam landed on Hardhouse, fighting like a schoolyard brawl—all fury and fists, no skill. They collapsed to the floor and thrashed from side to side, blundered against the wall. Hardhouse couldn't force Sam away. But he still had the 9mm.

He brought it around to shoot Sam.

In one long hard movement like the punch of a piston, Ginny stood up from her chair, swept forward, and stamped the heel of her boot down on Hardhouse's wrist.

I didn't know whether she broke his wrist or not. I couldn't hear any bones snap, Maryanne made too much noise. But the 9mm skidded away from his fingers.

Before he could do anything else, Ginny dropped her other knee into the center of his chest and jabbed her claw at the base of his throat.

"*Stop*," she hissed. "Stop, or I'll tear out your larynx."

He stopped. Gagging slightly, he lay still.

Sam retreated to his feet, panting hugely. His skin burned with exertion, but his eyes were full of fight instead of ruin. If Hardhouse had so much as twitched, Sam would've jumped back into the fray without hesitation.

Panting like Sam, but for a completely different reason, I stumbled forward. Almost falling, I landed on my knees beside Ginny. Just to be on the safe side, I poked the .45 at Hardhouse's nose.

"You all right?" I gasped out. "Did he hit you?"

She didn't turn her head or answer. She didn't need to. I could see a scorch mark spreading from the corner of her mouth in a fan along her cheek. Sam had deflected Hardhouse enough. The shot had only given her a powder burn.

By some miracle, the slug hadn't hit anyone at all.

When Maryanne quit screaming, I heard Connie murmur, "I'm sorry. I'm sorry. I couldn't do it. I panicked."

Ginny ignored her. Also Mile and Maryanne and Buffy and Rock. Leaning over Hardhouse, pushing her claw at the base of his throat, she demanded softly, "Why? What do you get out of it?" She didn't sound angry. She sounded close to tears. "Why did you make love to me?"

As far as I could tell, Hardhouse still wasn't scared. He didn't look caught or beaten. As much as possible with that dark, aggressive face, he seemed happy, almost beatified, as if he'd finally achieved a climax that released him from himself.

Swallowing against the pressure, he said, "Because it works."

Ginny and I stared at him and waited. She made no effort to wipe the black pain off her cheek.

"Life is sex. You don't understand that. You think sex is just fucking. But it's more than that, much more. It's passion and dominion and *life*." The words came out half choked, but he didn't ask her to ease back. "When you understand that, nothing ordinary works. Fucking doesn't work. It isn't enough. Women are just women. They don't mean anything. But a woman who needs me—a broken, maimed woman who needs me to make her whole— *That's* sex.

"When I learned that, I started living for the first time. I started looking for damaged women, women with physical and emotional injuries. Because they needed me.

"But it didn't help me with Lara. She didn't need me, not like that. And when you give people what they need, they stop needing you. I wanted more. *More.* I wanted sex that would make my whole body and mind flame with life.

"Part of what makes sex so potent is that you can give it or take it away. At first, I thought I wanted women who were going to die anyway. Women in the first stages of some terminal illness. Women who would lose what I gave them. That helped, but it wasn't enough. It didn't let me choose. And it still didn't help me with Lara.

"But *she* understood. She *understood.* She was the one who thought of killing my lovers."

Maryanne took one horrified breath. Buffy moaned softly.

Hardhouse's grin made him look like a malign saint. "Do you have any idea how sexy it is to know that the woman you're fucking is about to die? That she's going to die *because* you fucked her? That you can make her whole and doom her at the same time? When we started doing that, I had everything I could ever want. Damaged women, emotional and physical cripples—sex with them was vindication. And sex with Lara afterward was absolution.

"It's heaven.

"For her, the only problem was that we had to be so careful. Getting caught would ruin everything. That's what kills you. But for me, getting away with it is the crowning touch, the ultimate victory—the best part of being alive. And the more we lived, the more we wanted to live.

"When we heard about this mystery camp, we decided to risk it. The chance was too good to miss—the chance to do what we wanted in a camp full of 'detectives' and get away with it.

"You think you're so tough," he said straight to Ginny, "and you don't even know how maimed you are. Sex with you was the best I've ever had."

Her claw began trembling against his throat. Her shoulders shook, taken by sobs. His words hurt her worse than any bullet.

"You sonofabitch," she whispered back in the kind of husky voice lovers use. "I trusted you."

Nevertheless she fought to keep her grief to herself. Biting down on the unsteadiness of her voice, she asked, "Sam, have you got any tape?"

Sam's bag sat on the end table beside Queenie. He went to it promptly and came back with a wide roll of bandage tape. As he handed it to Ginny, he said harshly, "Tape his mouth shut. I don't want to listen to him anymore."

She nodded once, stiffly. That was all the acknowledgment she gave any of us.

Behind me, Rock and Buffy got to their feet. She looked like she wanted to sob, but that wasn't what she did. Facing him with tears in her eyes, she murmured, "Thank you."

He made a gentle shushing noise as if she'd asked him to comfort her.

"Is it over?" Maryanne asked like a frightened doll.

Connie stood up from behind the bed. "Yes," she answered. "It's over."

"Shee-it," Mile muttered thinly. "Shee-it." Then he growled at Maryanne, "Fool woman, you damn near got me killed."

"No, she didn't," Connie retorted. Apparently, she'd had all she could stand of Houston Mile. "She pulled you out of the line of fire. She saved your life."

That may or may not have been true. In either case, it shut Mile up.

Ginny gave me the roll of tape and took my gun to cover Hardhouse. It wobbled in her grasp, but she didn't need to worry about missing him. Against her pale skin, the powder burn looked dark and permanent, like a stain on her spirit.

With more strength than I knew I had, I flopped Hardhouse over onto his face so I wouldn't have to suffer his belligerent happy smile. Apparently his wrist wasn't broken after all—he didn't show any special pain when I strapped his forearms together. Then I did his ankles. I didn't stop until I'd immobilized him for good.

Because I agreed with Sam, I put a big strip of tape over Hardhouse's mouth. Maliciously I hoped that he was one of those people who had trouble breathing through his nose.

You think you're so tough, and you don't even know how maimed you are.

I like having sex with crippled men.

As I pried myself upright, I felt more than a bit stained myself.

As soon as I regained my feet, Ginny handed me the .45. Without a word to anyone, she left the room.

I wanted to follow her. In fact, I had to follow her. But when I looked around, I forgot that for a moment. The eight of us who remained were a shambles, no question about it. Too much fear had turned Maryanne's face raw and homely. Mile resembled a porker on the way to the slaughterhouse. Buffy and Rock lay on the floor again, cradling each other like lost kids.

As if she weren't aware of what she did, Connie righted up Buffy's rocker and sat in it. Her failure with Hardhouse had brought her anger to an end, or degraded it somehow. She didn't want it anymore. Mumbling to herself like an old woman, she closed her eyes.

Only Sam looked like he'd come through the experience with his soul intact. He'd saved Ginny and stopped Hardhouse. And struck a blow for his wife.

I envied him.

Through everything that had happened, Queenie slept on like the dead. If I hadn't seen the blanket move over her chest, I wouldn't have known that she was still alive.

I went to her side. I didn't ask Sam's permission. I didn't think I needed it. As if I were alone with her, I spent a moment studying her sweet unseeing face, waiting for her smile even though I knew that I might never see it again. Then I bent over her and kissed her on the mouth.

She'd told me once I owed her the story of my life. This was as close as I could get.

After that I went to find Ginny.

25

During the night Queenie regained consciousness.

Sam couldn't assess how badly she'd been damaged, of course. Only time would reveal how much of her brain still worked right. When she woke up, however, she smiled at him—just a ghost of her former vitality, but a smile anyway, a recognition. And like a good girl she drank the glass of water he put to her lips. Those were encouraging signs.

At about the same time, Truchi returned with a handful of distributor rotors. He'd found them in a chest in Reeson's attic, along with the missing guns and enough other munitions to equip a platoon.

Shortly after sunrise he left Deerskin Lodge on the snowmobile—and came back a couple of hours later with a heavy diesel plow chugging along behind him. He wasn't exactly elaborate in his explanation, but he let us know that he'd met the county road crew on its regular run up the mountain. The run hadn't been made sooner because this road wasn't used enough to be a high priority.

When he heard Truchi's story, the plow's operator had used his radio to call for help. Before another hour passed, the sheriff and several cars full of deputies arrived at Deerskin Lodge, along with two ambulances.

One of the ambulances left promptly, carrying a load of corpses for the coroner—Catherine Reverie, Mac Westward, Arthur Reeson. The other took Lara Hardhouse, Queenie Drayton, and Sam to the nearest hospital.

The sheriff arrested Joseph Hardhouse, naturally. He

also impounded Reeson's chest and Lara's cocaine, and asked the rest of us a lot of questions.

Those questions could've gotten me into trouble pretty quickly. Hours earlier, however—in fact, right after Truchi left on the snowmobile—Ginny had called the survivors together and told them how she wanted to save my life.

We didn't need much time, she explained. Just a few days, say until Sunday. For that long, she asked the Altars and Sam and Mile and Maryanne and Connie to tell the cops the same lie she did. On Sunday they could switch to the truth. They could even explain why they'd been lying. Unless the cops found Simon first, in which case the whole question would become academic.

Only Mile objected. He had a score to settle with Ginny and me—but mostly me—and betraying us to el Señor sounded fine to him. But Maryanne worked on him for a while. She spent the credit she'd gained by apparently saving his life. And when that didn't work, she let him know that if he refused Ginny she'd lose respect for him—which, she hinted broadly, would involve telling his friends back home about his sexual practices.

He gave in with his usual grace.

So Ginny introduced me to the sheriff as Simon Abel, and no one contradicted her. Under questioning, we all agreed that Mick Axbrewder had gone up into the hills tracking Reeson and hadn't returned. No one mentioned locking Abel in the wine cellar. Or the hole in Axbrewder's stomach, for that matter. The sheriff had no immediate reason to doubt us.

Which meant the police reports and newspapers would tell el Señor that I was missing and presumed dead. He wouldn't send anyone else after me until he learned the truth.

Ginny and I had that long to get out of the state.

Unless one of the Hardhouses decided to talk. But neither of them knew what we were doing. And they had both apparently concluded that silence was their best defense, at least until they could bring in some legal talent. Since they didn't say anything, they didn't give me away.

Some of the deputies started a search for the body. They weren't organized or equipped for the job, however, and the snow hampered them. Our lie might well last until Sunday.

While the sheriff asked baffled questions, groping to make sense out of what we told him, one of the deputies drove away with Joseph Hardhouse. On his way out to the unit, he passed Ginny and me in the den. As charming as ever, he paused under the heads of dead animals to tell her, "You still don't understand. That claw really is the most desirable thing about you."

His smile radiated happy malice in all directions.

I watched the muscles bunch and release at the corner of her jaw, but she didn't retort. He'd already had all the response he was ever going to get out of her.

I wouldn't have had any idea what was going on with her myself if we hadn't talked about it earlier.

When I followed her out of Sam's room after Hardhouse's confession, I'd found her in the kitchen, making a sandwich as well as she could with one hand and a prosthetic device, and munching vitamins like candy. She still hadn't tried to clean the powder burn off her cheek, and that impacted mark accentuated the pallor of her face, the vulnerability in her gaze. The damaged skin probably hurt too much to touch. Fortunately the wound in her shoulder hadn't resumed bleeding. Only her eyes bled. Tears streaked her face while she chewed.

Despite my own exhaustion, her distress went through my heart. Years had passed since the Ginny Fistoulari I knew had let me see her in a state like this—let me this close to her. For the time being, however, I'd apparently used up my fear of her. Of her and for her. I was willing to take risks that would've scared me to the core of my bones a day ago.

Propping my pain and fever on the edge of a counter, I said, "I don't think much of your taste in men."

A snarl twisted her mouth. "Is that your subtle way of reminding me that I made a mistake with Joseph, or are you just putting yourself down again?"

I shrugged. "Some of both, probably. I'm not terribly impressed with my contribution to this case. I've been in such a sweat about losing you that I couldn't think." I groped for the description I wanted. "Which is an expensive problem. I should've taken Connie's advice years ago."

And Sam's.

I guess I was being cryptic again. Ginny glared at me and demanded, "Huh?"

"I forgot, you weren't there. While you were out, Connie made a hell of a speech. To Joseph, of all people. If I heard her right, I've been treating everything you and I do together like a contest. I had to prove I needed you so much that you wouldn't have the heart to ditch me. And I had to prove I didn't deserve you so that I wouldn't hate you for letting me fear you'd ditch me anyway.

"But she said"—I remembered it exactly—" 'it is impossible to live on the assumption that any contest can exist between persons.'" Then I shrugged again. "I know what the words mean. I need to learn what it means to live like that."

Ginny's eyes continued to spill tears. The effort of seeing through them made her look furious. "And you think I don't?"

Well, at least she was listening. I shifted my weight against the counter, trying to find a more comfortable position. "Ginny, I don't give a shit whether you do or not. I've got enough problems of my own. I can't tell you what to do with yours. All I'm trying to say is, I intend to stop. I want to stop treating you like you're the enemy."

A quiver she couldn't control moved her lower lip. "What for?"

I faced her straight. "You and I will never get back to where we were. We used to love each other—it all used to seem pretty simple. We'll never get that back. But I can think of reasons to go on."

Her voice was so small that I almost missed the words. "Like what?"

"Like"—I paused to be sure that I was ready—"your claw isn't the most desirable thing about you." She flinched when I took that chance, but I didn't back down. Instead I stroked the tears on her undamaged cheek and showed her my wet fingers. "Neither is this. The most desirable thing about you is that you aren't Lara or Maryanne. You aren't Cat. You sure as hell aren't Faith, and you also aren't Connie or Buffy. You're Ginny by God Fistoulari, and no one can take your place."

That was honest, anyway.

Fortunately I didn't expect a gratified response. If anything, my assertion had the opposite effect. "Stop it," she murmured, fighting distress. "I can't deal with that right now. You're too far ahead of me. I thought I'd have to carry your self-pity and your stupid drinking around on my back for the rest of my life. I wanted to believe I was strong enough, but I knew I wasn't. I couldn't do it. That's why I didn't see what was wrong with Joseph. I felt like such a failure around you. He offered me a way out. He wanted me—and Lara wanted you, so that was all right. At least for a few days, I could stop carrying you around.

"I was helpless to really look at him. At what I was getting myself into.

"I don't know what to do with you if this isn't a contest."

I lowered my head. It felt too heavy anyway, and besides I couldn't pretend that what she said didn't hurt.

But I was braced for it. And the time had come to put up or shut up. If "no contest can exist between persons," I had nothing to lose. Sure, she could walk out of my life—but she couldn't take my life with her. And she couldn't take away the fact that I'd told her the truth at least once or twice.

When I felt ready to say it without sounding bitter, I looked back up at her and asked, "So what do you want to do?"

She didn't meet my gaze. With the same disdain she had for the burn on her cheek, she didn't wipe her eyes or her nose.

"You want the truth?"

"No," I said. "I prefer comfortable lies. The truth hurts. But I finally figured out that lies kill." Sam told me, actually. "I'd rather we both stayed alive, if we can manage it."

She nodded hard enough to hurt her neck. Harshly she answered, "The truth is, I don't know what I want. I don't know how I feel about you. I don't like *cripples*." She couldn't say the word without turning it into a curse. "I don't like being one, and I don't like you when you're one."

Then, before I could accept the implications and let her go, she added, "No, that isn't the truth. I mean, it is, but it isn't. It isn't enough."

Abruptly she raised her eyes. Tears blurred her gray gaze, confusing everything she saw. In a tight voice, she said, "I want you to go away with me. Somewhere out of el Señor's reach. Somewhere we can *think*. If we have reasons to go on, I don't know it right now. And if we're finished, I'm not going to admit it until I've had a chance to *think*."

Well, by God. And just when I was getting set to ride off into the sunset, too.

I was no Queenie Drayton, but I smiled with everything I had. "You devil. You always could sweet-talk me into anything."

That was honest, too.

For a while, she dropped her gaze. Without saying anything, she chewed on her ragged sandwich.

When she looked up again, her eyes had cleared.

"In that case, we need a better way to keep you alive. Doing security for mystery camps obviously isn't the answer."

Which wasn't exactly the same thing as a sign from God. But it sufficed.

After she finished eating, I went to my room for some sleep.

I remembered to take my pills before I climbed into bed. And again when I got up to see Truchi off.

The sheriff wasn't much fun to deal with. He had too much stubbornness, and not enough imagination to back it up. But eventually he allowed us to go home.

We were all ready by then. While the sheriff interrogated one or another of us, the rest made our preparations. Connie had packed the Draytons' stuff. Truchi put our bags in the van.

Ginny and I stood on the porch as if we were still in charge, supervising Murder on Cue's departure. We'd preceded the others by a minute or two, but the Carbones were out in the cold with us, sharing a brief vigil for the dead—and the living.

"Will you be all right with Faith?" Ginny asked Ama. "We could take her into town with us. If she has any family, we could get in touch with them."

Ama had worn a stony expression for days, but now her face softened. "I am the one to care for her," she replied. "I have known her long. And I have known Mr. Reeson." Apparently she'd never been on a first-name basis with her boss. "I can assure her that she was not wrong in him. His love was a thing to be trusted. Perhaps it will redeem him in her God's sight."

Ginny shrugged and let go of Faith's fate.

Houston Mile and Maryanne Green left first. He was in a hurry and didn't give her a chance to speak to anyone.

After them the Altars emerged from the lodge. In a forlorn murmur, Sue-Rose said a few words of thanks, but she didn't wait to see how Ginny and I took them. As if she'd aged a decade in the past few days, she went stiffly down the steps and climbed into the van. In the passenger seat.

Her husband scanned the hills to avoid our faces. Distantly he asked, "Where should I send your check?"

Ginny grimaced. "I don't want a check. I need cash."

This didn't surprise him. He knew what we were doing, and why. "I have money at home."

"That's fine," she answered. "We'll follow you there from the Camelot." Where we'd left her car.

He paused a moment longer, still gazing away. Then he said, "I don't know how to pick up the pieces after something like this. I think we're going to need help."

Mostly because I knew how he felt, I said, "There's nothing wrong with needing help."

He sighed. "I know. I'm just not used to it."

Stooped and gray, he trudged out to the van.

Constance Bebb came last. For both of us, Ginny asked her, "Will you be all right? I mean, without Mac? What are you going to do?"

Connie dismissed the first question. To the second, she answered, "I'll try to write another Thornton Foal novel. It will be difficult without him. He was always the better writer. But I've learned a few things I can use."

On impulse I leaned down and kissed her cheek.

The way she pulled back made me think that I'd frightened her. Then I saw her blush.

Nevertheless her dignity didn't forsake her. "Thank you, Mr. Abel," she said firmly. With a slight smile, she added, "Try to take better care of yourself on your next assignment."

With her head high and her back straight, she descended the steps.

Ginny nudged my arm. "Let's go."

I looked over at Petruchio Carbone. The antique droop of his mustache reminded me of our only conversation. As a way of saying good-bye, I remarked, "You were right. Everyone who comes here is crazy."

He looked at me with a mixture of sadness and contentment, like a man whose heart had been broken and healed so long ago that the cost no longer mattered.

"Not you," he said distinctly. After a moment, he nodded toward Ginny. "Not her."

He surprised me. But when I considered, I thought he might be right. Maybe Ginny and I were finally on our way to sanity.

Past my shoulder, she told him, "If you think that, you're loonier than he is."

I wanted to laugh. "I hope so."

Together she and I went to the van to make our getaway.